CON
HUSBANDS

From marriage of convenience to happy-ever-after…

Praise for three bestselling authors –
Helen Brooks, Jessica Steele
and Catherine George

About Helen Brooks
'Helen Brooks creates an emotionally
intense reading experience.'
— *Romantic Times*

About MARRIED IN A MOMENT
'Jessica Steele spins a new twist on a
favourite plot.'
—*Romantic Times*

About Catherine George
'Catherine George combines scintillating
characters and a nail-biting plot to keep
readers thoroughly enthralled.'
—*Romantic Times*

CONTRACT HUSBANDS

THE MARRIAGE SOLUTION
by
Helen Brooks

MARRIED IN A MOMENT
by
Jessica Steele

THE BABY CLAIM
by
Catherine George

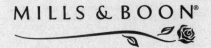

MILLS & BOON®

*MILLS & BOON and MILLS & BOON with the Rose Device
are registered trademarks of the publisher.
Harlequin Mills & Boon Limited,
Eton House, 18-24 Paradise Road, Richmond, Surrey, TW9 1SR*

CONTRACT HUSBANDS © by Harlequin Enterprises II B.V., 2003

The Marriage Solution, Married in a Moment and *The Baby Claim*
were first published in Great Britain by Harlequin Mills & Boon Limited
in separate, single volumes.

The Marriage Solution © Helen Brooks 1995
Married in a Moment © Jessica Steele 1998
The Baby Claim © Catherine George 1999

ISBN 0 263 83586 3

05-0103

*Printed and bound in Spain
by Litografia Rosés S.A., Barcelona*

Helen Brooks lives in Northamptonshire and is married with three children. As she is a committed Christian, busy housewife and mother, her spare time is at a premium but her hobbies include reading, swimming, gardening and walking her two energetic, inquisitive and very endearing young dogs. Her long-cherished aspiration to write became a reality when she put pen to paper on reaching the age of forty, and sent the result off to Mills & Boon®.

Coming next month:
THE PARISIAN PLAYBOY by Helen Brooks.
Don't miss this passionate, sophisticated story, in Modern Romance™

THE MARRIAGE SOLUTION

by

Helen Brooks

CHAPTER ONE

'I NEED to speak to David White *now*.'

Katie raised an eyebrow at the phone as she moved it back an inch or two from her ear before answering the hard male voice in a polite but firm tone. 'I'm sorry, I'm afraid my father can't be disturbed at the moment. Can I take—?'

'The hell he can't!' Now the voice was patently insulting with a thread of undeniable steel in its dark depths. 'Put me through, Miss White.'

'I can't do that.' She had straightened, her slim body held tight and still and her voice cool. 'I've told you, he can't be disturbed—'

'He'll be more than disturbed when I've finished with him.' She flinched visibly even as she wondered what on earth her father had done to make someone so mad. 'And I'm not asking, Miss White, I'm *telling* you. Put me through—'

'No.' There was a split-second of icy silence before she followed through. 'My father isn't well; the doctor is with him now.'

'The doctor?' She heard him swear under his breath, a particularly explicit oath which would have been quite at place in a rugby club changing-room, before he spoke again in clipped, measured tones that suggested barely controlled rage. 'Then when he has finished with the doctor I expect a call immediately. Is that clear?'

'Now look, Mr...?'

'Reef. Carlton Reef.'

'Well, I'm sorry, Mr Reef,' she said stiffly, 'but I have no intention of bothering my father with mundane business matters today. I presume it *is* business you wish to discuss with him?' she added icily.

'Dead right, Miss White,' he shot back tightly. 'And, for your information, the loss of a great deal of money due to your father's stupidity and crass ineptitude I do not consider mundane. I can be reached in my office for the next hour, after which the matter goes into the hands of my solicitors and I won't be accepting any calls from that point from either your father or his lackeys. Is that clear enough for you or shall I repeat it?'

'Mr Reef—'

'Which daughter are you anyway?' he interrupted her abruptly. 'Katie or Jennifer?'

'Katie.' She took a deep breath as she leant limply against the wall and prayed that the shaking which had begun in her stomach wouldn't transfer itself to her voice. This was incredible, monstrous—there had to be a perfectly simple explanation. 'Mr Reef, I'm sure there's a mistake here somewhere.'

'So am I,' he agreed coldly, 'and your father is the one who made it. I won't be made a fool of, Miss White, and I thought your father had the sense to realise that. One hour—doctor or no doctor.' And the phone went dead.

She remained staring at the receiver in her hand for a good thirty seconds before she recovered sufficiently to replace it and sink down on the nearest seat in the massive wide hall. This would have to happen today, with her father so ill.

The pains that had started in his chest during breakfast as he had read his paper had culminated within minutes in his writhing on the floor in agony, with Katie kneeling at his side as their housekeeper had frantically called the family doctor, who was also Katie's father's close friend, and fortunately lived in the same exclusive avenue of large detached houses. He had arrived within two or three minutes, just as the housekeeper, Mrs Jenkins, had taken the call from this Reef man, who had insisted on speaking to one of the family when Mrs Jenkins had told him that her employer wasn't available.

She had to get back to her father. She took a long, shuddering breath and levered herself off the seat before she hurried back to the breakfast-room, opening the door gingerly as she peered anxiously at him, now seated in an easy-seat to one side of the large bay window. 'What's wrong?' She spoke directly to Dr Lambeth as he turned to face her. 'Is he all right?'

'No.' Her father's friend's voice was flat. 'No, he isn't, I'm afraid, Katie. I've been warning him for months to get checked out but due to his own particular brand of bull-headedness he refused to listen to me. I'm going to call an ambulance.'

'No way.' Her father was as white as a sheet and his voice was a mere whisper of its normal, steel-like quality but his face was as determined as ever. 'If I have to go to that damn hospital, I'll go in your car, Mark.'

'You won't.' Even as her father spoke Mark Lambeth lifted the extension at his elbow. 'I'm not being responsible for your having another attack on the way, David, and that's final. There is equipment in the ambulance that you might need. Now don't be such a damn fool. If you are too stubborn to think of yourself, think of your daughters, man.'

'Dad?' Katie's eyes were wide as she stared down at the man whom she had always considered as unmovable as the Rock of Gibraltar. Her father was never ill; she couldn't remember him ever being less than one hundred per cent fit in the whole of her life. In fact, he looked on even the most severe illness as a weakness that was easily banished through sheer self-will, and was scathing with those lesser mortals about him when they couldn't accomplish what he apparently found easy to do. 'Dad, what's wrong?'

'It's his heart, Katie.' Mark Lambeth answered again,

and it was in that instant that Katie realised how serious things were. Her father wouldn't have tolerated being side-stepped in the normal run of things and Mark, old friend that he was, wouldn't have attempted it. 'He's had several warnings and now—' He stopped abruptly at the look of horror on Katie's face. 'Now he will have to come into hospital,' he finished flatly.

The ambulance was on the doorstep within four minutes and her father totally refused to let anyone but Mark ac-company him to the hospital. It hurt, but he had been hurt-ing her all his life and, if Katie hadn't exactly got used to it, she had learnt how to endure it without letting her feel-ings show.

She stared for some minutes down the long, wind-swept drive after the ambulance had departed, her thoughts in turmoil, before turning and re-entering the house where Mrs Jenkins was hovering anxiously in the hall. 'Oh, Katie, I can't believe it.' The small woman was nearly crying as she wrung her hands helplessly. 'Not Mr David.'

'He'll be all right, Mrs Jenkins.' Katie reached out and hugged the woman she had known most of her life and who had been something of a substitute mother since Katie's own mother had died when she was ten. 'You know Dad; he's as strong as an ox.'

'Yes, he is, isn't he?' Mrs Jenkins swallowed deeply and made for the kitchen. 'I'll fix us both a strong cup of coffee and then we'd better try to contact Jennifer. Do you know where she is?'

'On an assignment in Monte Carlo, I think, but the paper will have her number,' Katie said flatly as Mrs Jenkins' words reminded her of the telephone call of ten minutes ago. Carlton Reef. She'd have to phone him and explain somehow. He surely wouldn't expect her father to phone him from the hospital, would he? She recalled the hard, cold male voice and the barely controlled rage evident in every word, and shivered helplessly. But then again...

It took her nearly ten minutes to find his number in her father's address book on his desk in his study due to the fact that it was under a firm's name rather than his own. 'Tone Organisation. Chairman and Managing Director, Carlton Reef,' she said thoughtfully as she read the scrawly handwriting.

She had been sipping Mrs Jenkins' scalding hot coffee as she hunted and it had had the effect of stilling the trembling in her limbs and calming her racing heartbeat a little. In spite of her brave words to the housekeeper she was desperately afraid for her father, and the suddenness of it all still made her faintly nauseous as she made the call.

'Tone Organisation. Can I help you?' As the uninterested voice of the telephonist came on the line Katie took a deep breath and forced herself to speak quietly and coolly.

'Can I speak to Mr Reef, please?' she said politely. 'He is expecting the call.'

'I'll just put you through to his secretary.'

A few more seconds elapsed and then a cultured, beautifully modulated female voice spoke silkily. 'Mr Reef's office. Can I help you?'

As Katie gave her name and a brief explanation to the disembodied voice she felt her stomach tighten in anticipation of what was to come, and it was with a sense of anticlimax that she heard the secretary's voice speak again a minute or so later. 'I'm sorry, Miss White, I understand that Mr Reef was expecting your father to call.' It was said pleasantly enough but with just the faintest condemnation in the soft tones. 'He really can't spare the time—'

'My father has been taken into hospital,' Katie said tightly as she felt her face begin to burn with impotent anger. 'I'm fully aware of what Mr Reef was expecting but he'll have to make do with me, I'm afraid.'

'Just a moment.' There were a few more seconds of silence and then the secretary spoke again, her voice faintly embarrassed now. 'I'm sorry, Miss White, but Mr Reef said he did make it plain to you that it is your father he needs to contact. He doesn't think there is any point in talking to you.'

'Now just a darn minute.' Katie fairly spat the words down the phone. 'My father has been rushed to hospital with a heart attack and that creep you work for hasn't even got the decency to *talk* to me? Whatever he is paying you, it isn't enough for working for a low-life like him.'

'Miss White—'

'Look, this isn't your fault but I see no purpose in continuing this conversation,' Katie said stiffly before slamming the phone down so hard that the small table quivered under the force of it.

The pig! The arrogant, cold, supercilious pig! She tried to take a sip of coffee but her hands were shaking so much that she couldn't lift the cup, which made her still angrier. A combination of shock at her father's sudden collapse and rage at Carlton Reef's total lack of sympathy brought the tears she had kept at bay so far burning hot into the back of her eyes. She sat for long minutes trembling with the strength of her emotions before she wiped her wet eyes with a resolute hand and dialled the number of the local hospital with her heart in her mouth.

She was put through almost immediately to Mark whose calm, unflappable voice reassured her somewhat. 'It's as I expected, Katie,' the doctor said gently. 'His heart is struggling a little—I've recognised it for some time—but with certain medication or perhaps even an operation he can carry on more or less as normal.'

'Did he have a heart attack?' she asked nervously.

'I won't lie to you, Katie; you're over twenty-one and well able to take the rough with the smooth from what I've seen of you. Yes, it was a heart attack. He's all wired up at the moment and the results aren't too good but they're far from fatal, so don't let your imagination run riot. He's

been working too hard of late but you can't tell him. At
sixty he's no spring chicken.'

'No…' She smiled shakily. 'Can I come and see him?'

'Leave it for now,' he said gently. 'He'd hate you to see
him at the moment; you know how he is.'

Yes, she knew how he was, Katie thought painfully as
the shaft of agony that whipped through her body made
her gasp. If it had been Jennifer here he would have allowed her to see him, but the simple fact was that he didn't
rate his younger daughter at all. She shut her eyes tight
and forced her voice to remain normal. 'But he's in no
danger?' she asked quietly.

'Not now.' Mark's voice was soothing. 'I only wish I
could have got him in here months ago.'

'Thank you, Doctor.' She could feel the tears bubbling
to the surface and knew she had to finish the call quickly.
'I'll phone later, if I may?'

'Of course. Goodbye, Katie.'

'Goodbye, and thank you.'

She sat for long minutes in the overwhelmingly male
study before wiping her eyes for the second time, phoning
a local taxi firm and checking the address of the Tone
Organisation in her father's smart address book. Somehow,
during that telephone call with Dr Lambeth, something that
had been forming slowly through the last few years of her
life crystallised in her mind.

She was aware that her father treated her with an offhand, almost casual and often slightly caustic tolerance that
was totally absent from his dealing with her older sister.
Jennifer had chosen a career in the cut-and-thrust, dog-eat-
dog world of journalism and was doing wonderfully well.
This her father could both understand and respect. Whereas
she…

She blinked as she laid the book down on the desk. She
had chosen to work with physically handicapped children
in a local school after finishing her degree at university,

despite better, more up-market job offers. The hours were long, the salary low and the mental and physical exhaustion that were part of the job sometimes seemed too much to bear but the rewards… She straightened her back as she stood up. The rewards as the children under her care learnt to live to their potential were enormous and something that her father would never understand, she thought painfully.

'Where are you going, Katie—the hospital?' Mrs Jenkins met her in the hall as the taxi driver rang the bell. Katie's neat red Fiesta was sitting in the drive but she knew she was in no fit state to drive herself.

'No.' She smiled as she answered although it was an effort. 'Dad doesn't want any visitors although Dr Lambeth said he isn't in any danger.'

'Thank goodness.' Mrs Jenkins shut her eyes for a moment and then smiled mistily at her. 'I told you, didn't I?'

'Of course you did.' Katie smiled back at the homely face she had come to love over the years. 'I have to sort out some business affair of Dad's—you know, that other phone call? It's urgent and I can't really leave it but if anyone should phone you know nothing about it. OK?'

'Of course, my dear.' Mrs Jenkins understood her perfectly. 'Anyone' meant one person and one person only. 'I wouldn't say a word. We just want him to get better, don't we?'

Their house was situated on the outskirts of London, in a pleasant suburb with gracious tree-lined avenues and large houses in their own immaculate grounds. As the taxi ate up the miles into the capital the general vista changed to miles and miles of identical terraced dwellings, rows of shops broken only by the odd garage and, eventually, blocks of office buildings, neutral and blank in the cool March air.

The taxi stopped at a particularly imposing high-rise monstrosity and she saw the sign, 'Tone Organisation', with a little quiver of her nerves. But she wasn't backing out now. Her father might not think much of her but that didn't matter. This was something that needed to be done; Carlton Reef had made that plain. It wouldn't just go away—or, rather, *he* wouldn't just go away, she corrected grimly as she stared up at the tall building.

She needed to buy her father some time. She stuck out her small chin aggressively and leant forward to the driver. 'Could you wait?' she asked firmly. 'I shan't be long.'

'No problem, miss.' She received a toothy grin. 'You're paying.'

The offices were busy and full but by the time the smart lift had carried her up to the top floor all was hushed opulence and quiet elegance. She found the secretary's office with no trouble and prepared for battle as she opened the door, but the office was empty, the interconnecting door with the office on the left partly open.

'I don't care what it takes.' She knew that voice, she thought blindly as her stomach dropped into her feet. 'This is one hell of a mess, Robert, and you do what you can to get us out of it. Get back to me.' The sound of a receiver being banged down made her flinch but in the next instant the doorway was full of a big male body and a hard square face was staring at her with something akin to amazement in the narrowed eyes. 'Who the hell are you?'

She realised that she wasn't dressed in office mode, but the worn denims and thick jumper that she had donned that morning were ideal for her work, as was the no-nonsense hairstyle that held her long honey-blonde hair in a severe French plait at the back of her head. But in this world of pencil-slim skirts and the latest designer suits she was sadly out of place.

She lifted her chin a fraction higher and stared straight into the piercing grey eyes that were watching her so intently. 'I'm Katie White, Mr Reef, and I want a word with you.' She was glad her voice didn't betray her—inside she was a mass of quivering jelly. 'I have to say you are, without exception, the rudest, most objectionable man I have ever had the misfortune to come into contact with. My father is in Intensive Care at the moment with a heart attack—not that I expect you to be interested in that—and other than wheel the bed down here I had no alternative but to come here myself, as you wouldn't accept my call.'

'How did you get past Reception and my secretary?' he asked grimly, without the flicker of an eyelash.

There was something in the complete lack of response to her tirade that was more daunting than any show of rage but she forced herself not to wilt as she continued to face him. 'Reception was busy; a party of Japanese businessmen had just arrived,' she answered shortly. 'So I just slipped into the lift once I'd found your name and floor on the notice-board. And your secretary—' she glanced round the large room with her eyebrows raised '—is your problem, not mine.'

'I see.' He continued to survey her from the doorway and she was forced to acknowledge, albeit silently, that he really was the most formidable man she had seen for a long, long time. He was tall, very tall, with a severe haircut that held his black hair close to his head and accentuated the hard, aggressive male features even more. He could have been any age from thirty to forty—the big lean body was certainly giving nothing away—but the overall air of control and authority suggested that he had learnt plenty in the school of life.

'Well, Miss White, now you're here I suggest you come and sit down so we can discuss this thing rationally,' he said smoothly, after several seconds had passed in complete silence. 'You're obviously upset and I would prefer the dirty linen to be kept under wraps, as it were.'

'I couldn't care less about your dirty linen,' she shot back furiously, incensed beyond measure as he shook his dark head lazily, a mocking smile curving the full, sensual lips for a brief moment.

'I was referring to yours, not mine,' he said laconically. 'Or, to be more precise, your father's.'

'Now look here—'

'No, you look here, Miss White.' Suddenly the relaxed façade was gone and the man standing in front of her was frightening. 'You force your way into my office unannounced, breathing fire and damnation, when, by rights, it should be me squealing like a stuck pig.' He eyed her furiously. 'I'm sorry to hear that your father has had a heart attack, if in fact that is the case,' he added cynically, 'but that is absolutely nothing to do with me. The loss of a good deal of money and, more importantly, Miss White, my business credibility is, however, *everything* to do with *him.*'

'I don't know what you mean.' She had taken a step backwards without realising it and now, as he stared into the big hazel eyes watching him so fearfully, Carlton Reef forced himself to draw on his considerable store of self-control before he spoke again.

'Then let me explain it to you. Shall we?' He indicated his office with a wave of his hand, standing back from the doorway and allowing her to precede him into the room.

'How much do you know of your father's business affairs, Miss White?' he asked her quietly, once she was seated in the chair facing the massive polished desk behind which he sat.

'Nothing,' she answered honestly. 'My father—' She stopped abruptly. 'He isn't the sort of man to talk about business at home,' she finished flatly. Or, at least, not to her, she amended silently. Never to her.

'And this heart attack?' He eyed her expressionlessly. 'It's genuine?'

'Of course it's genuine,' she answered in horror. 'What on earth do you think—?' She shook her head blindly as words failed her. 'No one would make something like that up,' she finished hotly.

'You'd be surprised,' he said sardonically. 'When the chips are down most people would do just about anything.'

'Well, I wouldn't.' She glared at him fiercely. 'You can ring the hospital if you like and speak to Dr Lambeth, my father's friend. I presume you would trust a doctor at least?' she finished scathingly.

'I trust very few people, Miss White.' He shifted slightly in the big leather chair, leaning back and surveying her through narrowed grey eyes.

'Like my father.' The words were condemning and he recognised them as such.

'You don't approve?' he said mildly. 'You're an optimist, Miss White—a very dangerous thing to be in the business world.'

'Well, as I'm not in the business world I wouldn't lose too much sleep over it,' she replied carefully. 'And I wouldn't describe myself as an optimist anyway; I just think most people verge on kindness given a chance.'

He shut his eyes for a split-second as he shook his dark head slowly, the gesture more eloquent than any words, and then opened them to stare directly into the greeny-brown of hers. 'What world *are* you in?' he asked quietly, his eyes wandering over the pale creamy skin of her face and stopping for an infinitesimal moment on her wide, generous mouth. 'You do work for a living?'

'Yes.' She straightened a little in the chair as she rebelled against the questioning. 'But I don't see how that affects why I'm here today, Mr Reef. You said on the phone that my father had lost you some money…?'

'Lost me some money?' he repeated sarcastically. 'Well, that's one way of putting it, I guess. A little over-simplified but nevertheless… Have you read the morning papers?' he asked abruptly.

'The morning—?' She hesitated at the change of direction. 'No—no, I haven't. My father was reading them when he—' She stopped again. 'When he collapsed,' she finished flatly.

'They nearly had the same effect on me,' he said drily, and then shook his head at her outraged expression. 'And I wasn't belittling your father's condition, Miss White. Here—' He thrust a newspaper at her abruptly. 'Read that.'

She glanced at where he was pointing but the black letters were dancing all over the page as she tried to read them and she looked up after a moment, her eyes enormous in her white face. 'I'm sorry, I can't take anything in.'

'It's the total collapse of a certain economy that your father assured me was one hundred per cent solid,' he said coolly. 'I have invested a vast amount of money at his persuasion and within the last few months, too. I've been made to look ridiculous, Miss White, and I can't say it appeals.'

'But—' she stared at him desperately '—he wouldn't have done it on purpose, would he? No one's perfect.'

'"No one's"—?'

He held her eyes for several seconds before shaking his head again. 'This whole morning is fast beginning to resemble *Alice Through the Looking Glass*.'

A movement in the outer office caught his eye and he pressed the buzzer on his desk as he glanced towards the door. A second or two later, one beautifully coiffured head appeared round the door. 'I'm sorry, Mr Reef, I had to…' The well-bred voice died as the woman glanced in Katie's direction.

'Two coffees, please, Jacqueline, and hold all calls,' Carlton Reef said quietly.

'Oh, but I can't—' Katie glanced at him as he raised enquiring eyebrows. 'I've got a taxi waiting for me in the street. I can't—'

'Pay it off, Jacqueline.' He settled further into his seat as he raised one hand thoughtfully under his chin. 'And phone… What hospital is your father in?' he asked Katie abruptly. She told him quietly as her cheeks burnt scarlet. He thought she was lying; how *could* he think that? 'Tell them I want to speak to a Dr Lambeth,' he instructed his secretary quietly, 'and do it discreetly, there's a good girl.'

It was the first time that Katie had been able to examine him without having his piercing grey eyes trained on her and as she looked at him, really looked at him for the first time, she had to admit in a tiny, detached part of her brain that he really was devastatingly good-looking in a hard, macho sort of way.

His skin was dark, with the sort of even tan that suggested a recent holiday somewhere very hot and very expensive, and the dark grey eyes were fringed with short jet-black lashes under heavy dark brows. Big, broad shoulders suggested an impressive body under the beautifully cut suit and she had already seen that he was tall—well over six feet. And he was as hard as iron. She stiffened as the razor-sharp eyes switched back to her. He was the sort of man her father would respect and admire and whom she loathed.

'Now—' he didn't smile as the secretary shut the door without a sound and they were left alone '—why exactly did you feel it necessary to come here?'

'You phoned.' She stared at him with a mixture of bewilderment and anger. 'You made it clear that my father would be in some sort of trouble if he didn't—'

'He's in deep trouble already, Miss White, and I'm afraid there is nothing you can do about it.' There wasn't a trace of compassion in the deep voice and she knew, as she stared into the implacable, cold features, actual hate for another human being for the first time in her life. 'I am not sure of my facts yet, so I do not intend to say much more, but from the little I do know about this unfortunate episode it would seem to suggest that your father did not do the homework he was paid to do. Supposition is not an option in the market-place and for this to happen without any prior warning...' He shrugged eloquently. 'Something smells.'

'Are you saying that my father was dishonest?' she asked hotly. 'Because if you are—'

The buzzer on his desk interrupted further conversation and, as he took the call his secretary had put through, his face was blank and composed. It was obviously from Dr Lambeth and by the time he replaced the receiver, some minutes later, the dark face was thoughtful, although she had been unable to comprehend anything from his side of the conversation. As he finished the call his secretary knocked quietly and entered with the coffee, her face smooth and expressionless.

'Thank you, Jacqueline.' He glanced up once, busying himself with the tray. 'Can you arrange for the car to be brought to the main entrance in ten minutes, please?'

'Yes, Mr Reef.'

Something had been said during that phone call, something disturbing and relevant to her, Katie thought suddenly as she stared into the cool poker face op-posite. 'Is my father all right?' she asked quietly. 'He isn't worse?'

'No.' He handed her a cup of coffee and gestured towards the milk and sugar. 'Help yourself.'

'What did Dr Lambeth say?' she persisted, the trickle of unease gathering steam by the second. 'There's something you're not telling me, I know it.'

He stared at her for a good fifteen seconds before replying and she knew she was right. There *was* something—she could read it in the opaque blankness of his eyes. 'This is really nothing to do with me,' he said quietly. 'I feel it would be better if your father's friend explained in the circumstances, Miss White.'

'What circumstances?' She could feel her voice rising but there was nothing she could do about it as sheer un-diluted panic gripped her insides. 'He's worse? He's not...' She stared at him with huge eyes.

'No, nothing like that.' He waved his hand at her almost irritably. 'I'm satisfied that whatever your father did he did out of ignorance, incidentally. Not that that makes the results any different but—' He stopped abruptly. 'Why the hell did you have to come here today anyway?' he growled savagely.

'Why?' She glared at him, more angry than she could remember being in her whole life. 'Because you threatened me, that's why. You said—'

'I know what I said.' He stood up in one sharp movement and walked over to the huge plate-glass window where he stood with his back to her, looking down on the ant-like creatures below in the busy London street. 'I just didn't expect you to come here hotfoot like some guardian angel, that's all.'

'Well, all that could have been averted if you'd taken my call,' she said stiffly as her face burned still more. He was a monster, she thought, an absolute monster.

'Possibly.' He still didn't turn round. 'Well, perhaps the news would be better coming from a stranger, after all. I don't know. At least you would have some time to prepare yourself.'

'Mr Reef, you're frightening me,' she said in a very small voice and, at that, he did turn, swinging round to see her sitting on the edge of her chair, hands clasped together and face as white as a sheet. 'Whatever it is—could you just tell me?' she asked slowly.

'Your father is bankrupt.' He had taken a deep breath before he spoke but the smoky grey eyes didn't leave her face. 'He's lost the business, the house, the cars, every penny he owns in this deal. He's just unburdened himself to Dr Lambeth and asked him to let all interested parties know.'

All interested parties? Somehow that hurt more than anything else could have done. She lived at home, spoke to him every day, shared little moments of his life and he hadn't even hinted that things were bad. What had she ever done that her own father disliked her so much, trusted her so little? What sort of person did he think she was?

'Miss White, did you hear me?' He moved round the desk to stand in front of her, before kneeling and bringing his face into line with hers. 'He had suspected the worst for days but seeing it in black and white in the newspaper brought the heart attack on, so I understand. The house is mortgaged up to the hilt, there are debts mounting sky-high—'

'I understand.' She stopped him with a tiny wave of her hand as she spoke through stiff lips. 'And he bore all this alone; he didn't say a word to anyone.'

'He's a businessman, Katie.' She wasn't aware that he had spoken her name as her mind struggled to comprehend what he had told her. Their beautiful home that had been in her father's family for generations... The loss of that alone would kill him, she knew it. 'He has to make decisions that are sometimes difficult—'

'He's my *father*.' She raised her head to stare at him, her eyes drowning in the whiteness of her face. 'He should have been able to talk about it with me. What else are families for if not to share the hard times? If he could have told me, trusted me, he might not be in hospital now connected to a mass of wires and tubes—'

She wasn't aware that her voice had risen into a shrill shriek, but when the outer door burst open and the secretary rushed in she was conscious of a stinging slap across her face as Carlton Reef pulled her back from hysteria before lifting her body into his arms and signalling for the woman to leave with a sharp movement of his head.

'It's all right; shush now, shush...' He was sitting in the chair she had been occupying with her cradled on his lap as she moaned her anguish out loud, the hopelessness of endless years of trying to win her father's love and approval culminating in the devastating knowledge that he could have died and she wouldn't have known why. He hadn't wanted her, hadn't reached out, hadn't needed even a word of comfort from the daughter he seemed to despise so much.

'Why didn't he *tell* me?' she asked again, her head buried in the folds of his jacket. 'He should have *told* me.'

'He didn't want to worry you,' Carlton said comfortingly, somewhere over her head. 'That's natural in a father.'

'No.' She struggled away from him as she desperately tried to compose herself, suddenly horrified at the position she had put herself in. There was nothing natural about her father but she couldn't tell this man that—he wouldn't understand. She had never known her father share the smallest thing with her, never felt a fatherly hug, never had anyone to dry her tears as all her friends had. 'You wouldn't understand,' she said weakly. 'I'm sorry; I shouldn't have come. I didn't know—'

'Look, sit down and have your coffee.' He had risen as she had moved away and now took her arm gently, pushing her back down in the seat as he passed a cup to her. 'Drink that and then I'll run you home. It's been a tremendous shock for you.'

'I don't want it.' She stood up again and faced him, her face drawn and pale. 'And I'll make my own way home, Mr Reef.' She felt as if she could die of embarrassment at the ridiculous picture she made. Here she was, in the very centre of the hive that made up London's busy business world, behaving like some brainless schoolgirl. What on earth was he thinking and why, oh, why, had she come? She must have been mad, quite mad, but she hadn't been thinking straight. In fact, she hadn't been thinking at all!

She bit her lower lip hard. She'd made a bad situation wellnigh impossible. 'I'm sorry about all this,' she said stiffly to the hard, handsome face watching her so intently. 'I thought that if I came to see you and explained that my father was ill you would be able to wait a few days, that things could be sorted…' Her voice trailed away at the expression on his face. If cynical mockery could go hand in hand with reluctant sympathy then that was what she was seeing.

'And instead you found the very roof over your head was threatened,' he intervened softly. 'I do understand your predicament, Miss White. I'm not quite such an ogre as you seem to think.'

'No?' She faced him square-on now, a combination of shock and crucifyingly painful hurt making her speak her mind in a way she would never have done normally. 'Well, as you've pointed out, our worlds are very different, Mr Reef, and your standards and those of my father are not mine. The lust for power and wealth that masquerades as ambition is not for me.'

'I see.' His face had closed against her as she had spoken and now his mouth was grim. 'But, unless I am very much mistaken, you have enjoyed the benefits of this world that you seem to despise so much for a good many years without your conscience being *too* troubled?' His eyebrows rose mockingly. 'Or perhaps you live in a little wooden hut at the end of your father's property and indulge in hair-shirts and a monastic form of life?'

'Of course I don't.' Amazingly the confrontation was making her feel better, quelling the panic and fear that had gripped her since he had told her of their changed circumstances as fierce anger at his mockery left no room for any other emotion. 'And I am grateful to my father for all he's done for me—my education, our home, all the ''benefits'' you could no doubt list as well as I could. But—' she raised her chin and the large, clear hazel eyes that stared into his were steady '—I can manage without them without it being the end of the world. I don't *need* them in the same way that you do, Mr Reef.'

'Don't you indeed?' His face was dark with an emotion

she'd rather not dwell on now, and he crossed his arms as he leant back against the window, almost as though he needed to keep them anchored to his body rather than round her neck, she reflected silently. 'And how do you know what *I* need, Miss White? To my knowledge we have never met before today.'

'I know your type.'

'My "*type*"?' he barked angrily. 'My—' He broke off as he fought visibly for control before taking a deep breath and laughing harshly, the sound grating in the quiet air. 'You really do take the biscuit! You barge your way in here, flinging insults around as though they were confetti and then accuse me—'

He broke off again and shook his head before turning from her so that his hard features were in profile. 'You've had a bad day and I would guess that it's going to get worse. Let's leave it at that, and, despite the low opinion you obviously have of me, I would not dream of letting you find your own way home after the news I've just given you. The car will be outside now. Shall we?'

He turned and extended his hand to the door. She remained staring at him for one long moment before she moved forward. He was angry, very angry; that much she could see and she really couldn't take on any more now. It was simpler to accept this favour, however much it grated.

'Mr Reef?' His secretary's voice held a note of panic as he walked with Katie through the outer office, shrugging his big grey overcoat over his shoulders as he did so. 'You haven't forgotten the management meeting you called earlier? They're already assembling in the small boardroom—'

'Cancel it.' Her employer turned at the door to fix her with that cool gaze. 'Re-schedule for two this afternoon.'

'Is there a number where you can be reached?'

'No—' he was already shutting the door as he replied to the slightly dazed voice '—but I won't be long.'

'You don't have to do this.' As the silent lift sped swiftly downwards she ventured a glance at him through her eyelashes and then wished she hadn't. He looked mad—more than mad, she thought weakly, and she hadn't fully realised just how big and powerful that tall, lean body was until the close confines of the lift had emphasised it so threateningly. And his aftershave was gorgeous...

What was she *doing*, thinking such things at a time like this? she asked herself faintly, and about a man like him, too—the sort that populated her father's world in droves and the kind she had always abhorred. She was in shock. She leant limply against the wall of the lift and took a long, silent breath. That was it. That had to be it. Either that or she'd lost it completely.

He had ignored her hesitant voice as though he hadn't heard it but now the cold grey eyes pierced her, the expression in them anything but friendly. 'You aren't going to faint on me, are you,' he asked grimly, 'on top of everything else?'

'No, I'm not.' The adrenalin that sent fierce colour into her cheeks and an angry sparkle into her eyes also brought her jerking off the lift wall to stand rigid and stiff as they reached the ground floor. 'I've never fainted in my life.'

'Quite a formidable lady.' The thread of laughter in the mocking voice was unforgivable in the circumstances, and sheer anger kept her head up and her back straight as they walked through the reception area.

Out of the corner of her eye she was aware of one or two interested but veiled glances in their direction, but just keeping up with his large strides was more than enough to contend with for the moment. She had absolutely no intention of following in his wake like a whipped puppy, she thought tightly as they reached the massive automatic doors together. He was the epitome of the arrogant, dominant male but the Tarzan-Jane concept of male and female had never appealed less than at this moment.

The icy March wind was carrying chips of sleet on its breath as they left the hothouse warmth of the big building and she pulled her knee-length anorak more tightly round her as a big dark blue Mercedes purred to a halt in front of them, complete with chauffeur in matching uniform.

'In you get.' He opened the door for her and then followed her into the immaculate interior in one movement. 'Your address?' She gave it in a small voice that tried to be cool and assured but was merely...small.

'Are you going to the hospital?' They had travelled some minutes in complete silence but she had never been more aware of another human being in her life.

'Later perhaps.' Why couldn't he have been old and bald? she asked herself as she turned her head to meet his gaze. A sympathetic uncle-figure who would have met her halfway? 'My father doesn't—' She corrected herself quickly. 'The doctor thought it better to keep him quiet for the moment.'

'Right.' The intuitive grey eyes had narrowed at the slip but he made no comment, his face bland, and he turned to look out of the window into the grey world outside as the big car moved swiftly through the mid-morning traffic.

The journey home was accomplished in about half the time the taxi had taken earlier and as they drew into the smart pebbled drive she found herself looking, as though for the first time, at the house she had been born in. Mellow, honey-coloured stone, leaded windows and a massive thatched roof stared impassively back; the huge oak tree that stood in the middle of the bowling-green-smooth lawn at the front of the house was as yet bare and naked against the winter sky.

'You have a beautiful home.' She jumped visibly as he spoke, and dragged her eyes away from the sight that had suddenly become so poignant with a tremendous effort.

'Not for much longer, it would seem,' she said flatly as she held out one small, slim hand for him to shake. 'Thank you for bringing me home, Mr Reef. No doubt my father's solicitors will be hearing from yours in due course.'

'No doubt.' He hesitated for the merest second and then, instead of giving the handshake she had expected, leant forward and brushed her lips with his own. As she leapt backwards like a scalded cat he climbed out of the car and offered his hand, his eyebrows raised in a distinctly sardonic tilt. 'Allow me.'

She gave him her hand reluctantly—a fact which the dark eyebrows took full note of—and slid out of the car with as much dignity as she could muster, considering her cheeks were glowing bright red and her mouth was burning from the brief contact with his.

'Goodbye,' she said again, a little breathlessly this time, as she stepped backwards a few paces from his large bulk and edged towards the house.

'Goodbye.' He didn't smile or move and after a split-second of indecision she turned and ran up the steps to the front door, her only desire being to get into the safety of the house.

Mrs Jenkins must have heard the car because even as she fumbled in her bag for her key the door opened and she almost fell into the hall in her eagerness to get inside. 'Katie?' Mrs Jenkins peered out into the drive before slowly shutting the door and hurrying to her side. 'Who was that man?' she asked worriedly. 'And why was he looking at the house like that?'

'Like what?' Katie asked weakly, the relief at being home overwhelming. She didn't know why but during the last few seconds in the car she had felt undeniably threatened—terrifyingly so.

'Like...' Mrs Jenkins' voice faded away as she shook her grey head bewilderedly. 'I don't rightly know, but it wasn't normal.'

'He's not a normal man, Mrs Jenkins,' Katie said unsteadily just as the phone began to ring. It was the first of many calls that day from her father's colleagues and business contacts who were already beginning to demand their pound of flesh.

CHAPTER TWO

'KATIE?' Her sister's voice was more irritated than concerned when they finally managed to contact her in her hotel in Monte Carlo later that afternoon. 'What's all this about Dad being taken ill? He's never been ill in his life.'

'Well, he is now,' Katie said quietly, carefully keeping any trace of emotion out of her voice.

Jennifer was a duplicate of their father temperament-wise, scorning any show of sentiment or warmth, single-minded when it came to her career as a top reporter for one of the national tabloids, and utterly ruthless when it came to having her own way. At twenty-eight, she was five years older than Katie and well able to afford a luxurious flat in the heart of London, her own expensive sports car and a wardrobe of up-to-the-minute clothes that she changed like her nail varnish.

'It's his heart.'

'His heart?' Her sister's voice was scornful. 'I didn't know he had one!'

'Jennifer!' Katie's voice expressed her outrage.

Jennifer and her father had always held a mutual respect for each other's inexorable character while recognising that they were too alike to get on if they saw much of each other. The sort of comment that Jennifer had just made was exactly the type her father would have given if the situation had been reversed, and neither would have taken umbrage, but just now... Just now she couldn't take it, Katie thought painfully.

Despite his wishes, she had been to see her father after lunch, stopping for just a minute or two and driving away shocked beyond measure at the change which had been wrought in him in just a few hours. He had been in a semi-doze, never really waking, and to see his strong, lean and powerful body still and lifeless under the clinical hospital sheets had hurt more than she would have thought possible.

'I'm sorry, Katie.' Jennifer's voice was impatient, which made the apology null and void. 'How is he, then?'

'Hard to say.' She wasn't going to make this easy for her, Katie thought with an uncharacteristic flare of anger—besides which, it was true. 'He had a heart attack this morning but then, just before I got there this afternoon, he had another one. Lambeth said he'll be OK once they get the medication balanced but, as in most things medical, nothing is for certain.'

'Oh.' She could tell the news wasn't to her sister's liking. 'Well, I've nearly finished here so I suppose I could fly in in the next day or two,' Jennifer said reluctantly.

'There's something else.' Katie took a deep breath in preparation for the explosion. 'Dad's bankrupt.'

'*What*?' Now she really had her attention, Katie thought grimly. 'What do you mean "bankrupt"? You're kidding me.'

'I'd hardly joke at a time like this,' Katie said quietly. 'He's mortgaged the house, the business and even the weekend cottage he bought for Mum originally, and there is an absolute mountain of debts. The cars, his boat, everything will have to go. I saw the solicitor this afternoon after I left the hospital.'

'Oh, brilliant, just brilliant.' Her sister's voice was scathing. 'What happened to the Midas touch he was always so proud of, then?'

'Well, I think he's paid for the loss of it, don't you?' Katie ground out through clenched teeth as she strove to keep her temper. 'It was the knowledge of how bad things were that brought on the heart attack.'

'Well, there's no room in my flat for anyone else,'

Jennifer said quickly, after a moment's pause. 'I've got someone living in at the moment.'

'What's his name?' Katie asked tightly. Her sister was the original liberated woman, taking a new man into her life and her bed every few months and then kicking him out when she got bored, which was usually fairly quickly.

'Donald,' Jennifer drawled dispassionately. 'Hell, Katie, Dad'll hate the humiliation of bankruptcy, won't he? Not to mention losing the house. He really is a fool—'

'Don't you dare say that when you see him, Jen,' Katie hissed furiously. 'Not in words or one of those expressions you do so well. I'll murder you if you do.'

'Keep your hair on.' Her sister's voice was more amused than offended. 'Why you care so much about him I'll never know. You'll never learn, will you, Katie? You're just like Mum. Well, I've got to go, sweetie. I'll phone tomorrow and tell you what flight I'll be on. OK?'

'Goodbye, Jennifer.' Katie replaced the phone jerkily and strove for control. She should be hardened to it by now—she should, but her sister's total lack of emotion about anything but her precious job seemed to get harder to take as she grew older. And the casual reference to their mother... Katie could still remember the day she had died—the bleak, total despair and sense of loss that had never really dimmed through the years. She had learnt to live with the ache but had never really got over her mother's sudden death in a car accident when she was ten. They had been kindred spirits, totally different to look at but twin personalities and, in dark moments, Katie would still have given anything she possessed to gaze upon her face one more time and hug her tight.

It hadn't helped that her father and Jennifer had seemed almost unaffected either, although Katie had often thought, with her father at least, that it had been a way of coping with grief, to shut it in and refuse to acknowledge that it was there. But perhaps that was wishful thinking? She shook her head. Maybe Jennifer was right after all—she'd never learn, the eternal optimist always wanting to see the best in people. The thought brought the image of Carlton Reef into sudden focus before her eyes and she heard his scornful and derisive voice as though he were in the room with her.

'Right, enough is enough.' She rose determinedly from the chair. Tomorrow she would go into school, throw herself into the work there and face all the other mountains in her life when the time came. There was nothing she could do or say that would avert the catastrophe that had befallen them—it was far too late for that—but she was going to need to be strong for her father and herself.

How he would face the shame and humiliation she just didn't know; he was a fiercely proud man with unshakeable principles and this house in itself meant far more to him than mere collateral. Why on earth had he mortgaged it? She caught herself abruptly. No, recriminations were no good now; she needed to concentrate on the positive.

Over the next few days that resolution was to be sorely tested. News of the disaster travelled quickly in the business world and when she returned home from the school, often exhausted, the phone never seemed to stop ringing. Some of the callers were openly curious, digging for news, others faintly gloating that they themselves weren't in such dire straits; one or two were sympathetic and concerned and several verged on the abusive. The latter were mainly creditors who were doubting whether they would ever get paid.

Jennifer had called as promised, the day after her father's collapse, to say that the paper had contacted her shouting for a first-class reporter in France for a few days and would Katie mind terribly if she just did that little job before she came home? Katie had replied that her sister must decide her own priorities and Jennifer had finished the call quickly, saying that she had to run as the plane to France was going to be a tight one to catch.

Altogether, as Katie made her way to the hospital on Friday night for her regular evening visit, four days after her father's collapse, she felt tired in mind and body and sick to her soul. Her father hadn't improved as Dr Lambeth had hoped. Indeed, he seemed faintly worse each day, as though the will to live was ebbing away, and, forcing a bright smile on her face as she walked into the small side-ward, she dreaded what she would find.

'Hello again.' The deep, cool voice hit her at the same moment that her numbed gaze took in the dark, lean body lazily seated at her father's side.

'*You*?' She barely glanced at her parent, all her energy concentrated on the hard, handsome face watching her so intently. What was he doing here? The answer was obvious—he'd come to badger a sick man. How dared he? How *dared* he?

'Not the most charming of greetings but it will have to do, I suppose.' And the creep was laughing at her. 'How are you, Katie?' he asked softly as he rose and offered her his chair.

'I think you ought to leave, Mr Reef.' She forced her voice to remain low but her eyes, daggers of steel aimed directly at his, spoke volumes. 'My father is a sick man and I won't have him upset.'

'*Katie*!'

She ignored her father's horrified exclamation and continued to look at the tanned face in front of her, which had lost its mocking amusement as though by magic. 'Did you hear me?' she asked tightly.

'I'm not here to upset your father, Katie,' Carlton said coldly, 'although you seem to be doing a pretty good job of that yourself at the moment. Now would you please sit down and stop making a spectacle of yourself?' he finished coolly.

'Katie, for crying out loud…' Her father's agitated tones brought her eyes to his face for the first time and he nodded at the chair violently, his eyes lethal. 'Sit down, girl,' he barked angrily, more himself than he had been in days. 'Carlton is here purely as a friend, nothing more.'

'Really?' The word carried all the mistrust she felt for the man and her father shut his eyes for a moment in exasperation, shaking his head silently.

'Sit.' It was an order and she sat, but as Carlton moved another chair near the bed and stretched out his long legs to within an inch of hers it was all she could do to restrain the impulse to jerk away. She managed it—just. 'I'm sorry, Carlton.' David White waved his hand at her as he spoke. 'She isn't normally this way but my illness seems to have brought out the lioness-defending-her-cub mentality.'

'Not altogether a bad thing.' Carlton smiled back but, as the dark grey eyes moved to her, the smoky depths were as hard as iron. 'But the exterior doesn't quite prepare one for the fire and brimstone underneath.'

'Her mother was the same.' She glanced at him, utterly astounded as he spoke. She had never in all her life heard him compare her to his wife and it was still more amazing that his tone held a faint touch of embarrassed pride. 'She was sweetness personified, but if anyone threatened her family all hell was let loose. She was one special woman—'

He broke off, clearly horrified at having said so much, and there was a brief moment of charged silence before Carlton stepped into the breach. Katie was staring at her father open-mouthed, quite stunned. If a choir of heavenly angels had suddenly appeared in the room she couldn't have been more surprised.

Carlton glanced at Katie whose astounded countenance spoke for itself and then at David who was staring determinedly out of the window, his face ruddy with embarrassment, before shifting slightly in his seat and speaking in a cool, matter-of-fact voice that defused the awkward atmosphere.

'There are some papers in your father's study at home that might be important, Katie, and he'd like me to have a look through them in case there's a way out of this mess. Perhaps we could leave together and I could pick them up on the way home?'

'I'm in my own car,' she answered automatically as she dragged her eyes away from her father's stiff face with tremendous effort and turned to Carlton.

'No problem.' He smiled easily. 'I'll follow you home in mine. I'd really rather look at them as soon as possible. If anything's going to be done it's got to be quick.'

'You think there's a chance?' Katie asked quietly as she looked fully into the smoky grey eyes, receiving a slight jolt as the full power of the piercing gaze held hers.

'Possibly.' She couldn't read a thing from his face—it was a study in neutrality. 'From what David tells me, he was ill-advised himself and someone has certainly reaped a vast profit from this little deal. Now, whether it was actually illegal or not is another question and one that needs answering before the dust settles.'

'I see.' She didn't want him to come to her house; she didn't want anything at all to do with him, but in the face of what he was suggesting she had no choice but to smile, albeit painfully, and incline her head. 'Well, of course, if my father thinks you should investigate further—'

'I do.' David cut into the conversation sharply, his voice more alive than it had been for the last four days and certainly more full of energy than she had expected when she'd walked into the room that evening. 'Bankruptcy—' He stopped abruptly. 'I've never owed anyone a penny in my life,' he continued gruffly, 'and it doesn't sit well, Katie, dammit! If there's a chance—'

'If there is I'll find it.' Carlton's voice was smooth as he spoke but there was some inflexion, just something she couldn't put a name to, that made Katie stare at him hard. He was so cold this man, so in control. She didn't trust him; she didn't trust him an inch, and she was suddenly more sure than ever that there was an ulterior motive governing what appeared to be a straightforward request.

'Dad, these papers...' She hesitated and searched for a way of disguising the question she had to ask. 'Are there any you'd prefer to keep confidential? I could bring them all in here tomorrow and let you sort through them with Mr Reef if that would be more helpful. You must know what you're looking for, after all, and he might miss—'

'No, no. Let Carlton take anything he needs, Katie,' David said briskly. 'He probably knows what he's looking for better than I do.'

She didn't doubt it, Katie thought grimly, and that was exactly what was bothering her. She stared helplessly at her father, willing him to read her mind and know what she was thinking but he just smiled back at her before turning to Carlton with an easy gesture of thanks. 'Anything you can do would be appreciated, Carlton.'

Anything he could do? She felt a little shiver of premonition as her father spoke. He had never made a mistake before in the business world that was his lifeblood; it seemed very strange that now, suddenly, he *had* made one, and one of such gigantic proportions that it would leave them totally destitute. Exactly what part had Carlton Reef played in all this? she wondered suspiciously. And why this offer of help now, after the rage of a few days ago?

As she turned to the dark figure at her side she realised, with a sudden surge of panic, that if her father had been unable to pick up the waves she was attempting to send him Carlton Reef had had no such problem. The grey eyes were chips of stone in an otherwise expressionless face, the mouth a taut, sardonic line of enquiry.

'I have a photocopier in my study at home, Miss White,' he said coolly, the use of her surname a distinct put-down.

'Would you like to accompany me there tonight so you can keep the originals in your possession?' It was a definite challenge and one, in view of her father's comments, that he didn't expect her to take up.

She stared at him for a few moments, her natural politeness and gentleness warring with the feeling that possessed her where this man was concerned. 'Yes, I would,' she said quietly, hearing David's exasperated indrawn breath with a resigned sense of the inevitable. He would disapprove of her actions in dealing with Carlton Reef in the same way he disapproved of everything but she wouldn't have been able to sleep tonight if she hadn't followed through on her instinct.

She knew, without a shadow of a doubt, that the astute, intelligent mind ticking away behind those hard grey eyes was several paces in front of theirs. Quite what he had in view she wasn't sure, but if she had had to answer the old 'friend or foe?' question there would have been no hesitation. Carlton Reef was no friend of theirs.

For the rest of the visit Katie sat quietly listening to the two men talk. Carlton didn't broach the business difficulties again, concentrating on light, witty conversation that kept David amused without him having to make any effort himself.

Carlton Reef was a formidable adversary, she thought silently as the minutes sped by. She had never met a man who generated such an air of easy authority, who seemed so totally sure of himself. And she was forced to recognise, after nearly an hour had passed, that, in spite of her distrust and dislike for the man, there was something compellingly attractive about him that was both fascinating and frightening.

She remembered the feel of being in his arms and that light kiss as he had left her a few days before and shivered in spite of the over-hot room. This was ridiculous, she told herself sternly. She needed to keep all her wits razor-sharp around him and thoughts of this nature were definitely out of order.

The smoky eyes turned to her as the round, clinical clock on the wall ticked to seven o'clock. 'Would you like a few minutes alone with your father, Katie?' he asked quietly. She noticed that he hadn't asked David and surmised that he had gleaned enough about their relationship to know what her father's reply would have been.

'Thank you.' She smiled stiffly. 'I won't be long.'

'There's really no need…' The older man's protest was lost as Carlton rose and leant across the bed to shake him by the hand, making his goodbyes as he did so.

'It'll probably take a few days to sift through the correspondence, David,' he said easily as he walked to the door after replacing the chair near the wall, 'but if there's anything I'll call you immediately after the solicitors have checked it out. OK?'

'Fine, fine.' Her father was beaming as the door closed and for a moment, as Katie glanced at him, she knew a dart of intense irritation. 'What's the matter?' As his eyes switched to her face she tried to relax her features but it was too late. 'You don't like him, do you? Why?' he asked disapprovingly.

'I don't know him,' she prevaricated quickly.

'He tells me you went to see him on the day I was brought in here,' he said quietly, 'after he'd phoned the house. That took some guts, Katie, but why didn't you tell me?'

'There was no need.' She forced a bright smile to her face as she wondered where the conversation was leading.

'Katie…' Her father hesitated and then leant back against the pillows, his face more drawn now that Carlton's stimulating company had left. 'The situation can't get worse than it is, now can it? If there's the faintest chance he can pull it round, even if it means we're left with the house and nothing else, it's worth a try. I got greedy, girl...'

She stared at him in absolute amazement for the second time in an hour, aware that they were having the first *real* conversation of their lives.

'I'd always planned to leave the house to you, you know. Jennifer would have been looked after with an equal financial payment but I've always seen my grandchildren being raised in the old home, somehow. I know that's what your mother would have liked. She was always so upset she hadn't produced a son to carry on the White name that she didn't realise all I wanted was her—'

He stopped abruptly and there was a moment of deep silence before he continued. 'I don't know why I mortgaged the house—it was a crazy thing to do—but I thought I was going to make a killing.' He smiled grimly. 'And there was a killing all right.'

'Don't think about it now, Dad.' She stood up quickly; the expression on his face was too painful to watch. 'You've got to concentrate on getting better.'

'I didn't want to before Carlton came today,' he said thoughtfully, his expression introspective, 'but if there is a chance...' He looked up, his face touchingly hopeful. 'You do see we have to take it?'

'Of course.' She bent to kiss him goodbye and he turned his cheek to her as normal, the gesture as aloof as always. On the rare occasions in the past when she had gathered her courage and tried to hug or kiss him the response had always been the same—this formal offering of his cheek for a brief caress. 'Goodnight, Dad,' she said quietly, her voice bleak. Nothing had altered, not really. No wonder he liked Carlton so much. They were two of a kind—cold, reserved men who gave nothing of themselves and wanted no one.

Carlton was waiting for her just down the corridor, deep in conversation with one of the doctors. 'Katie?' He looked up as she carefully closed the door, and beckoned her to them. 'There's a chance that your father might be allowed home some time next week.'

'I understand you have a live-in housekeeper, Miss White,' the young doctor said quietly. 'So he would have someone with him at all times?'

'Yes.' She stared at him anxiously. 'You think he might have another attack?'

'We hope not.' She received the standard reassuring smile. 'But obviously he will take some time to recover from this one, you do understand that?'

'Of course.'

'And rest and quiet are essential,' he continued briskly. 'So, we'll think again after the weekend and give you a day or so's warning before he comes home.'

'Thank you.' As Carlton took her arm the doctor smiled and left them, to enter the main ward on their right.

'Encouraging news?' Carlton said softly as they walked towards the lift, his fingers burning her flesh as she strove to remain calm and cool. She was vitally aware of him, his touch, the timbre of his voice, and she allowed her head to fall slightly forward so that the thick, silky fall of her hair hid her face from his gaze.

'I suppose so.' There were several other people in the lift and she relaxed slightly as it sped to the ground floor, but once in the corridor leading to the car park she voiced what was on her mind. 'But I'm hardly going to be able to keep him quiet and calm with the house being sold over our heads and everything else that's going to happen.'

'Is there anywhere he could go while the worst of it takes place?' Carlton asked slowly. 'I understand your sister has a flat in London. Would she—?'

'No, she wouldn't,' Katie cut in flatly. 'The current boyfriend is in residence and, anyway, Jennifer is the last person to have her lifestyle interrupted in any way. She'd make my father miserable.' She shrugged. 'I'll think of something and perhaps, if you're successful, it won't be necessary anyway.'

'Right.' Again there was something, a slight inflexion in the bland voice, that made her glance at him sharply as they left the hospital.

'You meant what you said?' she persisted carefully as they walked down the path leading to the car park, a few thin flakes of wispy snow blowing in the icy wind. 'About trying to help?'

'Of course.' He stopped at the end of the path and turned to face her, his eyes veiled. 'It's in my own interest after all, isn't it? I do stand to lose as well by this deal, you know.'

'Some money, perhaps.' He seemed to tower over her as she looked up into his face, her honey-blonde hair blowing in silky tendrils over the satin-smooth skin of her face and her eyes huge in the dim light. 'But my father loses everything.'

'So do you.' His voice was very deep as his eyes followed the soft line of her mouth. 'But that has hardly occurred to you, has it?' There was a faint note of bewilderment in his voice but she was thinking about her father's face in those few minutes she had had alone with him and didn't notice.

'I have my work.' She looked up at him gravely. 'And I can find us a small flat somewhere but it will take time. How long—?' She paused and then continued painfully. 'How long do these sorts of things take to happen?'

'Not long,' Carlton said expressionlessly. 'David has to declare himself bankrupt first and then things move fairly swiftly, I understand.'

'It'll kill him.' She looked over the cold, dark car park bleakly, her face desolate, and missed the sudden tightening of his mouth at her distress. 'Well…' she turned to him again and indicated her car some yards away '…that's my car, so if you want to follow…?'

'Fine.' He stood still for a brief moment, observing her quietly before striding over to the Mercedes, lost in the night shadows at the far side of the car park. She unlocked her door and slid into the car, starting the engine and turning on her lights as she waited for him to join her. The snow was falling a little more heavily now, big, flat flakes beginning to outnumber the tiny, thread-like ones of a few minutes ago. She normally found the sight entrancing but tonight her heart was too heavy for the normal elation.

As the powerful headlights of the Mercedes drew up behind her she pulled carefully out of the dark car park, the icy conditions and the fact that Carlton was just behind her making her unusually nervous. Stop it, Katie, she told herself sternly. You're a big girl now and you've been driving for years.

It didn't help.

The journey home through a world fast becoming a winter wonderland was uneventful and as she drew into the winding drive, grateful for the scrunchy pebbles under the car's wheels instead of the black ice she had encountered more than once on the main roads, her heart plummeted right into her boots. 'Jennifer.'

She pulled up at the side of her sister's expensive sports car and glanced back to where Carlton had just entered the drive. What was her sister going to make of all this? And, more importantly in the circumstances, what was Carlton going to make of her sister?

She wondered, for a split-second, if she had time to dash into the house and warn Jennifer to be on her best behaviour or at least be civil, but as Carlton unfolded his long body from the front of the car and slammed the door shut she resigned herself to the fact that it was too late.

She was fumbling with her key when he reached her side, and he gestured behind her to the car as the door swung open. 'That's my sister's car,' she said hurriedly as the warm, scented air from the hall reached out a welcome. 'She must have just arrived.'

'Better late than never,' Carlton murmured sardonically as he followed her into the house. 'Or perhaps in your sister's case that old cliché doesn't apply?' he added wickedly.

She didn't have time to reply. As they entered the house both Jennifer and Mrs Jenkins appeared from the drawing-room, the former cucumber-cool and as regal as ever and the latter clearly flustered.

'Darling...' Jennifer's beautiful almond-shaped blue eyes rested briefly on her sister before transferring to Carlton's hard, dark face, whereupon they brightened considerably. 'We've only just arrived, Katie,' she continued as she remained looking at Carlton, 'so there was no time to visit father tonight.'

'The visiting doesn't end till ten,' Katie said automatically, stiffening as another figure sauntered lazily out of the drawing-room.

'Oh, this is Donald,' Jennifer said in an aside over her shoulder. 'And *this* is...?' She held Carlton's impassive glance for a long moment before turning briefly to Katie. 'Aren't you going to introduce us to your friend, sweetie?'

'I...' Katie found herself at a loss for words and tried desperately to pull herself together. Why on earth had Jennifer brought her current lover here now of all times? she thought helplessly. It had to be the worst possible timing.

Donald had come to a halt just behind her sister, resting a casual hand on her shoulder as he glanced nonchalantly in Katie's direction.

'You must be the little sister?' he drawled with a confidence that grated on Katie's nerves like barbed wire. 'Been holding the fort for Jennifer, then?' he added patronisingly.

'She's been doing a lot more than that.' Carlton's voice

was crisp and clear and both Jennifer and her swain stiffened at the tone. 'And today has been a hard day like all
the other ones before it, so might I suggest that we indulge
in further niceties over a cup of coffee in the drawing-
room?' The last part of the sentence he directed at Mrs
Jenkins with a warm smile that had been totally absent
when he had looked at Jennifer and Donald, and the small
woman nodded quickly, her eyes grateful at his mastery of
the situation.

'You go and sit down, my dear,' Mrs Jenkins said
quickly as she glanced at Katie's drawn face. 'I'll bring it
through in a minute.'

'Thank you, Mrs Jenkins.' Katie didn't know whether to
be pleased or angry at Carlton's control over them all but
it was simpler to be neither. 'I do feel exhausted tonight.'

'Poor darling.' Jennifer's voice was full of sweetness as
they all walked through into the drawing-room but the hard
blue eyes had difficulty in leaving Carlton's face for more
than a few moments. She turned as Katie sank down into
an easy-chair by the fire and held out her hand to Carlton,
her eyes frankly appraising. 'I don't think we've met,' she
said directly.

'I'm sure we haven't.' The mockery was back in
Carlton's voice and his eyes were cool as they looked into
the beautiful face in front of him. At twenty-eight, Jennifer
was in the full bloom of her beauty and she knew it. There
was no similarity between the two sisters except in the
colour of their hair, but whereas Katie's was soft and wavy
Jennifer's was cut into a sleek, expensive bob that framed
the lovely heart-shaped face in which the clear, vivid blue
eyes with their faintly oriental slant gave her a feline attractiveness that was infinitely seductive. 'I'm Carlton
Reef,' he continued coolly. 'A friend of your father.'

'A business colleague,' Katie added from her armchair.
'Carlton has offered to look through Dad's papers and see

if there is any way out of the mess we're in. He was involved in a considerable loss himself.'

'Oh, dear.' Jennifer reluctantly withdrew her hand as Carlton let go of hers. 'Not too bad, I hope?' she asked sweetly.

'I'll survive.' He glanced across at Donald who had been watching the little exchange with a faint frown on his good-looking face. 'You drove Jennifer down?' he asked pointedly.

'Not exactly.' Donald stiffened even as his eyes flickered beneath Carlton's icy gaze.

'Donald's a close friend of mine,' Jennifer said easily. 'Aren't you, darling? We thought it would be fun to have a few days out of the city together as I had to come down here anyway.'

'*Fun*?' Katie came back into the conversation with a vengeance as she saw red. 'You are supposed to be down here to see Dad, or had you forgotten?' she asked furiously. 'I hardly think ''fun'' comes into it!'

'Oh, don't be an old grouch,' Jennifer said with a total lack of heat, which told Katie that she had other fish to fry, and, as she watched her sister eat Carlton with her eyes, she had a good idea of what they might be. 'Donald can always take my car and disappear back to the flat, can't you, darling?' She glanced across at him and continued without waiting for an answer, 'And I'll stay here to help you, Katie.'

And pigs might fly, Katie thought balefully. She knew exactly what Jennifer had in mind—she had seen that predatory gleam in her sister's eyes before with more than one man. And she also knew the reason for the quick turnabout regarding Donald's visit. He would cramp her style if she were to indulge in a full-scale man-hunt.

'How sisterly.' Carlton's voice was bland, but as Jennifer's eyes returned to his face she saw the cynical mockery evident in every hard line and her mouth curved in a seductive little pout. This was the sort of man she both understood and appreciated.

'You don't mind going back tomorrow morning, do you, darling?' Jennifer turned to Donald with a languid wave of a limp hand. 'Perhaps it would be better with Father so ill.'

Donald obviously did mind, very much, but just as obviously he wasn't going to voice his protest with Carlton's piercing grey eyes trained on his face. He shrugged once, with a shake of his blond head, and said nothing but the pale blue eyes were malevolent.

As Mrs Jenkins bustled in with the coffee-tray the conversation came to a halt for a few moments, but once the housekeeper had left and everyone was seated Jennifer spoke directly to Carlton, her eyes curious. 'What exactly do you do, Mr Reef?' she asked sweetly.

'"Exactly"?' He was openly mocking her but she didn't seem to mind, Katie thought in amazement. She had never seen anyone treat her beautiful sister like this before; normally the boot was very definitely on the other foot. 'Well, "exactly" might take too long to explain,' he said easily, 'but among other interests I own the Tone Organisation. Perhaps you've heard of it?' he continued lightly as Jennifer's slanted eyes opened as wide as they could.

'I knew I recognised the name,' she breathed softly. 'I just knew it. You never told me,' she added accusingly to Katie who was watching the little by-play with some bewilderment.

'Told you what?' Katie asked in surprise.

'That you'd got *the* Carlton Reef down here,' her sister said breathlessly. 'I've been trying to fix up an interview with you for ages, you know,' she added as she turned the full hundred-watt smile in Carlton's direction. 'The paper has been doing a series on millionaires of the nineties. Perhaps you've read it?' she asked hopefully.

'I think not.' Carlton's voice was very dry.

'Oh.' Jennifer wasn't one to let a small put-down affect her. 'Well, your publicity department wasn't at all helpful,' she added with a faint touch of provocative helplessness. 'And it would mean *so* much to get a scoop at the moment.'

'Excuse me,' Katie interrupted as her stunned mind tried to make sense of what she had just heard. 'Are you telling me that you're a millionaire?' she asked Carlton flatly.

'I wasn't aware I was telling you anything.' His voice was guarded and very cool as he looked expressionlessly into her shocked face.

'But *are* you?' she persisted, still in the same flat voice.

'Do you mean to say you didn't know?' Jennifer laughed shrilly into the loaded atmosphere. 'Really, Katie, you live in a world of your own at that awful school. There is something beyond disinfectant and snotty noses, you know—'

'*Shut up.*' And for once in her life Jennifer did just that as her sister turned on her a glare that would have silenced Attila the Hun, before looking again into Carlton's dark face. 'What sort of man are you?' she hissed tightly as she rose slowly from her chair to stand over him like an avenging angel. 'To threaten my father like you did, to act as though the loss of that deal was the worst thing that had ever happened to you when all the time you're rolling in money...'

Carlton hadn't moved; in fact, neither had anyone else. The whole room had taken on the effect of a macabre tableau, frozen in time. 'He's lost everything—*everything*!' She could hardly get the words past her lips, so great was her fury. 'And you sit there like a big black spider with a hundred other webs, laughing at us!'

'I'm not laughing at you, Katie.' Carlton's voice was as flat as hers had been. 'And, if you remember, I thought your father had been...less than honest.'

'And that makes it all right?' she ground out through clenched teeth. 'To fool us—'

'Your father is fully aware of my financial position,' he cut in sharply, his voice icy now, 'which is one of the reasons why he approached me in the first place. I agreed to partner him in this venture at his insistence.'

'But the loss of the money doesn't mean anything to you,' she said furiously. 'Not really. How could you badger him—?'

'Dammit, girl, I haven't badgered him,' Carlton snapped tightly. 'If you remember, it was I who offered to help tonight, to try and find a way—'

'We don't need your help.' She saw Jennifer's hands flutter in protest with a soft exclamation of disagreement and turned on her sister like a small virago. 'And if you want your precious interview you have it, but not in this house. You don't care about Dad, not really. He could have died and you wouldn't even have been here. He could still die! What sort of world is this anyway where money is considered more important than a human being?'

She drew herself up and cast them all an icy look as she prepared to leave the room. 'We'll probably go under, Mr Reef,' she said at the door as she turned to hold his eyes across the room. 'But that needn't worry you at all, need it? As you said when you phoned this house the day my father had his heart attack, it was his "stupidity and crass ineptitude" that caused it all anyway.' His harsh words had been burning in her subconscious ever since they'd been uttered and Carlton's face whitened as she flung them back at him. 'But he's worth ten of you—of any of you.'

'Oh, really…' Jennifer's deriding voice wafted across the room. 'I can't see what all the drama is about, for goodness' sake. Anyone would think the old man was whiter than snow when in fact he's been a right so-and-so most of his life.' She stared at Katie scornfully. 'When has he ever been there for you, then? Answer me that. I don't understand you, Katie, I really don't. You're one of life's natural doormats.'

'No, I'm not.' Katie's face was as white as a sheet as the enormity of the confrontation began to sink in. 'I love Dad. I don't care what you think, Jennifer. You're incapable of love, and perhaps he is, but that doesn't make what I feel for him any different, and he *has* been there for both of us on lots of occasions in his own way.'

'Spare me the bleeding heart—' Jennifer's voice was cut off as Carlton ground out her name through clenched teeth before turning to Katie, his body tall and straight as he stood up and his face calm.

'You're thinking with your heart and not your head,' he said coldly as he walked across the room after picking up his coat from the back of his chair. 'Probably the result of the mental and physical exhaustion of the last few days.'

'No, it isn't.' He took her arm as she replied and led her out of the room, shutting the door firmly behind the other two. 'This is me; take it or leave it.'

'I'd prefer the former.' She had no warning as he enfolded her in his arms, his body hard as he held her close to him, forcing her head back in a deep, long kiss that she was powerless to resist, pinned as she was against his big frame. Her brief struggles were ineffectual, only serving to move her more intimately against his body as he moulded her into him, his mouth devastating as it held hers.

And then, shockingly, she felt a response deep inside to the sensual lovemaking, a warmth in her lower stomach and a tightening ache in her breasts as they pressed against his hard chest that frightened her far more than his embrace. She had never, ever experienced such a reaction to male chemistry and was unprepared for the violence of the assault that came traitorously from within.

His tongue moved caressingly along her lips before invading the sweetness of her mouth and she felt her heart pounding with the thrill of it. She couldn't believe that a kiss could draw forth such blindingly shattering sensations as she was feeling now. Her head was spinning, her body was pure fluid as it melted into his and the rest of the world was a distant thing with no meaning or substance.

'Hell, you're lovely…' His voice was thick and deep and a sensuous, teasing tool in itself as his hands massaged her back, slipping under her thin cotton sweater with an ease that suggested he had done this sort of thing a million times before. 'I don't think you know the sort of power you have over a man…'

She wasn't aware that her arms had drifted up to his neck or that she was straining into him, searching for closer contact, as he took her mouth again. She was drugged, drugged with sensations that she had never dreamed existed but then, as his hands moved to her hips to draw her further against the hard evidence of his desire, cold reason returned in an icy deluge.

'Let me go.' It was a whisper but he heard it; freezing for a single moment before he put her from him without a word, striding down the hall and out of the front door without a backward glance.

CHAPTER THREE

KATIE leaned against the wall of the hall for long moments as she struggled to calm her spinning mind, hearing the roar of the Mercedes' engine as it left the drive far too fast and died away into the night.

How dared he? How dared he kiss her like that? she thought weakly as she forced her trembling legs to move and carry her towards the stairs. She reached the sanctuary of her room just as her legs gave way. He knew she loathed him; how could he take advantage of his superior strength so blatantly?

She scrubbed at her mouth with the back of her hand but the feel of his lips and body were imprinted on her flesh, going more than skin-deep. He was quite without morals, principles of any kind—that much was clear, she thought bitterly. But then who was she to talk after the wanton way in which she had responded?

She shook her head as she began to undress, walking through to the pretty *en-suite* bathroom in pale lemon and standing for long minutes under the shower as she let the warm water flow over her skin and hair.

After wrapping herself in a big fluffy bath-sheet she walked through to the bedroom again, looking round this room that had been hers since childhood, with its wonderful view over the half-acre of garden at the back of the house. Soon it wouldn't be theirs any longer.

She frowned as the enormity of it all began to seep into her consciousness. She had been concentrating so much on her father these last few days, so anxious that he wouldn't have another relapse, that she had pushed the financial disaster to the back of her mind in order to cope. But it was

starkly in focus now and there was no escape from the
knowledge of the effect that losing the family home would
ultimately have on her father. He wouldn't be able to bear
it. She thought back to the last few days before Carlton
had given him a ray of hope and shook her head wearily.
He had been waiting to die, willing it almost. And she'd
sent Carlton away, insisting that they didn't need his help.

She groaned out loud, moving from the window to look
into the full-length mirror-doors on her wall-to-wall wardrobes. Why had he kissed her? She inspected her face crit-
ically. She wasn't a beauty, whereas Jennifer was quite
stunning. Large hazel eyes fringed with thick, dark lashes
stared back at her, her wet hair clinging in curling tendrils
to her shoulders.

She was averagely pretty, she thought with a little puzzled sigh, no more. Boyfriends had come and gone since
she had started dating at sixteen, some more ardent than
the rest, but none that had fired her with a grand passion.

She searched her face once more and then shrugged with
a defeated sigh, quite missing the soft vulnerability in the
hazel eyes and innocent appeal of her mouth that was more
sensual to a discerning male than any flamboyant glamour.
Maybe he had meant the kiss as a punishment for her harsh
words? As she remembered all she had said her cheeks
burnt with embarrassment. Oh, hell. She'd made a real
mess of all this.

It was a long, sleepless night and she only drifted off into
a heavy slumber as the birds began to sing in the old silver
birch outside her window. She awoke with a terrible start
a few hours later as Jennifer burst unannounced into her
room, looking as fresh as a daisy.

'Come on, sleepyhead.' Her sister plumped herself down
on the edge of the bed and shook her without ceremony.
'I've sent Donald packing, so are we speaking again?'

'What time is it?' Katie struggled out of a disturbing

dream that she couldn't recall and stared sleepily at her sister.

'Just gone nine,' Jennifer answered chirpily. 'Are you seeing Carlton today?'

'Carlton?' The name acted in much the same way as a bucket of cold water. 'I hardly think so after what I said to him last night.'

'You *were* a little emotional,' Jennifer said reprovingly, 'but perhaps he likes a bit of melodrama now and again. Anyway, it ought to be me who is mortally offended.'

'Why aren't you?' Katie asked shrewdly.

'Because you were only speaking the truth,' Jennifer answered disarmingly. Katie remembered this tactic of her sister's from the past—she always used it to devastating effect, especially when accompanied by the sheepish grin that, as she was doing now, melted the rather sharp features. It didn't mean anything but it *was* hard to resist, she thought wryly. 'Come on, Katie, I know I'm a pig but it's just the way I'm made,' Jennifer continued persuasively. 'Give me the gen on this Reef man, *please.*'

'There's not much to tell,' Katie said slowly, knowing she was being duped but beyond caring. 'Dad apparently approached him to go into this business deal with him and—'

'I don't mean *that*,' Jennifer interrupted caustically. 'What about his love life? Has he got a girlfriend? Is he keen on you? Any skeletons in the cupboard that you know of?'

'Jen!' Katie jerked upright in the bed as she brushed the hair out of eyes that were beginning to spark. 'Can't you forget you're a reporter for a few minutes?'

'Well, if I could, he's the man to make me,' Jennifer said dreamily. 'You must have noticed what a dish he is, Katie. I know your sex drive isn't particularly frenzied but that physique coupled with those incredible eyes of his must have caused a few tremors, surely?'

As Katie opened her mouth to deny it she remembered the kiss of the night before and the way it had fired her body, and blushed scarlet, the protest dying on her lips.

'I thought so.' Jennifer narrowed her eyes at her sister, her expression thoughtful. 'But he has a certain reputation, little sister, in business and out of it, for going straight for the jugular. I wouldn't mess with him, sweetie; leave it to the experts.'

'Like you?' Katie slanted her eyebrows at Jennifer even as she had to laugh at her sister's outrageous manoeuvring.

'Exactly.' Jennifer stood up gracefully, stunning in white ski-pants teamed with a pure white cashmere sweater that would have cost Katie a month's salary. 'You never know, I might be able to…persuade him to do something to help us out.'

'You really do have the morals of an alley-cat, Jen,' Katie said lightly, half serious and half teasing.

'I know.' Jennifer seemed pleased at the comment. 'But life's so short, sweetie, and I do find sex such fun.' The feline eyes narrowed still further at the expression on Katie's face. 'Oh, hell, I've shocked you again,' she drawled lazily. 'When were two sisters ever such opposites as you and I?' She sauntered over to the window and pulled the curtains wide open, gazing down into the shining white world outside. 'I suppose you haven't met anyone since we spoke last?' she asked idly, without turning round.

'If you mean am I still a virgin why don't you just come straight out and ask?' Katie said tightly, well aware of the hidden question in her sister's apparently innocuous words.

'Oh, Katie, you're going to grow old and die here without ever having any fun if you're not careful.' Jennifer yawned as she swung round and walked towards the door. 'What, or who, are you waiting for anyway? I haven't noticed many Prince Charmings beating a path to your door.'

'Jennifer, we're different; let's just leave it at that,' Katie said firmly. 'You can go from man to man without it bothering you an iota; I just couldn't. And I do have fun, anyway. I go on dates when I feel like it and I've loads of friends—'

'These are the 1990s, Katie.' Jennifer stopped at the door with her hands on her hips as she frowned across at her sister. 'People just don't go on dates without following through.'

'Well, I do.' Katie was determined to end the conversation as soon as possible. 'And now I want to get dressed, so if you don't mind vacating the premises...? And Dad is waiting for a visit, don't forget.'

'I know, I know.'

'And later you are going to have to go through some of the legal implications with me, Jennifer,' Katie added warningly.

'Oh, hell, darling, how tacky.' Jennifer wrinkled her nose disapprovingly. 'Can't we just leave it to Dad and the solicitors?'

'Jennifer, when are you going to get it through your head that he is an ill man?' Katie asked tightly. 'A very ill man. He shouldn't be worried—'

'Well, you refused Carlton when he offered to help,' Jennifer snapped back abruptly, 'and frankly I think that that was a hell of a moment to get on your high horse.' She flounced out of the room before Katie could respond, banging the door in her wake.

Katie stared after her, her face dark with anger, before she relaxed against the pillows with a deep sigh. Why did five minutes with Jennifer always resemble several rounds with Muhammad Ali? she asked herself silently, although in this case she had to admit that that parting shot had been justified.

She shut her eyes tightly as she forced down the sick panic in her chest. She would have to ring him and ask if he would still help them, to eat humble pie... She pictured the scene in the hall in her mind's eye and shook her head helplessly. He was going to just love this. He must think he'd got them all exactly where he wanted them.

Perhaps she ought to leave him to Jennifer after all? she thought numbly even as something in her repudiated the thought of her sister in an intimate embrace with Carlton Reef. He was the sort of man who could well want a particular form of thanks for his assistance. She felt a little shiver of excitement flicker down her spine and despised herself for it. All this was sending her crazy.

The ringing of the phone downstairs interrupted her thoughts abruptly and a few moments later Mrs Jenkins popped her head round the door. 'Jennifer said you were awake,' she said cheerily as she placed a cup of tea on the bedside cabinet. 'And Mr Reef is on the phone—wants to speak to you and you alone.' The housekeeper's face twisted in a rueful grimace. 'That didn't go down well with your sister.'

'No, no, it wouldn't.' Katie's stomach had performed a violent cartwheel and she took a deep breath before lifting up the bedroom extension at her elbow. He was going to be mad, so mad. Was he going to make her crawl for help?

'Katie?' It was the deep, impatient voice she would have known anywhere and again that subtle little shiver trembled down her spine. 'Are you free this morning to go over those papers?'

'The papers?' She must sound like a complete idiot, she thought desperately as she struggled to compose herself. 'Oh, the papers. Yes, this morning would be fine.'

'I'll be over about eleven.' He hesitated for a split-second and she expected a few caustic words of admonition. 'And I'm taking you out to lunch. No argument, please; you need to relax a little.'

'Lunch?' Please help me to stop repeating the last word of every sentence, she prayed desperately. 'But the hospital—'

'Let Jennifer do a turn.' This time the dark voice held a definite bite. 'And you can call in this evening, can't you?'

'I...' It was an olive-branch and, in the circumstances, more than generous, she thought rapidly. She couldn't refuse. But to suggest that lunch with Carlton Reef could be *relaxing*? 'Thank you,' she said jerkily. 'Lunch would be lovely.'

'Good try, Katie.' The words were said with surface amusement but she sensed something underneath. 'For a polite acceptance, that is, but I'm well aware that you loathe the very ground I walk on. I'll see you at eleven and please have all the necessary correspondence ready.' And as the receiver was replaced at the other end she found herself still holding the phone, with her mouth wide open and her cheeks burning.

Jennifer managed still to be around when Carlton called at eleven, and was first to the door, almost pushing Mrs Jenkins over in her rush to get there. 'Hi there.' She smiled up at him as Katie appeared in the doorway of her father's study. 'Thought any more about that interview?'

'Couldn't think of anything else,' Carlton said mordantly as he raised a hand of acknowledgement to Katie, who was in the background.

'And?' Jennifer asked hopefully, pouting her lips beguilingly.

'It seems an even worse idea on reflection than it did last night.' Carlton's eyes were cool as he stared down at the lovely blonde. 'I've seen what papers like yours do to interviews, Jennifer.'

'Perhaps in the normal run of things,' Jennifer admitted reluctantly, 'but you know me, Carlton; you're a friend of the family. I wouldn't dream—'

'Jennifer, I don't know you from Adam,' Carlton said cynically as he moved inside the house, forcing Jennifer to back unwillingly to one side. 'And as for "a friend of the family'' …?' He caught Katie's eye and the expression in his smoky grey eyes became positively derisive. 'Hardly.'

'But—'

'Now go and visit your father,' Carlton said drily as he walked towards the study without a backward glance. 'That *is* what you came down for, isn't it?' he added as he turned in the doorway and glanced at Jennifer's mutinous face. 'How long are you here for anyway?'

'Oh, whenever…' Jennifer murmured airily.

'Well, I'm sure we'll meet again.' Carlton smiled dismissively as he shut the study door very firmly and turned to Katie, watching her silently.

She stared back, acutely uncomfortable but determined that she wouldn't be the first to break the silence. Now that he was here, in the flesh, the sheer intimidating, sensual power of the man reached out to subdue and master her and the conciliatory feelings she had been experiencing all morning since his phone call took flight. She had never met anyone, her father included, who could challenge her with such absolute arrogance without uttering a word, she thought dazedly as the silence lengthened.

'Last night was not one of my better moves,' he said softly when the quietness reached screaming-point, 'but the only mitigation of what you would consider an act of gross boorishness was that it wasn't planned.'

It was the very last thing in the world that she had expected him to say and all coherent thought left her head as she stared dumbly back, quite unable to utter a sound.

'How mad are you?' he asked flatly, after a long moment.

'I—' She stopped abruptly as a feeling of utter bewilderment swept over her. She had flown at him, albeit vocally, in front of two other people and caused a scene, which was something she had never imagined herself doing in her wildest dreams. He had handled it with cool aplomb and amazing control in the circumstances, she reflected weakly, and even the kiss hadn't been unpleasant.

Far from it in fact, she thought silently as she turned and walked over to the desk where she had spread out all the relevant papers a few minutes before. He might have meant it as chastisement for her ill-chosen accusations, a lesson in discipline, but it had had quite a different effect on her nervous system.

'I'm not mad,' she said quietly after a long pause. 'I was way out of line, I know that. The important thing is that you're here now and prepared to try and help and I appreciate that.' She turned as she spoke and surprised an expression on the dark face that was gone an instant before she could catch it. Relief, hunger, a strange kind of vulnerability? But then he spoke, his voice cold and constrained, and the illusion was shattered.

'Good.' He joined her at the desk, careful to avoid the merest chance of any physical contact. 'Perhaps you wouldn't mind organising a cup of coffee while I glance through some of these?' He didn't look up as he spoke, his attention seemingly concentrated on the pieces of paper under his hands. 'And once I decide what's relevant we'll take them with us and photocopy them after lunch.'

'That's not necessary,' she said uncomfortably. 'If you just return them when you're done—'

'We'll photocopy them after lunch,' he repeated quietly as he raised his head and looked her hard in the face before resuming his perusal of the papers.

Jennifer was quite right, she reflected silently as she walked quickly from the room—those dark grey eyes of his *were* incredible. In fact, he was altogether too attractive for his own good and she had no doubt at all that he knew it. She could just imagine the women who must be after him and any man would get a swollen ego with all that he had going for him. Still...

She reached the kitchen and paused before she opened

the door, her hazel eyes uncharacteristically hard. She had seen him in action that first day and knew what he was *really* like, and no amount of physical attraction could make her fall for a man who was the epitome of all the things she disliked most in a male. And she wasn't stupid. Even if Jennifer hadn't told her of his reputation she would have known his love life was busy. That one kiss had spoken volumes.

They left the house at twelve, stepping into a frosty, snow-covered world where the air was pure and bitingly cold and the sky a white-gold contrast against the bare black trees. 'Oh, how beautiful.' Katie stood for a moment on the top step and gazed across the drive. 'It doesn't seem real.'

'No, it doesn't.' His voice was thick and low and she turned as he spoke to see his eyes fixed on her face, their depths unreadable. He moved in the next instant, walking down to the car and opening her door as he continued the conversation. 'The roads are pretty hazardous, though,' he said expressionlessly.

'Are they?' That look had unnerved her but she fought for normality as she slid into the car, taking a deep, calming breath as he walked round the bonnet to join her. She had to remember last night as a warning and keep her distance mentally and physically from this man, she thought, because somehow, in spite of his cold authority and distant coolness, he had a fascinating aura about him that was frighteningly compelling. But it was just an illusion. She almost nodded to herself and caught the action just in time.

'So…' As he manoeuvred the powerful car out of the drive he glanced at her swiftly before concentrating on the road ahead. 'Tell me a little about yourself.'

'Me?' She shrugged deprecatingly. 'Not much to tell really. I'm twenty-three years old; I've worked as a teacher for the last two years.'

'Which school?' he asked quietly.

'Sandstone.' She didn't expect him to know it but there was a brief pause before he nodded slowly.

'The special school?'

'You know it?' she asked in surprise and he nodded again. 'My father wasn't too pleased when I took a job there,' she said tightly; the subject was still painful to her. 'He thought—'

She stopped abruptly and then continued quickly as she realised that Carlton would probably have felt exactly the same. 'He thought it showed a lamentable lack of ambition,' she said flatly. 'I had a good degree and he thought I should use it in other areas, like Jennifer. But I'd always wanted to work with children and the fact that this school was so close was an added advantage. It all seemed right.'

'Does it continue to seem right?' he asked expressionlessly, and she glanced at him quickly but could read nothing from the hard profile.

'Yes.' Her tone was both defensive and guarded.

'Then you clearly made the right decision,' he said coolly.

'I know.' She glanced at him again. 'I suppose you think like my father? That I should have gone on to do a Ph.D?'

'Then you suppose wrong.' He overtook a small family saloon before he spoke again. 'What sort of degree have you got anyway?'

'Joint maths and chemistry—a first,' she said quietly.

'I'm impressed.' He smiled slightly. 'But I'm more impressed that you followed your own star and did what you felt was right for you and I've no doubt at all that the kids in your charge feel exactly the same.'

He had taken the wind right out of her sails and she stared at him in consternation before transferring her gaze straight ahead. What was this? Some sort of trick, a game? He must be a fiercely ambitious man to have got to where he was so young. Had he really meant what he just said—?

'Why the frown?'

'What?' She jumped as the dark voice sounded in her ear.

'You're frowning as though I'd just said something out of order.' He swore softly as a large thrush suddenly flew out of the hedge bordering the narrow road and skimmed the bonnet of the car, missing it by a hair's breadth. 'Stupid bird's got a death wish.'

'Well, in spite of being on the outskirts of London this is still in the country,' she said quickly, glad of the change of conversation. 'My father—'

'You haven't answered my question.'

'What question?' she prevaricated weakly.

'Why were you frowning?' he persisted quietly but with an intentness that told her he wouldn't be deflected.

She thought about lying for a moment, passing the incident off with a light, amusing reply, and then found herself speaking exactly what she had thought. 'I can't believe a man like you would approve of my actions,' she said flatly.

'Why? Because your father didn't?' he asked softly.

'Partly.' She licked her lips which had suddenly gone dry. 'And also...you are very successful and ambitious; I would have thought you would have approved of my going on to do more important work.'

'You don't think handicapped children are important?' he asked expressionlessly, his tone fooling her into thinking the conversation hadn't affected him.

'*I* do,' she answered hotly before she had time to think. 'I just didn't—' She stopped abruptly.

'You didn't think I did?' he finished for her. 'Charming. What exactly have you heard about me that you dislike me so strongly?' he asked grimly, his voice icy.

'Nothing,' she answered quickly, 'and I don't dislike you, not really. It's just that...'

'Just that?' he asked coldly.

'Just that your world is so different,' she said weakly. 'I didn't mean anything personal.'

'The hell you didn't.' He glanced at her once and she saw that the grey eyes were deadly. 'Well, in spite of what you may think, I consider your work very important, Katie, and I've just decided where we're going for lunch.' He had spoken as though the two things were synonymous and she stared at him, utterly bewildered, as he put his foot down on the accelerator, his face grim.

They drove for nearly half an hour in absolute silence and as the car ate up the miles she began to feel distinctly panicky. Where on earth was he taking her? she thought helplessly as the butterflies in her stomach began to do cartwheels. She glanced at him from under her eyelashes, intending to ask, and then bit her lip hard before she could form the words. She wouldn't give him the satisfaction but if he tried anything like last night again she would have the mental armour firmly in place.

She had seen her father in action too many times not to recognise that Carlton Reef was dangerous; men of their ilk regarded any show of compassion or tenderness as weakness and would capitalise on such vulnerability without the slightest stirring of conscience. It would seem that he was prepared to help her for the moment but she didn't doubt for a minute that he had reasons for doing so that she knew nothing about, or that he would be quite prepared to throw them to the wolves if it suited his purpose.

'We're here.' They were well into the heart of London now but in the last few minutes had turned off into a richly opulent area of the city where large, elegant detached houses stood impassively behind high walls surrounded by tree-filled grounds.

'Where's here?' she asked warily as he drove the car between two huge wrought-iron gates in a high stone wall and on to a small drive that finished in front of a particularly imposing residence in red brick.

'My house.' He cut the engine and settled back in his seat to survey her coldly through narrowed grey eyes.

'Your house?' she echoed in surprise. 'But I thought—' She stopped abruptly. 'Oh, are we photocopying the papers first, then?'

'Damn the papers.' He gave her one last long look before opening the door and walking round to the passenger side, his face grim. 'Come on.' He opened her door and offered her his hand.

'I don't think I want to come in,' she said warily as she glanced at his cold face. 'I'll just wait here.'

'You damn well won't.' He reached down and jerked her out of the car, his voice harsh. 'And frankly I couldn't care less what you want at the moment, Katie. I've never met a woman—' He stopped sharply. 'Like you,' he finished more quietly as he seemed to take hold of his temper.

She knew he had been going to say something more caustic and glanced at him once as he led her, still with his hand holding her arm, up to the wide semicircular area of concrete leading in a gradual slope to the front door. He bent down to insert the key in the lock and she noticed that the keyhole was exceptionally low but still the two things hadn't registered with any importance in her mind as the door swung open and they stepped into the hall.

'Carlton?' As the door directly facing them opened and a young man in a wheelchair appeared in the opening she froze. 'You're back sooner than I expected. Anything wrong?'

'Not at all,' Carlton responded easily as he drew her stiff body fully into the hall and shut the door quietly. 'I've just brought Katie home to meet you; anything wrong in that?' Her surprise was so great that she still couldn't formulate the right words in a mind that had suddenly gone blank. 'Katie, this is Joseph, my baby brother,' he added with a grin at the young man looking at them so interestedly. 'Joe, Katie.'

'Hi.' As the wheelchair scudded over to them Katie's wits returned in time with her heartbeat. 'Nice to meet you, Katie.'

'Likewise.' She smiled quite naturally, her eyes warm as she glanced down into a face that looked like a younger version of Carlton's but altogether more soft and gentle. 'Carlton didn't tell me he had a brother,' she added as she shook the hand held up to her.

'Then I'm way in front of you,' Joseph responded with a wry grin. 'I've heard quite a lot about a certain Katie White in the last week or so.'

'Have you?' Katie stared at him, her face expressing her incredulity as she tried to get her thoughts in order.

'I share all my business problems with Joe,' Carlton said smoothly as he took her arm again, leading her towards the room that Joseph had just left. 'And naturally the loss of a good deal of money was bound to come up.'

'Of course,' she answered quickly, missing the glance of warning that Carlton sent the younger man, who responded with a wicked grin and quick shrug of his broad shoulders.

'I'll go and organise some lunch.' Instead of following them into the room Joseph turned the wheelchair down the passageway to the left of the front door. 'I take it you *are* staying for lunch?' he asked Katie directly as she turned in the doorway to what was obviously the drawing-room.

'I don't know.' She glanced up at Carlton who was looking down at her, his face impassive. 'Are we?'

'If you'd like to,' he said quietly.

She looked at Joseph and nodded quickly, her warm smile in evidence again as her eyes met those of the younger man. 'I'd love to, thanks.'

'Right, I'll let Maisie know.' He nodded at his brother cheerfully. 'And you can pour me a beer. By the way, I'm not going out again today.'

'I thought you were visiting that site in Kent later?' Carlton said.

'Under a foot of snow.' The wheelchair turned and fairly flew down the passageway as Joseph's voice trailed back. 'Meeting cancelled.'

'Joe's an architect,' Carlton said in explanation as he followed Katie into the room, shutting the door behind him before walking across to a well-stocked drinks cabinet in one corner. 'Doing very well for himself, too.'

'You should have told me.' He turned round at Katie's quiet voice, meeting her eyes as he gave a small shrug.

'Probably.' He eyed her expressionlessly.

'I could have said something wrong, offended him.'

'I knew you wouldn't,' he said simply.

'No, you didn't.' She flushed slightly but kept to her point. 'People can say all sorts of silly things when they're surprised.'

'And you were surprised, weren't you?' he said flatly as he flung his black leather jacket on to a chair. He was wearing a thick sweater teamed with black denim jeans and the result made her nerve-endings quiver as he walked over to stand just in front of her, lifting her chin with the tip of a finger as he looked down into the greeny brown of her eyes. 'In spite of knowing nothing about me there are a whole host of preconceptions in there, aren't there?' He tapped the side of her head gently as he turned away. 'What would you like to drink?'

'Anything—white wine if you have it,' she said absently. 'Does Joe live here with you?'

'Uh-huh.' He passed her a glass of wine before speaking again. 'The same accident that killed my parents left him paralysed from the waist down at the age of thirteen,' he said quietly, meeting the shock in her eyes with an expressionless face. 'I was abroad at the time, bumming around Europe with a group of friends.' He waved to the big leather sofa behind her. 'Have a seat.'

'Thank you.' She moved to a big easy-chair to one side of the huge fireplace in which a log fire crackled and sparked, holding out a hand to the blaze as she sat down, as though she were cold. She wasn't, but the thought of sharing a sofa with him was definitely out of the question. 'You're a little older than him, then?'

'Ten years.' If he had noticed the manoeuvre he didn't comment on it. 'Joe's twenty-six.' So that made Carlton thirty-six, she thought quickly as she nodded at him, taking a long sip of wine as she did so. 'Once all the legal technicalities were sorted we bought this place and had it adapted for Joe, although he spent a good deal of his time in a special school in the early years.' The smoky grey eyes held hers hard. 'Learning what he could and couldn't do with people much like you, I suspect.'

'I'm sorry, Carlton.' She stared back at him as she nerved herself to make the apology. 'What I said in the car would have been right out of order whether there had been a Joe or not. It was cruel and stupid.'

'Yes, it was.' He walked back to the sofa with his own drink and sat down without taking his eyes off her face. 'The more so because I suspect you aren't usually like that. What is it about me that hits such a nerve, Katie?' he asked impassively. 'I don't think I've ever had anyone take such a violent dislike to me before and I'm curious to know why.' There was no emotion in his voice beyond faint interest but she was beginning to feel that he let very little of the real Carlton Reef show and wasn't fooled by the calm exterior.

'We just got off on the wrong foot, that's all,' she prevaricated quickly as she let her eyes drop from his. 'So Joe's an architect, then?' she continued, desperately searching for a change of conversation. 'He's done very well.'

'Four A levels and an excellent degree at Cambridge,' Carlton said quietly, unable to keep a note of pride out of his voice. 'He started a business with a friend of his when neither of them could get a job and it's going like a bomb now; he's hardly able to keep up with the amount of work. They're thinking of taking on a third colleague soon.'

'That's good.' She didn't know what to say. She had never felt so out of her depth in her life. The Carlton she had built up in her mind over the last few days, the harsh, uncaring, worldly philanderer, was metamorphosing in front of her eyes and she didn't like it; she didn't like it at all. It had been far easier to hate him when all was black and white; suddenly the amount of grey was more than a little disturbing.

But nothing has *really* changed, she told herself silently as she took another swallow of wine. He might be good to his brother but even the most selfish of men have the odd Achilles' heel; it doesn't mean anything in the overall run of things.

Suddenly the desire to leave, to get out of his presence and just run and run, was overwhelming and she bit her lip hard as she fought for control. No reason to panic, she told herself firmly; no reason at all.

The relief on her face was transparent a moment or so later when Joseph opened the door and wheeled himself in, and as she turned from smiling at him she caught Carlton's eye and saw that his face was icy. 'Steak and salad OK?' the younger man asked cheerfully as he took the beer Carlton held out to him. 'You've sent Maisie into something of a spin.'

'Maisie?' Katie asked him enquiringly.

'Our chief cook and bottle-washer,' Joseph said, with a wicked grin. 'We had a succession of live-in helps before Maisie turned up but Carlton was never satisfied with any of them. Mind you—' he turned from Katie and nodded at his brother's impassive face before grinning at her again '—when you see Maisie you'll understand why Carlton let this one stay.' He made an outline of the female figure with his hands. 'Real good to look at, eh, Carlton? As well as being the best little housekeeper this side of the Thames,' he added cheekily.

'Maisie is good at her job, that's all, Joe,' Carlton said with a slight bite to his voice. 'As you very well know. Now drink your beer and stop casting aspersions on the girl's character.'

Katie was surprised at how quickly the next half-hour sped by as she talked and laughed with Joseph, Carlton joining in the conversation once or twice but sitting slightly back from them as he surveyed them through cool, narrowed eyes.

She couldn't really take Joseph seriously—he was the original clown with a slightly childish sense of humour that nevertheless appealed—but he was exactly what she needed to relax. It amazed her that in spite of all he had gone through there wasn't a trace of bitterness or regret in anything he said, and in fact he seemed to have a confidence that was unshakeable coupled with an unswerving belief in his own fortitude.

She wondered how much of this positive mental attitude was down to Carlton and suspected that it was quite a lot. There was no doubt that the two brothers were exceptionally close but then that was only to be expected in the circumstances, she told herself as she watched Carlton raise sardonic black eyebrows in silent amusement at something Joseph had just said.

When Maisie tapped on the drawing-room door to call them through to lunch Katie saw exactly what Joseph had meant as Carlton called her in to meet her. The girl was stunningly attractive, with huge liquid brown eyes and a long fall of sleek black hair almost to her waist. She smiled timidly at Katie and scuttled away after the briefest exchange of pleasantries, and Carlton smiled ruefully as they walked through to the dining-room just across the hall.

'She's very shy,' he said in a soft undertone as they

followed Joseph, who was teasing Maisie about something as they entered the room, 'but she has one of the sweetest natures I've come across.'

Katie nodded and smiled even as a sudden dart of something gripped her heart. So he *was* attracted to the girl, she thought slowly as she sat down in the chair indicated. Well, it was only to be expected and absolutely nothing to do with her.

The room was exquisitely furnished in the same traditional style as the drawing-room, with heavy velvet drapes at the large full-length windows and expensive Persian carpets on the floor. This room was at the back of the house and the window overlooked a wide sweep of lawned garden, trimmed with large bushes and trees that had taken on a Christmas-card prettiness under their mantle of snow.

The meal went well, largely due to Joseph's irrepressible banter, and it was only as they were finishing coffee that Katie thought to check the time.

'It's nearly three o'clock.' She turned to Carlton in surprise. 'We ought to do that photocopying and then I must get back to the hospital.'

'How is your father?' Joseph asked quietly, his face completely serious for once.

'So-so.' She smiled but it was an effort. 'He's a very proud man and the thought of losing everything in the full glare of bankruptcy is hard for him to come to terms with.'

'It would be for anyone.' Joseph's eyes had darted to his brother as she had spoken but now centred on her face again. 'It's a wretched situation.'

'Yes, it is.' Carlton spoke dismissively as he stood up abruptly and indicated for her to do the same, resting his hands on the back of her chair and pulling it away from the table as she followed his lead. 'Let's go into my study and see to those papers.'

Joseph raised his eyes slightly as she followed Carlton out of the room and she smiled but said nothing, wondering what had caused the sudden departure but not caring to voice her confusion. Being around Carlton was like living on the edge of a volcano, she thought as she followed him down the hall and into a beautiful book-lined study at the far end of which a large coal fire was glowing bright red, giving the very male room a warm, comforting glow.

It had started to snow again outside, large feathery flakes falling thickly out of a laden grey sky, and Carlton stood looking out of the window for a few moments with his back to her before turning round suddenly and staring her straight in the face.

'Sit down.' It wasn't an invitation, more an order, and she did as she was told, sensing that something momentous was about to happen as she looked into his cold, grim face. 'It isn't much use photocopying those papers, Katie.' His voice was so devoid of expression that the portent of the words didn't sink in at first.

'It isn't?' She stared at him numbly.

'No.' He was still holding her eyes with a piercing gaze which she couldn't have broken if she had tried. 'I saw immediately I looked at them today that there is no hope of a reprieve. Your father signed several documents that were…skilfully worded and in doing so lost any chance of compensation. It was a forlorn hope at the best of times,' he added quietly.

'I see.' Her face had whitened as he'd spoken, but other than that she kept an iron grip on her emotions that wasn't lost on the tall, dark man watching her so intently. The brave tilt of her head, the dark anguish in the huge green-brown eyes with their liquid appeal caused his mouth to tighten into a hard line before he turned to look out into the winter's afternoon again.

'You understand what I'm saying?' he asked tautly after a few seconds had ticked by.

'Yes.' She stared at the broad back and wondered how she was going to dash her father's hopes without breaking down herself. It would have been better if Carlton hadn't offered the little ray of hope, she thought desperately as she remembered the painful appeal in David's face the last time she had seen him. It would be almost as though he had lost everything for the second time.

'But there is a way…' He turned and faced her again as the grey eyes narrowed on her pale face. 'There is a way we could turn things round.'

' "Turn things round"?' She rose jerkily from her seat— she really couldn't sit still a moment longer—and walked over to the fire, feeling as though she would never be warm again. 'What do you mean, "turn things round"?' she asked again, swinging to face him as his words sank through the grey blanket that had descended on her mind. 'We're talking thousands and thousands of pounds' worth of debts, aren't we?'

'Yes.' He was completely still as he watched her, an almost menacing tenseness in his body that sent a fluttering of chilling fear through her system as she looked into his dark face. 'Several million if you take the house into account too.'

'Then how—?'

'I could pay the debts for you and give your father the house.'

'What?' The word came out as a breathless sigh but he seemed to hear it none the less.

'I could pay everything off,' he said again. 'You needn't even tell David the real circumstances if you don't want to.'

'But we could never pay you back.' She felt very strange as she spoke, the room and his big dark figure taking on an unreal quality that made the dream-like impossibility of his words even more insubstantial.

'Not in a financial sense, no.' He walked over to her as her heart began to thump frantically, an awful presentiment of what he might be trying to say freezing her mind and body. But he couldn't mean that, she told herself helplessly as he stopped in front of her. He didn't have to buy sex like any back-street voyeur in the less reputable parts of Soho; he could have any woman he wanted with just a raise of his eyebrows—and women far more beautiful and experienced than she was, at that.

'I don't understand,' she said weakly.

'I think you do.' He raised his hand slowly, as though in spite of himself, and touched the soft silk of her hair with one finger as his eyes moved slowly over her face. The sensual, expensive smell that seemed a part of him set her senses aflame as she stared up into his face, her eyes enormous. 'I want you, Katie. I want you very badly.' It was said without any emotion, a cold statement of fact that sent a shiver of fear flickering through her limbs.

'You're seriously saying you want to buy me?' she asked numbly, unable to take it in. 'That you want me to be your mistress?'

'Hell, *no*!' The explosion was immediate and she flinched at the anger on his face even as she knew a moment of profound relief that she had misunderstood him. Of course he couldn't have been saying that—she should have known. What would a man like him want with someone so naïve and ordinary as her, after all? She must have been crazy—

'I want to marry you, Katie.' Now she really *was* losing her mind, she thought as she stared at him in torpid insensibility. 'I want to marry you—a full marriage in every sense of the word with everything that that entails.' She knew her mouth had fallen open but there was nothing she could do about it. 'After which every debt would be cleared, every last penny paid off, the whole slate wiped clean.'

He stood back a pace and eyed her sardonically as his eyes registered her horrified shock. 'So it's really over to you,' he said slowly as he crossed his arms over his muscled chest and narrowed his eyes like a great black beast waiting to pounce. 'The grand sacrifice or disaster; a way of escape or a long walk down the painful road of financial ruin that you've been trying to save your father from so desperately.

'Decision time, little Katie White; decision time.'

CHAPTER FOUR

'YOU can't be serious.' Katie stared up at him helplessly. 'I mean...' Her voice trailed away as she found herself utterly lost for words, her face portraying her horror at the suggestion.

'On the contrary.' His brief smile was quite without humour and didn't touch his eyes at all.

'But why on earth would you want to marry *me*?' she asked weakly. 'You must know loads of women who would be only too pleased to jump at such an offer.'

'Must I?' He considered her quietly through narrowed eyes. 'Perhaps that's the problem.'

'I don't understand.'

'Then let me explain it to you.' He indicated the chair that she had vacated with a wave of his hand and as she sat down he turned to look out of the window with his back to her and his dark face hidden from her gaze. 'I'm a wealthy man, Katie, a very wealthy man, and that in itself brings a certain set of...difficulties. As you just pointed out, a certain type of woman who is looking for an easy ride for life would appreciate a tailor-made meal ticket to keep her in the style to which she is accustomed.' The deep voice dripped sarcasm. 'I want children but I want something more than a clothes-horse as their mother, you understand?'

'No.' As he turned to face her she shook her head slowly. 'I don't. Surely you must have met someone you liked, someone who would be suitable—'

'You're suitable.' The piercing grey eyes were unreadable. 'You are beautiful, spirited, and your attitude to life

75

and values are in line with what I would look for in the
mother of my son.'

'Your son?' This was getting out of hand, she thought
desperately. 'Look, I really don't think—'

'Joe will never be able to have children,' Carlton continued quietly as though she hadn't spoken. 'The succession of the Reef name is down to me and I do not intend
to leave my estate to a cats' home.' He eyed her consi-
deringly. 'I am thirty-six years of age and I feel the time
is right to settle down and produce a family but as yet I
haven't met a female I would consider suitable—or I
hadn't until you came on the horizon. Besides which—'
He stopped as she twisted restlessly.

'But we don't even like each other.' She spoke quickly
before she lost her nerve, still unable to believe that he was
really serious. 'You can't possibly think a marriage between us would work? It's... Well, it's—'

'The only way out of your problems,' he finished coldly,
the dark veil that had settled over his face as she had spoken masking his thoughts. 'Unless of course you would
prefer to see your father lose everything he has worked for
all his life? The decision has to be yours.'

'But we don't even *like* each other,' she said again, her
voice urgent. 'And I don't want to marry anyone.'

'I do not dislike you, Katie.' Just for a moment something dark and fierce burst in the depths of the grey eyes
and then a shutter banked down the fire and his face was
ruthlessly implacable. 'And, like I said, I want you. You
cannot deny that there's a certain physical chemistry between us?'

'I—' She stopped abruptly. How could she explain to
an experienced man of the world like him that she had
thought every woman reacted the way she had to his maleness, that her response to him would have been something
he would have expected, nothing out of the ordinary?

'If the physical side of a marriage is OK everything else

will fall into place,' he continued smoothly, 'and with us it would be, I can assure you.'

'How can you know?' she asked weakly. 'You don't—'

As he pulled her up and into his arms she was too dazed by recent events to resist, although her body tensed, expecting a fierce, overwhelming assault on her senses. But his kiss was delicate, meltingly, deliciously delicate, as he traced the outline of her mouth and her closed eyelids with soft, butterfly kisses that were achingly sweet.

And then his mouth found the hollow of her throat where a pulse was beating frantically and she heard her little moan of desire with a throb of embarrassment even as she tilted her head further, allowing him greater access.

This was crazy... But the thought couldn't compete with what his mouth and body were doing to hers. Sensation after sensation washed across her closed eyes as a trembling warmth shivered through her limbs. He was good at this, oh, he was very, very good, she thought helplessly as his fingers explored the length of her spine in a sensuous, warm caress that made her aware of every inch of her body, her breasts heavy and full as they pressed against his hard chest and her lower stomach achingly hot.

'So perfect...' As his mouth took hers in a deeper, penetrating kiss he moved her more firmly into his body, his arousal hard and dominant against the softness of her hips, leaving her in no doubt as to what she was doing to him. 'Now do you doubt it?' He moved her slightly from him as he spoke to look down into her face, his eyes glittering. 'We would be good together, Katie, I know it.'

She came back to reality with a hard jolt as she opened her eyes to stare into the dark, triumphant face in front of her. All this had been a cold-blooded exercise in proving a point? But of course, what else? And she had fallen into his arms like a ripe plum? Self-disgust was bitter on her tongue as she adjusted her clothes with shaking hands, her cheeks burning.

'Do you doubt it?' he asked again, his voice almost expressionless now as she glared at him before turning away, mortally embarrassed.

'I don't know.' She shook her head blindly as she walked over to the fire, holding out her hands to the warm blaze as she kept her face in profile to him. 'I've never—'

She stopped abruptly and then forced herself to go on. He had to know, after all. He'd probably assumed that she had slept with other boyfriends, that she was at least a little experienced. 'I'm not used to the physical side of a relationship,' she managed stiffly, her face hotter than the fire now. 'I've nothing to judge by.'

There was utter silence in the room for several moments and then he spoke again, his voice quiet and low. 'Does that mean what I think it means?'

'Yes.' She wanted to curl up and die with embarrassment but the need to justify her statement was paramount. 'And not because I haven't had offers,' she said tightly. 'I just haven't happened to meet anyone I liked enough, that's all, and for the last few years my job hasn't left me much time for socialising.'

'You don't have to apologise—'

'I'm not!' She interrupted his quiet voice sharply as she turned to face him, expecting mockery, contempt, even derision, but the hard face was completely expressionless—curiously so. 'I'm not,' she reiterated more quietly. 'But you're used to more experienced women. I wouldn't be able to…' Her voice trailed off as she found herself completely unable to finish what she wanted to say.

'I get the message.' His voice was very dry. 'You think I'm looking for a cross between a performing chimpanzee and a modern-day Jezebel between the sheets, is that it?'

'Well, aren't you?' His cool composure was the last straw. 'From what I've heard—' She stopped abruptly, aware that she had been about to be less than tactful.

'"From what you've heard"?' he repeated softly—so

softly that she was fooled into thinking that he was unconcerned until she looked into his eyes. 'And what exactly have you heard, Katie?' he asked grimly, his voice quiet and even. 'And who from?'

'It isn't important.' She shrugged with a lightness she was far from feeling.

'The hell it isn't.' He moved the two steps to the fireplace in a moment, his face tight with controlled rage. 'Someone has been filling your mind with stories and I would like to know who.'

'It isn't like that.' She raised her gaze to his as she spoke, her hazel eyes jade-green in the dim light. 'And you have no right to question me like this, no right at all,' she added quietly as she forced herself to stand her ground and not flinch away from his rage. 'You're a millionaire and people are bound to be interested in your private life. It's human nature.'

'Jennifer…' He breathed the name between clenched teeth as he looked down into her face. 'Of course, I might have known.'

'I didn't say—'

'You didn't have to.' He nodded grimly. 'And you believed every word which came from such a reliable source?' he asked cuttingly, his voice icy and his narrowed eyes tight on her face.

'Look, this is ridiculous.' She sat down in the chair as her legs began to tremble, taking a deep breath as she did so and forcing her voice to remain calm. 'It doesn't matter one way or the other, does it? I can't marry you; you must know that. We barely know each other and, anyway, the whole thing is…immoral.'

'"Immoral"?' he repeated savagely. She watched him take an almost visible hold on his emotions as he glared down at her, his eyes glittering hotly, and when he next spoke his voice was cool and controlled, only his eyes betraying his inner fury. 'Hardly, Katie,' he said softly.

'People marry for much less reason than we have, I do assure you. There are still countries where arranged marriages are the normal procedure and the rate of success is very high, much higher than in the Western world where so-called ''love'' dominates the game.'

'You don't think it's right to marry for love?' she asked quietly, appalled by his cynicism.

'I didn't say that.' Something flickered in the back of his eyes and was gone. 'But love is a transient thing, all too often here today and gone tomorrow. If you married me I can assure you that I would never look at another woman and I would expect absolute fidelity from you in return. I can make you that promise in the cold light of day without any messy emotion gilding my words. You would gain immediate solvency for yourself and your father and my protection both physically and financially for you and yours for the rest of your life.'

'You really *are* serious,' she whispered slowly. She moistened suddenly dry lips with the tip of her tongue and as his eyes followed the gesture, a dark heat flaring briefly in their grey depths, she felt her stomach tighten in response to his desire. The full enormity of what marriage would mean, in all its intimacy, flooded her senses and she shut her eyes for a moment as its rawness overwhelmed her.

'Oh, I'm serious, Katie.' Her eyes snapped open to meet his cool, sardonic gaze and their eyes held for a full ten seconds before she broke the spell, lowering her head quickly as she took a shuddering breath. 'I've never been more so,' he added.

How could he be so cool, so unemotional about it? she asked herself weakly in the few seconds before she raised her head again. He was treating the whole thing almost like a business deal, a clinical merger. Even her father had more emotion than this man. And however he dressed the proposal up he was buying her as a breeding machine for his offspring. No more, no less.

She steeled herself to look at him calmly and keep her voice steady. 'I'm sorry, Carlton, but I can't accept your offer, generous though it is,' she said stiffly. 'And I'm sure you will be able to find someone far more suitable for the perpetuating of the Reef name.'

Her father would understand, he *would*, she told herself desperately as she met the cool grey gaze that was carefully blank. He wouldn't expect her to make such a sacrifice…would he? 'I really think I'd better go now,' she added uncomfortably when he still didn't speak. 'I'd like to visit Dad tonight.'

'Of course.' She could read nothing that indicated his feelings in either his face or voice; they could have been discussing the weather a few minutes previously instead of the joining together of their bodies and future in matrimony. 'Would you like me to drop you at the hospital or at the house?' he asked quietly as he walked across the room and opened the door, his body relaxed and controlled.

'The house, please.' She smiled nervously, but as he opened the door and stood for her to pass through the grey gaze didn't centre on her face. 'I want to pick up my car.'

The drive home was the sort of unmitigated nightmare Katie wouldn't have wished on her worst enemy and the tense, electric atmosphere in the car wasn't helped by her growing panic at the thought of what she had refused. They had been given a way out, something she had imagined impossible just days earlier, and she had thrown it away without even considering it.

She sneaked a quick glance at Carlton's harsh, dark profile from under her eyelashes and her stomach churned painfully. But she'd had no choice. To marry him, to actually *marry* him? She couldn't.

She glanced at his large, capable hands on the steering-wheel, the dark body-hairs disappearing into his sleeves, and again that little thrill of something hot and alien shivered down her spine. What would it be like to be made love to by such a man?

She caught the thought firmly and locked it away before it could develop. She would never know. She didn't *want* to know. But even as she chastised herself the elusive smell of his aftershave was doing crazy things to her hormones.

'Goodbye, Katie.' He had left the car, intending to open her door, but she was too quick for him, almost falling out of the luxurious interior in her eagerness to escape before he could touch her. He paused to lean against the bonnet as she backed away towards the steps, his face cool and sardonic and his eyes veiled. 'The offer still stands, you know.' His voice was cold and formal. 'I'd prefer you to think about it for a day or so before you make a definite decision. It would be advantageous to both of us.'

'I—'

He interrupted her by dint of raising one very autocratic hand. 'Goodbye, Katie.' The dismissal was very definite.

She watched him slide back into the Mercedes as she stood at the bottom of the steps and although the air was already redolent with the tang of frost she still stood there long after the car had vanished, her mind whirling in a maelstrom of fear and excitement and confusion. Just a few days ago she had never heard of Carlton Reef. Her normal, safe little world had been ticking on in the same old way, no big highs and no lows.

She turned to look up at the house, mellow and lovingly familiar in the dusky light of the dying day. And now this could go, along with everything she had always thought of as theirs. She shook her head slowly. And she still wasn't convinced her father was going to get well. She put her hands up to her head, feeling as though it would burst with the force of her thoughts.

'No more thinking.' Her breath was a white cloud in the

bitingly cold air as she spoke out loud into the silent, snow-covered evening. 'Just one step at a time.'

Her father was alone, dozing in an armchair next to his bed, when she reached the hospital half an hour later. She had been unable to see Jennifer's car in the car park but as it had been almost full she hadn't paid too much attention.

'Katie?' David White opened tired eyes as she sat down quietly next to him. The sight of him rent her heart. For the first time that she could remember he looked every inch his age, his big, broad-shouldered body strangely vulnerable in the old, thin hospital blanket that someone had tucked round his waist, and his head bowed, as though the effort to hold it upright was too much.

'Hi, Dad.' As she bent to kiss him she prepared herself, subconsciously, for the usual turning away of his head, but tonight it didn't happen. Instead she found her kiss accepted, welcomed even as his mouth met hers, and the shock robbed her of conversation as she leant back in her own chair. 'How are you feeling?'

'How do you think I'm feeling?' The irritable, exasperated voice was the same, however. 'These damn nurses are forever fussing in and out; it's like Piccadilly Circus in here most of the time. How they expect anyone to get better in this place is beyond me—you need an iron constitution just to survive.'

'Well, you'll be fine, then.' She smiled at him as he glared his irritation. 'Did Jennifer come in to see you?'

He indicated a bowl of grapes on the top of the hospital locker with magnificent disgust. 'She stayed long enough to give me those and then went off in a huff because I told her what to do with 'em,' he said testily. 'If she had to bring anything at all a half-bottle of Scotch would have gone down well.'

Katie closed her eyes for a moment and prayed for patience. 'And you needn't look like that,' he continued flatly. 'You know as well as I do that the only reason she came was out of duty and because you'd badgered her to make the effort.'

'Dad—'

'I know Jennifer, lass.' The pale blue eyes were cynical now. 'And there's no need to make any excuses for her. Unfortunately she inherited most of me and very little of her mother, unlike you.' She stared at him in surprise, her mouth falling open in a little O. 'And she's astute enough to know I read her like a book,' he added quietly. 'Jennifer will always do unto others before they do unto her, whereas you…' His voice faded as he shook his grey head slowly. 'You worry me to death.'

'I worry you?' For a moment she thought she was hearing things. 'Why do I worry you?'

'No matter.' He waved his hand at her, clearly embarrassed, his voice gruff and his face scowling. 'How did you get on with Carlton? Did he find anything of interest?'

'Well…' She hesitated, unsure of how much to say.

'I feel in my bones there is a solution, Katie.' It pained her to see the eagerness in his face, the light of hope in the tired blue eyes. 'And if there is one Carlton is the man to find it. He's one of the hardest men I've ever come across but he's fair. Oh, yes, he's fair,' he added almost to himself, nodding with his thoughts. 'He'll find a way out.'

How was she going to tell him? She bit her lip as her stomach turned over. It would have to be now. He would know sooner or later anyway and it would be better hearing it from her than from someone else.

'I was born in that house, you know, lass.' He raised his eyes to hers again and she was shocked to see the suspicion of tears in their watery brightness. 'Your grandparents were never around much, always partying here and there or away out of the country, but although I didn't have any brothers or sisters I was content with my nanny, living

quietly at home. That house sort of became father and
mother to me, I suppose.

'Your mother understood that; yes…' he nodded again
'…she understood. And first Jennifer and then you were
born under its roof.'

'And here was I thinking you weren't sentimental,' she
teased softly, taking refuge in lightness as the ache in her
chest threatened to spill out in tears, and when a knock at
the door sounded a second later, followed by the entrance
of two of her father's old cronies, she had never been more
pleased to see anyone.

She sat with the three men for a few minutes before
leaving, promising her father that she would call in the next
afternoon, and walked out to the car park feeling as though
she had just received a death sentence.

She knew what she had to do; she had known it all
along, really, from the moment Carlton had made his
amazing offer. If her father lost everything, if he was
stripped of even his pride and dignity along with the house,
he would give up and die. She knew it. And Carlton knew
it too.

She remembered his face in the study and clenched her
hands together in tight fists as she took big gulps of the
icy cold air. He was attracted to her physically, he wanted
a certain type of wife quickly, and she fitted the bill. And
he was prepared to pay an exorbitant amount of money for
the privilege.

She walked slowly to her car, her head spinning. Money
was no object to him; he could probably buy and sell them
ten times over without even noticing. But it was all so cold-
blooded.

She sat in the driving seat without starting the engine,
her mind numb and desperate. Cold-blooded and inevitable. Could she go through with it? She sat for a moment
more before starting the engine suddenly, her face white
but her mouth determined. Of course she could. There was

no other choice. She would face this as she had faced all the other twists and turns of life over the last thirteen years and draw on her own strength and determination to get her through.

But Carlton Reef? She pushed the sudden panic and fear aside with a ruthlessness her father would have been proud of. He was a man, just a man, whatever her fanciful mind tried to make of him. This feeling that he was different in some way, that he could affect her as no other man ever could or would, was merely the result of long, sleepless nights worrying about her father and their financial catastrophe, of trying to find a way out of the maze of problems and difficulties that formed a living nightmare whether she was asleep or awake.

And now she had a solution. She negotiated the car out of the hospital gates as her stomach turned over. And she would take it without flinching, with no more hesitation, because lifelines such as this were only thrown once, and if the dark waters of despair and misery closed over her father's head because she had let her fingers slip on the rope she would never forgive herself.

CHAPTER FIVE

'CARLTON?' She had rung him as soon as she'd got home. There was no point in delaying the decision and she didn't want him to visit her father and tell him the truth. 'It's me—Katie.'

'Katie?' The deep voice held a note of concern. 'Is anything wrong? Your father is all right?'

'I've changed my mind.' There was a blank silence at the other end of the phone and, after waiting a moment, she plunged on, her voice trembling and her nerves quivering with a sudden fear that it was too late, that he'd already regretted what was, after all, an amazingly generous offer. 'If you still want to marry me, like you said this afternoon, then—' She took a deep breath and prayed her voice wouldn't betray the thick panic that was consuming her. 'Then I agree.'

She waited with bated breath for his reaction and couldn't have explained even to herself what she wanted it to be. Just hearing his voice sent shivers down her spine.

'Why?'

'Why?' she repeated. His voice had been strange, thick and husky, and now she felt a sick dread that he *had* thought again, and had realised that he was giving far too much and receiving very little in return. He could have almost any woman he wanted; it had been madness to think he was for real. She should have known—

'Why have you changed your mind?' he asked in his usual voice now, the tone slightly wry and definitely cool. 'I presume you've been to visit your father tonight?' he added quietly, as though the two things were linked.

'I've just got back.' There was no point in lying. If this

crazy idea was going to get off the ground, and it didn't
seem too promising at the moment, then at the very least
she was going to have to be completely honest about everything. 'He wasn't too good,' she continued painfully,
'and I don't want... I don't want him to lose this house,'
she said slowly. 'It means far more to him than you could
realise, more than even I knew. I'm frightened he won't
get better if he has to see it go,' she added when he still
didn't say anything, her voice very small. 'In fact I'm sure
he won't.'

'I see.' There was a brief pause. 'Did you say anything
to him?' he asked quietly, his voice devoid of any expression.

'No.' She took a deep breath as her heart began to thud
so hard that it actually hurt. 'He had other people there.'

'So he doesn't know yet? Are you going to tell him
about...our arrangement?' he asked flatly.

'No.' The answer was immediate and instinctive. 'That
would make everything just as bad. He has to think that
you've found something, done something that enables him
to keep the house through his own good fortune. We'll
have to tell him that we—we've fallen in love,' she added
painfully.

'And you think you can fool him?' Carlton's voice was
gentle and for some reason that very fact made her knees
tremble. 'You think you can act that well?'

'We'll have to.' She closed her eyes tight and prayed
for calm.

'I didn't say "we",' he said slowly. 'I can do my part,
but can you do yours?' There was a strong element of
doubt in the deep voice.

'Of course.' She still wasn't sure if he was saying yes
or no. 'I can do anything at all if it helps him to get well.'

'I'm not so sure, Katie.' There was a moment's silence.
'Unlike nearly every other woman I know, you would not
make a good liar.' There was a note in the deep voice she

couldn't identify and she would have given anything to see his face at that moment. 'You know I want you and I'll agree to anything you want regarding David but he is not a fool. He's a very astute and intelligent man, and, more than that, he loves you. That makes him particularly perceptive where you're concerned.'

'Carlton, just because I'm his daughter, it doesn't automatically mean he loves me,' she said with a flat pain that wasn't lost on the man listening to her. 'You don't understand—' She stopped abruptly. There was no way she could tell him how the years had been since her mother had died. She couldn't tell anyone—it was too complicated, too harrowing to put into words. 'Things aren't always black and white,' she continued slowly.

'No, I know that,' he said blandly.

'It has to be as I've said.' She paused, searching for a way to make him understand. 'If he thought he'd been bailed out, that in some way he had still failed and lost the house through his own misjudgement, he wouldn't try again,' she finished painfully.

'And he's not trying now, is he?' Carlton said gently. 'You've noticed that too. He's in danger of giving up.'

'Then you agree?' she asked carefully, her nerves jumping wildly.

'Yes.' The answer was immediate. 'I told you, I want you, Katie. I want you very badly.' There was that thickness in his voice again that sent a little shiver flickering down her spine. 'And you're aware of exactly what you're promising?' he asked slowly.

'Of course.' She couldn't keep the note of indignation out of her voice. She was twenty-three years of age, for goodness' sake, and after several years at university she was well aware of the facts of life, in all their diverse branches, even if she hadn't actually participated herself.

She remembered the paper-thin walls of her small room on campus and the energetic activities of one of her friends next door, whose morals had matched Jennifer's, and smiled mentally. Carlton would be amazed at what she knew! There had been mornings when she had found it difficult to face Sally without blushing!

'Shall I come round now?' he asked quietly.

'*What*?' For a heart-stopping moment she thought he was demanding his proposed marital rights immediately, and from the note of unforgivable amusement in his voice when he next spoke she knew he had recognised her blunder.

'Relax, Katie…' His voice was soft and deep and she shut her eyes against its seductiveness. 'I was merely asking if you would like me to come round to iron out the details tonight.'

'No.' She took a deep breath and prayed for dignity. 'The morning will do.' The morning will more than do, she thought weakly.

'I'll see you at eleven.'

As the phone went dead she blinked in surprise, standing with the receiver in her hand for a good half-minute before she replaced it slowly and glanced about the wide, spacious hall.

Everything looked the same. The beautiful wood panelling still gleamed and shone in the dim light, the expensive water-colours in their gilt frames, which her mother had loved so much, still hung silently in place, and yet everything was irrevocably, frighteningly different. She had just promised to marry a man she didn't love and who didn't love her. A marriage of convenience.

She heard Jennifer's car draw up outside and then the sound of her sister's key in the lock at the same time as Mrs Jenkins appeared from the kitchen at the end of the hall.

Well—she squared her shoulders as she prepared to tell them her news—this was where the acting began and it had better be the performance of her life. If she couldn't convince them she would never convince her father and too much depended on her for her to fail.

Carlton arrived dead on eleven the next morning and, inevitably, it was Jennifer who got to the door first, opening it with a dramatic flourish and smiling up at him with as much charm as she could muster, considering she was green with envy.

'Have I got the scoop of the year or what?' She slanted her eyes at him with more than a faint touch of malice in their light blue depths. 'I take it I can print the news Katie told me last night?' she added smilingly. 'Especially as you are going to be my brother-in-law.'

'I thought you'd be pleased.' Carlton's voice was very dry.

'Oh, I am, I am.' She watched him carefully, her eyes speculative. 'Mind you, I think you're marrying the wrong sister.'

'Is that so?' He smiled down at the slightly feline face in front of him, recognising the social repartee and a little amused by it, but as he opened his mouth to say more Katie walked down the stairs, and when Jennifer saw the look in his eyes as he gazed at her sister she accepted defeat.

'My, my, my, so it's really true...' she drawled softly as Katie reached the bottom of the stairs, and as Carlton sent her a swift glance from narrowed eyes she smiled again, her face even more cat-like. 'Wedding-bells and orange blossom even? I have to admit I did wonder if anything untoward was going on last night when Katie told me you were going to get married.'

'Once the reporter, always the reporter, Jennifer?' Carlton asked as Katie joined them. 'Sorry to disappoint your fertile imagination but this is just a case of good old-fashioned romance, isn't it, sweetheart?' As he bent to take Katie's lips in a swift but possessive kiss she didn't have to act the immediate response her body made to the intoxicating smell and feel of him.

'Love at first sight?' Jennifer asked softly, her eyes tight on Carlton's face as he drew Katie to his side, his arm round her waist. 'Just like all the best stories?' she added cynically.

'For me, most certainly.' He smiled lazily as he held Jennifer's gaze. 'Katie took a few days longer but I convinced her she couldn't live without me in the end.'

'Lucky old Katie.' Jennifer smiled sweetly but the pale blue eyes remained as hard as glass. 'Who would have guessed? It looks like Dad's little bit of misfortune was destiny, after all.'

'And that's not as bad as it could have been.' Katie entered the conversation for the first time, treading warily. Her sister was too cute by half and the years of being a reporter had honed her natural sense of shrewd cunning to rapier-sharpness. It was clear that she was suspicious of this whirlwind romance, although Carlton's easy, assured handling of the affair this morning had mellowed the edge of hard scepticism in the slanted blue eyes.

'Storm in a teacup,' Carlton agreed smoothly. 'Now, if you'll excuse us, Jennifer, I've got a few things to discuss with my new fiancée.'

'Oh, don't mind me.' Jennifer looked distinctly put out as Carlton turned from her with a dry smile. 'I'm just part of the furniture.'

'I'm taking you out to lunch.' As the dark grey eyes rested fully on her face Katie felt her senses leap helplessly. 'Can we leave now?' he asked softly, his voice warm on her overwrought nerves.

'I'll get my coat.' Anything to escape Jennifer's hawk-like stare! she thought hurriedly.

As they drove away Katie was aware of Jennifer's face at the window and raised a hand in farewell which was ignored. 'Your sister doesn't approve of me?' Carlton had noticed the little by-play with some amusement, a cynical smile curving the hard sensual mouth.

'Oh, she approves of *you* all right,' Katie answered candidly. 'It's me she doesn't think much of. She thinks she'd make a far better Mrs Reef than I.'

'And what do you think?' he asked her softly.

'I think she's right,' Katie answered honestly, after a moment of hesitation. Well, he had asked, and that was exactly what she did think, after all.

'That devastating honesty.' He glanced at her briefly and she saw that although his mouth was smiling his eyes were cold. 'I shall have to remember only to ask you questions I might like the answers to. I don't know how much of this my ego can take.'

'I didn't mean—' She stopped abruptly. 'Well, you know women find you attractive, don't you?' she said uncomfortably. 'And Jennifer—'

'What about you?' he interrupted her coolly at the same time as he pulled off the main road on to the verge and cut the engine almost in one movement. 'How do *you* find me?'

She stared at him warily. She hadn't seen him in this mood before. The cold, ruthless, austere Carlton Reef of the business world was gone but in his place was someone... Someone she wasn't sure how to react to. His eyes were still veiled, giving very little away, his face cool and slightly mocking, but there was something... She swallowed silently as fire trickled down to her nerve-endings.

'Katie—' He stopped as though searching for the right words as she gazed at him. 'We're entering into this thing for our own reasons; you know mine and I know yours.'

He paused and glanced away out of the window, his eyes remote. 'And I'm aware that I'm not your ideal man, so don't worry that I shall expect any protestations of undying love, either now or in the future.' The dark eyes swung back to her for a second but she couldn't read anything in their cool greyness. 'But if I've misread the signals, if you don't find me even physically attractive...well, human sacrifices were never my scene.' He eyed her as her cheeks burnt scarlet.

What on earth did he expect her to say? She could feel her face growing hotter and hotter. 'I do.' When the ensuing silence got too much to bear she forced the words out. 'Find you physically attractive, that is.' Too much for comfort, she added silently.

'Well, that's a start.' He raised her chin with one finger so that her eyes met his. 'Isn't it?' he asked softly.

'Yes.' She was amazed and horrified at what the light contact of his skin against hers was doing to her and even more so at the dizzy confusion his words had produced. She *knew* he was marrying her simply because he had decided, in a cold, logical, emotionless way, that it was time for him to have children, and she fitted the requirements he had laid down for his future wife. He wanted her physically, and he had bought her when the opportunity had arisen. She wanted to close her eyes against the knowledge but it was there, hot and vibrant, in her soul.

So it was imperative that she keep her own space, that she didn't let any little part of the real her become vulnerable or exposed. He didn't love her; he had never pretended that there was any chance of that now or in the future; he had been totally honest.

But she wasn't a man. And now she did shut her eyes for a fleeting moment. She didn't have his cool, logical, predatory approach to life and love, and already she wasn't sure how she was beginning to feel about him. It wasn't just his looks, impressive though they were—it was *him*. There was a magnetism, a fascinating aura about the man that was dangerously compelling and although she knew it would be sheer emotional suicide to fall for him—

'Katie?' He interrupted her racing thoughts by reaching

into his pocket and extracting a small, and obviously old, dark velvet box. 'I'd like you to wear this.'

'What is it?' She lifted the tiny lid carefully and then stared astounded at the exquisite antique ring that the box held. 'Carlton...' Her eyes shot to his face. 'It's the most beautiful ring I've ever seen.'

'It was my mother's, and her mother's before her.' He took the ring out of its snug setting and reached for her left hand. 'May I?' There was a thickness in his voice, a husky warmth that turned her insides to melted jelly, and as she obediently held out her hand he slipped the ring on to her third finger and held her eyes with his own before leaning forward and drawing her into his arms.

His mouth was caressing, arousing, bringing an immediate hot, aching response from her that frightened her half to death. What was this power he seemed to have over her? she asked herself, panic-stricken, but as his hands moved over the small of her back, warm and knowledgeable, she ceased to think and just let herself feel.

The kiss was hot and sweet and full of a subtle awareness of her own needs that made it devastatingly irresistible. Not that she wanted to resist. She had never felt like this before, never known it was possible to feel like this.

As his lips moved to the pure line of her throat she felt herself shudder, but she was helpless under his caress, no more able to hide her response to his lovemaking than fly.

There was passionate heat in his mouth now as he bit sensuously at her lower lip before plundering the sweetness of her inner mouth. His hands moved from her back to cup her breasts through the soft wool of her sweater, his thumbs stroking their tips, which hardened and swelled at his touch, and when she heard the soft moan that hung trembling in the air for an instant she didn't realise for a full ten seconds that it was her voice.

And then he moved away, settling back in his own seat

almost lazily as she struggled to come to terms with how he could make her feel with seemingly very little effort.

'I thought we'd drop in at the hospital on our way to lunch.'

'What?' She gazed at him for a moment as though he were talking in a foreign language and then forced herself to respond normally as she pulled her coat around her, the engagement ring heavy and alien on her hand. 'Oh, yes, fine,' she agreed dully.

'It can only hasten David's recovery to know everything's under control,' Carlton said evenly, his voice cool and contained, and for a moment she could have hit him for his impassive countenance. How dared he sit there so cool and relaxed when she was a shivering wreck? she asked herself angrily. And everything was far from being under control. Light-years away in fact. 'Do you feel up to it?'

'Up to it?' She felt a flood of pride and burning humiliation at his quiet words. He thought his lovemaking was so wonderful that she would collapse at his feet, did he? That it would render her incapable of talking to her father? 'Of course I feel up to it,' she said with an icy coolness that made his eyes narrow. 'I'd rather get it over and done with as soon as possible. I've never lied to my father about anything before.'

'And now you've got to convince him that you're madly in love with a guy you don't even like,' Carlton drawled mockingly, his eyes tight on her profile as she smoothed her hair into place with the help of the small make-up mirror in her bag. If she had been looking at him she would have seen a tenseness to his mouth that belied the easy voice, but she wasn't, and his tone fired her temper still more.

'Exactly.' She turned her head to look out of her side-window, allowing the silky fall of her honey-blonde hair to shield her face from his gaze. 'But needs must.' He might have women falling at his feet from every direction but she was blowed if she was going to add to their number, she thought silently.

'Quite.' He started the engine without another word and as they drove in absolute silence along the icy roads, heaped on either side with banks of snow that the snow-ploughs had cleared, she stared blindly out of the window at the white world outside until her gaze was drawn to the ring again.

It *was* beautiful, she thought miserably. Exquisitely so. The centre was a large diamond that flashed with breath-taking majesty over a circle of tiny rubies and pearls that surrounded it and in between each stone the gold was worked in lacy folds that enhanced the clearness of the jewels. And it had been his mother's, and his grand-mother's... Perhaps she shouldn't have accepted it in the circumstances, she thought suddenly. An ordinary ring, just a token, would have done.

'Carlton...' She didn't know quite how to put it but she had better say something. 'This ring.'

'Yes?' His tone wasn't exactly forthcoming but she glanced at the hard profile and took a deep breath.

'If you would prefer to keep it I wouldn't mind. I'd be quite happy with something less expensive, even a dress-ring if you'd rather—'

As the car slammed off the road and on to the verge for the second time in ten minutes her stomach turned at the look on his face. He was angry, furiously angry, but what had she said?

'Let's get one thing absolutely clear here and now, Katie,' he said tightly, each word punched into the air with such force that she shrank from them. 'This is going to be a real marriage and as my wife you will be expected to wear the Reef ring. There will also be much more expected of you, not least from me, I might add.' He glared at her angrily. 'When I make a deal I stick to it and I expect those I'm dealing with to do the same.'

'I know that.' After the first moment of shocked surprise she had straightened proudly, her eyes flashing.

'Good.' He glared at her a moment longer and then ran a hand through his hair in a gesture of utter exasperation. 'Oh, hell, I don't want to frighten you—'

'You don't,' she lied promptly, two spots of colour burning in an otherwise pale face. 'I just wondered if you'd felt that you had to offer me your mother's ring, that's all—if you felt obliged—'

'Katie…' Her name was a sigh, but in the next instant his voice held that mocking, caustic note that she had heard before. 'No, I don't feel I "have" to do anything,' he said slowly as he flicked the ignition again. 'When you get to know me better you'll understand I never do anything I don't want to.'

They arrived at the hospital without having spoken another word and Katie felt her stomach churn at the prospect ahead as Carlton parked the big car and cut the engine. He took her arm as they entered the building and she forced herself not to flinch from his touch although her nerves reacted violently to his closeness as he drew her into his side.

'A smile might help,' he said softly as they came to the door of her father's room. 'If you can't quite manage the dewy-eyed bride approach.'

She flashed him a glance of pure venom and then stitched a smile into place as he opened the door, his mouth twisted with cynical amusement.

She was amazed at how well things went—mainly due, she had to admit, to Carlton's easy mastery of the situation. David was delighted, transparently so, at their news, although there was one nasty moment when Carlton left them alone at the end of the visit.

'Katie?' Her father took her hand in his, the first time

she could ever remember him voluntarily touching her. 'This is all very sudden, isn't it?'

'Dad, we're two grown adults, not a couple of teenagers,' she replied carefully. 'There's no need to wait if we're sure, is there?' She looked into the eyes of this man whom she had always loved but had remained steadfastly remote from her since the death of his wife, and forced a smile from somewhere. She hadn't really expected him to question her; she hadn't thought he would care that much.

'And you are? Sure, I mean?' he asked urgently, his pale blue eyes searching her face. 'Don't get me wrong—I like Carlton. In fact he's one of the few men I like as well as respect. When he makes a commitment to anything or anyone it's made and that's rare these days, but...' He paused, his face thoughtful. 'You're young and your heart rules your head. You aren't doing this out of some sort of misguided gratitude because Carlton helped us find a loophole, are you?'

She forced an easy laugh from somewhere even as it registered that he was still holding her hand tight and that the soft light in his eyes was something he hadn't allowed her to see in a long, long time. 'As if I would...'

'Oh, you would, Katie White, you would,' her father said quietly. 'I know you, lass. You're too like your mother in the things that matter. I was always glad I'd met her almost before she was out of pigtails so that I could protect her from herself,' he added with a flat, hard pain that caught at her heartstrings.

'Were you?' Something of her utter amazement must have shown in her face because he shook his head slowly, shutting his eyes as he lay back against the pillows and letting go of her hand as his face flushed a dull red with hot embarrassment.

'I'm tired, Katie.' It was the normal sort of brush-off she had received over the last thirteen years if she ever tried to break through his hard outer shell, but it still hurt.

She stared at his lined face for a long moment before rising from her chair and placing a careful kiss on the side of his cheek.

'OK, Dad.' The years of training kept her pain from showing in her voice. 'I'll call in later.'

'No need.' He opened his eyes, his face straight and his eyes veiled now, the softness gone. 'Jennifer is coming this afternoon, so I understand, and no doubt there'll be other visitors. Enjoy the day with Carlton.' The withdrawal was complete.

She smiled but said nothing and left quietly to join Carlton who was waiting in the corridor outside. 'OK?' His eyes were piercing on her face. 'No problems?'

'Not really.' But her mouth was tremulous and the dark grey eyes missed nothing.

'He didn't buy it?' Carlton asked quietly.

'Yes, yes, he did.' They began to walk towards the lift some yards away and she lowered her head in the gesture he was beginning to recognise.

'Katie?' Just before they left the warmth of the centrally heated building he took her arm, turning her to face him, his eyes searching her face. 'He cares very much for you, you know. He just finds it hard to express it.'

'Does he?' She wasn't going to crumble, she told herself tightly as the unexpected sympathy constricted her chest. 'You don't know him like I do, Carlton; you don't understand.'

'Perhaps you know him too well. Sometimes an outsider can see things more clearly,' he said with a gentleness that made her instinctively gather her defences before she crumbled in front of him.

'Sometimes,' she agreed bitterly, forcing the weakness aside.

'But not in this case?' he asked carefully.

'Definitely not in this case.' She shook off his arm wearily and opened the door to the blast of arctic air outside.

'But he likes you, Carlton; he likes you very much indeed,' she said quitely as they walked towards the car. 'You're very like him, you see; he understands you.'

'And that's another black mark against me.' Her eyes snapped up to his face then but she could read nothing from his expression to indicate how he had meant the cool statement.

'No, of course not—'

'You don't lie well, Katie, like I said before, so just stick with the big whopper for now,' he said grimly. 'I'm aware that you disapprove of me and I don't altogether blame you so let's leave it at that for now. Is there anywhere in particular you'd like to eat?' he asked abruptly as he opened the car door for her.

'I—n-no…' The change of conversation had her stammering like a schoolgirl, she thought with a sudden burst of anger that banished the ache in her heart over her father. Why did this man always reduce her to a quivering wreck anyway? It just wasn't fair. She wanted to be cool and calm and in control.

They lunched at an olde-worlde pub that was all horse brasses and copper warming pans but the food was surprisingly good and Carlton proved to be an entertaining companion when he set his mind to it, with a sharp, slightly cruel wit that had her laughing more than once, even though she slightly resented the fact without understanding why. But she did understand that he was dangerous, she thought to herself as she watched him return with their drinks, after they had walked through to the bar from the charming little dining-room. Dangerously attractive, dangerously male, *dangerous*. And she was going to marry him.

'Have you a date in mind?'

'What?' It was almost as though he had read her mind, she thought faintly as he sat down beside her at the little carved wooden table, depositing her dry white wine in front of her with an easy smile.

'For the wedding.' The black eyebrows rose fractionally. 'And do you want all the trimmings? A white dress, bride-maids and so on?' he asked with indulgent easiness.

'I haven't really thought about it,' she prevaricated quickly, mortified at the touch of colour she could feel in her cheeks.

'Then think.' He was still smiling but there was a touch of steel about his mouth now. 'I thought the beginning of June would be suitable. That will give you a few weeks to fuss about your dress and all the other details and we could have a month's honeymoon at my villa in Northern Spain and get to know each other.' She blushed bright red now at the immediate picture in her mind, but if he noticed he didn't comment on it. 'Later we could perhaps take a cruise, spend the winter abroad if you would like that?'

'I—' She was floundering again and hated herself for it, but the careless ease with which he spoke of their future plans left her breathless. 'I don't mind. Whatever you think.'

'Submissive as well as beautiful?' The dark voice was both amused and mocking and grated on her nerves like barbed wire. What did it matter what she thought anyway? she asked herself painfully as she averted her eyes from his. She was nothing to him beyond a body in which to nurture his precious heirs; he had made that perfectly clear, and she would have to come to terms with that.

But somehow… Somehow, the more she got to know him, the harder that became. She wanted him to see *her*. The self-knowledge was frightening, opening her as it did to a vulnerability that she was sure he would capitalise on if he sensed it.

But he couldn't read her mind. The thought enabled her to raise her head and smile with a composure she was far from feeling. 'But of course.' She took a sip of her drink and carefully placed the glass back on the table, pleased to see that the trembling inside was hidden and that her hand was perfectly steady. 'You are paying a great deal for me, Carlton. It's only fair that I give value for money.'

As his mouth straightened into a thin line and his eyes took on the consistency of splintered glass she realised that she had gone too far, but there was no way she could take the words back. They had been a defence, a desperate cover for her bruised feelings, but she hadn't liked their ugliness and she suspected that Carlton liked them still less. But it was too late now. There was nothing she could do but brazen it out.

'Is that how you really see things?' he asked coldly after several seconds had ticked by in deathly silence.

'What other way is there?' she asked dully.

'Dammit, Katie!' The explosion was sudden and frightening but even as she shrank back from him and the heads of the only other couple in the bar turned their way the perfect control was back in place, the only betrayal of the rage burning inside in the glittering darkness of his narrowed eyes as they fixed on her white face.

'You're making this harder than it needs to be,' he said quietly. 'You do see that? If you give yourself half a chance you might even find you like me.'

That's what terrifies me, she thought painfully. She had gone through the whole gamut of emotion since the first moment she had heard his voice on the day her father collapsed, but none had been as frightening as the one that was creeping insidiously through her veins now.

She *knew* he was like her father—cold and austere and devoid of normal human warmth. She *knew* that he was ruthless, that he had had lots of women—hadn't Jennifer confirmed that very thing? He would find it easy to mould her to his will, to pick her up and drop her whenever he felt like it. She had seen her father do it time and time again with different females since her mother's death. She knew all that. It was a solid weight in her chest that was there night and day.

So why, knowing it, did she still have the urge to reach out and touch his face and ask if they could begin again as though the last few days had never happened? To beg him to look at her, really look at her, and see her for what she was rather than the future mother of his children?

She had spent thirteen years trying to win her father's love and approval; she couldn't spend the rest of her life trying to win Carlton Reef's, and for that reason she had to keep herself detached, remote from this thing that was going to happen to her. It would be hard, but the alternative was unthinkable.

CHAPTER SIX

THE next few days rushed by at breakneck speed, for which Katie was thankful. It gave her less chance to think and that way she could function on automatic. She explained to the headmaster at the school that it would be necessary for her to leave after Easter, and although he was reluctant to see her go he was more than understanding about the position she was in.

'We shall miss you, Katie, but I didn't think we'd hang on to you this long,' he said warmly as she sat across the desk from him in his small office. 'And you know that there's always a place for you here.' The brown eyes smiled with real friendliness.

'Thank you.' His kindness had touched her. 'And I'll always be available to help out now and again once I'm married if anyone is sick. I'll let the office have my new address and telephone number.'

'That'd be useful but we know you've got a lot on your plate, what with your father and all.' Mr Mitchell patted her arm as she rose to leave. 'But if you wouldn't mind doing the odd bit of supply teaching in the future it would be a great back-up for us. Your fiancé wouldn't mind?'

'No, no, of course not.' Would Carlton object? she thought as she left the orderly little room and walked back to the general staffroom. She had no idea. She stopped still in the corridor as the full enormity of it all swept over her again. She didn't know him, what he thought, how he would behave as a husband...

She pushed the whirling thoughts back into the box she had kept them in for the last few days and closed the lid firmly. She wouldn't think about it now. All that would have to wait. Just getting through each day was enough for the moment, what with the host of arrangements and plans to discuss each night and with her father expected home at the end of the week.

Carlton insisted on coming with her to fetch David the following Friday evening and she was glad of his hard male strength as they wheeled him to the Mercedes outside the main hospital doors. 'Damn fuss!' David White was red with anger at the ignominious position he had been forced into. 'There's nothing wrong with my legs.'

'It's not your legs we're worried about,' Carlton said mildly as he opened the passenger door and helped him into the car. 'And stop acting like such an idiot, David. You've had a couple of major heart attacks in as many days and you either knuckle down to good advice or you break your daughter's heart. Which is it to be?'

Grey eyes met pale blue ones and neither was prepared to give an inch. As Katie watched them she felt a bubble of laughter for the first time in days. It looked as if her father had met his match at last. The thought sobered her instantly.

Once he was home, Mrs Jenkins fussed around him, patently ignoring his bark and avoiding his bite, helping to establish him in his study, which she and Katie had converted to a bedsit over the last few days. Katie sat on the end of his bed while he ate a light supper.

'You do see it's better for you to avoid the stairs for the time being?' she asked him warily as Carlton walked in with a bottle of Scotch that made David's eyes light up. 'And this room is huge, and it looks on to the garden, and the cloakroom and loo are right next door—'

'All right, all right, all right...' He raised a hand in protest. 'I give in—for the moment,' he added quickly.

'And you promise you'll take your pills and rest?' She thought she might as well press the point while she had Carlton for back-up. 'It's important, Dad.'

'He knows that.' Carlton had poured two hefty measures of whisky into two tumblers as she had been speaking and handed one across to him with a wry smile. 'He might be a cantankerous old so-and-so but he's not stupid.'

'Well, thank you.' David's voice dripped sarcasm. 'I was beginning to wonder if everyone thought my brain was addled as well as my body.' But he accepted the whisky with a nod as Carlton sat down on an easy-chair by the side of the bed and stretched out his long legs.

'Should you have that?' Katie asked anxiously but as both men gave her a withering glance she acknowledged defeat, took her father's tray from the bed and left them to it.

Much later, after a short phone call to Jennifer, who was back in her flat in London and preparing to dash off the next day to the wilds of Scotland on some story or other, and after checking the guest list for the wedding, Katie was sitting finishing the wedding invitations when Carlton walked into the drawing-room. 'He's asleep.'

Ignoring the tightening in her body that his presence always induced, she lifted what she hoped was a calm face and smiled carefully, but it was hard not to betray what his big body, clothed casually in jeans and a black sweat-shirt, did to her nerve-endings. 'Thank you for staying with him tonight, Carlton.'

'No problem.' He shrugged as he flung himself down in a chair opposite the large sofa, where she was sitting with the invitations spread around her. 'I thought he needed some sort of normality after all those days in hospital so we chatted about business and so on.' His eyes were fixed on her face. 'He's totally accepted our explanation, by the way, even congratulated me again on acquiring you for my future bride. He hoped I realised that I was the luckiest man this side of heaven.' Her eyes shot to his face and Carlton smiled easily.

'Did he say that?' she asked with a painful casualness that wasn't lost on him.

He nodded slowly. 'That he did,' he said softly. 'Do you want to know how I replied?'

The room had become still, very still, and she found she was holding her breath as she looked into the dark, handsome face opposite her. 'I—' But then she jumped violently at the shrill intrusion of the telephone ringing loudly at her side and lifted the receiver to the sound of Carlton's muttered curse in the background. 'Yes.'

'Katie, is that you?' It was Joseph's voice. 'Is Carlton still with you? There's some emergency or other with his American office.'

'Just a minute.' As she handed the telephone to Carlton she rose quickly, scattering invitations over the floor. 'Would you like a coffee?' she asked quickly.

'Fine,' he nodded before speaking into the receiver and she left the room quickly as though the devil himself were on her heels. There had been something in his face during those last few seconds, something dangerously hypnotising. Was that how he looked at his other women before he made love to them?

She found that she was clenching her hands tightly against her side and forced herself to relax them slowly, finger by finger. But he'd said that once married to her he would be faithful. Did she believe that? She toyed with the question as she busied herself fixing the coffee. She really didn't know. What if he fell in love with someone else? The thought caused her heart to jump violently. What would he do then?

'Why such a deep frown?' She nearly jumped out of her skin as his voice sounded just behind her, and turned to see him leaning in the doorway, his hands thrust into his jeans pockets and his dark eyes glittering as they wandered over the soft gold of her hair.

'Carlton, what if—?' She stopped abruptly. She had almost been going to say ''you''. 'What if either of us falls in love with someone else?' she asked quickly, before she lost her nerve. 'What happens then?'

He straightened, anger darkening his eyes and stiffening his body as he moved to stand in front of her. 'Is this a rhetorical question or is there something you're trying to tell me?' he asked softly as he lifted her chin to look into the soft greeny brown of her eyes, his mouth hard.

'No, I'm not trying to say anything,' she protested quickly. He smelt good; he smelt so, so good. 'I just wondered—'

'Quit wondering.' As his mouth came down hard on hers she realised that there was more than a touch of anger in the kiss—almost a fierceness that bruised and punished, but it didn't seem to make any difference to her traitorous body, which leapt into immediate and vibrant life.

In fact, the only time she was alive, fully and completely alive, was around him, she realised helplessly as he ravaged her mouth with a raw desire that was shockingly pleasurable. His hands firm in the small of her back, he moulded her into the length of him and shaped her against his arousal so that the embrace was almost like an act of physical possession.

It should have shocked her, she knew that, but, instead of anger or self-disgust at her wanton response to his aggressive domination, she gloried in it, gloried in the fact that she could make him want her so badly.

When he released her they were both breathing heavily, and as she touched a finger to her swollen lips his eyes followed the gesture, self-contempt turning his eyes black. 'I'm sorry, Katie; I didn't mean to hurt you,' he said thickly as he turned and walked to the doorway.

'Carlton?' Her voice stopped him as he was about to leave. 'I didn't mean—I haven't met anyone.'

He turned to face her and nodded slowly, his face expressionless now and his eyes veiled. 'Good.' His eyes

stroked over her face, flushed and warm, and over the tousled silk of her hair. 'Because I don't share what's mine,
Katie, not now, not ever. And I would kill anyone who
tried.' She stared at him, her eyes wide. 'Does that answer
your question? And skip the coffee; it's getting late. I'll
see you tomorrow.'

Once Easter had come and gone and she no longer had to
work each day, Katie found that she was dividing her time
between her own house and Carlton's most of the time.
His limitless wealth had smoothed the arrangements for the
wedding like magic in spite of the comparative haste.

The church was booked and she had chosen her dress—
a fairy-tale concoction of ivory silk and old lace over a
wide hooped skirt and tiny fitted bodice. The staff of the
madly expensive hotel where Carlton had booked the reception for over two hundred guests had fallen over themselves in an ingratiating desire to satisfy his every wish,
and even Jennifer's dress—her sister was her only bridesmaid—was hanging ready and waiting in her wardrobe at
home.

The fact that all that side of things was taken care of
had left Katie free to organise some changes at Carlton's
home—a suggestion that had come from the man himself.

Since that night when David had come home Carlton
had maintained a cool, almost distant approach to her when
they were alone that Katie didn't understand. In company
he was the perfect fiancé—charming, attentive and always
ready to please—but when they were alone… Katie wrinkled her brow as she smoothed the last fold out of the new
curtains in the room that was to be their bedroom. He was
reserved, wary even. Always holding himself in check.

'Hi.' She turned to see Joseph in the doorway. Carlton
had had a chair-lift installed in the early days of Joseph's
accident so that he was able to move about the house
freely. 'Maisie says lunch will be ready in twenty minutes.'

'Lovely.' She smiled warmly at Joseph. The more she had seen of Carlton's brother, the more she liked him, and the two had found that an easy, friendly relationship had developed between them almost without their realising it.

Maisie she found harder to communicate with. The girl was an excellent housekeeper but painfully shy and the only person she really seemed to open up to was Carlton, a fact which Katie had to admit, in the odd moment of self-analysis, she didn't like. And the way he was with Maisie—gentle, protective even… She brushed the thought aside as Joseph wheeled his chair into the room.

'What does Carlton think to all this, then?' he asked cheerfully as he glanced round the room that had been Carlton's. He had been sleeping in one of the spare bedrooms while she redecorated this one. 'Does the master approve?' he asked cheekily.

'Uh-huh.' She smiled down at the face that was so like her fiancé's, and waved her hand expansively at the dusky grey curtains and carpet, and deep scarlet duvet that covered the large four-poster bed. 'It was a compromise.'

'Bodes well for the future.' She nodded but the shadow that passed over her face wasn't lost on him. 'Anything wrong, Katie?' he asked casually as he wheeled his chair across to the large full-length window and looked out into the garden, lit with soft May sunshine.

'Not really, it's just that—' She hesitated, unsure of how much to say. Although she and Joseph got on well he was still Carlton's brother and fiercely loyal. She didn't want him to think that she was criticising Carlton behind his back. 'He's a very private person, isn't he?' she murmured quietly. 'It's hard to know what he's thinking.'

'Persevere.' There was a note in Joseph's voice that made her join him at the window and as she sat on the carpet at his side he looked down at her, his face open and direct. 'The last thirteen years or so haven't been easy for him, Katie, looking after this house, the business, being father and mother to me.' He hesitated, then continued slowly and quietly as though he found his thoughts difficult to express.

'I went through a bad patch after the accident. I was just a kid, Mum and Dad were gone and I couldn't bear to think I'd never walk again, that I was a cripple for life.' The last few words were full of pain and she put out a hand to him, her eyes soft. 'At the time I took all the care and love Carlton gave me as my right; kids can be very selfish...' He paused, his expression reflective.

'Carlton dedicated himself to me in those early days, gave me the will to fight, to go on, and I slowly came to terms with it all. It was a long time later that I realised just what he'd had to sacrifice too.

'He'd been involved with a girl, Penny, at the time of the accident. They'd been going to get married. Oh, it wasn't official—' he flapped a hand '—nothing like that but he'd told me and they'd started to make plans.

'Well, like I said, he put in a lot of time with me in the early days and Penny began to object. A helpless little kid brother wasn't her idea of the best start in the world to married life. She made his life hell for a time, trying to make him choose between what she saw as a millstone round his neck and herself, and then one day he found her in bed with someone else and that was that.'

He eyed her warily and she forced herself to keep her face blank and betray none of the pain that had hit her like a ton of bricks. 'It hit him hard—he's the original still waters that run deep—but he'd never talk about it after he told me what had happened. But from that point—' He paused abruptly. 'Well, he played the field, I guess. You know that.'

'Yes.' It hurt. It hurt far, far more than she would have thought possible and everything in her wanted to ask him if he thought Carlton still loved his first love, but she couldn't. She was too frightened of what the answer might be.

'And then he met you.' Joseph looked up at her as she rose slowly to her feet. 'And I could see straight away you were the real thing.'

'Could you?' For a moment she almost told him—told him that this whole thing was a sham and that Carlton was merely acting a part, but she bit back the words before they passed her lips.

'Sure.' He grinned as she forced a smile to her face. 'The way he looks at you, his voice when he speaks your name—I never thought to see him like this but, like I said, still waters run deep. But it's difficult for him to open up, Katie; he's always been like that, but more so after Penny. Don't give up on him.'

She nodded blindly. Well, she'd brought this on herself; she should never have started the conversation in the first place. But oh—she found she was gritting her teeth as she followed Joseph out of the room to go downstairs for lunch—why couldn't she have affected him the way this Penny had?

The thought shocked her and she immediately tried to explain it away. Of course it would be better if he had some feeling for her—they were going to be married for goodness' sake. That was all she wanted, just some sort of normal human warmth. She didn't love him and she knew he didn't love her but they were going to commit a good part of their lives to each other. It was only natural that she wanted some solid basis to build on, wasn't it?

She continued to talk to herself all the way downstairs and into the kitchen where the three of them ate at lunch-time at the huge wooden kitchen table that Maisie kept scrubbed snow-white.

Maisie glanced up as they entered, her beautiful velvety brown eyes lowering swiftly as she quickly began to place the cold meat, jacket potatoes and salad on to the table.

For the hundredth time since she had first come into this house Katie found herself wondering about the relationship between Carlton and his housekeeper.

She couldn't fault Maisie. The girl was sweet and quiet and almost painfully timid and yet there was something… Something in those big brown eyes that she couldn't quite fathom. And Carlton was…different with her. Whereas Joseph would tease and chaff Maisie he always managed to keep her at a distance too, but Carlton… He was defensive, protective even.

The thoughts that had been forming for weeks solidified. She wasn't imagining it, she *wasn't*. But she couldn't ask him about it. Her wedding was only three weeks away and yet she couldn't really talk to the man she was marrying. The urge to scream and shout at the tangle she had made of her life was overwhelmingly fierce but she bit it back painfully.

By the time she arrived home later that afternoon the tension had culminated in a pounding headache at the back of her eyes. Carlton was taking her out to dinner that night and she had never felt less like seeing him. There was such a mixture of emotions swirling about in her head that she couldn't identify just one and yet she knew that if he cancelled the evening she would be unbearably disappointed.

'You look tired.' Her father raised his head as she glanced into his room where he was sitting reading a book. He was much better although he still tired easily and the fact that he hadn't insisted on returning to his old room upstairs before now told Katie that he was aware of his weakness. 'Doing too much, no doubt, just like your mother.'

He had taken to mentioning his wife more and more in the last few weeks and Katie loved it. The fact that she could talk about her mother with him, for the first time since she had died, was beginning to ease the ache in her heart that always accompanied thoughts of the woman she had loved so much.

'I'm OK.' She walked over and bent to kiss him and he raised his face to meet hers. It had happened several times now but it always stunned her. He had changed and mellowed since his illness, she thought. He wouldn't thank her for saying so but it was true. She sat a while with him, discussing her day and making something out of nothing to entertain him, and then wandered upstairs to shower and change.

At eight, when she heard Carlton's voice downstairs after an imperious ring of the doorbell, she was ready to join him. After the snow and blizzards of March May had entered as gently as a lamb and the night was warm and soft, the scent of summer hanging heavy in the air. He had warned her that he would be taking her to a nightclub so she had dressed accordingly in a chic sleeveless cocktail dress in midnight-blue with a short silky jacket that she had spent hours finding a few days before. It had cost the earth, but the expert cut of the material and the much needed confidence the dress gave her was worth every penny, and now she stared at her reflection in the mirror anxiously.

She'd left her hair loose to wave in soft tendrils about her shoulders, and had used just a smudge of eyeshadow to enhance her eyes, which now stared back at her, wide and speckled with light beneath fine, arched brows. She wished she looked older. She frowned at the artless reflection irritably. Older and sophisticated and more... More cosmopolitan.

She grimaced at her thoughts, snatched up her bag from the chair and left the room quickly, running down the stairs on light feet.

'Hi.' It had only been twenty-four hours since she had seen Carlton last but as she entered her father's room and he turned towards her, drawing her into him with a casual arm round her waist and kissing her lightly—for her father's benefit, no doubt, she thought testily—her senses went haywire. Her response to him only intensified the feeling of vulnerability, of unworldliness she had felt in the bedroom and she didn't like it but…there was absolutely nothing she could do about it either.

'Hello.' She moved away from him as soon as he released her in the pretence of folding back the covers on her father's bed. 'You won't be late to bed, Dad?'

'Fuss, fuss, fuss.' David fixed her with hard, gimlet eyes, clearly annoyed at being treated like a child, and Carlton surveyed her through narrowed grey slits that told her he had recognised her manoeuvre and didn't like it. She stared back at them both as an unfamiliar recklessness snaked through her veins. Just at this moment in time—and she knew it wouldn't last—she didn't care about what either of them thought.

'Well?' She smiled with dazzling brightness at them both before settling her gaze on Carlton's dark face. 'Shall we go?'

'Of course.' She saw the narrowed glance he gave her as they walked through the hall and realised, with a little thrill of gratification, that for once he wasn't quite sure where she was coming from. Her satisfaction at her little show of defiance ebbed drastically once they were in the car, however, and the magnetic pull of his big, powerful body took full sway over her senses.

'You look very beautiful tonight.' His voice was as cool and controlled as always but she caught a husky edge to it that had her glancing into his dark face. His expression was implacable and she could read nothing in it but as he looked back at her, just for a lightning moment, the brilliant intensity of his eyes made her breath catch in her throat.

Why did he want to marry her? she asked herself silently. Was it just because she fitted some preconceived idea he'd had of what his future wife, the mother of his children, had to be like?

She imagined the weight of his powerful body holding her prisoner, his hands and mouth moving over the softness of her feminine curves and felt weak with a strange mixture of excitement and fear and a hundred other emotions that flushed her skin and made her unutterably glad that he couldn't read her mind.

She had never thought, even in her wildest dreams, that she could feel this way about a man she didn't love but then Carlton was no ordinary man. The poor excuse for her annoying weakness was unsatisfactory and she knew it.

'You can return the compliment, you know.' His voice was mocking now, dry and sardonic, and that made it easier for her to respond in like vein.

'You want me to say you're beautiful?' she asked in tones of exaggerated surprise.

'It'd be a start.' He shot her a glance of derisive cynicism. 'Frankly, I'd take anything I could get at the moment.'

'I'm sure your ego is quite big enough as it is,' she said tartly. 'It doesn't need any help from me.'

'Oh, it does, Katie.' There was a rueful note in the deep voice now. 'I hate to disappoint you but I'm only human, you know.'

'You don't seem it half the time.' The moment the words had left her lips she regretted them, thinking that they would spoil the evening before it had started, but surprisingly he didn't fire back with a caustic rejoinder. Instead he pulled the car off the road into a quiet, gated pull-in and cut the engine as he turned to face her.

'Don't I?' His hand tilted her chin as he looked deep into her eyes. 'Then that is my misfortune, perhaps, because I assure you I am very human, Katie. I bleed when I'm cut and I feel pain as keenly as the next man.'

'But you wouldn't let anyone see like the next man might,' she whispered tremblingly as his hand moved to the nape of her neck and stroked the silky skin gently.

'Ah, now there you might be right...' As his mouth moved over hers in a kiss that was all-consuming she felt almost as though she was melting into the hard male body pressed against hers, but within moments she was free as he moved fully into his own seat and the big car growled into life.

'I've booked a table for half-past eight,' he said quietly, his tone so matter-of-fact that she could have kicked him.

He was an impossible man! She studied him from under her eyelashes as the car moved away. Every time she thought she had a glimmer of insight into that hard, intimidatingly male mind he did or said something that completely destroyed the illusion. And it was beginning to hurt.

Her eyes narrowed as her subconscious tried to bring something to the surface even as her mind rejected the shadow of disquiet. She was in a situation that had been forced upon her; she had had no choice, and all she could do was make the best of things. That was all she was trying to do. She nodded mentally. Just get through as best she could.

Their entrance into the nightclub caused a discreet little ripple of commotion that was not lost on Katie and she knew it was all due to the tall, dark man at her side. The manager appeared at their elbow with a beaming smile as a waiter scurried ahead, almost clearing the way to a table for two in a prime position to one side of the small dance-floor.

She saw that a bottle of champagne was already waiting, nestled in an ice bucket; their chairs were pulled aside for them to be seated with an air of deferential humility and she could almost feel several pairs of female eyes boring into her back as she slid gratefully into her seat.

'OK?' His eyes were dark on her flushed face and she

nodded quickly before forcing herself to glance around the room with studied nonchalance. What a place! And what an entrance! Was it always like this with him? For the first time the fact that he was something of a celebrity due to his enormous wealth and power fully registered on her senses. As her gaze travelled full circle she saw that the smoky grey eyes were still trained on her face, their dark depths intuitive. 'You'll have to get used to it, Katie,' he warned her quietly.

'Get used to it?' She didn't like it, this ability of his to read her mind, and there was more than a thread of antagonism in her voice. 'I don't know what you mean.'

'I think you do.' He leaned back in his chair slightly, his eyes speculative. 'There is great interest in my wealth, the significance of which is fuelled almost weekly by people like Jennifer writing their rubbish in the tabloids.' The deep voice was bitingly acidic. 'Now, other than become a recluse, the prospect of which does not appeal in the slightest, the only option open to me is to live life exactly the way I want to, ignoring that which can be ignored.'

'And that which can't?' she asked quietly as she looked into the hard, handsome face opposite with a little shiver.

'Is dealt with.' His eyes had a flinty coldness that chilled her blood. 'I don't go looking for trouble, Katie, but I can deal with it when I have to.'

She didn't doubt it. Not for a minute.

'I see.' She kept all shadow of apprehension out of her voice.

'Not yet, perhaps,' he said grimly, 'but you will. As my wife you will come under my protection but unfortunately the tentacles of the media are pernicious. You will learn to say little and be on your guard—'

'Wonderful,' she interrupted wryly. 'It looks like all this is going to be a bundle of laughs. I take it Jennifer is included in this strategy?' she asked carefully.

'Especially Jennifer.' He raised sardonic black eyebrows. 'Your sister is a barracuda on two legs, in case you hadn't noticed. It is fortunate that the two of you have little to do with each other, although having her in the immediate family is a problem I could well do without.'

'Then why—?' She caught herself up abruptly and subsided back in her seat, aware that she had been about to ask the question that had been tormenting her for days but had become more urgent since her conversation with Joseph earlier that day. The knowledge of that other love burnt like fire at the back of her mind.

'You would like me to open the champagne now, Mr Reef?' She could almost have kissed the portly little manager who appeared at their side again, complete with two massive menus, which he handed to them with elaborate ceremony before proceeding to open the champagne and fill their glasses with the sparkling, effervescent wine that tasted quite wonderful.

Once they were alone again Carlton surveyed her thoughtfully over the top of his menu as she took another sip of the delicious drink. 'I seem to have got something right for a change,' he remarked quietly. 'Champagne is obviously your drink.'

'This particular sort is,' she said appreciatively, 'although, to be honest, I didn't think I liked champagne. I've only had it a couple of times at weddings and so on and it didn't taste anything like this.'

'No—' there was a wry amusement in the dark face as his eyes wandered from her pale, creamy skin to the shining silk of her honey-blonde hair '—it probably wouldn't have. That is a very good vintage that you're guzzling so shamelessly. One advantage of the terrible position you find yourself in is that you won't have to drink mediocre champagne, at least.' The grey eyes were mocking. 'What were you going to say before we were interrupted?'

'Say?' She had hoped he'd forgotten but she might have known that that razor-sharp mind never let anything slip, she thought resentfully as hot colour flooded her face. 'I don't remember—'

'We had been discussing Jennifer and then you asked me why...?' She wasn't going to get away with it. She knew it and he knew it.

'It was nothing.' She lowered her eyes to her menu, raising it so that her face was hidden from his gaze as she searched her mind for something to say that wouldn't suggest that she was in any way interested in either his love life or what he thought of her.

'Katie...' The deep voice was insultingly patient. 'In the short time I've known you you have never opened your mouth without *something* emerging,' he said softly. 'Now spit it out.' She saw him wave the waiter away as he approached for their order and knew her last pretext for hesitating was gone.

'I just wondered, in view of your disliking Jennifer and everything...' She found it hard to continue as the dark eyes held hers, and took a deep, hidden breath before speaking the thought that had been stinging unbearably since the mention of his first love's name. 'I just wondered why you wanted to go ahead with the marriage,' she finished in a little rush, lifting the glass of champagne as he leant back in his seat, his face expressionless, and finishing the contents in two gulps.

'I'm not marrying Jennifer.' He looked devastatingly handsome, she thought helplessly, the dark evening suit a perfect foil for his particular brand of harsh maleness, the dangerous attractiveness that was an essential part of him accentuated by the formal clothes.

'But there must have been other women with fewer complications?' she asked hesitantly, her heart thudding as he watched her so carefully. 'I mean—'

'I know what you mean,' he assured her drily, his tone almost bored. 'But I've already told you, a pretty little socialite with nothing in her head but pound signs doesn't fit the bill for what I have in mind.'

'You don't seem to have had any such compunction in the past from what I've heard,' she said tartly as aching hurt and furious anger at her own vulnerability made her voice tight.

'That's enough.' The easy, bored façade was ripped apart in an instant as he leant forward, his voice low and cold but his eyes fiery. 'If you will listen to rumours and gossip, Katie, then don't expect to hear anything good. Of course I have had relationships with women. At my age I think there would be more justification for anxiety on your part if I hadn't, don't you?' he queried softly with cutting mockery.

'However, if only half of what has been printed about me were true I'd have long ago burnt myself out, and I can assure you I haven't.' The glittering eyes held her own wide ones as if in a steel vice. 'As you will discover in due course.'

He settled back in his seat again as an almost visible mask settled back in place, hiding his thoughts and emotions. 'Now, the poor waiter is getting restless. What would you like to eat?'

In spite of the shaky beginning, halfway through the evening Katie was surprised to find that she was beginning to relax. The food was superb, the service faultless and the clientele… She found herself holding her breath as yet another well-known name, the third in as many minutes, strolled into the dimly lit nightclub. 'Isn't that…?'

'Blake Andrews?' Carlton's voice was smiling and as she turned to him she saw that his face was lit with unconcealed amusement at her wide-eyed enthraldom, and the cynical mockery that was usually evident in the dark face for once was totally absent. 'Yes, it is. I'll introduce you later if you like.'

'You know him?' she asked quietly, hearing the breathless note in her voice with a feeling of self-disgust. He must think that she was so naïve, so stupid, but this place, this whole scene, was so overwhelming that she couldn't disguise the effect it was having on her nervous system.

'Not intimately,' he drawled lazily. 'But Blake is the sort of entertainer who is always pleased to meet a fan, especially one who is both young and beautiful.'

Although the teasing was light, playful even, it hit a raw spot and she flushed violently, lowering her eyes immediately to her glass. Why was she forever destined to make a fool of herself in front of this man? she asked herself painfully.

'Katie?' His hand covered hers as he leant forward. 'Look at me.' She raised eyes that were jade-green with chagrin to stare into grey ones that were soft with an emotion she couldn't name. 'Be yourself.' It was an order and spoken with a quiet intensity that made her hold her breath. 'I can't—' He hesitated as though searching for the right words. 'I can't drop the habits of a lifetime in a few weeks—they're too deep and too strong—but I'm not trying to humiliate you. Do you believe that?'

'Yes.' It was a whisper but he heard the note of bewildered surprise as she voiced what was obviously the truth and was satisfied, leaning back in his seat again as he surveyed her through narrowed grey eyes.

'There isn't a woman in this place to touch you tonight,' he said softly. 'I mean that.'

She couldn't respond; it was taking all her control, all the fortitude she had built up through the long years since her mother's death to cope with the knowledge that had suddenly burst into her consciousness as though his words had been a key that had unlocked a door she had kept tightly bolted.

She loved him.

As she forced a careful smile to her face and took a small sip of champagne her mind was screaming the truth at her. Quite when this physical attraction, the fascination she had felt since the first moment of seeing him had changed into something deeper she didn't know, but she had been fighting the knowledge for days, weeks even. How could she have been such a fool as to let it happen?

'Katie? Are you all right?' he asked quietly.

She stood up quickly as he spoke, keeping the smile in place even as the muscles in her jaw hurt with the effort. 'Fine, just fine. I'm just popping to the cloakroom for a moment; I won't be long.' She had left the table even as she spoke.

He was too knowledgeable, too intuitive for her to remain sitting there. She found the ladies' cloakroom and collapsed on to one of the velvet-covered seats in front of an ornate mirror, overwhelmingly thankful that she had the small room to herself.

The worst thing, the very worst thing in the world had happened and she was powerless to do anything about it. She looked deep into the haunted eyes staring back at her from the mirror and shook her head wearily as she let the truth permeate her mind. Most women would have given everything they possessed to be in her place—the fiancée of Carlton Reef. And the fact that she loved him? They would look on that as natural, inevitable even with a man like him who was larger than life in every way.

But he didn't love *her*. The face in the mirror could offer no comfort. He had made that perfectly clear. A deep sexual attraction, a satisfaction in the type of woman she was and her standards and morals maybe, but that wasn't love. She had experienced years and years of trying to win the love of one cold, ruthless, hard man and had never won. And now the process was to begin again but intensified a million times because what she felt for Carlton made any other emotion in the past seem lukewarm by comparison.

What was she going to do? She groaned and leant her head against the cool glass, only to straighten almost immediately as the door opened and two women, elegance personified, glided past her in a cloud of expensive perfume. That was the sort of woman Carlton should have married.

She watched them in the glass as they purred and wriggled, stroking already immaculate hair and glossing beautiful lips like two sleek, expensive cats. They would know how to survive with a man like him but her sense of self-worth, already badly damaged by her father's constant rejection, was too fragile to endure a life of walking on eggshells.

She bit her lip as the women disappeared and she was left alone again. Stop it. She glared into the greeny brown eyes as she spoke the words again out loud. 'Stop it.' She was going to be his wife, bear his children, be at his side both publicly and privately. And he had said, promised, that there would be no other women.

She would make him love her. Somehow, even if it took years, she would reach that cold, cynical heart and make it her own. Time, if nothing else, was on her side.

CHAPTER SEVEN

THE next three weeks sped by in a whirl of last-minute arrangements and minor panics. May had been a beautiful month, full of warm spring sunshine that heralded the approach of a perfect summer, new life bursting out in a frenzy of curling new leaves, the heady perfume of a thousand spring flowers, and, best of all, the steady, reassuring improvement in her father's health that meant the world to Katie. And she was miserable. Desperately, frantically miserable.

She couldn't fault Carlton's handling of their relationship. He was attentive, affectionate to a point, introducing her to many facets of his life and work in easy stages so that she absorbed each one without too much effort, but...

Her brow wrinkled as she arranged a bowl of fresh dawn-pink roses which she had just picked from the garden, their rich perfume scenting the hall with their promise of summer.

He was remote, in the same way he had been since that night they had brought her father home. It was as though he was deliberately keeping her at a distance, controlling his emotions in a way she found impossible. His lovemaking was still intoxicating—he only had to touch her for her to melt in a heady, trembling fever that she strove to conceal—but even in that, or perhaps especially in that, he allowed himself to go so far and no further, his control absolute.

And tomorrow she would become his wife in the eyes of God and man. She stifled the flood of panic as her hands shook, dislodging a rose, which fell to the floor, its velvet petals scattering in a little arc at her feet.

'Katie?' Her father came carefully down the stairs, his steps slow but steady, and she glanced up at him as she knelt to gather the petals in her hand. 'Come and talk to me for a while.'

Since his graduation from the study to his bedroom upstairs, her father seemed to have accepted that he was really going to get well and the realisation had made life easier for the rest of the White household.

'Come on.' David held out his hand as she rose, and led her into the drawing-room, walking through the wide French doors, open to the early June sunshine, and into the garden beyond, drawing her down beside him on the old wooden bench just behind the house. 'Jennifer will be here soon and that will be the end of any peace and quiet,' he remarked with his customary causticity.

'You don't like peace and quiet,' she chided softly as she smiled up into his face. 'Look at you this week, sorting through all your papers, discussing the business with Carlton all the time, and working into the night when you should be in bed.'

'I'm going to let Carlton run it in future, Katie.' She stared at him, too surprised to speak. 'Or, at least, he's putting one of his managers in to do the job. I'll still be around in an advisory capacity but the heat will be taken out of the job.'

'And that's what you want?' she asked quietly, her eyes fixed on his. 'That's what you really want?'

'Katie…' He paused and, to her amazement, reached out and took both of her hands in his, his eyes soft. 'I've been doing a lot of thinking over the last few weeks when I've been laid up in that damn bed and I've made a hell of a mess of the last few years, haven't I, girl?' He shook his head slowly. 'A hell of a mess.'

'No, I—'

'Don't deny it, lass. Carlton and I have done some honest talking which I didn't thank him for at the time, but

I've faced some personal demons that have been on my back for years. I've only loved two people in my life, Katie—your mother was one of them and you are the other.' His eyes were intense on her face.

She had wanted to hear it, needed to hear it for years, but now the reality left her stunned and speechless, her heart thudding painfully as she stared back at him, her eyes enormous.

'I ought to love Jennifer, I know—she's my own flesh and blood—but I don't.' He shook his head. 'No, I don't.'

'Dad—'

'When your mother died I felt my world had ended. Can you understand that?' He gazed at her and the pain in the pale blue eyes mirrored what her own had been at that time. 'The only way I could cope with it and go on was to shut it away, ignore it,' he continued quietly. 'But you were there, Katie, the very image of your mother in your ways and emotions, a kindred spirit, a constant reminder of all I'd lost, and so I shut you out too. Not consciously— I didn't realise I was doing it—but I did it nevertheless. Can you forgive an old fool, lass?' He shook his head slowly. 'Because I can't forgive myself,' he finished with a break in his voice.

'Oh, Dad…' She turned into his arms and he hugged her close, the tears that were streaming down his face wetting her hair as she lay against his chest, her heart full and her eyes moist.

'I want to see my grandchildren, Katie, for your mother as well as myself. I want to make up to you for all the years I've wasted.'

'Dad…' She drew herself back slightly and looked into his face, her own wet with her tears. 'There's nothing to make up for. I love you—I've always loved you.'

'Coals of fire.' He drew her to him again and sighed deeply, his voice husky. 'I'm a hard man, lass. Your mother knew that when she married me but she still went through with it, bless her. Because she loved me as I loved her. Katie—' he moved to look into her upturned face '—do you love Carlton? Really love him?'

'Yes.' In this, at least, she could be honest even if the reason for their marriage had to remain forever hidden. She took a deep breath and smiled through her tears. 'I do love him.'

'That's all I wanted to know.' He settled her against him, the June sunshine warm on their faces. 'I know he loves you—what man wouldn't?—but it's important for a woman to feel absolutely sure, with everything that the physical side of a marriage entails. You know what I mean?' he added uncomfortably.

'Yes, Dad.' Her face hidden from his gaze, she smiled at the touch of fatherly advice, but in the next instant the smile disappeared as Jennifer's voice sounded from within the house, high and authoritative and strident.

'Here we go.' He straightened, moving her gently to one side, but it didn't hurt at all. She knew how he felt now. That was all that mattered. She didn't need effusive shows of affection.

'I know he loves you—what man wouldn't?' The irony of his words stayed with her all that morning and into the afternoon, when, her father having retired for his afternoon nap, Jennifer dragged her into her bedroom so that she could watch her try on her bridesmaid's dress again.

'Do you think the colour is really me?'

As her sister turned and pirouetted in front of the mirror, the deep wine-red of the dress swirling round her feet in a cloud of silk, Katie stifled an irritated sigh. Jennifer hadn't once asked about her father's health, the state of their finances, even any details about the wedding except those directly concerning her.

'It's the dress you chose,' she said patiently. 'We went through the whole shop if you remember.'

'And what a shop…' Jennifer gave one more twirl and

then reluctantly took the beautiful dress off and replaced it on its hanger. 'I've got to hand it to you, Katie, you've got your head screwed on all right. I used to wonder—but to make a catch like Carlton Reef must have taken some planning.'

'Planning?' Katie stared at her sister with distaste. 'I didn't plan anything.'

'Oh, come on.' Jennifer laughed unpleasantly. 'He's had more women than I've had hot dinners and his mistress is really something, as you probably know. You can't tell me that this all happened by accident. You'll have to give me some advice on—'

'What do you mean, "mistress"?' Katie asked through suddenly numb lips, her blood freezing in her veins.

'Whoops!' Jennifer's slanted eyes narrowed still more as she placed her hand over her mouth in affected horror. 'You mean to say you didn't know? I'd have thought that he'd at least have told you...'

'Told me what?' She wanted to walk out of the room, pretend she was unaffected by the malicious envy that was suddenly so apparent in Jennifer's almond-shaped eyes, but she was held rooted to the floor by some power stronger than herself. 'I don't believe there's anything to tell,' she said flatly, her stomach churning.

'About his mistress or all the other women?' Jennifer asked with catty innocence. 'Well, I can assure you it's all true. One advantage of my job is that I get to know all the inside titbits...

'Carlton has been keeping a woman in a flat in Mayfair for several years now although it's all supposed to be hush-hush. They're never seen out in public together but then she probably serves a more useful purpose inside, if you know what I mean,' she said with crude spitefulness. 'And he's still had other women on the side; the man must have a voracious appetite.' The pale blue eyes narrowed further.

'But then you'd know all about that—or would you, my sweet, virginal little sister?'

Katie ignored the obvious question as she turned away, her legs trembling and the blood pounding so violently in her ears that she felt dizzy. 'It's not true,' she whispered. 'I don't believe it. You're just jealous.'

'Too true, sweetie; I've never tried to hide it. I—' As Katie turned back to face her something in her eyes caught Jennifer's words in her throat and for a moment she looked acutely uncomfortable.

'Oh, don't take it like that, Katie. What did you expect anyway? He's hardly a shy little flower, is he? Look, perhaps I've got it wrong,' she added urgently as Katie sank down on the bed, her legs finally giving way. 'Perhaps this woman is—is—' She ran out of words. 'A friend,' she finished, with a wry, embarrassed little laugh. 'Anyway, he's marrying you. That's more than enough, isn't it? All the women I know are pea-green—'

'What's her name?' Katie asked flatly. 'This woman, what's her name?'

'I don't know.'

'You know.' Katie looked hard into the beautiful face in front of her. 'You're a good reporter, Jennifer—you find out all the sordid details before you let rip,' she accused bitterly.

Jennifer tossed her head, the tone of Katie's voice erasing all guilt from her face. 'A Mrs Staples. Penny Staples. She used to be a model before Carlton took up with her but then she dropped out of sight. Perhaps he didn't want her working or seeing other men; I don't know. She's the original recluse now, anyway, but Carlton pays the rent each year; that much I do know for sure. And I thought it was my duty to make sure you knew,' she added tartly. 'We are sisters after all.'

'Yes, we are sisters,' Katie agreed dully as she rose slowly and left the room, her heart thudding so hard that it was a physical pain. Penny. *Penny.* It was too much of a coincidence for it not to be the same Penny whom Joseph had told her about. So he had loved her all these years, biding his time until he could persuade her to belong to him again. But why hadn't he married her?

The thudding had transferred itself to her head now and she felt nauseous as she collapsed on to her own bed after locking the door. Perhaps she was already married; perhaps the 'Mrs' was real? Or maybe…

She sat up, the room spinning, as another thought occurred to her. Perhaps he had some hold on her too? Something that had forced her to leave the catwalk and all the glamour and allow herself to be incarcerated in what virtually amounted to a prison, just waiting for the moments when he could spare her some time and ease her solitude. Was it some form of weird punishment? A form of retribution for a love he couldn't let go?

And Maisie? The pain in her heart was so fierce that it was catching her breath. How did she fit into the scheme of things? Her knowing about his mistress suddenly made the close relationship Carlton had with the beautiful brunette even more suspect. She felt that there was something between them, some secret; she had felt it all along but had tried to put it out of her mind. Perhaps she was his mistress too? A hundred little incidents she had noticed but dismissed returned to her mind with renewed vigour. He was so different with Maisie in a way she couldn't quite pinpoint.

When the tears came in a burning, blinding flood they didn't help. Even after she had cried herself dry the ache in her heart was savage. She lay on her bed, careless of all the hundred and one things she still had left to do, and watched the afternoon sky with blind eyes until the bedside clock told her it was five o'clock. He would be home now and she had to go and see him, confront him with the truth and tear away all the lies and meaningless promises he had made. 'Absolute fidelity'. She clenched her teeth and forced back the sudden rush of tears before washing her face and fixing her hair into a knot high on top of her head. When she faced him she wanted to be cool and controlled—an ice woman to match the ice man.

Jennifer was waiting in the hall when she ventured downstairs. From the pile of magazines by her side it looked as though she had been there all afternoon. 'I told Mrs Jenkins you had a headache and wanted to sleep,' she whispered nervously as Katie reached her side and picked up her car keys. 'And where on earth do you think you're going now?'

'Where do you think?' Katie asked dully.

'I wouldn't—'

'I'm not interested in what you would or wouldn't do.' Jennifer was still standing in the hall open-mouthed as she left the house. She had never spoken to her in such a cold tone before. Perhaps she should have done so a long time ago.

Carlton was in his study when Maisie led her through and as he looked up from his desk, his face breaking into one of his rare smiles when he saw her framed in the doorway, she knew a rage so strong that she had to restrain herself from leaping at his face like a wild animal. How dared he smile at her like that when all the time—?

'Katie?' His smile faded at the look on her face and as Maisie shut the door, leaving them alone, he rose swiftly from the desk. 'What's wrong? Is it David?'

'My father is fine.' Something in her voice brought him to a halt just in front of her, the arms that had reached out dropping back by his sides as he looked down at her. 'Who is Penny Staples?' she asked with icy control, and as she saw the blow register in his eyes she knew that Jennifer hadn't been lying, and the last tiny scrap of hope died.

'I don't know what you've heard, Katie, but I can explain.' He motioned her to the seat facing his desk but she remained standing, her eyes set tightly on his face. 'Penny is an old friend—'

'The old friend you were going to marry once?' she asked acidly, willing the anger to hold the trembling that was threatening to take over and render her useless. '*That* old friend?'

'Someone has been very busy.' The surge of angry red colour that fired his high cheekbones didn't intimidate her at all—she was way, way past that. 'Dare I make a guess that Jennifer is home?' he asked coldly. 'The fount of all knowledge?'

'Do you keep an old friend in a flat in Mayfair?' she spat at him as she felt her control slipping and the urge to scream and tear at him with her hands grow. 'And I want the truth, Carlton,' she warned bitterly.

'Sit down, Katie.' As she still stood swaying in the middle of the room he reached out and forced her into the seat, only to have her spring up and away from him as his hands left her shoulders.

'Don't you touch me.' So great was her rage that she hit her hip on the corner of his desk and didn't feel a thing. 'I want to know about your mistress, Carlton—this old, old friend.'

'She is not my mistress.' The words were punched out into the room as he watched her through narrowed eyes. 'I can explain it all if you'll just sit in the damn chair and listen to me. Penny and I were close once but that was a long time ago—'

'And she left you for someone else.' Katie stared at him, seeing all her tentative hopes for the future crashing down about her ears. 'I know that. All I want to know now is if you pay the rent for her flat in Mayfair.'

'Yes.' His eyes never left her face as he spoke. 'I pay the rent. I was going to explain it all when we had some time alone together in Spain after the wedding, when I could make you understand.'

'I'll never understand.' She drew herself up as her heart slowly broke, and faced him with an icy composure that was the result of shock and pain. 'I hate you, Carlton Reef. I thought that at least you would keep your word in this monstrous farce of a relationship but I might have known you would run true to type. You disgust me; everything about you disgusts me.' She was lashing out through her own bitter hurt and humiliation, trying to scourge the love from her heart with cruel words and an icy front, but inside she was screaming, dying.

'I know that.' As his control broke he leapt at her so savagely that her head jerked back on her shoulders when he caught her arms in his hands, shaking her like a dog with a bone. 'Don't you think I don't know that?' he snarled rawly, his eyes glittering with an unholy fire and his face black with rage. 'I've felt the way you tense every time I so much as lay a finger on you, seen the reproach and wariness in those damn great eyes every time you look at me. I *know* how you feel, Katie.

'You were just waiting for something like this, weren't you—some excuse to get out of the commitment you made of your own free will?' He shook her again, his eyes lethal. 'You wouldn't unbend an inch, damn you. I've been turning inside out trying to keep to the softly-softly approach, to show you I'm not quite the animal you seem to imagine. I thought you'd begin to understand, that I could show you—' He made an exclamation of disgust as he threw her to one side.

'I've been trying not to come on too heavy, to frighten you, and where has it got me?' He swore, softly and succinctly, as his eyes washed over her white face.

'This is not my fault—'

He cut short her protestation with a bark of a laugh that grated harshly. 'I didn't say it was.'

Before she knew what he was going to do he had closed the gap between them, gripping her wrists as he hauled her against the hard wall of his body with ruthless ease. 'And you know the thing that really has been driving your ice-cool brain crazy, the thing you couldn't forgive me for?' he asked thickly as he looked down into her trapped eyes. 'You want me. Physically you want me as much as I want you. You might not like to hear that, my cold, suspicious little fiancée, but we both know I could have had you at any time over the last few weeks and you would have been there all the way.'

'No—' As he took her mouth in a fierce, contemptuous kiss that forced her head back she was conscious of one piercing moment of thankfulness that he hadn't guessed the truth—that she loved him—and then all her energy went into fighting him. The cold control of the previous weeks had melted like ice before fire and the raw, primitive desire that had him in its grip made him blind and deaf to everything but his own need as he sated his passion on her twisting form.

She was moulded into his body, the evidence of his desire hard and fierce against her softness, and although she fought him with all her strength he hardly seemed to notice. And then, through the anger and shock and self-contempt, she felt herself respond to his need as it fired her own passion.

She hated herself even as she trembled against him, all resistance gone; she hated herself for her incurable weakness where he was concerned, but she just couldn't help it. She loved him. It had no rhyme or reason, and he would never understand that it was more than mere physical lust, but she could no more resist him than fly.

As he felt her submission the tempo of his assault changed, his mouth immediately persuasive and sensual as he kissed her throat and ears, his hands removing her light blouse with experienced ease before she even realised what he was doing, and cupping her full breasts in their brief lacy covering, his thumbs running over their swollen peaks. She gasped, her body alive with sensation after sensation as he continued to kiss and caress her, making her tremble with hungry expectancy.

She wanted him—she needed him... Through the maelstrom of tormenting desire that thought was uppermost. But like this? After what she had just discovered? Where was her pride? Her self-respect? But even as the warning formed it was gone in a turmoil of touch and taste, his devastating experience and knowledge in the sensual arts combining with her love to render her helpless and quivering in his arms.

'Now do you doubt it?' Suddenly, shockingly, the warmth of his body had left hers and she almost whimpered with the betrayal. He held her at arm's length, desire turning his eyes into glittering black onyx, his face hard and set. 'I won't take you until we are legally married— that's one thing at least you won't be able to accuse me of—but tomorrow you *will* become mine, Katie. Do you understand that?'

She was unable to speak, staring at him with great bruised eyes as he bent and retrieved her blouse from the floor. 'Put it on.' She struggled into the cotton material hastily, her cheeks burning, but when it came to fastening the small pearl buttons her fingers wouldn't obey. He watched her fumble for a few moments and then brushed her hands aside, doing up the tiny buttons with perfectly steady hands, his face expressionless.

'I hate you.' And for an infinitesimal moment she did. How could he stand there, with that iron control firmly in place once more, and act almost as though this was all her fault? It just wasn't fair. None of this was fair. He had things all his own way, far more than he realised.

The sting of tears at the back of her eyes brought her

head up sharply and straightened her trembling mouth. Oh, no, she would have none of that. No tears in front of him.

'I think we can take that as read,' he said grimly. 'But you are going to sit and listen to me, Katie, whether you like it or not.' He indicated the chair with an abrupt nod of his head. '*Now*. You are making an appearance at that church tomorrow come hell or high water and I'm not giving you an excuse to change your mind because nothing has altered—nothing at all.'

She sat. There was nothing else she could do and, besides, she had the awful suspicion that if she didn't she would collapse at his feet as the trembling that was situated at the very core of her body threatened to take over.

'As your evil-minded sister informed you, I do pay the rent on an apartment which Penny Staples occupies,' he continued coldly as he walked round the desk and sat down facing her in the massive leather chair he had been occupying before she had interrupted him. 'But she is not my mistress.'

As she twisted restlessly in her chair, half rising, he motioned her back with a sharp wave of his hand, his voice a bark. 'Sit, damn you! You've made one hell of an accusation tonight and you will listen to me even if I have to tie you in that chair. Now…'

He took a deep, shuddering breath and she realised, for the first time, that he wasn't quite as in control as he would have liked her to believe. It helped—not a lot—but it gave her the courage to sit still and watch his face silently as he talked.

'As I said, I intended to tell you about Penny on our honeymoon when I'd made you understand how I—' He stopped abruptly and shook his head, rising from his seat to stand with his back towards her as he looked out of the window into the mellow evening sunshine.

'I knew Penny from my university days,' he continued flatly, 'and, as your informant's already told you, we'd planned to get married one day. Then the accident changed everything. Suddenly I had the responsibility of my father's businesses and all that that entailed, plus a badly hurt younger brother who needed all my spare time and attention. Penny didn't like it.'

He paused for a moment and she saw the broad back stiffen. 'The final break came when I went round to her flat one night thinking to surprise her and found her in bed with a friend of mine. It was a surprise all right,' he added grimly. 'I called her all the names under the sun and left and that was that. But I felt bitter, very bitter, for a long, long time.

'Joe stabilised. I found I had a flair for business and everything I touched turned to gold, and I made sure my private life was run exactly the way I wanted it. On my terms. No commitment, no promises; I took what I wanted when I wanted it and if they didn't like it they could always walk. Not very pretty but that's how it was.'

'And Penny?' she asked stiffly, the pain that had flooded her heart at the thought of those other women keeping her back straight.

'She'd become a model—a successful one,' he said slowly. 'A different guy for each new outfit—that sort of lifestyle. I'd seen her around at a distance but then one night about five years after the split, she came across to my table in a crowded nightclub and we talked about old times. She laid it on the line; she wanted me back.'

He paused. 'But there was nothing there—nothing. It had taken me all that time to realise the girl I thought I'd loved was a figment of my imagination, an illusion. It scared me to death. How could I have been so mistaken? I'd have *married* the girl, for crying out loud. So I became even more determined that any relationship I had would be on my terms, that this so-called love was merely a short-lived feeling in one's imagination that died as quickly as it was given life.'

'But the apartment?' she asked bewilderedly. 'If you don't love her...'

'I haven't slept with Penny Staples since I was twenty-three years old,' he said coolly as he looked straight into her eyes, a shaft of sunlight from the window behind him turning his hair fiery black. 'But five years ago I got a call from a London hospital to say they'd got a patient who had tried to commit suicide, had no next of kin and had given my name as the only contact. It was Penny. I went to see her and she was in a mess.'

He shook his head slowly. 'She had skin cancer, badly; she'd left it far too late to do anything about it because she was scared an operation might ruin her looks for the modelling circuit. What would have been a small scar on her jaw ended up as a major operation to remove half her face.'

'Carlton...' As her face whitened he nodded slowly.

'I know. She had no friends, no money; her looks were gone and she wanted to die. But I wouldn't let her. Rightly or wrongly I wouldn't let her. The plastic surgeons did what they could but the results weren't good. But one thing came out of all the months of hospitalisation—she found she could paint. Water-colours. They're damn good too.

'So I provided the apartment when she was well enough to leave and she supports herself in everything else with her painting. She has a few close friends now among the artist community and is content in her own way, although she never leaves the apartment. Her life is her painting, her friends and her two cats.'

'Do you visit her?' she asked painfully, her head whirling. Whatever she had thought, it wasn't this. 'To see how she is, I mean.'

'Occasionally.' He gestured abruptly with his hand. 'She asked for my help knowing I didn't love her and that she didn't love me. It was an appeal from the past, in memory of two young kids who had fun for a time before it all went sour. And it was in that vein that I responded.

'There is nothing there beyond a strange feeling of duty, not even friendship, but I couldn't have turned my back on her when she had nothing and no one. And the financial side is a drop in the ocean to me but means security and stability to her. I'd have done the same for anyone in that position.'

'I see.' She rubbed a shaking hand across her eyes before rising to face him. 'I'm sorry, Carlton; I made a terrible mistake. But I didn't know.'

'No one does.' He shrugged slowly. 'Penny didn't want anyone to know about her face and what had happened. The world is cruel but the modelling world even more so and the media would have had a field day for a time until some other poor so-and-so took their attention.

'She just disappeared from sight, changed her name to Staples, added the ''Mrs'' and cauterised the wound of her old life. Her artist friends have no idea who she was previously but they're a good bunch—they don't care. How did Jennifer find out about it?' he asked abruptly. 'I presume it was Jennifer?'

'Yes.' She stared at him miserably, loving him more than she would have thought possible and terrified that he might read it in her face. 'I don't know how she found out but she is jealous about—about us,' she finished painfully. 'I suppose, knowing Jennifer, she dug and dug away until she got something; she has contacts you wouldn't dream of.'

'Oh, yes, I would,' he said grimly.

'And since Penny you've never fallen in love again?' She had to ask now, while he was actually talking to her. She had been wrong about Penny, criminally wrong, but there was still Maisie and, by his own admission, several other liaisons through the years. She had to know it all, face the worst now.

'I—' He had been facing her, his face taut and strained, but as she asked the question something flickered in the smoky depths of his eyes for an instant and he hesitated before turning to look out of the window again. 'Why do you ask?'

'Because—' Because I love you, I can't live without you, I'm going to marry you tomorrow knowing you don't love me, but you've reduced me to this creature who will take anything she can get, she thought wildly. 'Because it's only fair that I know,' she continued bleakly. 'You know everything about me—not that there was anything much to know,' she added bitterly.

'Yes, I see.' She saw him straighten, as though he had taken a deep breath, before he faced her again. 'Do you want me to be honest?' he asked with a grim seriousness that stopped her heart.

'Of course I do.' She stared at him, sheer will-power keeping her face cool and still and her eyes veiled.

'Are you sure?' he asked heavily. 'You might not like what you hear.'

'I want to know.' Her heart was thudding so hard that she was sure he must be able to hear it.

'Then the answer has to be yes,' he said tiredly. 'Yes, I have. I think you've known for some time deep down inside, haven't you?'

'Oh.' If the world had stopped spinning at that moment she wouldn't have cared. It was Maisie; it had to be. All the hundred and one little incidents from the past, the tender gestures, the gentleness, the innate kindness. It had to be the beautiful, shy brunette.

But why couldn't he marry her? What was stopping him from taking her as his wife? Didn't she return his love? Perhaps they hadn't been lovers. Perhaps Maisie had held him at a distance, unable to love him in return except as a friend. Or was there an obstacle she knew nothing about?

'And now you've had it confirmed.' He stared at her

across the room, his eyes holding hers as her face registered her awareness. 'And it hasn't helped, as I knew it wouldn't. You're more shocked, more panicky—'

'I have to go.' She spoke through numb lips as she backed from him, the look on his face piercing her heart like a sword. She didn't want to hear more—hear the details about another woman who had captured his cold heart for her own. She wouldn't be able to bear it. What good would it do anyway?

She knew now that she would marry him tomorrow whether or not he gave help to her father. She would marry him because she loved him, because a life without him in it would be pointless and empty and cold, even as a life as his wife would be an unending torment of pain and grief. But it would be better than knowing he was alive somewhere, walking and talking on this planet without her.

'Katie—' As he took a step towards her she found her hand on the doorknob and wrenched open the door savagely.

'No, don't come near me.' She couldn't bear to hear more. 'I'll be there tomorrow—you have my word—but I need to go home now.' And as she slammed the door behind her, a sob catching in her throat, it was as though she was slamming a door on all her hopes and dreams.

CHAPTER EIGHT

SHE was a beautiful bride—everyone said so—but as Katie drifted through the day on Carlton's arm—the ceremony, the reception—it was as though it were all a dream, indistinct and unreal. She knew her father was worried about her but she couldn't seem to find the words through the fog in her mind to reassure him, although she caught him looking at her time and time again, his pale blue eyes narrowed with concern.

There was dancing after the meal at the lavish hotel that Carlton had booked for the reception and as he raised her to her feet, the guests clapping as they took the floor, she felt her footsteps falter, and in the same instant his hand came firmly round her waist. 'Don't faint on me, little wife.' His eyes were glittering with some dark emotion as he looked into the speckled light of hers. 'See it through to the bitter end.'

Her eyes were wide and dazed as they looked into his, her skin a pale, translucent cream that complemented the ivory silk dress with its mass of tiny seed-pearls and old lace, the skirt wide and hooped and the bodice fitting like a glove. 'I'm not going to faint,' she said quietly, the tiara of tiny pink rosebuds in her hair reflecting the colour of her pale lips. 'I told you once before, I've never fainted in my life.'

'And I called you formidable.' He looked down at her as they began to dance, the full skirt of her dress preventing close contact. 'I had no idea then just how formidable.'

'Formidable?' She stared up at him in bewilderment. He thought this mass of bruised emotion and trembling flesh that he held in his arms 'formidable'?

144

'You don't think so?' he asked softly as her face mirrored her thoughts. 'Innocence is a terrible weapon, my love; don't ever doubt it.'

'My love'? It was the first time he had used such an endearment and it cut like a knife. She would have given the rest of her life for one hour in his arms with him meaning those two words, she thought painfully.

The revelations of the day before had meant a sleepless night and an aching heart, and as she had sat and watched the night sky change from dark velvet blue to a dawn streaked with pink and orange she wept until there had been no more tears left. The magnificent wedding-dress on its hanger on her wardrobe door had seemed like a mockery then, the fine veil with its intricate lace and pearls an abomination, but she was married now.

She glanced up at him as the music came to an end and their solitary dance finished with the assembled throng clapping and cheering as they began to take to the floor. 'For better for worse, for richer for poorer, in sickness and in health'—

'You are breathtaking.' His eyes were waiting for her glance. 'Ethereal, exquisite, so delicately beautiful I'm afraid you might break.'

'Don't.' It was too much after the day before, spoken as it was in a deep, husky voice that sent shivers down to her toes and made her weak.

'I'm sorry.' His expression instantly hardened into granite, the familiar mask hiding his emotions as he looked away from her and round the crowded dance-floor. 'I didn't realise my mere words would be so distasteful.'

'They aren't.' She didn't know what to say, how to handle this powerful, hard man who could turn from ice to fire and then back again all in the same breath and leave her trembling in confusion. 'It's just that…'

'Just that?' he asked softly, his eyes veiled as he looked down into her troubled face. 'Just that you're frightened, nervous, wondering how you're going to face the night ahead and all the other nights?'

'I didn't say that.'

'Don't be frightened, my formidable little wife. Physically, at least, we will be compatible,' he said thickly. 'I will make you want me as you've never dreamed it possible to want a man, in spite of how you feel about me in the cold light of day. You will tremble in my arms, plead, moan for that which only I can give. I promise you that.'

'Carlton...' She was trembling already, the dark, fiery side of him that she had only glimpsed now and again raw and naked in front of her eyes as his gaze roamed over her face and body with a hunger that was voracious and quite at odds with the very English, formal tailed suit.

'I've wanted you from the moment I saw you,' he whispered softly as the other dancers swirled and moved around them. 'From the second I saw your photograph on David's desk.'

'My photo?' She tried to pull away a little but he was holding her too tightly, his hand like a band of steel on her waist and his body rigid as he crushed her closer against him, careless now of the beautiful dress.

'You were sitting with Jennifer in some park or other and while she laughed into the camera, her face tilted for the best pose, you gazed into the lens like a little lost dove, your eyes wide and beckoning and your hair loose about your shoulders like raw silk. As it will be tonight.' His gaze moved to the tiny curls and waves on top of her head which had taken the hairdresser over an hour to accomplish.

How could he love one woman and want another the way he wanted her? she asked herself bitterly. Were all men like this? Able to detach their bodies so completely from their emotions? Her eyes chilled with resentment and humiliation and she turned her head away, her body stiff and unyielding and her face cold with hidden pain.

'Stop frowning.' The expression on his face as she raised her eyes to his again made her catch her breath. There was hunger there, rage, a strange kind of bitterness and, she would almost have thought, pain. 'This is your wedding-day; you are the radiant bride. At least try to act the part for a few hours, if only for David's benefit.' He gestured with the merest inclination of his head towards her father, sitting at the top table in the distance, and she saw that although he was talking to Joseph his eyes returned every few seconds to her face and his lined face was worried.

From that point she threw herself into the allotted part with all her might, circulating on Carlton's arm and chatting happily with all their guests, her lips smiling, her eyes bright and her nerves stretched to breaking-point. Just before they left the party later that evening she found herself in a quiet corner with David, her facial muscles aching with the effort it had taken to keep the smile in place all day.

'Is everything all right, lass?' He took one of her hands in his as he looked into her face. 'You seem a sight too het up to me.'

'It's my wedding-day, Dad.' She forced a light laugh from somewhere. 'Surely a girl has a right to be excited on her wedding-day?'

'And that's all it is?' he asked quietly. 'There's nothing wrong?'

'Nothing.' If he said much more with that loving look on his face she would burst into tears, she thought frantically, and then all this would be for nothing. He mustn't find out the truth or the price she had paid to give him peace of mind.

'Have you ever seen such a beautiful bride?' Carlton's deep voice over her shoulder made her sag with relief as her father's eyes moved from her face and up to his.

'Never.' The two men smiled at each other before

Carlton's hand under her elbow raised her gently to her feet.

'Time to say our goodbyes, darling,' he said smoothly.

The last twenty minutes seemed the worst but at last it was over and she went upstairs with Jennifer, who was going to help her change in the room that Carlton had reserved, before they left the hotel, where the festivities were going to continue into the early hours.

'You looked lovely today, Katie.' As Jennifer unhooked the tiny buttons at the back of the dress and helped her step out of it, her voice was full of reluctant admiration. 'Things went OK last night, then?' she asked with heavy casualness.

'Yes.' As the flurry of silk and lace was laid on the sofa at her side Katie reached for the simple cream linen dress and jacket she had chosen to wear and slipped into the dress quickly. 'Help me take the flowers out of my hair, would you? This tiara is fixed with a thousand pins; it kept slipping out of my hair without them.'

'You don't want to talk about it?' Jennifer asked quietly.

'No.' Katie turned and looked her sister straight in the eye. 'Not now, not ever. It's OK and I want to leave it at that.'

'Fine, fine.' Jennifer's hands deftly removed the tiara without disturbing the upswept curls. 'I'm sure you know what you're doing,' she said tartly, with a faint trace of spitefulness.

As she left the lift in the reception area a few minutes later, Jennifer just behind her, and caught sight of Carlton, big and dark as he towered over all the other men present, Katie thought that she had never in her life been less sure of what she was doing than right now. She loved him. She ached with love for him and as she walked to his side and he smiled down at her, devastatingly attractive in his dark morning suit, she felt a sudden fierce determination to make things work whatever the cost, to turn this fiasco around and make him if not happy, then at least content.

That spirit of sacrificial nobility lasted exactly five minutes until Carlton shook hands with Joseph, who had been his best man, and then turned to take Maisie in his arms, kissing her gently before whispering something quietly in her ear that made the lovely brunette flush and drop her eyes shyly.

And then they were being showered with confetti as they ran for the car, parked outside the huge glass doors of Reception, and the last goodbyes were said, her bouquet of fresh pink rosebuds and white freesias thrown over her shoulder into the waiting crowd, and the big car with Carlton's chauffeur at the wheel glided away as she waved frantically to her father, the tears that had been threatening to fall all day spilling over at the sight of him standing slightly to one side of the rest of the throng, hand raised in farewell, his eyes suspiciously bright.

'Here.' A large white handkerchief was thrust under her nose as Carlton pulled her into his side with his other arm. 'Just shut your eyes and relax for a while. It's a little way to the hotel where we're spending the night, but I thought it would be better to get right away somewhere where the practical jokers couldn't find us.'

'Yes.' What had he said to Maisie in those last few seconds? she asked herself bitterly as she wiped her eyes, trying not to smudge the delicate eye make-up that the beautician had been so painstaking over earlier in the day. *What had he said*?

It was a full twenty minutes later that the Mercedes glided into the small courtyard in front of a rambling country-style hotel with leaded windows and old, mellow stone. The smell of wood-smoke was heavy in the dusk-laden air as Carlton helped her from the car.

'What a lovely place.' She forced herself to speak normally, conscious of the chauffeur extracting their cases from the back of the car, and Carlton nodded slowly. They hadn't spoken a word to each other on the drive from the reception, but he had seemed content to sit quietly with his arm around her and her body leaning against his as she had shut her eyes and let her thoughts torment her.

'I thought you'd like it. I've arranged a taxi to pick us up tomorrow morning and take us to the airport. Now…' He turned to the chauffeur and smiled. 'Not a word as to where you brought us, Bob. Joe still has enough of the boy about him to try some damn silly trick.'

'Mum's the word, sir.' The young man grinned at them both conspiratorially. 'I'll let 'em cut my tongue out first.'

'A somewhat extreme expedient but I appreciate the thought,' Carlton responded drily as the three of them walked up the steps and into the small foyer where he was greeted with the normal rapturous welcome that Katie was beginning to expect.

'Would you like dinner served in our room or in the restaurant?' he asked her quietly as Bob and the porter walked to the lift with their cases.

'The restaurant,' Katie said quickly—too quickly. The thought of being alone with him was doing strange things to her insides and the prospect of delaying it a little longer was welcome. She caught the narrowed glance he shot at her but he said nothing, indicating the lift, where Bob and the porter were waiting with the doors open, with a wave of his hand.

'But I thought… I mean—weren't we going to have dinner?' she stammered nervously. 'You said—'

'I thought you would like to freshen up a little before we come down,' Carlton said smoothly as he took her arm and began to lead her towards the waiting lift, but not before she had seen the flash of anger in the smoky grey eyes. The lift travelled upwards silently and once on their floor, which was thickly carpeted and discreetly elegant, the porter led the way to the first door and opened it before handing the key to Carlton and allowing them to walk through.

'Oh, it's beautiful…' They had entered a suite of rooms luxuriously furnished in cream and gold, the air redolent with the perfume from several bowls of fresh flowers, and the full-length windows in the small sitting-room open to the gentle evening breeze that drifted in from the gardens below. Aware that he had thought carefully about their first night together and had tried to please her, she turned impulsively to him as the chauffeur and porter left the room. 'Thank you; it's lovely here,' she said shyly as he looked down at her with unfathomable eyes.

She had expected him to kiss her as soon as they were alone but he merely smiled carefully before walking through to the small bedroom and indicating her overnight case on the huge double bed. 'Would you like me to wait downstairs while you freshen up?' he asked quietly, his back towards her and his voice strangely thick.

'No, no, it's all right,' she said hastily. 'I'll just fix my hair and then we can go down. I won't be a minute.' Nerves made her all fingers and thumbs but just as she finished combing out her hair from the intricate style that the hairdresser had laboured over that morning, and which had been making her head ache for the last few hours, a light touch on her shoulder made her nearly jump out of her skin.

'Dammit, Katie!' Carlton had jumped too at her reaction and now she saw, in the reflection in the dressing-table mirror, that his face was dark with rage. 'What the hell do you think I'm going to do to you? Leap on you at the first opportunity and rip off all your clothes? Credit me with a little finesse at least.'

'I'm sorry.' She rose and turned from the stool where she had been sitting as she spoke, her cheeks pink. 'I'm just tired, I think; it's been a hectic day. I didn't mean…'

Her voice dwindled away as she strove to bite back the hot tears at the back of her eyes.

This was awful; everything was awful. Why couldn't he love her? Thousands and millions of really plain women were loved. Was she so unlovable? Couldn't he see the real person under the skin he seemed to desire so much? Why did there have to be a Maisie?

'Don't cry. I can just about stand this if you don't cry,' he said thickly as he reached out and pulled her roughly into his arms, holding her against his chest for a long moment before pushing her away and placing a small box in her hand. 'I just wanted to give you this.' His face seemed to hold a wealth of pain. 'A wedding-gift.'

'But you've paid out so much for me already,' she murmured, meaning nothing beyond that she was grateful for all he'd done for her father, but even as she lifted the lid to the box her eyes still held his and she saw that he had misconstrued her words.

'You're never going to let me forget it, are you?' he ground out savagely through clenched teeth. 'Even though you know how I feel there's going to be no lowering of the drawbridge, dammit.'

How he felt? How did what he felt alter anything? she thought dazedly before she glanced down at the exquisite dark gold locket that the box held, a work of art in intricate, fine, worked gold and delicate engraving that was truly magnificent. 'It was my grandmother's,' Carlton said quietly, his voice smooth and controlled again. 'Open it.'

She flicked the tiny little catch and then froze, staring down at the tiny pictures either side of the hinge. Her mother's face smiled back at her, the minute photograph beautifully sharp and clear, and on the other side her father had his customary scowl which appeared whenever he looked into a camera. She continued staring down at her mother's face, at the photograph she had never seen before and hadn't known existed, as burning tears began to flood down her cheeks and shake her body.

'Katie, Katie, Katie… Don't. Don't feel so intensely; don't hurt so much…' And then she was in his arms again but this time she raised her head to his, searching for his lips, his gesture concerning her mother's picture cutting through all the hurt and pain he had inflicted, was still inflicting, and would continue to inflict. 'Your father loves you, you know that, don't you?' he murmured, still not taking her lips although she strained up to him, her eyes liquid.

'I know.' As she pulled his head down there was a brilliant heat in his eyes and then his lips met hers, his breath escaping in a deep groan of need. His arms tightened as he felt her response and then he was raining burning kisses over her face, her throat, her closed eyelids, his breathing harsh and ragged and his body taut and hard.

'Katie—' he raised his head, pushing her away slightly as he fought for control '—I can't—I've waited so long. You don't understand what you do to me. If we don't stop now I shall take you, and your chance for dinner will be gone.'

It was a poor attempt to lighten the situation but she had felt the trembling in his body, sensed the desperate waiting in him, and her love for him filled her with a crazy kind of exhilaration that she could affect him so badly. But his desire wasn't love. The thought didn't have the power to stop her lifting up her arms towards him. Her love would have to be enough for them both.

'Katie…' He breathed her name with a soft groan. 'Don't say I didn't warn you; I want to eat you alive…' She smiled, a wild excitement at the knowledge of her power over this hard, fierce man giving her face a primitive sensuality that made his breath catch in his throat.

'I was going to wine and dine you, coax you—'

'Well, coax me, then.' Her voice snapped the last shred

of his control and he pulled her into him desperately, moulding her against the length of him, his arousal hot and fierce as his hands explored the length of her. She was hardly aware of her dress sliding to the floor but when her bra followed and he knelt before her, his mouth erotic on her full, taut breasts, she moaned softly, her fingers entwining in the short, crisp black hair of his head as she trembled and shook.

'I told you how it would be between us...' As he rose, lifting her into his arms and carrying her across to the massive bed, she felt a moment's sadness at his whispered words. Yes, he had told her. Told her that their bodies would be good together, that they would be... What had he said? Oh, yes, 'compatible'.

What would he say if she told him it was her love that made her flower at his touch, her love that had evoked a raging thirst for them to become as one? But he must never know. That humiliation, more than any other, would be too much to bear.

He undressed quickly, his eyes never leaving hers as he drank his fill of her, lying pale and trembling in the dusk-filled room, and then he was beside her. His hands removed the last barrier between them, sliding her pants down her legs slowly as he kissed their path with warm, searching lips, and she was unable to stop the shivers of desire shaking her limbs. His body was strong and hard as he took her in his arms again, the feel of his nakedness strange and thrilling even as its alien ability frightened her. She wasn't ready for this... His maleness was too fierce, too powerful...

'Relax, my sweet darling, relax...' He had sensed the sudden surge of fear at the unknown and his voice was soft and tender against her mouth. 'We have all the time in the world.'

And slowly, surely, he fed her desire with lips that blazed fire over every part of her body as she lay helpless and warm in his embraces, his mouth and hands hungry and sensual, cajoling an aching pleasure that was almost pain until she found herself arching and pleading for a release from the sweet, subtle torment. His lips were demanding as they found and explored all her secret places, the fire that was consuming her burning away any shred of shyness or fear.

And as his hands lifted her hips to meet his body he still continued to ravage her mouth, catching the gasp of fleeting pain as he possessed her fully and kissing away the brief moment of panic with deep, tender kisses until she began to move in rhythm with his maleness, a shuddering ecstasy rippling over her being in greater and greater intensity until it seemed as though she was on fire.

'You are mine, fully mine,' he groaned harshly as he took her with him to the heights that were filled with blinding colour and light, the world exploding into a million glittering pieces that were piercing and hot against her closed eyes.

'Have I hurt you?' His voice was thick and warm with a rueful tenderness as she stirred beneath him, her senses slowly returning as he moved off her and drew her into his side. 'I had promised myself that I would be patient, restrained, that tonight I would let you sleep so that you would be ready to accept my advances tomorrow in the security and warmth of our villa in Spain.'

'Our villa'? Somehow those two words meant more than the physical act of possession in all its intimacy. She was his wife. He had told her that she would be his wife in the full sense of the word, that their lives would be intrinsically linked from this point, and she believed him; she did.

And with such closeness, such familiarity, surely that other love would cease to keep its hold on his mind and his heart? He had promised her that there would be no other women and she knew he believed that was enough but she wanted more than a commitment of bodily faith-fulness—she wanted his heart too.

'Katie?' He rose slightly on one elbow to look into her flushed face and she knew in that instant that she must be patient. He wanted her physically; he had shown her to-night that he was capable of tenderness and understanding even in his overwhelming need of her body. From that she would have to cultivate the first seeds of love.

'Yes, you hurt me.' She slanted her eyes at him in mock-severity even as she wanted to reach up and pull his face to hers, to kiss his mouth without passion getting in the way, to trace each line and contour of his hard face with her lips. 'But I forgive you.'

'You do?' He smiled down at her, his eyes lazy as they stroked over her naked body. 'Well, that's a good omen for the future, wouldn't you say?' There was some inflex-ion, just a shred of emotion she couldn't quite place, in his voice, but she could read nothing from his face and decided she must have imagined it.

'Maybe.' She smiled up at him as he brushed a tendril of hair from her cheek with one finger. She must keep this relaxed and easy; she was feeling too vulnerable for any deep talking, too exposed and close to tears.

'No, not ''maybe''.' His eyes darkened as he let his finger trail down the length of her body. 'You are mine now, completely and utterly. You belong to me. You made it clear last night that you don't want to talk about how I feel but surely you can see that we need to discuss things? Our future is bound up together, Katie, you can't deny that, and after what we just shared—'

'Please.' She shook her head as she went to move from his side and in the same instant he pulled her back against him, his face suddenly still as his eyes travelled over her troubled face.

'No, don't turn away from me,' he said huskily.

'Can we just take things a day at a time?' she asked

weakly as his power over her swamped her afresh. She couldn't, she just couldn't listen to any explanations about Maisie now; even if he didn't put a name to his love she would know whom he was talking about.

He had made it clear at the start why he was marrying her. In that she had no reason to complain. He had laid it fair and square on the line and she had walked into this with her eyes open but... But it hurt like hell.

She didn't want to listen to a reiteration of his promise of physical faithfulness, not now, not when the need for reassurance was so strong that she could taste it. He was a possessive, ruthless and hard man. What he had he kept and he didn't share. She knew that. And as his wife, the vehicle by which his future heir would be born, she was of more value than anything else he possessed.

'Go to sleep, Katie.' His voice was quiet and flat but his arms were gentle as he drew her into him, stroking her hair softly as they lay together in the gathering darkness until the warmth of his body and the steady beat of his heart under her cheek sent her into a deep, dreamless sleep.

She had never seen anything more beautiful than the area of Northern Spain where Carlton's villa was situated.

They left the hotel early the next morning after a huge breakfast and she found herself painfully tongue-tied in the cold light of day when she remembered the intimacies of the night before, although Carlton chatted with an ease that gradually relaxed her taut muscles and freed her tongue.

The plane flight was uneventful and when they landed at the Spanish airport the usual formalities were dealt with quickly and efficiently. As they left the terminal, stepping into the brilliant heat beyond the air-conditioned building, Carlton guided her over to a powerful, low-slung sports car parked in a reserved spot just outside the massive doors.

'Is this yours?' she asked in surprise as he extracted a

key from his pocket and opened the back of the car, slinging their cases into the area beyond.

'Uh-huh.' He moved round to open her door, his eyes narrowed against the piercing quality of the light. 'I keep it garaged in the town here and have it brought to the airport when I arrive.'

'Oh, right.' The power of money, she thought to herself as she slid into the luxurious seat and watched him walk round to the driver's side. His wealth seemed to open magic doors, smooth all the normal little irritating difficulties of life clean away. 'That's very convenient,' she added as he slid into the seat beside her and started the engine, which responded immediately.

'Yes, it is.' He extracted two pairs of sunglasses from the front of the car and handed one to her with a smile, the lazy warmth of which took her breath away. As he slipped his own pair on, and his eyes were masked from her gaze, she thought again of the things his mouth and hands had done to her the night before and found her cheeks were burning as she remembered the majestic power of the big male body sitting next to her. She felt vulnerable, helpless, but also more feminine than she had ever done in her life, as well as wonderfully, vitally alive.

They travelled through the town nearest to the airport, and out on a long, winding road the other side, and Katie was spellbound by the intensity of colour in all that she saw: villages of golden stone perched amid pine-clad hills, tall towers of brown churches in the distance with great bells outlined against the startling blue sky, fields of almond, olive, lemon and orange trees shimmering gently in the midday sun and glimpses of picturesque fishing harbours and fine golden beaches set in secluded bays on either side of rocky headlands.

They passed small whitewashed houses set among orange and lemon groves with flowered, walled gardens adjoining the orchards, and several villages where the houses had balconies of wood or iron covered in scarlet geraniums, pink begonias and trailing purple and red bougainvillaea which were a blaze of colour against the white-washed walls.

'Magnificent, isn't it?' Carlton had been aware of her breathless appreciation of the dramatic scenery and now his voice held a note of indulgent, amused pleasure as she turned to face him, her face flushed and her eyes sparkling behind their protection of dark glass.

'It's just wonderful.' Her eyes studied the dark, impassive profile. 'How long have you had a villa here?'

'My parents bought it before I was born,' he answered quietly. 'My maternal grandmother was Spanish and although my mother was born in England the family were always visiting their relatives over here. Most of them are scattered about the world now—Canada, England, France—but there are a few who still prefer the Spanish sun to any other.'

'I can see why,' she breathed softly as the car began to climb into the mountains. They had just passed a small village, where Katie had been enchanted to see an old brown donkey with a small barefoot child on its back in a square packed with market stalls overflowing with produce, when Carlton drove the powerful car through an open gateway set in a high, ancient wall and into a large garden bursting with trees and shrubs, before drawing to a halt in front of a shadow-blotched, rambling, hacienda-style villa.

'La Casa.' Carlton turned to her as he cut the engine and kissed her very thoroughly before leaving the car to open her door.

'La Casa?' She emerged pink and ruffled to stand beside him, conscious as ever of his great height and the restrained power in his lithe, impressive body.

'Home.' He smiled down at her, suddenly very foreign in the shimmering sunlight, his black hair and smoky grey eyes with their thick black lashes sending shivers down to her toes. 'My mother might have been English but in here—' he tapped his chest gently '—she was always Spanish. She loved it here. Every holiday I had from school, whatever time of the year, we would fly out to La Casa even if it was just for a few days.

'My father rarely came—the businesses took up most of his time and attention—but we would content ourselves nevertheless. At first it was just the two of us but when Joe was born he loved it too.

'I brought him out here after the accident once he was well enough to travel and it turned out to be wonderful therapy. He had been holding on to the past too hard. The last memory he had of my mother and father was their bodies after the crash, before he was cut free, and it was impeding his recovery. It took a few months but eventually La Casa helped him to remember them with more peace than pain.'

'La Casa and you,' she said softly, watching the play of emotions across the hard face. 'It was a terrible time for you too, wasn't it?'

He shrugged, turning away immediately, but she had seen the flash of raw pain in his face before he could speak. 'I survived.' His voice was dismissive, abrupt, but even as she shrank from the rebuff he turned back and touched her face with his hand. 'I'm sorry, Katie; I didn't mean…' He shook his head slowly as he held her hazel eyes with his own. 'I don't find it easy to express my emotions; I never have.'

'You trust very few people,' she whispered softly, repeating the words that he had stated at their first meeting and which had stayed in her mind ever since. And it would appear that she wasn't one of them yet.

'You can't have it all ways.' He stared at her, his eyes very dark in the white light. 'You've made it clear what you want, or don't want, from me, and I'm doing my damnedest to play by the rules, but I can only be pushed so far, Katie. Even this block of stone has his limits.'

'I don't understand.' Her eyes were wide with hurt as she gazed into his face. What had she done now?

'No matter.' He shrugged and smiled and suddenly he was the Carlton of the night before and that morning, relaxed, easy, with a lazy charm that was fascinating. But that wasn't how he was really feeling. As she held his eyes one more moment before he moved to take her hand and lead her into the villa she knew her sixth sense was right. He was playing a part, but why?

The villa was quite breathtakingly lovely inside, with an old, rustic feel to it that hadn't been spoilt by the fine furnishings and modern amenities which Carlton explained had been added at a later date. Most of the whitewashed walls were covered in an array of fine plates, decorated with coloured animals and flowers and glazed thickly like Arab pottery, as well as a host of exquisite pictures.

The front door led directly into the massive sitting-room, which was a blaze of colour in red and gold and stretched the length of the house. The leaded French windows at the far end of the room led out on to a large patio surrounded by orange and lemon trees and gently waving palms. There was also a very large and well-stocked kitchen, with fine oak cupboards and a red tiled floor, a breakfast-room, a more formal dining-room and a downstairs cloakroom complete with a large double shower.

Upstairs, the five bedrooms seemed to stretch for miles, three with their own *en-suite* bathrooms, and all with large balconies covered in red and white bougainvillaea, deep green ivy and the fragile, lemon-scented verbena. The master bedroom and one other overlooked the grounds at the back of the house where an olympic-size swimming-pool, just beyond the fringe of trees surrounding the patio, shimmered gently in the blazing sunshine.

'I can't believe it.' As she stood with Carlton on the

balcony of the master bedroom she felt as though she had been transported into another world. All this would have been so perfect, so utterly enchanting if the tall, dark man standing silently by her side had been truly hers with his heart as well as his body. At this moment she would have given every last penny of the Carlton fortune to live with him in a little shack if he had spoken one word of love. 'It's just so lovely.'

'We have two girls in the village who come and air the house periodically and do a little housework,' Carlton said quietly as he stood at her side, his profile dark and austere as his eyes gazed straight ahead. 'If the family are in residence they come each afternoon to prepare and serve an evening meal and attend to the household chores. I've never wanted anyone living in but I can hire a housekeeper on a permanent basis if you would prefer that.'

'No.' As the image of Maisie flashed before her mind she spoke quickly and instinctively. One housekeeper was more than enough.

Katie was always to remember the next few days with a bittersweet enchantment that even in the years ahead could bring tears to her eyes with their painful poignancy. They spent the mornings lazily by the pool, alternately swimming in the cool, silky water and dozing on the luxuriously upholstered sun-loungers scattered round the tiled edge. After a cold lunch they would set out to explore the surrounding countryside, Carlton's face often relaxed and animated in a way it had never been in England as he showed her the country he loved.

They travelled through mountain villages where patient donkeys still carried the occupants along cobbled, flower-decked streets and twisting, narrow lanes, wandered in green meadows beside peach and cherry orchards set against a mountainous backdrop of jagged limestone, bathed in golden bays of warm, crystalline water and returned home each evening, as the soft, gentle dusk began to mellow the fierce sun, to a delicious meal served by the two giggling, dark-eyed girls from the village.

But it was the nights that were the most bittersweet of all, timeless and enchanting as Carlton gradually introduced her to a potent, bewitching world she had only guessed at. As the hours unfolded in all their intimacy she realised that during that first night he had been wonderfully patient and controlled, his passion curbed in view of her innocence, and the knowledge made her love him all the more.

In fact, each day she loved him more as she discovered the man behind the mask. And still there were no words of love in all the passion and desire; still the days and even the nights were marred by moments of electric tension, strain and unease.

It was after one such moment early in the morning, when she had woken to find him leaning on one elbow watching her face in such a way that she had immediately imagined that he was wondering how it would be if his love were there beside him, and had reacted accordingly with veiled eyes and an almost visible withdrawal of her body, that the telephone call came.

She had already gone downstairs and Carlton was in the bathroom, shaving, and so she took the call, wondering nervously if a flood of incomprehensible Spanish was going to meet her ears. 'Hello? This is Katie Reef.' The name was still strange on her tongue. 'Can I help you?'

'Katie?' Joseph's voice was strained and tight. 'I have to talk to Carlton; is he there?'

'Yes, of course, I'll just get him.' She put the receiver to one side and ran quickly up the open, winding stairs that led to the first floor of the villa, her heart thudding as her senses recognised the note of distress and panic in Joseph's voice. What now?

Carlton turned as she entered the bathroom and, as always, her heart went haywire at the sight of him. He was stripped to the waist with just a pair of jeans covering his lower half, and his muscled chest with its light covering of dark body-hair was bronzed and powerful in the light-coloured bathroom. 'Was that the phone I heard?'

'It's Joe,' she said breathlessly as her eyes drank him in.

'Joe?' His eyes narrowed as he shook his head. 'You don't mean to say he's calling us on the first week of—'

'There's some sort of trouble, I think,' she said quickly. 'He seemed upset, Carlton.' Even as she spoke he reached for a towel and wiped the shaving-foam from his face, pushing past her and running down the stairs, Katie following at his heels.

'Joe?' His voice was anxious. 'What's wrong?' He listened for a few moments in silence and then barked a particularly explicit oath down the phone that made Katie jump. 'Why the hell did you let her?' he growled angrily. 'What's the matter with you, anyway?' There followed a few more terse sentences that Katie couldn't make head or tail of, although she gleaned enough to realise that Carlton was furiously angry with his brother, and as he banged the phone down and turned towards her she saw that his face was black with rage.

'The young fool. The stupid, blind young fool,' he muttered grimly. 'If anything's happened to her—'

'What *has* happened?' she asked softly as a terrible sense of foreboding rose like a thick cloud over the magic of the last few days.

'It's Maisie.' As his eyes focused on her face she saw the deep concern and her heart began to pound like an express train. 'She's left the house, disappeared in the middle of the night.'

'In the middle of the night?' She had heard the expression of blood turning to ice but it was the first time she had experienced it.

'She could be anywhere considering the state Joe says she was in.' He ran a hand distractedly through his hair. 'There was no need for this, no need at all. What on earth was Joe thinking of?'

'You can't blame this on Joe!' She was suddenly furiously, fiercely angry, her rage so intense that it swept away every other emotion in its path. So the lovely brunette *was* his mistress and she hadn't been able to stand by and see him married to another woman. She felt sick with impotent fury. What was he doing, playing with all their lives like this? Just who did he think he was?

'You don't understand.' His voice was preoccupied, absent, and the final humiliation was that he was looking through her as though she weren't there. 'Joe—'

'Oh, yes, I do,' she said tightly. 'I'm not a fool, Carlton, and I understand far more than you think. I do have a pair of eyes in my head, you know.' Her blood was pounding in her ears but her eyes were as dry as dust.

'You know?' he asked as he seemed to force himself to concentrate on her. 'Did Joe tell you?'

'No.' She didn't know where this strength that kept her upright was coming from but she was more than thankful for it. 'I just put two and two together—'

'Joe was supposed to put things right,' Carlton muttered as he walked past her as though he hadn't heard her. 'She must have been in a damn awful state to clear out like that. Hell, he promised me—'

'*He promised you*?' She was shrieking now, all control gone as the absolute unfairness of it all made her quite literally see red. He had left Joseph to do his dirty work, placate his mistress while he played his games thousands of miles away, and now, it having gone all wrong, he was laying the blame on the younger man's shoulders? 'I don't believe I'm hearing this.'

'You don't believe you're hearing what?' The pitch of her voice had got through to him and he turned with his foot on the first step of the stairs and glanced across at her. 'What the hell is the matter with you anyway?'

'What do you think is the matter with me?' she asked furiously.

'I don't know, Katie; that's why I'm asking you.' If she had been rational she would have noticed that he had gone curiously still, his dark eyes intent on her face and his voice low and controlled, but she was too mad to observe the subtle body language and the sudden awareness in the smoky grey eyes that narrowed with disbelief at his own suspicions.

'You expect me to just stand by and say nothing,' she asked incredulously, 'while you panic about where your mistress has gone?'

'My *what*?' And then she realised, as she stared into his face which had gone as white as a sheet, his eyes glittering with a fury that surpassed her own, that she had made a terrible, unforgivable mistake.

CHAPTER NINE

'YOU think Maisie is my mistress?' Carlton asked with a deadly quietness that was more lethal than any roar of rage. 'You've been thinking that all along?'

'I...' Katie's voice faltered and died at the look on his face. 'It seemed like that; I—' She shook her head as she searched for words. 'You were always so nice to her... You—' Her words strangled in her throat. 'You were kind, gentle...'

'And because those attributes are so alien in me, so unnatural, the only conclusion that you could draw was that if I was nice to anyone I was sleeping with her?' he asked softly. 'I'm such an animal in your eyes, so abnormal that I can't feel friendship or warmth or any of the normal human emotions that the rest of the human race takes for granted?'

He hadn't moved any nearer, made any threatening gesture, but she was rooted to the spot with an overwhelming fear of what he might do if she moved so much as an inch. 'You thought I would marry you, commit myself to you when I was using another woman in that way, forcing her to watch us together and even expect her to keep my house?'

She stared at him, her eyes enormous in the chalk-white of her face, as his lips drew back from his teeth in a contemptuous snarl that paralysed her with fright. 'And my fumbling attempts to make you understand how much I loved you—you thought they were all part of the act?' he asked acidly. 'No wonder you cut me dead each time I tried to make you understand how I felt.'

His eyes narrowed still more into black slits that gave

his face a sinister, panther-like darkness. 'And you were prepared to marry me, thinking all that? Sell yourself to such a man as that? What are you, Katie? Who are you? Did your flesh creep each time I touched you? Was all that passion, all that desire an act to keep the buyer happy?'

'Carlton, it wasn't like that.' She was frightened, desperately, helplessly frightened, her mind still reeling from the revelation that he loved her—he loved *her*—but that she had ruined it all, destroyed anything they might have had because he would never forgive her for this. His eyes told her so.

'The hell it wasn't.' His face was grey now, his mouth a hard white slit in a face that was as cold as ice. 'I thought I could *make* you love me, Katie.'

He gave a harsh bark of a laugh. 'Funny, isn't it? The ultimate irony. I couldn't believe that, feeling as I did, you wouldn't respond. Oh, I know you hated me at the beginning, that circumstances conspired to make it all wrong, but the physical chemistry was real—or I thought it was.

'You hit me like a ton of bricks that day you came to the office, when I sat with you on my lap and you sobbed out all your insecurities and pain. But we'd got off to a bad start so I thought I'd play the waiting game, persevere, be around.

'But every time we met there were fireworks and then the solution was dropped in my lap. I could help your father, keep you near me at the same time and show you the man I really was. I was going to be patient, believe it or not.' His face was caustic with self-contempt. 'I wasn't going to force my unwelcome attentions on you, I was going to wait until you were ready, however long it took, because once you had married me I had all the time in the world. No one else could touch you. But then...'

He shook his head slowly. 'What the hell was that on our wedding night, Katie? You didn't have to give satisfaction for money like some whore in a brothel.'

She deserved it. She knew she deserved it but his words were more punishment that she could bear. The bitter hurt and pain that had turned his face into a stone mask cut her like a knife. What had she done? *What had she done?* She had seen so many glimpses of his caring side even before they were married and the tenderness he had displayed since they had been man and wife had touched her time and time again. She should have known he wasn't capable of this thing—she should have known, especially loving him as she did.

'Please, Carlton,' she whispered brokenly. 'Let me explain.'

'You've had your revenge, Katie.' As she went to walk towards him he lifted his hand to stop her. 'You've shown me what an arrogant fool I am, but just at this moment the urge to wring that beautiful neck of yours is overpowering so just keep your distance for an hour or so,' he warned with chilling grimness.

'But I want to talk to you,' she pleaded desperately. 'This isn't what you think—'

'I don't want to talk to you,' he said bitterly. 'In fact I don't want to look at you, think about you—' He turned and strode past her, walking to the French doors at the end of the room and opening them savagely before striding out on to the patio and disappearing behind the trees.

'*Carlton*!' She screamed his name but there was no reply, just the bright, sun-filled room and warm, scented air that was a mockery in itself when she could hardly breathe for the agony that was tearing her apart.

How long she stood there in the screaming silence she didn't know, but eventually she walked slowly across the room and up the stairs, entering their bedroom and walking out on to the balcony that was already hot underfoot with the heat of the sun. She looked up into the clear blue sky first, her eyes narrowed against the piercing light, and then down into the garden below, gazing blindly into space as her mind whirled and spun.

He had said he loved her. The thought was drumming loudly in her head along with the sickening, weak feeling in her stomach which the sudden confrontation had produced. Why hadn't he told her before? Then none of this would have happened.

Her mind searched its memories, like a computer compiling data, and suddenly several little incidents, when he had tried to do just that, were stark and clear in front of her. But she had been too blind, too stubborn to deviate from the verdict her brain had decided to reach and now she had lost him.

She whimpered out loud as she gripped her arms round her waist and swung back and forth in an agony of grief, the locket that he had given her on their wedding night moving gently against her throat.

A sudden movement below focused her eyes on the swimming-pool and she saw Carlton's powerful body cutting through the water like a machine, his arms and legs keeping up an unbelievable speed as he swam relentlessly up and down it.

He was nearly an hour in the water and her eyes didn't leave him for a moment, and when at last he hauled himself out to stand naked and magnificent for a moment in the blazing hot sun she saw that his shoulders were bowed as though with an unbearable weight, and the pain was so intense in her throat that she thrust her fist into her mouth to stop herself crying out. She had hurt him, hurt him as no one else had ever done. The knowledge was crucifying.

She watched him as he pulled his jeans on slowly, running a hand through his wet hair as he straightened, and then the big, lean body stiffened, his shoulders squaring and tensing, and she knew he had come to a decision of some kind.

*   *   *

'Pack your things, Katie.' As he joined her in the bedroom she turned to face him, her heart pounding. 'I'll check the first flight to England.'

'We're going back?' There was a lump in her throat that was making speech almost impossible.

'I hardly think there's any point in continuing this travesty, do you?' he asked grimly as his eyes flickered briefly over her tear-stained face before he turned to leave the room. 'Besides which I want to make sure Maisie doesn't do something silly—something Joe might have to live with for the rest of his life.'

'Carlton—'

'Don't offer any platitudes, Katie.' He swung round so savagely that she took an instinctive step backward, her hand going to her mouth as she realised that his veneer of self-control was paper-thin. 'I don't want to listen to a word you might say. Just keep quiet and pack your things.'

They left that day on an evening flight, the tall, dark, stony-faced man and pale, fair-haired slip of an English girl, and no one looking at their faces would have guessed that they were on their honeymoon.

Katie was in the grip of a fear so overwhelming that she was functioning purely on automatic, the guilt and horror of what her hasty words had produced in Carlton almost unbearable. He had retreated behind that invincible authority and coldness that had so misled her in the early days, unassailable and proud and quite unreachable.

All she could hope for was that there would be an opportunity, just a slight mellowing of that icy calm, for her to tell him the truth and bare her soul. But somehow, looking at his face and remembering all he had told her of his past life, she feared he wouldn't let her in even for a moment.

She had tried to talk to him once more before they had left the villa, but at her first words he had cut her off with such bitter ferocity that she hadn't dared try again. He was a fiercely proud man—that much she had known—but now she realised that in acting as she had she had ground that pride into the dust and he was finished with her. It was in his every action, every gesture, every icy glare.

Joseph was at the house when they arrived late that night and the sight of his face, strained and white, reached through Katie's grief and made her want to take that much younger Reef into her arms and soothe his distress like a mother with an unhappy child.

'What happened?' It was clear that Carlton had no such feeling as he put their suitcases down in the hall and spoke directly to his brother who had just wheeled his chair from the sitting-room. 'And I want it all, mind, straight down the line.'

'I didn't expect you to come back.' Joseph glanced from one to the other, his eyes red-rimmed and exhausted. 'Carlton, this is all my fault; you can't say anything to me I haven't already said to myself,' he groaned desperately.

'I wouldn't bank on it,' Carlton said grimly, but his face had softened somewhat at the younger man's obvious desolation. 'I thought you were going to go for it at long last— forget all these damn stupid ideas about being half a man and unable to give her children and so on? You know she's loved you since the moment she put a foot in the house, dammit. What more of a guarantee could you want for a marriage? You've held her at arm's length, made her as miserable as hell ever since I can remember and still she hasn't looked at another man. If that isn't love I don't know what is.'

'I know, I know.' Joe raked his hair desperately, his eyes bleak.

Katie stared at their faces in stupefaction. Maisie and Joe? *Maisie and Joe*? They had loved each other for years but Joe had refused to admit it to her, she thought helplessly as all the little incidents from the past slotted neatly into place. It was clear that Carlton thought they would be the ideal match and all his gentle concern for Maisie, his encouragement to the painfully shy beauty and, she saw now, fatherly affection had been to compensate for Joe's discouragement and rejection. What a mess. She gazed at the two men flatly. What a terrible, hopeless mess.

'Don't say "I know",' Carlton bit out angrily. 'We had this conversation a couple of days before the wedding and you assured me that once you and Maisie were here alone you would set things straight with her and put both of you out of your misery. Hell, I hinted as much to her at the reception just before we left, when she looked so damn miserable. Don't you realise what that day must have been like for her, feeling the way she does about you?'

'I told her we needed a year apart,' Joe admitted bleakly, his broad shoulders pathetically slumped. 'I *was* going to propose to her, Carlton. I even organised a meal with wine, roses, the lot, but then I looked at her across the table and she was so damn beautiful. I couldn't face tying her to a cripple for the rest of her life.'

'So in effect you sent her away?' Carlton asked caustically.

'She asked me why the year apart and I told her she ought to meet someone else,' Joe said flatly. 'Someone who could love her like a real man.'

Carlton ground out an oath as he shook his head in disbelief. 'Dammit, man, you *can* love her like a real man,' he said more softly now. 'The accident only interfered with your procreative ability; everything else down there is in prime working order.'

They seemed to have completely forgotten about Katie, for which she was supremely thankful as the more intimate aspects were discussed.

'You can adopt, can't you? Private adoption, anything. We aren't exactly short of a penny or two in case it's slipped your mind, Joe. Maisie has faced and accepted that she won't have children of her own, you know that. All she wants is you.'

'What am I going to do?' Joseph stared up at his brother helplessly. 'The last twenty-four hours have made me realise I can't live without her, Carlton. What the hell am I going to do?'

'Pray that I find her,' Carlton said grimly. 'Did she take all her things?'

'Everything personal.' Joseph's voice broke and Carlton bent to hug him swiftly, his own face working for a second before he stood up, his eyes thoughtful.

'There's one place she might be—that friend of hers from the children's home that she's kept in touch with through the years,' he said quickly. 'Have you spoken to her?'

'I tried her number,' Joseph said bleakly. 'She said she hadn't seen her.'

'She's a friend, Joe; she would,' Carlton answered drily. 'I'll go round there myself. If she isn't there it'll be down to private detectives—the police won't want to know—but we'll find her, however long it takes.' He patted his brother's shoulder. 'And when we do just keep your mouth shut and take her in your arms, boy, OK? She had one hell of a life in that children's home from when she was a baby; the only thing she wants from you is love.'

His compassion, his understanding rent Katie's heart into ribbons as she stood in the shadows to one side of the hall, watching them. And he had loved her. The only trouble was that she had the sick feeling that the past tense was right. Had.

She sat and listened to Joseph talk through the next few hours in between making them endless cups of coffee and forcing him to eat some sandwiches she prepared. She didn't mention the situation between Carlton and herself;

it wouldn't have done any good, and the younger man looked on the verge of collapse as it was.

Dawn was just breaking and Joseph had fallen into a light doze by her side when she heard Carlton's car pull up outside. She rose quickly, careful not to brush against the wheelchair and wake him, and walked out into the hall just as Carlton opened the front door and stood aside to let Maisie walk in.

The lovely brunette looked shattered, drained, and without even thinking about it Katie walked across and hugged her tight, and after a moment of startled surprise Maisie hugged her back. 'He's in there,' Katie said quietly as she gestured towards the sitting-room. 'He's been asleep for a few minutes.'

'I won't wake him.' Maisie looked at her with eyes that were swollen with crying. 'I'll just stretch out on the sofa in there and then I can be around when he wakes up.' She smiled at them both before walking into the room and shutting the door softly after her.

'You found her, then,' Katie said nervously even as she thought what an inane remark it was.

'Yes.' He stood looking at her through shuttered eyes and Katie thought he had never looked more attractive, or more unapproachable. 'She was with her friend. It took me a while to persuade the girl to let me in, but once she realised I wasn't going to go she obliged. She's not too thrilled with the Reef name; I can't blame her.' He shook his head slowly. 'But she is a good friend to Maisie and good friends don't happen too often in a lifetime.'

'No…' She felt glued to the spot and then forced herself to speak quickly before she lost her nerve. 'Carlton, about us—'

'Leave it, Katie.' The armour was back in place instantly. 'I'm damn tired and I don't want any post-mortems right at this moment. I'll move into one of the other bedrooms and I suggest you get a few hours' sleep yourself; you look done in.'

'But I don't want you to move into one of the other bedrooms,' she said rapidly. 'I—'

'I don't care what you want, Katie,' he said flatly, his eyes cold and remote. 'Later on we can discuss how best to handle this—whether you want a divorce straight away or a separation for a time to give your father time to reconcile himself to the situation—but right now I'm going to bed—alone. OK?'

'A divorce?' Somehow, in spite of all that had happened, she hadn't been expecting this and his words hit her like a physical blow. She put a hand to her mouth in protest.

'Don't worry, the financial side will remain as I promised,' he said coldly, misunderstanding her gasp of shock and white face. 'Whatever else I am I don't welsh on a deal. All your father's debts will be cleared and I'll continue to support his business with a nice healthy bank balance to keep him thinking he's winning. Your settlement we can discuss separately, but you won't have to work again or do anything else you don't want to for the rest of your life.'

'I don't want a divorce,' she said numbly.

'A separation, then.' He was already turning and walking up the stairs as he spoke. 'You can play this exactly how you want to. You kept your end of the bargain after all—you married me and fulfilled all your marital duties.' His voice was derisive and tight but even through the cynicism her new awareness of him heard the agonised pain he was trying to hide.

'You won't listen to me, then?' she asked quietly, moving to stand at the bottom of the stairs. 'Hear how sorry I am?'

'I accept your apology, Katie.' His eyes were narrowed and veiled as he looked down at her from the first floor. 'And I absolve you of all guilt, all blame; how about that?

You are free to leave if that's what you want or stay until the legal formalities are completed. I probably got exactly what I deserved after all in forcing you into a situation I knew you didn't want. But it's over now.' There wasn't a shred of indecision in his voice. 'Finished.'

For one more moment he watched her standing, pale and small, in the hall below, then turned without another word, and as she heard the door to one of the bedrooms close a few seconds later it was as though it was synonymous with all she could expect from the future.

CHAPTER TEN

KATIE remained standing staring upwards in the dimly lit hall for a long time. There was no sound from the sitting-room where Maisie and Joe were or from the bedrooms upstairs. All was quiet and still. She fingered the locket at her neck, her mind too heavy and dull with exhaustion and pain for coherent thought.

She found herself in the sleeping garden almost without being aware of getting there, sinking down on to a wrought-iron bench beneath the sweeping fronds of an old weeping willow tree as her trembling legs finally gave in.

The June morning was just beginning to stir, the birds twittering and calling in the trees surrounding the green square of lawn and a few insects buzzing quietly on their early morning call to the flowering bushes and plants perfuming the summer air. She sat there as the last of the dawn's shadows were banished by the sun overhead, its mild heat gentle on her arms already browned by the fierce Spanish sun.

'What am I going to do?' She spoke her thoughts out loud, her voice flat and slow. 'I love him. Doesn't that count for anything?' As her gaze wandered round the hushed, tranquil garden she touched the locket again, unfastening it suddenly and opening it to peer at her mother's face.

'Help me, Mum.' She felt like a little child again, tiny and alone. 'Tell me what to do. I can't let him go; I have to do something.' The tears were raining down her face; it was probably that which gave the minute face a different expression for a moment, but suddenly she heard her mother's voice in her mind as clearly as though she were in the garden with her.

'Tell him.' The tone was urgent. 'Tell him how you feel.'

'He won't listen,' she answered wearily. 'He's finished with me; he's had enough.'

'He'll listen.' The voice was persistent. 'He loves you. Did you have enough of your father over the years? Did you finish with him because he was wrong, cruel even? You loved him and love is stronger than disappointment and bitterness and hurt—yes, and even betrayal. He'll listen. You have to make him listen and then he will understand. He loves you, pumpkin; he'll never love anyone else. You owe it to him to make him see how you feel, how wrong you were.'

'Pumpkin'. The old pet name, forgotten through the years, brought her to her feet. 'Mum?' But there was no answer, no soft hand on her brow or fleeting shadow that she could touch, just the silent, peaceful garden and her own tears.

He was sleeping when she slipped in beside him after shutting the bedroom door quietly, her heart in her mouth. The strong, hard face was younger, boyish in sleep; the harsh lines of experience and life had eased and mellowed. He stirred very slightly, murmuring her name, before his breathing regulated and quietened again.

How could she have thought him capable of what she'd accused him of? she thought as she lay propped on one elbow, watching him sleep in the same way he had done with her only the morning before. First Penny and then Maisie…

She shut her eyes tight as she groaned in her mind. He had given her so much and she had thrown it all in his face, and if she had to debase herself now, crawl and plead and beg, she would. Pride and self-preservation had no place in her feeling for him any more—they couldn't have.

She had intended to keep awake, fighting the warm blanket of sluggishness every time it descended on her as she lay curled up by his side, knowing she had to stay awake to confront him the moment he woke, but when something heavy brought her out of a deep inertia she knew by the length of the afternoon shadows that she had slept.

Carlton's arm had landed across her middle and a moment or two later his eyes opened slowly, their lids heavy with sleep. As he saw her by his side he smiled lazily for a split-second and then, as realisation hit, sprang upwards so violently that the bed bounced.

'What are you doing here?' he asked harshly, but she had seen him glance at her naked breasts, seen the hunger in his eyes before he'd swung his legs over the side of the bed, intending to move away.

'Don't go.' She flung her arms round his neck as she pressed herself against his back. 'Please don't go, Carlton, please.'

'Let go of me.' His voice was thick and husky. 'I don't know what you think you're doing but I'm fully aware that this is beyond the call of duty.'

'Carlton, I love you,' she gabbled rapidly, keeping her arms tight round his neck although he had made no move to stand once she had touched him. 'I've loved you for ages but I thought you didn't love me—'

'Katie—' his shoulders tensed, the muscles hard and tight against her soft nakedness, but still she wouldn't let go, hanging on to him as though her life depended on it '—what is this? Some extreme form of guilt? You don't have to lie. I know how you feel and I can handle it. I'm a big boy now—'

'You don't know how I feel,' she said desperately. 'Every time I try to tell you you walk away, and I don't blame you, not after what I thought. But you have to listen.

'I didn't understand before—about you loving me, I mean. I thought you were talking about Maisie, not me.

You never made it plain. You never *said*,' she added breathlessly as she tried to fight the sobs that were constricting her throat. 'You'd said at the beginning that you wanted me because I was suitable, that you wanted children, but you never said you cared about me. I know you wanted me physically but then I started to care about you and it wasn't enough. I could see how you were with Maisie—so gentle and protective...'

'Joe was ripping her apart,' he said gruffly without turning his head. 'She was an emotional mess.'

'I now that *now*.' She was frantic. 'But at the time, when you admitted there was someone you loved, it seemed only logical that it was her.'

'Katie, I don't believe you.' He took a deep breath and tried to raise himself but she was a limpet round his neck. 'I've seen the way you look at me, for crying out loud. If all this is through some misguided sense of pity—'

'I won't let you go,' she said brokenly. 'I won't. I love you; I'll always love you even if you hate me. I loved you when we made our marriage vows and they meant exactly what they said to me.' Her arms tightened around him as she covered his neck in desperate, frantic kisses and when he stood he raised her with him, her arms clinging round his neck.

'Let go, Katie,' he said softly. 'This is doing neither of us any good.'

'No, you have to stay with me.' She began to sob even as she fought to stay in control. 'If you leave me, if you make me go there will never be anyone else for me, Carlton. I'll grow old all by myself and I've been by myself so long...' Her voice ended in a wail that wasn't in the least attractive but there was nothing she could do about it.

As he loosened her hands from about his neck, forcing her arms apart as he turned to face her, she couldn't see his face for the tears blinding her eyes. But he was going to go. That thought was uppermost and with it went the last of her fragile control. 'Don't you dare leave me!' she stormed through her sobs. 'Don't you dare. I can't live without you—'

'Shush, my formidable little wife, shush…' And suddenly, miraculously, she was held close to his hard, strong body as he joined her on the bed, pulling her to him as he kissed the hot, salty tears before taking her mouth in a deep, long kiss, parting her lips and exploring its full sweetness with his tongue. 'No more. No more tears.' His hands cupped her face as he raised himself slightly to look down into her drowning eyes, his voice husky and not quite even.

His hands moved over her body slowly and sweetly and he kissed where they lingered, his lips warm and sensual as they made her nerves quiver and melt with a flood of tiny, intimate caresses that were delicate and skilfully erotic.

There wasn't an inch of her body that he left unexplored, his hands and mouth taking their time as they slowly brought her to fever pitch, and then the need was raging, overpowering, taking control of her thoughts and senses and burning away the agony of the previous twenty-four hours with its fire. And for the first time endearments and sweet, intimate phrases of love were spoken as they touched and tasted and enjoyed.

As molten fire burnt in the moist, warm centre of her being her body began to tremble and shudder for the release only he could give, and he moved over her, entering her fiercely and possessively, murmuring her name against her lips, and the universe shattered into a million blinding fragments for them both.

When it was over he held her close for a long, long time without speaking, stroking her hair as she lay entwined with him, her eyes shut and her mouth content. 'Don't leave me!' Her voice was urgent and intense when at last he stirred, her eyes opening wide and shooting to his to read his expression, displaying her vulnerability for him to read.

'I wouldn't dare.' His lazy smile held both tender amusement and rueful wistfulness as he kissed her mouth gently. 'I can't remember the last time I was shouted at like that. You have no respect for your husband, Mrs Reef.'

'Carlton?' She nestled into his shoulder, wrapping her legs round his as though to anchor him to her side forever. 'You believe me? You aren't going to send me away?'

'I don't think I would have been able to let you go in the final analysis, Katie.' The dark face was very serious. 'It does me no credit but the thought of another man touching you makes me want to commit murder.' She moved to look into his face and saw that he wasn't joking.

'I don't want any man to touch me but you,' she said lovingly, her fingers tracing an idle path across the strong, muscled chest. 'I *do* love you, Carlton. I never want to face another twenty-four hours like the last—'

His mouth descended on hers with a passionate ferocity that stopped further talk, and her desire rose to meet his, her response without inhibition now that she knew she had his heart as well as his body. They soared into a timeless, enchanted world of their own where there was no yesterday or tomorrow, only the present in all its richness. And this time their union had a sweetness, a depth that was like nothing she had ever imagined.

'I wonder if we just made a baby?' She was still enfolded in his arms and now the night sky was dark and strewn with a million tiny, sparkling pinpoints of light, the bedside lamp at the side of Carlton bathing the room in a rosy, subdued glow that gave their naked bodies the texture of silk.

'I hope not.' His words startled her and in spite of the reassurance of the last few hours she raised her head sharply to look into his eyes, relaxing when she saw that they were lit with a soft, tender warmth that melted her bones. 'I'm selfish enough to want you all to myself for a while,' he admitted softly. 'You've married a very possessive man, my love.'

'I know.' She sighed happily. 'Tell me again when you first fell in love with me.'

'Little toad...' He turned her over and slapped her rounded behind before drawing her to him again. 'You put me through hell on earth and then you expect compliments? Just like a woman.'

'Have there been many—women, I mean?' she asked carefully, although his eyes noticed the flash of pain on her quiet face.

'None that has touched my heart.' His dark face was suddenly very still. 'I thought I loved Penny for a time but it only took a little while for me to realise that what I had felt was a blind infatuation, a youthful dream of something that never really was. And then I was searching, without realising it, without ever admitting it to myself—searching for the one woman I could love and want for the rest of my life.'

'Me,' she said with great satisfaction, the last lingering doubts from the past laid finally to rest.

'You.' He raised himself on one elbow and searched her face with his eyes. 'Even your face in that photograph pierced my heart in a way that was both uncomfortable and disturbing and when I met you, breathing hell-fire and damnation, I still told myself that what I felt was a strong sexual attraction—until the minute I took you in my arms, that was. From that moment on I knew I loved you, but it would have been more than my life was worth to try and make you understand how I felt at that time.'

'I wouldn't have believed you,' she admitted ruefully. 'I thought you were like my father, hard and callous, and by the time he explained why he'd been so cold over the years there was Penny and Maisie.'

'And now there is just us.' He kissed her hard. 'And from this moment on we talk about every little thing, every worry, so there can be no misunderstandings between us again.'

'You think you can do that?' she asked in loving disbelief.

'I will try,' he promised gravely. 'And now we should go and see if this stupid brother of mine has finally done the thing I have been urging him to do for years. I'm surrounded by stubborn people in this family.' He eyed her with mock-severity. 'When will you all understand that I know best?'

It was much later, as the four of them sat having a midnight supper in the soft warmth of the June night, that Joseph and Maisie outlined their plans for the future.

'That house I designed for the Croxleys is up for sale,' Joseph said quietly as he sat holding Maisie's hand, their faces relaxed and at peace as though they had just come through a great storm. 'I'd like to put in an offer. With their son being disabled, all the alterations another place would need are already taken care of and they'll be glad of a quick sale now that his new job in America has been finalised. There's a massive downstairs study which would be ideal for my work and the garden is a pocket handkerchief that Maisie will easily cope with.'

'Are you sure you want to leave here?' Carlton asked Joseph softly, although Katie sensed he had been pleased at the proposal.

Joseph had obviously caught the same notion because there was a twinkle in his eye and a wicked tilt to his head as he gazed back at his brother. 'I don't think Maisie and I could stand the noise,' he murmured innocently, with a sidelong glance at Katie that held both respect and admiration. 'I have the strangest feeling you've met your match in Katie, Carlton. I've often longed to shout at you but I've never had the bottle.'

Katie blushed to the roots of her hair but Carlton's face was lazy and unconcerned as he grinned back at the younger version of himself. 'It wouldn't have had the same effect,' he admitted drily.

'We'd like to get married in a few weeks. Neither of us wants any fuss—just a few close friends and family,' Joseph continued quietly, with a long glance at Maisie's lovely face. 'But you'll be my best man?'

'Well, I sure as hell wouldn't let anyone else be,' Carlton said with a flash of his old arrogance, which made Katie smile and Joseph grin wryly.

'And the Croxleys' house…?'

'That'll be down to you to sort out, Joe, my lad,' Carlton said firmly as he stood up, pulling Katie up with him and wrapping a possessive arm round her waist. 'Just in case anyone has forgotten, this is supposed to be our honeymoon and we're back out on the first plane to Spain tomorrow morning.'

'We are?' Katie queried breathlessly.

'We are.' His eyes were dark and hot as they left the others and mounted the stairs to their room. 'I want to hold you in my arms all night and most of the day without anyone else around, my sweet love. I want to look at you spread out before me in the moonlight and know that you are mine to touch and taste and love. I want to feel your body quiver and tremble beneath mine as I possess every part of you until the only thing you can think of is me.'

As they entered the bedroom he pulled her against him fiercely, his eyes glittering with desire. 'I can't get enough of you, do you know that? You're like a drug, a hypnotising, powerful drug that has enslaved me.'

'Carlton…' Her legs were ready to give way beneath her, so sensual were his words, spoken in that deep, husky voice that made love to her all by itself.

He ran his hands over her skin, satin-soft and honey-brown from the heat of the Spanish sun, as he stripped her swiftly until she stood naked and trembling before him. 'You are my love, my life,' he whispered softly as his eyes blazed over her body. 'My yesterdays, my tomorrows, my wild, sweet destiny…'

And then there was nothing but the blinding, hot darkness of the night as love consumed them both.

Jessica Steele lives in a friendly Worcestershire village with her super husband, Peter. They are owned by a gorgeous Staffordshire bull terrier called Florence, who is boisterous and manic, but also adorable. It was Peter who first prompted Jessica to try writing, and after the first rejection, encouraged her to keep on trying. Luckily, with the exception of Uruguay, she has so far managed to research inside all the countries in which she has set her books, travelling to places as far apart as Siberia and Egypt. Her thanks go to Peter for his help and encouragement.

MARRIED IN A MOMENT

by

Jessica Steele

CHAPTER ONE

ELLENA stared at the television screen in stunned horror, her brain numbed by what the newscaster had just announced—an avalanche in the Austrian Alps. An avalanche in the very area where Justine was spending a ski-ing holiday with her boyfriend Kit!

Ellena didn't seem able to think as the newscaster carried on solemnly about tons of snow, rocks and boulders, and no chance of anyone surviving such circumstance! Having done with that piece of news, he went on to the next item.

Though still disbelieving, she was starting to recover sufficiently from her initial shock to tell herself that she was panicking unnecessarily. Only that morning she had received an 'our hotel'-type of picture postcard from her sister... But—that must have been posted days ago!

Hurriedly Ellena found the card, feverishly scanning it and looking to see if by any chance there was a printed hotel telephone number. There was! In next to no time she was busy dialling. If she could just speak to Justine...

The line was engaged. For a half-hour the line was engaged. Ellena accepted that she was not the only anxious relative wanting to get through, though the waiting was unsustainable.

Perhaps Justine was trying to get through to her. She would know that Ellena would be anxious. She put her phone down. It did not ring.

All lines were probably swamped anyway. Perhaps Kit had managed to get through to his family. He had two brothers; the middle one, Russell, and his wife, Pamela, were looking after their baby while Justine and Kit were away.

Ellena was enormously thankful that she'd insisted on having Russell's address in Hertfordshire and phone number before Justine left. Ellena had never met any of Kit's family, but—interfering though it might be, or perhaps because she was so used to looking out for Justine—she had already phoned once to see if baby Violette was settled without her mother. Pamela, Russell's wife, had been more than a shade frosty, she recalled. But Ellena cared not for Pamela Langford's frostiness just now and, finding the number, she dialled.

'Hello, Russell. Ellena Spencer—J-Justine's sister.' Striving to keep calm, she announced herself—and hesitated, suddenly realising that if he had not had a telephone call from Kit, nor had he been watching the news, she was going to have to break the news to him herself.

But, 'Bad do,' he replied, and she knew that he was aware of the avalanche.

'You haven't heard anything from Kit? He hasn't phoned or anything?' she questioned urgently.

'We had a card from him this morning, but that's all.'

'Oh,' Ellena cried faintly, starting to feel a shade frantic. 'I've tried to phone the hotel, but I can't get through.'

'Try not to worry. Pamela says you'll hear soon enough if Kit and your sister are involved.' Russell attempted to soothe her, and she wondered how they could be so passive. Not worry…! 'According to the news report we were watching, that area was out of bounds—there shouldn't have been anyone in that area.'

Oh, heavens! Ellena was two years older than Justine and had done her best to take care of her when their parents had been killed in a mountaineering accident five years ago. Ellena knew from experience that anything labelled 'out of bounds' was a magnet for Justine. There shouldn't have been anyone in the avalanche area! When had that ever stopped Justine?

'I think I'll keep trying to get through to the hotel,' she

stated, starting to feel torn. If she went to her office and sent a fax there'd be no one at her flat to take any incoming call. 'If Kit rings you, would you…?'

'Look, if you're seriously worried, why not ring Gideon? He'll know how to get through.'

Gideon Langford was the eldest of the three brothers. By all accounts he was successful in everything he did, a high-flyer making the engineering firm started by his father into the vast empire it was today. Popular with the opposite sex—but light on his toes, apparently, when it came to marriage talk.

All the same, it defeated her to know how he could get through to the hotel if she couldn't. But she was beginning to feel quite desperate. Desperate enough to try anything. 'Have you got his number?' she asked.

Ellena tried the hotel again first, but when she again couldn't get through she dialled the number Russell had given her. It was engaged, as it was on her second and third attempt. On her fourth attempt, however, it rang out, and was answered.

'Langford!' an all-male voice answered abruptly. So abruptly, Ellena just knew that her call was most unwelcome.

'I'm sorry to bother you—' then no more formality; she was almost past caring whom she bothered '—my name's Ellena Spencer—I'm Justine's sister.'

'Justine?' he demanded clarification.

'Justine and Kit, your brother,' she inserted, too het up to feel foolish, because he'd know Kit was his brother, for goodness' sake! 'They're on a ski-ing holiday together and—'

'You've heard the news?' Gideon cut in tersely, clearly a man who had little time to waste.

'About the avalanche. Yes,' she said. 'I've been trying to get through to the hotel, but—'

'They're missing!' he stated shortly.

'Missing?' she gasped. How Gideon Langford had come by that information totally irrelevant as she clutched hard onto the phone receiver.

'My brother and his companion left their hotel first thing this morning—they haven't been seen since.'

'Oh, no!' she whispered, tears springing to her eyes. 'They might have gone anywhere,' she choked, clutching at straws. 'Russell said that the area of the avalanche was out of bounds.'

Gideon Langford took in that she had been in touch with his other brother without commenting on it. 'Did he also tell you Kit would merely see that as another rule to be broken?' he snarled harshly.

'J-Justine and Kit are—well met,' Ellena answered, her voice starting to fracture, the realisation hitting her that Gideon Langford's harshness might stem from the fact he was keeping a lid on his own emotions about his youngest brother. 'Is that all you know?' she questioned.

'I'll find out more when I get there.'

'You're going to Austria to—?'

'I'll have a plane standing by in a couple of hours,' he butted in grimly. Then he paused for a moment and, still in the same grim tone, asked, 'Do you want to come?' He didn't sound very enthusiastic.

'Yes,' she answered without hesitation—it didn't require any thinking about.

'Where are you?'

'My flat near Croydon.'

'Your address?' he demanded, barely before she had finished speaking. She gave it to him. 'I'll send a car. Be ready in an hour,' he instructed, and rang off.

An hour ago she'd been watching the television. Now she was on her way to Austria! At any other time she might have taken exception to Gideon Langford's bossiness. But not now. At this moment she was only grateful that he was taking charge. She felt a desperate need to be near Justine. Anything was better than sitting at home worrying.

As instructed, she was ready an hour later when a chauffeur-driven limousine arrived to take her to the airport.

And it was at the airport, in a private waiting area, that she caught her first glimpse of the man who ran that mammoth concern, Langford Engineering—Kit's brother! Gideon Langford was tall, about ten years older than Kit, well over six feet, dark-haired and, as they shook hands, she felt pinned by a direct look from his unwavering slate-grey eyes.

She felt herself being checked over, starting with her straight blonde hair, now held back in a neat chignon. Then his eyes took in her creamy skin, her slightly hollowed cheeks and photogenic high cheekbones that sometimes caused her to seem aloof. She wasn't particularly aloof, she didn't think. It was just that she usually had some problem on her mind—most often something to do with Justine.

'I don't suppose you've heard any further news?' she enquired, as he let go of her hand.

He shook his head. 'We'll just keep hoping,' he said shortly, and that was about the sum total of their conversation until someone came to show them to the private jet.

They had little to say to each other throughout the journey, either. While she knew Gideon Langford was busy with his own thoughts, Ellena lapsed into thinking of her years with Justine since their parents' deaths. They had been killed on a mountainside—she couldn't bear it if Justine, too, perished… No, no, she wouldn't think that way; she just wouldn't.

She had been just seventeen; Justine fifteen—and on the point of being expelled from school for some misdemeanour. Which of her misdemeanours it had been exactly was lost under the weight of all the others when word had reached them of their parents' accident.

They had both been much loved by their lively, bubbly

parents, but Ellena had had to do some instant growing up.
Prior to the accident, she had been hopeful that her father,
as he had before, might have been able to persuade
Justine's school from taking such drastic action as expul-
sion. But, he didn't come back and, while they were both
devastated at losing their parents, it was Justine who had
adored her father—he who, it had to be said, had indulged
her endlessly and had refused to see anything wrong in a
few high spirits and who had been inconsolable for months.

During this time Ellena had realised that her plans to go
to university to study accountancy were not going to happen. Although in the light of the tragedy the school had
relented, and allowed a much subdued Justine to stay with
them, Ellena had felt there was no way she could leave her.

Hiding her own heartache, she'd set about the practicalities of living without their parents. Out of necessity she'd
checked into their financial security.

Their finances weren't brilliant, but they weren't too bad
either, she'd discovered. Both she and Justine were aware
of an investment which their father had made for them both
in the years of their birth. They would each receive a quite
substantial amount—but not until their twentieth birthdays.

Meantime, their parents' house was heavily mortgaged
and there were a few debts outstanding; they had all lived
well, but there was nothing left over for a rainy day.

Ellena had left school straight away and, excelling at
maths, obtained a job with a firm of accountants. She was
reasonably well paid for her junior position, but it was nowhere near enough to pay the mortgage.

'The house has got to go. Do you mind very much?'
she'd told Justine gently.

'Without Mummy and Daddy here—I don't care at all,'
Justine had replied listlessly.

'We'll find a lovely flat to rent,' Ellena had decided with
a brightness she was far from feeling.

'If that's what you want...'

It wasn't, but facts had to be faced. So the house had been sold—with just enough money left over to settle all bills and, Ellena hoped, pay rent—if they were careful for the next three years—until her twentieth birthday when she could claim the money from her father's investment.

Justine had not cared for the first four apartments they'd looked at, but had started to perk up when Ellena, trying not to despair, found a flat at the more expensive end of the market.

'The rent's a bit more than I'd calculated.' Ellena had thought it wouldn't hurt to let Justine know there would have to be a few economies.

'I'll leave school and get a job too,' Justine had declared.

'I think we can manage while you finish your education,' Ellena had smiled, and, because Justine was just Justine, she'd given her a loving hug. Justine had clung to her.

It had been a wrench for Ellena to leave the rambling old house she had been brought up in, but, with more than enough furniture to spare, she and Justine had moved into their new home and started to try to rebuild their lives.

On the plus side, Justine had begun behaving herself at school, and, joy of joys, Andrea Keyte, the head of A. Keyte and Company, the accountancy firm Ellena worked for, had called her into her office one wonderful morning. Mrs Keyte, then a divorced lady of thirty-seven, had interviewed her personally for the job, so knew all about her present qualifications, and that she had hoped to study accountancy. Mrs Keyte had, she'd said that wonderful morning, observed how much Ellena enjoyed her work and how easily she seemed to grasp complicated issues. How, she'd enquired, would Ellena feel about being articled to her?

'You mean—train to be an accountant—to gain my qualifications here?' Ellena gasped, suddenly starting to see light, unexpected, wonderful light, after the darkness of recent months.

Apparently, that was exactly what Mrs Keyte—who was later to invite Ellena to call her Andrea—did mean. 'It will mean a lot of hard work,' she cautioned. 'Study in the evenings when you'd probably much rather be out with your boyfriend.'

Ellena didn't have a boyfriend. What time did she have? Before her parents' deaths she'd spent evenings and weekends either swotting over homework from school, or on some mad adventure with them. Since their deaths, Justine had taken precedence.

'I can do it,' she said eagerly. 'I *know* I can do it.'

'It will take all of five years for you to be ready to take your finals,' Andrea had warned.

'I want to do it; I really do.' Ellena, fearful that her employer might change her mind, promised this earnestly.

'Then you shall.'

And she had. It had not been easy. Left alone to cope with the work and the studying, Ellena knew she would have coped with only minor panics. But, in avowing, 'I *know* I can do it', she had not taken Justine—or rather Justine finally coming to terms with the loss of their parents—into consideration.

By the time Justine's sixteenth birthday had approached, it seemed she was close to being expelled from school again.

'I'd better find time to go and see if your headmaster will overlook your truancy one last time,' Ellena stated when, having arrived home from the office with a load of studying to do, Justine owned up to not having been to school for a while.

'I shouldn't, if I were you,' Justine grinned, 'I've no intention of going back—even if they'd have me.'

'Justine!'

'Don't go on, there's a love. I've been awfully good today.'

Ellena did not trust the word 'good'. ' ''Good'', as in…?'

'As in, I've been and got myself a job in a boutique. I start tomorrow.'

'You're not sixteen yet!' Ellena gasped.

'I told them I was. And I will be, by the time they find out I wasn't.' She laughed. She was infectious. Ellena remembered she had laughed too.

Dear, dear Justine, she couldn't be dead! Ellena choked on a sob of sound, and caught Gideon Langford's sharp glance on her from across the aisle. She hastily turned to look, unseeing, out of the aircraft window at the night sky.

He looked pretty bleak too, she realised, and strangely felt she wanted to help his suffering in any way she could. She realised her sensitivities at this dreadful time must be bouncing about all over the place, and strove again to calm her emotions. She had no idea what lay before them—it could be the best or the worst of news—so she must gather what strength she could.

Determinedly she pushed the weakening worst thoughts from her. Concentrate on the good things, she instructed herself. That time Justine... Her thoughts were at once back with Justine: Justine laughing, Justine crying; Justine bringing her first boyfriend home, the great unwashed group of her friends who had—to the dismay of their neighbours—almost camped on their doorstep; Justine starting new jobs, lasting a day, a week—miracle of miracles one job had even lasted three months! Justine's taste in boyfriends improving—her boyfriends starting to look as though they bathed and changed their clothes regularly.

By the time Ellena was twenty, and their finances were at last buoyant, however, she'd had enough of chasing halfway around London on what transport she could find, looking for Justine when she didn't come home at night. Ellena had found time to have driving lessons, and bought a car. She'd had many qualms about letting Justine have driving lessons as well—she was hard enough to keep tabs on. But, as ever, her soft heart had won over her sensible head, and

Justine learned to drive too—and Ellena bought her a car also. Then Justine fell in love—and the man she fell in love with seemed equally fluffy-minded.

Kit Langford wasn't too keen on work either, by the sound of it. 'What does he do?' Ellena had asked.

'Do?' Justine seemed to have no idea what she meant. 'Oh, you mean *work*! Oh, he's not working at the moment; he's having too good a time spending the money he came into on his twenty-first birthday from his father's estate.'

Ellena was sorry that Kit was without a father too. But she couldn't help but feel responsible for her younger sister. 'Does he live at home with his mother?' she asked.

'His mother remarried a year after his father died—she's living somewhere hot—the Bahamas, I think.'

'So where does he live?'

'He's got a flat; his brother bought it for him when he booted him out of his house.'

'His brother…'

'Well, it was rather a riotous party, and Gideon was away. But we did try and clear up all the mess.'

Justine had no need to go on. Ellena saw the picture quite clearly. She had herself come home from a late evening office function one time to find all hell had been let loose in her absence—music blaring and all sorts of people, no two with hair the same colour—pinks and greens all competing. Justine had decided to have a party. It had taken all of a week to restore the flat to good order, and a month to be on speaking terms with the neighbours again.

When Justine had fallen in love with Kit, though, no one else seemed to exist for her but him. Gradually Ellena had learned a little more about Kit's family. They were well to do, by all accounts, though Justine had never met either of his brothers. Kit saw his eldest brother occasionally, and there were frequent phone calls between the two, but Gideon Langford had a busy life on all fronts. Kit, who seemed as besotted with Justine as she was with him, wanted to spend all his time with her.

They had been going out with each other for quite some while when, as happy as you please, Justine had come home, holding a bottle of champagne aloft.

Ellena had broken off from her studies. 'We're celebrating?' she teased, joy in her heart that, by the look of it, her little sister had just become engaged.

She should, she'd later realised, have known not to prejudge anything where Justine was concerned. For, grinning madly, and obviously delighted, 'We're pregnant!' she announced.

Ellena was studying hard for her finals just then, though, had she thought that being pregnant might calm Justine down to lead a quieter life, she discovered she was much mistaken—Justine's relationship with Kit entered a stormy phase. And while Ellena had been mentally adjusting to the fact that her sister might soon be leaving to set up home with Kit—of that there had been no sign.

Justine still met Kit occasionally, but, more often than not, would come home needing to be soothed. When Ellena wasn't calming Justine's agitation, she was coping with her being unwell—and wondering what to do for the best. Her tenancy agreement stated definitely, no children. By the look of it, they would have to find somewhere else to live.

Then everything seemed to be happening at once. Ellena took her final accountancy exam—and with joy and not a little astonishment learned she had passed with an exceptionally good mark. But, even while she was relaying this news, Justine went into labour.

'I want Kit!' she'd cried.

Ellena contacted him and was warmed by his caring. He must have broken all records—he was at the hospital only minutes after Justine and Ellena—she didn't know which of the three of them was the more panic-stricken.

Kit stayed with Justine when the time arrived, and Ellena

paced the waiting area fearing she was going to break down in tears and disgrace herself at any moment now if she didn't hear something soon.

Then Kit, his grey look gone, grinning from ear to ear, was coming to find her. 'What do you think of Violette Ellena?' he asked—and, uncaring that she might disgrace herself, Ellena waited only for him to add that mother and daughter were doing fine before she burst into tears.

She had thought Kit seemed to grow up a little then. In any event he wouldn't hear of anything, other than Justine and their daughter moving in with him. In the short time Justine was in hospital he turned his spare bedroom into a baby's room, complete with crib and fluffy toys.

Justine was the happiest Ellena had ever seen her. She was but a few weeks away from her twentieth birthday. 'You feel all right about moving in with Kit?' Ellena felt she had to ask. 'You needn't. If you're worried about our tenancy agreement, we can look for...'

'I'm very all right about it,' Justine answered, and it was clear that such a small thing as having a landlord come down on them like a ton of coals for breaching their tenancy agreement had never for one moment bothered her. 'I want to live with Kit.'

'In that case, since you'll have enough to do looking after the baby, I'll pack your clothes and—'

'No need to bother with that, Ellena-Ellen,' Justine interrupted sweetly, using a pet name for her sister she always used whenever everything in her world was rosy. 'It'll take a little while for me to get my shape back, I expect, so I'll have to manage with a couple of these tents you bought me! But, as soon as my inheritance comes through, I intend to dump my old wardrobe and buy new clothes.'

In Ellena's view, Justine had some lovely garments in her wardrobe and it would be a sin to throw them out. But Justine had just been a very brave girl, and had presented her with a most beautiful little niece. Justine could do no wrong. Even when, as the weeks went by, she spent money like it was going out of style.

Kit had a single bed fitted into the minute box-room in his flat. It came in useful when, more and more frequently of late, they asked Ellena to come and baby-sit her niece.

Ellena had babysat the adorable scrap a week ago last Saturday evening. But it was on Sunday morning, as she was preparing to return to her own home, that she learned that Justine was as irresponsible now as she ever had been.

Ellena said goodbye to Kit, cooed a 'bye-bye' to the wonderful little girl who had so soon won her heart, and was about to make her farewells to her sister when Justine said she'd come out to her car with her.

Oh, dear, knowing her of old, Ellena suspected Justine had something to say which she feared she might not like to hear. She'd had an hour in which to say something—yet she was leaving it until Ellena was on her way out!

'We're going away tomorrow,' Justine announced as they walked to the parking area. 'We'll—er—probably be away for a month or so.'

Given that it was January, and had seemed a long winter, a month somewhere warm might do them all the world of good. 'Where are you going?' she asked, her thoughts on Violette and how they would have to guard her. 'You don't think you should wait until the baby's a little older?' she queried. She didn't want to put a damper on their plans but, apart from the time factor, and what would be involved in getting any vaccinations done—wasn't Violette a little young for such treatment?

'Oh, we're not taking her with us!' Justine answered blithely. While Ellena was starting to be concerned that there was no way she could look after baby Violette for 'probably a month or so' and at the same time do her job, Justine was going on: 'Kit's heard of this wonderful place in the Austrian Alps. We're going ski-ing. And don't worry, Kit's brother's going to mind the baby while…'

'His brother! Gideon? The one who, according to reports, works all day and parties all night?' Ellena exclaimed aghast.

'No, not him! Kit's other brother.'

Ellena was only marginally relieved. 'Russell, the married one?'

'Mmm, Russell,' Justine confirmed. 'Kit hasn't seen him in ages, and he's a bit of a dream—while his wife, Pamela, she's a bit of a shrew, with a nose for money like no one you've ever met! When I mentioned I'd be prepared to pay handsomely—and for the cost of a temporary nanny—she couldn't offer her services fast enough.'

Apparently Kit had used up all the money left to him by his father. But Ellena didn't think she liked the sound of this arrangement at all. Perhaps she could employ a temporary nanny herself to take care of the baby during the day and look after her herself at night. But complications stirred before she could so much as voice her thoughts. Apart from the fact that children were not allowed where she lived—crying babies with massive lung power in particular—since qualifying as an accountant she was starting to take responsibility for her own clients; hers was no longer a nine-to-five job.

'But—but—what about clothes?' She was putting obstacles in the way on purpose, she knew she was, but somehow she couldn't bear the thought of them going away and leaving the baby with strangers.

'Oh, heck, Ellena, I've put on an inch or two since Violette arrived; my old salopettes were never going to fit me anyway. Besides, what are credit cards for?'

By the sound of it Justine, who was still replenishing her wardrobe, intended to purchase all she required at her holiday destination.

Ellena knew she was on a losing argument, even as she suggested, 'Don't you think Violette's a little young to be left with strangers? She's only…'

'Oh, Ellena!' Justine exclaimed impatiently. 'I knew you'd be like this, which is why I didn't tell you straight away when Kit and I decided to take off. Besides, Violette has met Russell and Pamela—we went there one day last week when we were wondering who best to leave her with. Ideally it would be you, but you're going up in the world with your job and, having wrecked your social life over the years—I know I've been sheer murder for you sometimes,' she put in, her flare of temper dying as she became loveable, charming Justine again, 'I just didn't want to be responsible for wrecking your career so soon after you've qualified.'

'Oh, Justine!' Ellena said helplessly.

'Austria's not the moon,' Justine smiled winningly.

That had been the last time she had seen her. How glad she was now that she had asked for Pamela and Russell Langford's address and phone number, that she and Justine had said goodbye on friendly terms. She had managed to wish her a happy holiday, Ellena recalled—and without realising it, took a shaky breath.

'We're about to land,' the stern-faced man sitting across the aisle cut into her darkening thoughts.

'Thank you,' she mumbled, made hastily aware that she was in an aircraft and that in the next hour or so she could be hearing news that she did not want to hear.

Icy cold air hit them as the plane door opened. Ellena was glad of her thick trousers, sweater and sheepskin coat. Glad, too, of Gideon Langford's assistance because, for all he didn't seem to say much, and what he did say was curt and to the point, it was he who made what explanations were necessary. He took over, asking questions—though there was no more news now than there had been then.

She had brought only the barest minimum in the way of luggage, and without humour wondered if perhaps she was more like her younger sister than she realised.

But then Ellena discounted this, realising that, unlike

Justine, her reasons were practical. Gideon Langford had said, 'I'll have a plane standing by', so she'd known it might only be a small aircraft with little room for a heavy and bulky suitcase.

Gideon saw to the small airport formalities and she followed him out to a waiting car. The cold no longer bothered her. It was late, dark and her nerves were stretched. She got into the car with no idea where they were going—she just wanted to find Justine.

Kit's brother was highly efficient, she discovered, for after they had been driving some while the driver pulled up outside a smart hotel. It was not the same one that had been pictured on Justine's postcard.

The driver got out and opened the door for her. She found herself standing beside Gideon Langford while he relieved the driver of their small amount of luggage.

'What are we doing?' she asked, her wits seeming to be numb.

'I've booked a couple of rooms here,' he replied. He had taken care of her accommodation too, apparently, and he was already turning to go into the hotel.

'I want to go to...' She wanted to say Justine's name, but was caught out by an emotional moment and could not. 'The other hotel.'

'So do I—we'll check in first,' he decreed, and Ellena realised, as she followed him into the smart hotel and he summoned someone in authority, that Gideon Langford, once he'd had an update on the situation, had always intended to go and check out the other hotel whether she went with him or not.

Ellena stood by him aware that he, or someone in his employ, must have phoned ahead so they'd have somewhere to stay. The local police had been informed that their plane had arrived, apparently, and they, with the hotel manager, adjourned to a private room—but only to hear that there were no new developments, that everything was as bleak as had been forecast. A well-rehearsed plan had been put into operation, with rescue teams combing the area—they had reported back that there was absolutely no chance of anyone caught in that avalanche surviving.

Ellena strove valiantly for control. She could not believe it, would not believe it. Nor, apparently, would Gideon Langford. Stiffly he thanked everyone for their efforts and, flicking a glance to where Ellena stood dry-eyed and taut with control, said, 'And now, Miss Spencer and I would like to see where our relatives were staying.'

She hated that word 'were', the past tense, even if logic said loudly and clearly that since Justine and Kit were not around to occupy their hotel accommodation, 'were' very clearly fitted.

They left their luggage to be taken up to their rooms, and drove away from their hotel in the same car in which they had arrived. This time, though, with a police escort. The reason was explained—and also why they were booked into a different hotel—when they got to the place where Kit and Justine had been staying. Regardless of the lateness of the hour and the risk of frostbite, some of the press, having been blocked at the small airport, were keen to have an interview with the missing man's brother.

Ellena had been aware that Gideon Langford was well known. How well known was borne out by the fact that he knew some of the newsmen by their first names. 'You know as much as I do, John,' he answered one reporter, while at the same time ushering Ellena inside the hotel.

'Who's the lady?' someone else asked—they did not get a reply.

The hotel manager showed them up to the room which Kit and Justine had used. 'I have not had the room disturbed,' the Austrian assured them, and, receiving their polite thanks, sensitively went out, closing the door behind him.

Only then, alone with Gideon Langford, did it dawn on

Ellena, having been in his company for some hours now,
how little conversation had passed between them.

Nor did she feel like talking then. She stared round the
twin-bedded compact room, imagined she could hear
Justine and Kit's laughter, the way they had been laughing
that last Saturday—abruptly she blanked her mind off, and
became aware of Gideon Langford opening drawers and
poking about in wardrobes.

'There are a few clothes here—but no suitcases,' he
stated matter-of-factly.

Ellena went over to the open wardrobe and, standing next
to him, observed a couple of ancient anoraks which she
recognised as belonging to Kit and Justine.

'M-my sister was going to buy new,' she informed him
chokily. 'She was—is—oh, dammit...' Her voice broke;
she turned from him, determined to gain control. Justine
wasn't dead, she wasn't, and she wasn't going to cry.
'Justine is going to buy a whole new wardrobe,' she made
herself continue.

She guessed Gideon was having a hard time with his
emotions as well, when he retorted shortly, 'Kit didn't have
any money!'

Even so, that annoyed her. It gave her the stiffening she
needed, anyhow, as she retorted straight back: 'Then perhaps it's just as well Justine had her own money—she probably paid for this trip.' Immediately the acid words were
out she felt contrite. She flicked a glance at him, saw he
didn't seem to view her as his favourite person, and at once
she apologised, 'I'm sorry, Mr Langford, I'm trying so hard
not to go to pieces. I d-didn't mean to give you the rough
end of it.'

Whether he accepted her apology she had no idea, for
he just stood and stared at her from those steady slate-grey
eyes. But she rather guessed she had been forgiven when,
turning from her, he grunted, 'Gideon.'

She felt she should curtsy, then wondered if stress had

made her light-headed. But she forgot everything save
Justine when she spied in one of the open drawers a sweater
she had lent her one time.

'No, definitely no suitcases,' Gideon announced, sounding positive.

'If you're thinking that they may have packed up and
left—and you can't wish it any more than I—I have to tell
you, Justine in the main is so happy-go-lucky. She planned
to buy anything she needed here—she's just as likely to
have arrived without luggage.'

'Or followed Kit's example and packed anything she
might have thought of in a plastic carrier,' he documented,
adding, 'As you remarked, a pair well met.'

They stayed another few minutes in the room but there
were no more clues to be picked up; only a few toiletries
were left in the bathroom. Ellena could feel her emotions
on the brink of spilling over, and had not Gideon suggested
they leave she would have made the suggestion herself.

They had chance of a private word with the hotelier, who
promised he would contact them instantly, should his guests
return. Then, again running the gauntlet of a couple of
hardy pressmen, they returned to their own hotel.

Gideon Langford had a room opposite hers and, having
escorted her up in the lift, he went into her room with her.
'Will you be all right here?' he enquired courteously.

'Yes, thank you,' she replied politely.

He didn't leave straight away, but stayed to suggest,
'You'll want to phone your parents.'

'My parents are dead,' she answered tonelessly.

'You're on your own?'

'No,' she denied. No way was she ready to accept that
Justine wasn't coming back.

'You live with someone?' he asked sharply, and she just
knew he meant some man.

'I live alone,' she responded curtly.

'Goodnight!' Gideon Langford turned away from her, obviously fed up.

'I'm sorry,' she found herself apologising. 'I'm—on edge.'

He halted at the door and turned round, relenting, 'We both are.' And then proceeded to instruct, 'Try and get some rest. Have anything you need brought to your room. With a few pressmen around, you'd better stay where you are until I come for you.' He made to leave, thought for a moment, and then said, 'I may be out some time tomorrow. I'll contact you as soon as I get back.'

'Where are you going?'

He hesitated, but then did her the courtesy of being honest with her. 'Out to the avalanche site.'

'I'm coming with you,' she said at once, no please or thank you.

'I don't think—'

'I'm coming!' she butted in. If he thought she was going to stay here while he went there—where Justine and Kit might be—he could think again!

He shrugged, 'Suit yourself,' and left her.

Ellena supposed she must have slept at some time—it didn't feel like it. She was up at six, showered and dressed and waiting for Gideon Langford's call.

It wasn't long in coming. He would see her in half an hour's time. Meanwhile, he had some breakfast sent up to her room. Ellena wasn't hungry, but drank some strong hot coffee and belatedly remembered work she was supposed to be doing that day.

She put through a call to Andrea in England and explained why, and where she was. 'I'm not sure when I'll be back,' she warned.

'Don't worry about it,' Andrea answered warmly. 'Take as long as you need, Ellena,' she suggested gently. 'We'll all be hoping for you.'

Gideon Langford, when he knocked on her door, was not in talkative mood. 'There's no news?' she asked urgently.

He shook his head. 'Ready?'

Wordlessly she went with him out of the hotel and to the waiting car, and said not another word in the hour-long drive to where the disaster had occurred.

There were some officials waiting for them, but when, after walking some way, they stood back and pointed and explained about the mass of snow, and the boulders and rocks it had brought down in its wake, Ellena could see for herself that anyone foolhardy enough to chance ski-ing in that area would not have stood a chance.

She felt what little colour she had in her face drain away, felt gut-wrenching pain and wanted to scream, and to go on screaming. She turned away, collided into someone. It was Gideon. His arms came around her. He held her. They held each other, two human beings in need of solace. She guessed that, like her, he had always looked out for his younger sibling and it had been a role taken on willingly. She wanted the holding to go on.

Ellena broke from him, her mind in a turmoil. Somehow she got back to the car; somehow Gideon was there too. The car was moving, she staring unseeing out of one window on one side, he staring unseeing out of the window on the other side.

They had been driving on the return journey for some while. Ellena was still feeling stunned, shaken, and still not ready to believe it, to believe that she had lost her sister, that poor little Violette had lost her parents, when suddenly it hit her that the poor little scrap might have been orphaned.

'Oh, no!' escaped her on an anguished cry of sound, and as Gideon Langford turned from his non-contemplation of the view, she whispered, 'What about the baby!'

'Baby?' he echoed, and sounded so startled that Ellena

came to, realising she was not alone. 'What baby?' he questioned tautly.

She moved from her own non-contemplation of the view to look at him. And it was her turn to be startled. For clearly Gideon Langford had no idea that Kit had a baby daughter. A daughter of four months old.

Astonished, she realised that Gideon Langford had no idea at all that he was an uncle!

CHAPTER TWO

'You didn't know?' Ellena gasped.

'Baby?' he clipped, clearly wanting to know more, and quickly.

There was no way to dress it up, nor, a shock though it might be to him, try to hide it. 'Justine and Kit have a four-month-old daughter,' she replied, and saw a muscle jerk in his strong, good-looking face. Saw him take what she had said on board—and realised that a dozen and one pertinent questions were on their way. But then she saw him flick a glance at their driver, who understood a little English—and Gideon turned from her to renew his non-contemplation of the view from the vehicle's side window. He had obviously swallowed down those questions but Ellena did not doubt that she would be on the receiving end of them the moment there were no other ears around to overhear what they were saying. Gideon Langford was well known but, indisputably, he valued his family privacy—and there were pressmen about.

A cold, stiff silence stretched between them and lasted until they arrived at their hotel. Gideon Langford asked for the keys to their rooms. He hung onto them as they went up in the lift and inserted the key into the door of her room. He pushed the door open. She preceded him into her room, knowing that he would follow.

Ellena went over to the window, again looking out but registering nothing very much. She heard the sound of the door behind her being closed. She turned. She was not mistaken, she saw: Gideon Langford had not merely opened the door and left her to it, he was right there with her. Those questions weren't going to wait any longer—he wanted an-swers.

Why she should feel hostile to his questioning she had no idea, a self-defence mechanism perhaps? But when he began, 'This child…' for short, pithy starters, she discov-ered an aggressiveness in her that rushed out to meet any-thing he had to say head-on.

'Kit and Justine's baby, you mean?' she challenged before he could get further.

Her aggressiveness glanced off him, barely touching him, though she didn't miss the way his eyes narrowed slightly at her tone. 'You're saying my brother is the father of your sister's child?'

'Of course he is!' she erupted.

'You're sure of it?'

How dared he? 'Listen, you,' she attacked hotly, 'Justine may have been a bit wild, a bit of a rebel, and their rela-tionship may have had its—its stormy moments, but there's been no other man for her but Kit, since the moment she met and fell in love with him!'

'But they're not married?'

'Grief—he's your brother—don't you know anything about him?'

'I know a whole lot about him, including the fact that there was no woman on the scene when I last visited him six months ago.'

'Your bi-annual visit, was it?' she threw in tartly, though she almost apologised for that remark when he flicked her an acid look. Then she wondered why the hell should she? Who did he think he was, trying to deny Kit was the baby's father? 'Justine lived at home with me until the baby was born—Kit collected them from the hospital and there didn't seem to be any question that he would take them back to his flat.'

'They live together?'

'Happily,' Ellena declared frostily.

'Happily unmarried?'

'I don't think getting married occurred to either of them,' she replied honestly.

'That sounds like Kit,' Gideon muttered, and asked abruptly, 'Where is it now—this infant?'

She felt annoyed. 'Violette,' she informed him stiffly. 'Her name's Violette.'

'Violette?' he echoed—much in the same vein as if she'd told him they'd called the child Rover.

'They chose the name, not me!' she snapped, and wondered if the stress was getting more than she could take, because her sense of humour seemed to be twitching for a smiling release at his reaction to the baby's name. She did not smile, however, but informed him, 'Your brother Russell and his wife are looking after Violette while—'

'Your sister left a four-month-old baby with that hard-nosed, money-grubbing bitch!' he interrupted on a snarl.

Ellena blinked in surprise—all too evidently Gideon Langford had little time for his sister-in-law. She recalled that Justine had called Pamela a bit of a shrew; the one and only time she had spoken with her herself, she hadn't taken to her, either.

'Your brother left the baby too!' she defended. 'Anyway, as well as paying Pamela, Justine also engaged a temporary nanny.'

'Huh!' he grunted, and Ellena started to actively dislike him. 'I phoned Russell just before I left—he didn't say anything about looking after Kit's infant!'

'That's hardly my fault!' she flew, her emotions all over the place, her temper seeming to be on a very short fuse. 'Since you're a family who only visit every six months, it's a wonder to me you tell each other anything.'

The chill factor went down another ten degrees as Gideon Langford favoured her with an icy look for her trouble. 'You know nothing!' he rapped curtly.

'I know…' she went to explode. But then was suddenly

so overcome by the events that had taken place that she
came to a full stop, words failing her. She swallowed hard,
emotion threatening to overwhelm her.

She turned swiftly about, her grief private, not to be
shared. She looked down at the windowsill, concentrated
hard on it, striving with all she had for control.

So hard was she battling not to break down that she
momentarily forgot she wasn't alone in the room. A reminder of Gideon Langford's presence arrived, though,
when, just as if he knew of her every thought and feeling,
he moved behind her and took hold of her.

She felt his firm grip on her upper arms and began to
like him again, even though all the evidence pointed to the
reverse. 'Hang on, Ellena,' he instructed low in her right
ear, using her first name, making them more friends than
the enemies they'd been a minute ago. 'They're not dead.
I won't believe they're dead.'

She swallowed hard, but did not turn around. 'I can't
believe it either,' she said huskily.

For a minute more Gideon held her in that steadying grip.
Then he was saying, 'We have to think of leaving.'

'I don't want to leave—I can't,' she answered.

'Yes, you can,' he countered. 'I'll instruct everyone you
can think of to contact me the moment they have the barest
hint of news.'

She tried to be sensible. 'You've business to get back to,
I expect.'

'It seems incidental,' he replied—and Ellena knew that
she really did like him. He had a multi-million pound con-
glomerate to run, but it meant nothing to him when his
youngest brother was missing.

She realised, common sense giving her a nudge, that they
could achieve nothing by staying. 'When do you want to
leave?' she asked, and felt him give her arms a small
squeeze of encouragement.

'As soon as you're ready,' he answered, letting go his hold and moving away.

Ellena turned and looked at him. The icy look he had served her with before had gone, and, for all he was un-smiling, he seemed less harsh than he had been. 'I'll just get my things together, settle up here, and...'

'I'll settle,' he stated, and, when she looked likely to proudly protest, 'You're family,' he said, and went, not knowing how warmed she felt. For, apart from Justine and Violette, she had no other family.

It took her next to no time to gather her belongings together. But in that short period Gideon Langford had settled their account with the hotel and organised their flight.

They were on their way back to the small airport when she realised he'd found time to speak with other people too. 'The minister from the local church was kind enough to call,' he informed her quietly as they reached their destination. 'He wondered if we would like him to carry out a service for Kit and Justine.'

'You thanked him, but said no I hope,' she answered jerkily.

She realised that she and Gideon Langford must be pretty well near on the same wavelength when he replied, 'I did. It sounded too final.' He, by the sound of it, was not ready to admit to that finality yet—and neither was she.

In contrast to the silence that had existed between them on the journey out, they had been in the air around ten minutes when Gideon Langford looked across the small aisle at her and enquired, 'You mentioned your sister has money of her own; does that mean that neither of you has to work?'

'Justine never did get the hang of working,' Ellena replied truthfully. 'Though the way she's spending, she'll be lucky if her money lasts her longer than a couple of years.'

'It was an inheritance?'

'Money our parents invested for both of us to have when we reached twenty.'

'You're—how old?'

Ellena stared at him from frank blue eyes. Nothing like asking! He'd be demanding how much the investment was next. 'Twenty-two,' she answered. 'I received my money two years ago.'

'But you've still some of it left?'

Was there a purpose behind his questioning—it escaped her if there was. 'Some of it went—cars for Justine and me, clothes, and… But, yes, there's still a little left,' she owned.

'From your remarks about your sister not getting the hang of working—and that's not a criticism,' he slipped in, causing her to realise she must have bridled a touch without knowing it, 'Kit is very much the same,' he soothed any ruffled feathers. 'But, to get back, I take it that you *do* know the meaning of the word ''work''?'

'I enjoy my job so much I hardly think of it as work,' she owned.

'What sort of work would that be?'

He had a certain kind of charm, she realised. Sufficient, anyway, to have her put her present worries to the back of her mind for a short while. 'I'm an accountant,' she answered, and, because that sounded a little like showing off, 'Though I've only recently qualified.'

'Who are you with?' he wanted to know.

'A. Keyte and Company,' she replied, and, realising it was a very small business compared with the enormous accountancy firm he must deal with, she added, 'It's only a tiny company, but I love it there.' Agonising thoughts and worries were soon back as she relayed, 'I rang Andrea this morning. She said to take as much time as I…' Her voice tapered off. Ellena looked away from him as she fought for and gained control of her emotions. 'Anyhow, much as I enjoy working for her, I may have to look else-where.'

'You have some problem?'

She glanced across at him again. He had seemed so much on her wavelength about almost everything, it surprised her that he wasn't this time. 'Well, I'll obviously try to make some arrangements that will mean I don't have to leave my present employer, but if all else fails, I shall have to try and find a firm that has crèche facilities. V—'

'You're thinking of taking that baby to live with you?' He seemed astounded at the very idea!

But that he should be astounded at something which, to her mind, was a foregone conclusion, annoyed her. 'Natu-rally, I'm taking her,' she stated forcefully. Adding, for good measure, '*That* baby is my niece!'

Only to be left staring at him open-mouthed when, 'And mine!' he stated quietly, purposefully.

Ellena closed her mouth, but was still staring at him in-credulously, still not believing the deliberate intent behind his quietly spoken words. She just could not take in that he seemed to be saying that he wanted charge of Violette. Then her feeling of shock gave way to a feeling of fury—fury born of panic. Over her dead body! 'You can't possibly want her!' she erupted furiously. 'You've had nothing to do with her. I've seen her most every weekend!' she staked her claim. 'In the week, too, if her parents needed a babysitter,' she tacked on for extra strength. 'Why,' she hurried on, barely pausing for breath, 'you didn't even know of Violette's existence until I told you about—'

'So now I do know,' he cut in calmly. 'And I have as much right as you to…'

'No, you haven't!' she denied. 'You don't know her, you don't love her, you…'

'You live in a *flat* near Croydon.' When had she told

him that? She was too het up to remember. 'I have a house in open country.'

Who said her flat wasn't in open country? It was a wasted argument, she realised. 'You led me on!' she accused him furiously.

'How the devil did I do that?' he challenged harshly.

'You know!' she hurled back. 'Finding out that while I have some funds they're peanuts in relation to your wealth. Finding out that I have to work, so I won't be able to be with Violette all the time. You're despicable! You're…'

'You're off your head!' he countered. 'It hadn't so much as occurred to me that you'd want guardianship of that infant when I indulged in a little—polite conversation—to help the flight along.'

'Polite conversation, my aunt Fanny!' she tossed at him rudely, not believing it for a minute. 'Well, you may make a claim for her, *Mr* Langford, but I'm having her!' No way was she going to let the poor mite live with this brute!

'I'll see you in court,' he drawled—and that infuriated her. Just because he had more money, a house in the country, he thought he could ride roughshod over other people. She loved the baby but he didn't even know her!

'You won't stand a chance!' Surely love came before money?

'How do you figure that?'

She hadn't yet. But, thus challenged, she slammed at him, 'I've an unsullied reputation, for one thing!'

His look said, How boring. 'You mean with the opposite sex?' he drawled, and she wished she'd kept her mouth closed. But that How boring expression niggled her, forcing her on.

'Which is more than can be said for you!' she attacked sniffily.

'It's true, I've had my moments,' he admitted mockingly. 'But are you saying that you've *never* had any member of the opposite sex—er—staying over?'

'That's got nothing to do with you!' she retorted hotly, starting to feel a shade warm around the ears.

'It has, if you intend to stand up in court and swear to it,' he derided.

He was infuriating. True, her experience of men was limited, though she was certain that there couldn't be many around like him! 'I'm prepared to do that if I have to,' she told him snappily.

'Ye gods!' he exclaimed, seeming to find it incredible that she'd reached twenty-two without being tempted.

And that annoyed her. 'From what I hear, you were chief practitioner of the love 'em and leave 'em ethic.'

He shrugged. 'Charm has its own reward,' he owned modestly. But, apparently done with ribbing her, 'Straight up—are you a virgin?' he wanted to know.

It wasn't just her ears that felt warm. She was certain her cheeks positively glowed. 'It's nothing to be ashamed of!' she snapped.

'Did I say it was?'

He hadn't. But she didn't want this conversation, though she wasn't sure if it hadn't been her who had started it. 'We're getting away from the point,' she said heatedly.

'Which is?'

Give her strength! 'The point is, you, with your lifestyle. Well, you're hardly the type to be responsible for the upbringing of a young girl, are you?'

'If she's only four months old, I'd guess she isn't even walking yet!'

'She'll grow!' Ellena retorted, glaring at him, feeling panickily that she was somehow getting the worst of this.

She was positive of it when, having tired of the argument, it seemed, he decreed, 'Perhaps we'll leave it for some judge to decide.'

Ellena did not answer. Suddenly it dawned on her that she and Gideon were talking as if Justine and Kit weren't coming back—and they were. *They were!* Whether the same thought had just struck Gideon she couldn't have said, but she thought she caught a glimpse of a bleak look come to his expression a moment before he turned his head away.

Ellena turned her face to her window too. Conversation between them, polite or otherwise, was done with, and she spent the rest of the flight on trying to keep thoughts that Justine might be dead out of her mind. Instead she endeavoured to concentrate on what must be done to ensure that Violette had a safe, warm and loving upbringing.

From the sound of it, Gideon Langford was fully prepared to go to court to battle for custody of the baby. With his money, he was going to be able to afford to employ the very best of lawyers.

What she must do, she realised, was to get herself in a position to combat everything he threw at her. Had a house in the country, did he? Well, albeit that hers would probably be pokey by comparison, she'd get a house in the country too.

She'd probably got enough money left to put down a deposit on something small. And she was earning more now, so a mortgage of not too vast proportions was within her means. She'd got enough furniture to furnish somewhere modest and—and…

Her thoughts fractured and her mind hurried on to taking the baby's cot and all necessities from Kit's flat. She gained control and decided she would only *borrow* them for the short term, until Kit and Justine came for Violette.

Ellena fought another battle for control—and managed to win. She was making all these plans unnecessarily. Justine and Kit would be back soon. As likely as they were to take themselves off ski-ing in a prohibited area, they were equally as likely—leaving bits and pieces of clothing behind—to up sticks and move on somewhere else, if the mood took them. The very worrying thing about that, though, was that whatever else Justine was or was not, she was scrupulously honest. No way would she dream of doing a flit without paying her hotel bill, Ellena just knew it. It just wasn't in her sister's make-up—and yet, that hotel bill had not been paid.

Telling herself that everybody was allowed one lapse, and that, what with having just had a baby and everything, Justine's hormones were probably still all over the place—sufficiently, anyhow, for her to act in a way she wouldn't normally—Ellena suddenly had one very bright positive thought, that was startling in its simplicity.

Possession, it was said, was nine-tenths of the law. So what was to stop her from going to Russell and Pamela Langford's home and taking possession of Violette? To hear Justine tell it, and Gideon Langford too, for that matter, Pamela Langford was only interested in money.

No problem. If Justine had not settled with her and the temporary nanny in advance, then she could easily do so. Did she have any proof with her that she was who she said she was? Of course, she had her passport with her. And both Pamela and Russell Langford, from the two times she had telephoned, would know the name Ellena Spencer. Though, come to think of it, she would have to call at her flat first to pick up Russell Langford's address and her car.

The plane started to descend. Ellena couldn't wait to be on her way. Andrea had said, 'Take as much time as you need…' There was a lot to do. First things first, though; she was making tracks for Hertfordshire…

Gideon Langford's organisation was highly efficient, she discovered, after they had landed. Someone—the pilot or whoever—must have notified someone of their estimated time of arrival. In any event, there were two chauffeur-driven cars waiting for them.

'George will drive you to your home,' Gideon Langford explained, plainly heading in another direction himself, no doubt to some high-powered business meeting.

'Thank you,' she answered politely.

'I'll be in touch.'

You mean your lawyers will! But civility cost nothing and, even if Gideon had sprouted horns, give the devil his due, thus far she had reason to be grateful to him. She extended a hand. 'Thank you for everything,' she said sincerely.

They shook hands. 'Goodbye,' he said.

She turned away. She had urgent business to attend to. She doubted the next time she saw him—in court—that they would be so civil with each other.

In the limousine she gave thought to what must be done. She didn't want this fight, this tug of war. Please God, Justine and Kit would be back before the fight got started.

She vaguely remembered something in the newspapers only recently, about a magistrate or judge sitting in emergency session of the family division of the court when someone needed an instant decision on what was best for a child. Ellena had only her own love-filled childhood to go on. But surely it was better for a child to be brought up where love was?

Worriedly, she instinctively knew where love *was not*, and that was with Pamela and Russell Langford. It was possible that in future—if he could spare time away from his other non-work activities—that Gideon might get to know and love his niece. Though she doubted he would see much of her. It went without saying that he would hire a nanny… All this wasn't going to happen, though. Bearing in mind that Violette's parents would come home—she must believe that; *she must*—Ellena sincerely felt she would be letting Justine down if she allowed anyone to have guardianship of the baby but herself.

At her flat Ellena thanked George very much. 'It's not heavy,' she smiled when it seemed he would carry her bag indoors for her.

Once she was in her flat, Ellena raced around finding the address she needed, and was again on her way. She could, she realised, have left Violette with Pamela and Russell

Langford for the duration Justine had contracted with them. But fear that Gideon Langford would take pre-emptive action spurred her on. Should it come to a court hearing, she wanted it established that Violette—a healthy, happy Violette—lived with her.

Ellena stopped briefly on her way to buy a baby car seat and a few other essential purchases for Violette, and was soon speeding on again. She did wonder if she should ring the Langfords to let them know she was coming. She decided against it. Gideon might ring Russell at any time to tell him the latest concerning Austria. She didn't want Russell revealing that she'd phoned. She didn't want Gideon knowing anything until after her visit.

She arrived at the address she was seeking, a very smart house in its own grounds, with hope in her heart that her own neighbours would bear with her when she brought a baby home to her flat. There was a very sleek and expensive car on the drive of the Langfords' home which hinted that, for all they were accepting payment for looking after Russell's niece, they weren't too badly off.

Ellena rang the doorbell, with her thoughts on the early possibility of maybe renting somewhere where children were allowed; only on a short lease while she got somewhere more permanent arranged.

The door was opened almost at once. 'Good...' she began as part of her greeting, but the rest didn't get said. The sleek and expensive car didn't belong to Russell Langford, she swiftly realised. It belonged to his brother, Gideon! Gideon Langford, having changed the chauffeur-driven vehicle for his own car, had got there before her!

'Traffic's a nightmare at this time of day, isn't it?' he murmured blandly.

It wasn't funny! The fact that he had beaten her to it wasn't funny at all so why did she find his remark amusing? Not that she'd let him see, of course.

'What are you doing here?' she demanded.

He looked ready to put her in her place for trying to demand anything. But, to her surprise, instead he clipped out the words, 'Just leaving!'

He was still there, though, when a man, not so tall as Gideon by a couple of inches, and fair haired, with the same features as Kit, came along the hall with a sharp-looking auburn-haired woman in tow. The woman looked hostile before they even started. 'Yes?' she challenged irritably.

Ellena opened her mouth but, to her surprise, heard Gideon Langford say pleasantly, 'Ellena, I don't think you know my brother, Russell, and his wife, do you?' Smoothly, he introduced them, and, while Ellena was seriously wishing that he would just clear off, he stayed to hear her business.

Russell Langford invited her into the sitting room—of the baby and her temporary nanny there was no sign. Gideon returned to the sitting room with them. Ellena tossed him an Afraid-of-missing-something? kind of look. He smiled back, though it was an insincere smile.

'G-Gideon will have told you the news concerning Austria,' she began.

'Bad do,' Russell replied, the way he had when she had telephoned him. Was it only last night? It seemed weeks ago!

'The thing is that while I c-can't believe...' she took a shaky breath '...that we'll never see Justine and Kit again,' she gained control to continue, 'I feel, with your permission, of course, that they would want me to look after Violette until they get back.'

'Now isn't that strange? That's more or less exactly what Gideon said!' Pamela Langford answered for her husband waspishly.

Ellena guessed she should have expected, from what he'd said on the plane, that Gideon would not drag his heels in taking some action. What was unexpected, though, was that Pamela Langford would look at her with such blatant hostility. Then it was that Ellena recalled Gideon saying something about Pamela being a money-grubbing bitch, and, although she was wishing that Gideon would just get to his car and go, there seemed nothing for it but to conduct her business in front of him.

'I'm sorry,' she apologised as pleasantly as she was able. 'I know there are some—er—money matters outstanding.' She knew nothing of the sort, but realised that if Justine hadn't paid Pamela in advance, then outstanding the matter of money must be. 'Naturally I'll settle what Justine owes y—'

'That child was left in our charge!' Pamela Langford cut in loudly, coldly. 'And in our charge is where she'll stay!'

Oh, heavens! Ellena felt tremendously taken aback. She hadn't expected this sort of reception! 'I appreciate that you want to do what's right,' she began, forcing herself to be placatory—she had not the smallest intention of leaving her niece with this cold, unfeeling woman. 'But...'

'But nothing. The child stays here,' Pamela Langford cut in sourly. Ellena looked from her to Russell—he was looking anywhere but at her or his brother—no use appealing to him! Not that she wanted to set husband and wife against each other. And, given he wanted the same as she wanted, she couldn't expect any help from Gideon. Which was just as well, because, while silently absorbing everything that was taking place, Gideon Langford was not offering her any help. 'I'll show you out,' Pamela stated frostily.

'I'd like to see Violette if I may.' Ellena refused to budge.

'She's upstairs asleep. I'm not going to have her disturbed again; it will take hours for her nanny to shut her up.'

Ellena was aware that Violette's needs were nothing in this alien household, and felt a desperate need to check that the little mite was being properly cared for. 'I won't disturb her,' she stated, still refusing to budge.

'That's right, you won't,' Pamela Langford answered nastily.

Ellena felt frustrated beyond bearing by the woman's attitude. She couldn't leave without seeing the baby, she couldn't. Then, just as she was about to insist that she must see her, Gideon Langford chipped in, to tell her quietly, 'I've seen the baby, Ellena; she seems well looked after and healthy.'

Ellena turned to him swiftly, not knowing why she trusted him when she didn't feel she could trust his sister-in-law. 'She's all right?' she asked urgently. 'She looks happy?'

He gave her a slightly sardonic smile as though to say, What do I know about four-month-old babies? 'She wasn't crying,' he said.

Ellena turned back to Pamela Langford. 'Perhaps you'd tell me when it would be convenient for me to spend some time with my niece.'

'We'll arrange visiting rights through the courts,' was the vinegary reply—and as the import of those words took root, Ellena didn't trust herself to answer.

She went to the door. Pamela Langford, as though she didn't trust her not to dart up the stairs, went with her. Ellena was forced to accept then that she was not going to see Violette that day, and took what solace she could from the fact that Gideon had seen the baby and, albeit that his knowledge of infants was limited, he thought she seemed well looked after and healthy.

She half expected him to follow her out. After all he had been about to leave when she'd arrived. But he was obviously staying behind to have a word more with his brother.

Ellena drove home in a very upset frame of mind. Over the last few hours she had received one shock after another. Last night she had learned that Justine and Kit were missing; earlier today she had learned that Gideon was prepared to go to court over the guardianship of their child. And now, here was Pamela Langford—a woman she had found it impossible to warm to—talking of court action! What chance, Ellena wondered, did she have of loving and nurturing Violette until Justine and Kit came home?

After another fretful night, Ellena awoke on Friday morning with the same thoughts going around in her head. She was in two minds about going to her office. But realising that, if she didn't change her job—and her plans of yesterday seemed to be getting further and further away from her—she was going to need time off work for court appearances; no way was she going to give up Violette without a fight. Ellena decided she had better go to work.

'We didn't expect to see you!' Andrea Keyte exclaimed when she walked in.

'I may need time off later,' Ellena replied without thinking.

'Want to talk about it?'

Andrea had been a wonderful friend and very forbearing with regard to previous crises Ellena had had over Justine. And normally Ellena might have confided in her this time. Only now, depending how things went, there was a possibility that in the interest of Violette's daycare, she might have to resign. Andrea had enough to worry about running her business, without Ellena giving out hints at this early stage that she might, or might not, be leaving.

'Thanks, but not just now.'

Ellena went to her own office, suddenly realising that if she hired a nanny herself, that would solve the problem of Violette's daycare. She wouldn't have to leave. She took out some work, though her thoughts became desperate that she might not need a nanny if Pamela Langford or her brother-in-law, Gideon, were granted guardianship, and her concentration wasn't all it should be. What she needed, Ellena realised, was some legal advice.

She was just contemplating ringing the solicitor who had always handled her parents' affairs, and who had handled

the legalities of selling their house for her and Justine, when
the protector of the firm's switchboard rang.

'I've a man named Langford on the phone for you, are
you available?' Lucy asked.

Langford? Which one? With hope in her heart that it was
Russell, calling to tell her that he and his wife were prepared to let the baby go, she requested, 'Put him through,
Lucy,' hearing the click as she did so. 'Russell?' Ellena
asked.

'Gideon,' came the reply—and her thoughts went racing
in another direction.

'You've heard something—from Austria?' she questioned urgently, half in fear of bad news, half in hope of
good news.

'Afraid not,' he answered instantly.

'Oh,' she said dully. But he hadn't taken time out of his
day merely to chat. 'What can I do for you?' she asked,
knowing in advance that she wasn't going to lift a finger
to help if he was still insistent on claiming guardianship of
Violette.

'I'd like to see you,' he stated.

Why her heart should give a little flip just then, she had
no idea. He wasn't asking her for a date, for goodness'
sake! Not that she'd go out with him if he was. 'I've a full
appointments book today.' She countered that peculiar little
heartbeat—why should she want to see him? Grief!

'I meant outside of business hours. I'd like to call round
at your flat this evening. Unless, of course, you'd prefer we
shared dinner while we…'

'My flat will be fine,' she said hurriedly, too late realising
that in her haste to show him she had no wish to have
dinner with him, she had taken another option she didn't
want either. 'Presumably this is in connection with the
baby?' she queried, just to let him know that she wasn't
interested in entertaining him socially.

'Of course,' he replied, just as if the notion of seeing her socially had never for a minuscule moment so much as occurred to him. 'Seven-thirty?'

'Seven-thirty,' she agreed. Simultaneously their phones went down.

Ellena seemed to take a queue of phone calls after that, some of them needing action, so it was lunchtime by the time she got round to ringing her solicitor. 'Mr Ollerenshaw has left for the day on other business,' his secretary informed her. 'He'll be out of the office until Monday—can anyone else help?'

Ellena declined, but made an appointment to see Mr Ollerenshaw on Monday. She liked the fatherly man and, as well as having a first-class legal head on his shoulders, she remembered him as being warm and kind. She'd wait and see what Gideon Langford had to say that evening, and perhaps would have more to check with Mr Ollerenshaw on Monday.

She was late getting home. That wasn't unusual on a Friday. She liked to clear her desk, and, having had Thursday off work, there had been yesterday's work to catch up on. She just had time to make herself a sandwich and ponder on whether she should make Gideon one too. She raised her eyes skywards—was she going mad? This man was coming to try and talk her into forfeiting any claim she intended to make for Violette. If he hadn't had dinner—let him starve!

Ellena did consider changing from her smart all-wool light navy suit and into trousers and shirt. She decided against it. She had an idea that to take away her business suit for something less formal might give him the edge, make her oddly vulnerable somehow. Oh, rot, she was letting her fear that the Langford family would take Violette from her get to her.

Gideon Langford arrived a minute after the appointed time. 'You found the address all right, then,' she commented. He was in her home and good manners decreed she was polite to him to start with—even if he'd be leaving with a flea in his ear! 'Coffee?' she enquired, her good manners working overtime. She had never thought her sitting room tiny, but he seemed to fill it.

'Thanks,' he accepted, and wandered out to her kitchen and watched her while she made the coffee.

In her view, depending on what he had to say, he might not be around long enough to drink it, but—painful though it was to remember—he need not have offered her a lift to Austria in his private jet on Wednesday.

She made herself a coffee as well and carried a tray to the sitting room. 'Take a seat,' she invited and, sitting down herself, looked at him opposite her, his long legs stretched out some way. 'Have you seen Violette today?' she asked by way of an opening as he drank some of his coffee.

'No,' he replied, and asked sharply, 'Have you?'

She shook her head, and saw no harm in revealing, 'I'm taking legal advice on Monday.'

'An excellent idea,' Gideon answered to her surprise. 'Though I may be able to save you the trouble.'

'I don't think…' she began stiffly—bubbles to him and his saving her anything! He was a Langford—in this instance, he was the enemy!

'I took legal advice myself last night, as a matter of fact,' he cut in, stunning her somewhat.

'Well, don't let the grass grow!' she retorted crossly.

'Now, don't get angry,' Gideon said calmly. 'Russell I can handle, but if you knew his wife better than you do, you'd know to have your ammunition ready to spike her guns and get in there first.'

By the sound of it, Gideon Langford was going to fight his sister-in-law with everything he had. And while one meeting with Pamela Langford was sufficient for Ellena to know she would fight with everything at her disposal too, to ensure that Violette was brought up in a far more loving home, she was also aware that that meant opposing Gideon.

Ellena swallowed down her crossness. Gideon had finished his coffee, and they hadn't really begun their discussion yet in earnest. 'You don't sound as if you like your sister-in-law very much,' she commented.

'I don't,' he stated bluntly. 'Among other things, she's taken over the ruination of my brother from his mother, and…'

'Oh!' Ellena exclaimed, startled. 'Your mother—um—spoilt him?'

'Like you'd never believe! Well-intentioned though she was, she had an unshakeable belief that the middle child in any family was grievously disadvantaged. I'm afraid she over-compensated to extremes.'

Ellena stared at him, fascinated by this insight into his family. Somehow she knew that wild horses would not normally have dragged this information from Gideon. So, without knowing quite how, she realised that his telling her this much must have some relevance to why he had called to see her.

'The result being that you and Kit missed out?' she suggested.

Only she realised that what Gideon was more interested in talking about just then was Russell, and the woman Russell had married. 'The result being that Russell has grown perfectly content to let women run his life—his mother, his wife.' He ignored her question to state, 'He doesn't seem able to think for himself, though before Pamela came along and smelt his inheritance, he was quite capable of earning a living.'

'He doesn't have a job?'

'At the moment he doesn't need to work. His inheritance from his father kept him afloat to start with. Then, when he was twenty-five, he came into a small fortune left to him by my grandfather. He's thirty-two now and, I'd hazard a guess, has said goodbye to most of that fortune.'

'It—er—doesn't take much spending,' Ellena volunteered, knowing very little about it.

'Not when you're married to a woman who, cunning about everything else, gambles wildly on the stock exchange, it doesn't!' he said shortly. He paused, and then, to Ellena's amazement, added 'So, having gone through Russell's fortune, she's now after Kit's!'

'Kit's! Kit's fortune!' Ellena exclaimed.

'You didn't know?'

'He hasn't got any money!' She was certain of that. 'I know that for a fact! He had some, from your father, but that's gone and they're now living off Justine's money. Not that it matters to either of them—me neither—whose money it is, but Kit hasn't any now—' She broke off. Gideon was looking at her with something akin to a smile on his face. He was a man who didn't seem to smile a lot, though it was true he hadn't had a lot to smile about of late. But he was sort of smiling now, and, she owned, she liked the look of him.

'What a nice family you are,' he commented quietly, and she felt a flurry in the region of her heart and wasn't sure her cheeks didn't go a bit pink.

'I don't know about that... Well, yes, I do. Justine's lovely, and...'

'And her big sister's not so bad either.'

Oh, heck, he *did* have charm. 'You were saying that Kit has money, but...'

'Doesn't have now, but, like Russell, like I did, Kit inherits a third share of our grandfather's estate when he's twenty-five.'

'But—but, that's in about six months' time,' Ellena calculated.

'Exactly. Which is why, if I know my sister-in-law, and—' He broke off. 'I'm not giving up hope, Ellena, far from it,' he said gently, 'but we have to face the possibility that we may not see Kit and your sister again.'

She knew he was speaking only the truth. She nodded, and, when she thought she could speak, took up his suggestion, 'You think your sister-in-law will…'

'I know she will. By the time that six months is up, she'll have worked hard to ensure that she and Russell are legal guardians to Kit's child, and…'

'No!'

'And legal guardians to the child's inheritance.'

Ellena felt winded. 'But,' she gasped, 'she wouldn't be able to spend any of it!'

'You think not? Expenses, phoney and otherwise. Schools, holidays, clothes, new furnishings for her room…'

'Heavens!' Ellena could barely believe it. But, on thinking of that sour-expressioned woman, remembering her hostility, her coldness—not to mention remembering Justine saying that Pamela Langford had a nose for money and hadn't been able to offer her services fast enough in the context of it—she realised that believe it she could. 'I can't leave Violette there!' she exclaimed anxiously, ready to fight tooth and nail. 'It was just convenient at the time for Justine to leave her baby with your brother and his wife, but Justine wouldn't want her brought up by them—I just know it.'

'Neither would Kit. Which is why yesterday I checked out his writing desk hoping, now he has the responsibility of fatherhood, that he hadn't taken himself off on a ski-ing holiday without leaving some instruction with regard to his wishes for her.'

He meant a will, she knew he did, and realised that for all Gideon had said they should face the possibility of their siblings not returning, he was having an extremely tough time doing just that. So was she.

'You—' She broke off, her voice husky. She made a small coughing sound. 'You've been to his flat. You have a key?' The question was of small consequence, but it gave

her the few seconds she needed to pull herself together after
a weak moment.

'I'd all but forgotten I'd got it. To all intents and pur-
poses the flat's Kit's…'

'You bought it for him after a bit of a wild party at your
house while you were away?'

Gideon favoured her with that hint of a smile again. 'The
flat is Kit's to live in,' he agreed, 'but mine to dispose of.'

'Ah!' she murmured, realising then that, though he loved
his youngest brother very much, Gideon wasn't blind to the
fact that, given the deeds to the property, he wouldn't have
put it past Kit to sell the property if he had felt like it. 'Has
he been very much of a headache to you?'

'What can I tell you? You've got one in the same
mould.' He was right there, Ellena mused—it wasn't surprising Justine and Kit should have fallen in love with each
other; they were equally as hair-raising. 'For the most part
he's enjoyable to have around but I've had to come down
hard on him on occasions.'

'The last time being six months ago?' she questioned.

'My oath, you're bright,' he answered, as if remembering
that he'd told her he'd last visited Kit in the flat six months
ago. 'I've spoken briefly to him over the phone since then,
of course. But we've been a bit distant since I took him to
task for being content to take and take, but not thinking of
getting a job, or even of looking for one.'

'You couldn't find one for him in your organisation?'

'He had one—he doesn't like work. He gave it up.'

'I'm sorry,' Ellena said, realising that, for a man who
worked so hard, it must have been increasingly difficult for
him to find excuses for Kit.

'It's not your fault,' Gideon replied charmingly. 'I just
feared he would go down the same shiftless road as Russell.
Kit,' he added, 'has a fine brain if he troubled to use it.'

'He'll—er—perhaps he'll grow out of it.' They were

both talking as if there was every chance that Kit had not perished.

'He's taking a long time about it!'

Ellena guessed that at close on twenty-five Gideon had already made great strides into a successful career. 'Perhaps…' she began, but left it there. Perhaps when Kit and Justine came back… Perhaps Kit would have grown up somewhat. Perhaps, perhaps. Abruptly she switched her thoughts away from 'perhaps'. That was in the future; she must concentrate on the present. 'Did you find anything, any instructions in Kit's desk?'

Gideon Langford shook his head. 'What I did find was a birth certificate in which Kit named himself as Violette Ellena's father.' His slate-grey eyes were steady on her when he added, 'The fact that the baby's parents thought well enough of you to give their child your name might well go towards being a deciding factor when my legal team take proceedings to…'

'Just a minute!' she halted him. She was, she felt, of normal and sometimes quite sharp intelligence. But she had lost him somewhere. Gideon had been talking of *her* name on Violette's birth certificate aiding in some way *his* application for guardianship! Ellena realised she must have missed something. 'You've as good as said,' she attempted to backtrack, 'that Russell and more particularly, his wife are out to get what money they can from—er—Kit's estate.' It hurt—but it was a possibility they might not come back.

'Russell will go along with whatever his wife tells him. And, as legal guardians of Kit's heir, they'd be in an ideal position to drain whatever they could in phoney expenses.'

'But—they won't get custody of her! I'm going to…'

'Russell is brother to the child's father. It was to him and his wife that Kit entrusted his daughter when he went on holiday,' Gideon pointed out levelly.

'Yes, but they wouldn't have taken Violette if they

hadn't been handsomely paid to do so. They did it for the money! Justine as good as told me so! They—'

'Purely to cover expenses,' Gideon cut in. 'At least that's how Pamela will make a judge see it.'

'But-but…' She was floundering and they hadn't even got started yet! 'But she's not a blood relative! I am! I'm Violette's aunt—her mother's sister! Don't I…?'

'Her unmarried aunt,' Gideon tossed in.

Ellena wished he hadn't—it gave her something else to worry about. 'Do you think it will make a difference—my being unmarried?' she asked anxiously. Suddenly, though, she realised from *that* point of view Gideon Langford was in no better a position. 'Hang on—I thought you wanted Violette too!'

'I do,' he answered. 'Her unmarried uncle.'

Ellena hadn't slept much in the last forty-eight hours, so she blamed that for the fact that she had again lost Gideon somewhere. She admitted as much. 'What are you getting at?' she asked.

He shrugged. 'Merely that I, too, am the brother of the child's father.' Gideon paused, and studied her for a moment, those slate-grey eyes steady on her. Then, somehow deliberately, Ellena felt, he went on, 'According to the lawyers, my chances of being awarded the infant's guardianship would be greatly enhanced were I married.'

Ellena's mouth went dry. She was sure she didn't give a light that he might marry. But the thought that he and his wife—not withstanding that Russell and his wife might put in their claim—could jointly apply for Violette's care caused her to feel quite dreadful.

She swallowed hard. 'Are you going to get married?' she made herself ask.

That steady slate-grey-eyed look was still fixed on her. She met his gaze unwaveringly. But her jaw very near hit the floor when he replied coolly, 'I hope so. According to that same legal team, I would be more or less home and dry, were I, in fact, married—to the sister of the child's mother.'

Ellena's eyes shot wide. Open-mouthed, she stared at him.

CHAPTER THREE

ELLENA was still staring dumbfounded at Gideon after what seemed an age later. So *this* was why he had come to see her! She was only glad they were in her flat and not, as he'd offered, in some eating establishment. For in no way could she hide her absolute astonishment! He was saying nothing more. Having delivered his bombshell, he was silently watching, waiting to hear what she had to say about it.

'You're serious?' was what she did say when she found some breath.

'Never more so,' he replied evenly.

Ellena began to recover from her initial shock, but she still couldn't believe it. Then questions started queuing up that demanded answers. 'Let me get this right,' she began carefully. 'You're suggesting that, in order for you to gain legal guardianship of Justine and Kit's baby, you are prepared to marry me?'

'Got it in one,' Gideon answered—but it was about then, as the rest of her shock began to evaporate, that Ellena's brain started to function again.

'Er—forgive me for being dim, Gideon,' she apologised with polite sarcasm, 'but while it's extremely gallant of you to be prepared to marry me, could you give me one good reason why you think that I should so much as consider being prepared to marry you?'

Gideon Langford stared at her, was still staring at her when, unbelievably to her watching eyes, he remarked, 'Oh, my word, Ellena Spencer, I bet you're hell on earth once you get going!'

Her eyes mirrored her stupefaction, and it was her turn

to stare. Her devil-may-care parents had occasionally been hell on earth. Justine frequently so. But quiet, studious and coping Ellena? Hell on earth—never! 'Untrue!' she retorted. And, since he hadn't answered her admittedly sarcastically-asked question, she unsarcastically rephrased it. 'Do you intend telling me why you think I should do this—er—marriage thing—for you?'

'You'd be doing it for yourself too,' Gideon answered seriously, and, while she failed to see how, he went on to explain, 'You want Violette. But, as things stand, you have about the same chance of getting her as me. I've thought about it a great deal, though in actual fact it didn't take long for me to see that I'd stand a much better chance of defeating Russell's cold and calculating wife if you and I joined forces.'

'Two against two, as opposed to one and one against two,' Ellena mused out loud. It was an insane idea, of course it was—and yet, she was a blood relative, Pamela wasn't; of the two married couples, wouldn't she and Gideon stand a better chance? Didn't it make sense? At least, it would if... 'You'd agree to my having Violette living with me?' she questioned abruptly, a beam of light suddenly appearing in the denseness of her darkness.

'Children are allowed here?' he returned before she could blink.

Clever hound! He thought he had her. Think again, Langford! 'No, but then I hadn't planned to take care of her here. I'd planned to buy a house in the country.' Pick the bones out of that! 'And—'

'Were we to marry, you'd naturally come and live with me,' Gideon cut her off. And, while she was thinking he could go and take a running jump, he was going on, 'For our—partnership to have any credence at all, we'd have to be seen to be living together, have to appear to be a loving couple, devoted to—'

'I get the picture,' she interrupted him quickly.

'Talking of love worries you?' he queried, seeming to be quite interested in her psyche.

'Obviously you do it every day!' she snapped crisply—and couldn't believe it when, for the first time, she heard him laugh, a short amused bark of laughter.

'As a point of fact, I don't,' he commented easily. But he was serious when he went on, 'It's important that no one suspects the true reason for our marriage.' She hadn't said she'd marry him yet! 'It's important we look as though we married for love.'

Ellena owned that she was not the madcap one of the family and never would be. Yet to marry Gideon Langford as he suggested would, in her view, be even more madcap than anything Justine had ever done. 'Couldn't we just pretend to be engaged?' she wriggled.

Gideon shook his head. 'No. It wouldn't do.' He turned her suggestion down flat. 'Russell's wife will be watching from every angle. Once she realises her get-rich plans are looking decidedly rocky, she'll stop at nothing.'

'She sounds dreadful!'

'Believe me, there are women like her in the world. Anyhow, you've met her!'

That she had. Without Justine's comments about the avaricious woman, Ellena, from her own observations, saw Pamela Langford as a cold and nasty type. Certainly not a type to whom she would entrust anything so precious as her niece—which was, of course, what the whole of this was about. Pamela Langford, with or without a temporary nanny to take care of Violette, was not going to have charge of her!

'Marriage—could be the answer,' she agreed slowly.

'It is,' he stated firmly. 'The two basic criteria are that we need to be married, and you need to be living in my home.'

Ellena tried to look beyond the facts that to marry Gideon Langford and to live in his house were the last things she wanted to do. She wanted Violette to be brought up with love. 'Er…' He waited. Thinking of love activated her imagination into the realms of the loving relationship she would supposedly have with him. Grief—they'd only met two days ago! 'We'd—um—have to make believe it was love at first sight,' she spoke her thoughts. 'For anyone to believe it, we'd have to pretend we were attracted from—' She broke off. As he'd earlier spotted, she wasn't very comfortable talking of love. And yet she continued when the next rapid thought swiftly landed, 'What if we fall in love…?' Her voice faded when his right eyebrow ascended aloft. 'With other people, I mean!' she finished crossly.

'You do like to meet crises head-on—precipitate them before they happen,' he drawled, and that annoyed her some more.

'You can talk!' she erupted. 'You had your lawyers wiping the dust off their law books before we'd barely landed yesterday!'

Gideon inclined his head to acknowledge, *Touché*, but did her the courtesy of answering her question. 'In the event of either of us falling in love, you and I will amicably discuss that situation when it arises. But the child's interests must come first.'

'I wouldn't argue about that,' Ellena agreed.

'You agree, then—we marry?'

'No, no,' she said, panic attacking her. 'Hold it a minute! You've had all night to sort out the pros and cons of what you propose. There are a dozen and one things I need to have clear first.'

'Such as?'

'Look, you've only just dropped this on me, I can't think of all I need to know at once!' she protested. He did not look impressed. She felt forced to go on. 'Well, for one thing, I was thinking of having a nanny take care of Violette Monday to Friday while I'm at work. How would any judge view that, do you think?' Her question had little to do with any plans to marry, she realised that, but it was something that had worried her, and had just sort of come out.

'I think your industry would be viewed far more favourably than the indolent lifestyle of my brother and his wife,' Gideon answered unhesitatingly.

That cheered her, but though that one very big worry was now somewhat lessened, she wasn't very comfortable with the next question that sprang to mind—it was a very gigantic one from where she was seeing it. 'This marriage...' she began, and got stuck before she started.

Whether Gideon had any idea of what she wanted to ask she had no idea, but she did mentally thank him that his look softened, and his tone was gently encouraging when he prompted quietly, 'Don't be afraid, Ellena. Ask whatever bothers you.'

Thus invited, she took a long breath, and plunged. 'This marriage... Oh, grief, I wish I knew more about men and their... But, what with studying and keeping an eye on what Justine was getting up...' This was ridiculous, she fumed, cross with herself, with him. It was all his fault—he had put her in this position and she shouldn't have had to explain anything about herself, for goodness' sake! 'I'm not having a proper marriage with you!' she told him bluntly. 'Not that I've said I will at all yet,' she tacked on hastily.

'By "proper", you mean consummated?' he queried—with not a sign of a blush about him.

Not so Ellena; had she been answering, she might have dressed it up a little, but not him! Though it did come down to that very thing. 'That's what I mean,' she agreed, feeling very pink in the face.

'Do you have a steady boyfriend?' he asked.

'What's that got to do with anything?' she flared. He knew she hadn't. She felt sure he knew—did that make her a lesser mortal?

'I wouldn't put it past my sister-in-law to have you followed.' Gideon revealed what it had to do with his question.

'Oh!' Ellena exclaimed—heavens, was he two streets in front of everyone else? Ellena owned that, up to now, though mainly by choice, her dates had been few and far between. But should some hired private detective follow her if she dated someone, then Gideon's sister-in-law would soon have evidence she could use to show their 'love marriage' was not what it should be, that their home was an unstable one in which to rear a child. 'There's no one special,' Ellena owned, and, wondering why some detective should follow her and not him, 'How about you? Are you seeing anyone?'

'I'm resting,' he replied, with such a look of mock sorrow that she had the strongest desire to laugh. She glanced to the floor for a moment so he shouldn't see the amusement in her eyes, but looked up again when, his tone serious, he stated, 'While we were married we'd have to agree not to date anyone else.'

'How long would it last?' she asked and, some imp of mischief catching her unawares, added, 'And could you "rest" that long?'

His answer was to grin—oh, heavens, how it changed him! She saw in him a kind of wickedness she had never noticed before, and for the first time saw something of Kit there too. Perhaps he had been a lot more like Kit at one time. Perhaps, before his father's death and before he'd had to take on the responsibilities of running and then expanding Langford Engineering, Gideon had been as happy-go-lucky as Kit. That Gideon took his responsibilities most seriously was beyond doubt, given the facts that not only was Langford Engineering the thriving concern it had become, but also that Gideon was so determined to have responsibility for his brother's child, that he was prepared to go through a marriage ceremony to help achieve that aim.

'So?' she asked when he still hadn't answered her question about how long the marriage would last. 'It could go on for years!'

'I'm doing nothing special for the next year or two,' Gideon answered. 'By which time, if Kit and Justine haven't returned,' he inserted gravely, 'the child will be in a more stable and kind environment, and we can review what we both want for ourselves, and for her.'

'Amicably,' she inserted, borrowing his word.

That hint of a smile touched the corners of his mouth again. 'How does that sound?' he asked.

Ellena, save for getting on with her career, had nothing special planned for the next year or two either. 'I've no quarrel with that,' she answered.

'Good,' he replied, going on, 'So, the ground rules are that neither of us dates anyone else until we're certain my sister-in-law has given up.'

'There's no other choice.' She could see that.

'So you agree—we marry?'

Whoa, there! Panic started to throw spiteful, tummy-churning darts at her. Ellena had the feeling of being hurt-led along. Yes, she could make quick decisions, but this wasn't a new coat she was buying, or a client about whom she was making decisions in her professional capacity. Naturally she was prepared to devote all her energies and time to Justine's baby, but to tie herself up with Gideon Langford for a couple of years—oh, pray God, Justine was all right and came home!—was something she wanted a little more time to consider.

'Do you do everything at a gallop?' she questioned, a shade aggressively, it was true.

'I don't have time to delay,' he retorted. 'I want everything cut and dried when next I contact my sister-in-law.' Ellena looked across at him. He was trustworthy, she knew that. And he wanted what, in his view, was only the best for his infant niece; she knew that too. But, as she stared at him, his look softened again, 'You'd be able to carry on with your work, just the same,' he assured her. 'I'd engage a nanny…'

'Only from Monday to Friday,' she interrupted him quickly. 'I'd want to take care of Violette myself at weekends. Let her know she's much loved—' She broke off, afraid she was revealing too much of the emotion she felt. 'It sounds good,' she admitted. 'There has to be a snag—oh!'

'You've just thought of one?'

'I've been talking as though our winning custody of Violette is a foregone conclusion. But—what if we went so far as to get married only for some judge to rule against our claim for Violette?'

'We appeal!' Gideon replied unhesitatingly. It was a rare occasion, she was sure, but he allowed her a peep into his own emotions as he revealed, 'Kit means more to me than allowing his child to be reared in a home where, were it not for her monetary value, she is unwanted.'

Ellena went along with that, all the way, and felt more than a little emotional herself just then. But, with difficulty, she made herself be practical. 'And if any appeal fails?' she asked.

He looked at her steadily. 'The marriage would be annulled,' he decreed.

She'd go along with that too. She tried to think if there was anything else she should ask, but felt she had covered everything. 'When do you need to know by?' she queried, guessing from his statement that he wanted everything cut and dried he'd require her answer sooner rather than later.

But she stared at him witless when he replied, 'As soon as I have your answer I'll apply for a special licence. We can be married by this time next week.'

'Good heavens!' she exclaimed, and darts of panic started to attack again. 'Justine and Kit could be back from their holiday in two or three weeks!'

'While I don't want to accept it either—they may not be,' he stated heavily. 'And then I'll have given Pamela Langford two or three weeks head start!'

So be it. Ellena gave a shaky sigh. 'May I sleep on it?' she asked.

His answer was to stand up. Ellena left her chair too, and was in receipt of a direct no-nonsense sort of look from his steady slate-grey eyes as he informed her, 'I'll ring you first thing in the morning.' He delayed only long enough to take her home phone number, then he left her—with a whole lot of thinking to do.

She paced the floor, going over everything—and tried to be strong when she thought of Justine. She swallowed down tears and made herself think only of Violette. She remembered the money-grabbing Pamela Langford—who had no love for the infant—and Ellena knew that she was going to have Violette in her safe keeping and caring, or die in the attempt. Which suddenly made her realise that if to marry Gideon Langford increased her chances by over twenty-five percent, which surely it must, then marrying him was not the gigantic hurdle it had seemed at first.

Ellena went and showered and got into bed, but lay wide awake with too much on her mind to give sleep a chance. How could she sleep?

At midnight she got out of bed and made herself a warm drink. At three o'clock she left her bed again and put the kettle on for a cup of tea. She sat down at the kitchen table and tried to analyse what—apart from the very real fear that she might never see Justine again—she was so worried about.

She wanted Violette. Fact. She stood a much better chance of getting her if she threw in her lot with Gideon. Fact. What did she know about him? He was trustworthy, honourable and, with all he had going for him, would, whether she married him or did not marry him, fight with

all he had to gain guardianship of his brother's child—
which meant that she would have to fight him too.

Ellena didn't doubt he would put up a tremendous battle.
Wasn't he—bachelor of the year—prepared to go so far as
to give up his freedom in that fight? Would she do less?
No, by thunder, she wouldn't!

At four o'clock, realising that it wasn't as though she
hated him, for goodness' sake, and, thank heavens, she
didn't have to love him either, Ellena went and found his
phone number. She knew she wasn't going to get any sleep
until she'd got this first hurdle settled. And, on the basis
that since it was his call to her stating the proposed merger
that had kept her sleepless, she didn't see why he shouldn't
be sleepless too.

She dialled and, despite not being the harebrained one in
the family, saw nothing at all wrong in getting someone
out of bed at four in the morning. Gideon Langford had
said he'd ring her first thing—so she'd saved him the
bother.

The phone rang out only briefly and was answered almost immediately. 'Gideon?'

'Couldn't you sleep either?' His voice was even, calm.
She pictured him, tall, good-looking—she was going to
marry him!

She swallowed and, while praying that Justine would
come back—come back early—and that she would not have
to take the colossal step of marrying him, she, who had not
done a reckless thing during the last five years, took the
plunge. 'Do I need to take a day off work?'

'Make it Thursday,' he answered. Ellena put the phone
down. Today was Saturday. She had a lot to do—she was
getting married on Thursday!

After a few hours' sleep, Ellena got up and pattered into
the kitchen. She put the kettle to boil, and while making a
cup of tea—and while still feeling somewhat shaken when
she realised that she had, at four o'clock this morning,

agreed to marry a man she barely knew—she set about being practical.

Strangely, though, when practicalities suggested that, since she would be leaving her flat for the duration of her marriage, she should spend the day sorting through what to pack and what to leave, she discovered she didn't want to do anything of the sort.

She was getting married on Thursday, for goodness' sake! Suddenly Ellena discovered that the practical side of her nature was up against a recently awakened incautious side. Harebrained it might be, but she wanted something nice to wear at her wedding. She had another four days in which to sort out her clothes!

Ellena spent the day shopping. She had long legs and the warm, blue, above-the-knee dress she purchased showed them off to advantage. With the dress came a matching boxy jacket, which complemented the colour of her eyes perfectly.

Naturally, even though Violette would not be at the wedding, Ellena bought her a dress too. She let herself into her flat, experiencing an urge to go and see the baby, to hold and love her. The phone rang.

Ellena dropped down her carriers, hope in her heart that Justine, an alive and well Justine, had taken it into her head to give her a call.

She picked up the phone, forgetting completely that Justine had never thought to telephone when she'd been away on holiday before. 'Hello,' she said huskily, emotion getting to her.

'You've been crying!' Gideon Langford accused.

'No, I haven't!' Ellena denied sharply, any stiffening she needed there at his tone. Then, feeling she had overreacted, 'I thought you might be Justine,' she explained, and at once felt foolish; grief, he was an all-practical male!

There was a pause, and Ellena knew that she really liked

him when he answered sympathetically, 'It's unbearable, I know.'

'You've heard nothing from Austria, I suppose?'

'Not a word,' he answered, and, not giving her time to dwell on sad thoughts, he continued, 'At a guess, I'd say you've spent the day packing.'

Oh, heck—he thought she was as practical as she had thought she was herself. Somehow she didn't like that. Somehow she wanted to be non-practical. She'd had years of being practical.

'You'd guess wrong,' she answered, and, because all at once it seemed unbelievable, she questioned, 'Are we really getting married on Thursday?'

'We are,' he assured her straight away. 'Which is part of the reason for this call. In the cause of our "love at first sight" engagement, it's occurred to me we should be spending a little more time together.'

'I hadn't thought of that,' she confessed.

'You're slipping,' he answered, his tone light. Grief, what did he think she was? Some mastermind? 'I wondered if you'd like to come and see your future home tomorrow? If you do have anything packed you could bring it with you.'

'I suppose going to see Violette tomorrow is out of the question?'

'I'm afraid so. Trust me on this, Ellena,' he said gently. 'I promise you—once we have our certificate of marriage things will move fast. Hold back until then.'

She gave a shaky sigh. 'Roll on Thursday!'

'That's what I like—an eager bride!'

'Get you!' she scoffed—but found she was laughing, which, she realised, was far better than the near tearful state she'd been in at the start of his call.

'I'll pick you up tomorrow at—'

'No need for that,' she cut him off pleasantly. 'Just give me your address, tell me what time, and I'll be there.'

Gideon told her how to get to Oakvale, his home, and Ellena gave him the information he requested which he thought he might need to make their marriage application.

After his call she went and hung up her new dress and jacket. Her new outfit wasn't exactly bridal, she had to own, but neither was it funereal. She had to believe Justine was alive. She couldn't bear to think that she wasn't.

Ellena could not remember ever being so interested in clothes before. But the very next morning she found she was in a dilemma about what to wear to go to Sunday lunch at Gideon's home.

By ten-thirty that morning she was dressed in a fine wool suit of pale mustard, with her blonde hair silky about her shoulders. She had been going to pull it back in the chignon which she sometimes wore but, on thinking about it, would any newly engaged woman go and meet her 'love at first sight' fiancé with her hair dressed so formally?

Ellena pulled up on the wide drive of Oakvale and took a deep breath. In acres of its own grounds, the Georgian house with its many windows was larger than she had anticipated—and beautiful. Oh, heavens, she was going to live here!

She got out of her car—and looked up to see Gideon had left the house and was crossing the gravel to meet her. 'Ellena,' he smiled and, reaching her, took hold of her upper arms. She stared at him, startled. 'My housekeeper is extremely loyal, but you never know who's watching. May I?' he enquired, and before she could begin to think what he was about, he bent his head—and touched his lips to hers.

They were walking across the drive to the open front door of the house before she had her head anywhere near together again. She had been kissed before, but—given that Gideon's mouth on hers had been but a brief meeting of lips—never had she felt so all over the place afterwards!

Her thoughts were still tangled up with the very far-fetched notion of newspaper photographers with telephoto lenses—and also with the fact she had packed a suitcase and left it in her car but had been too witless, after Gideon's light kiss, to remember it—when he escorted her inside his home.

'Your house is beautiful.' She felt she should say something.

'I think so,' Gideon answered. 'Let's go to the kitchen and say hello to Mrs Morris. She and her husband, with outside help, keep the place going for me.'

'Have you lived here long?' Ellena asked, going through a large hall towards the rear of the house with him.

'I was brought up here. It's the family home,' he answered. 'I had my own place after university, but purchased the house from my mother when she remarried.'

He really must love it, Ellena realised. 'Your mother lives in the Bahamas, doesn't she? Does she know about—?' She broke off as they halted by a door.

'We're in daily contact,' Gideon revealed, and while Ellena's heart went out to Kit's poor mother, who must be suffering agonies over him, Gideon opened the door and guided her into the kitchen where he introduced his plump, fiftyish housekeeper, Mrs Morris.

'How do you do?' Ellena smiled, shaking the housekeeper by the hand.

'I hope you and Mr Langford will be very happy,' Mrs Morris beamed.

'Oh!' Ellena exclaimed, startled, and knew she was handling this first outside reference to their planned marriage very badly. She was, she owned, absolutely hopeless at deception.

But smooth wasn't the word for it! Gideon was there before she could draw another breath. 'I hope you'll forgive me, Ellena, but since you're going to be mistress of Oakvale from next Thursday, I felt you wouldn't mind if I shared our good news with Mrs Morris.'

'Of course.' Ellena smiled, refusing an offer of coffee.
A minute or so later, they crossed back over the hall to
Gideon's drawing room, Ellena trying to cope with the notion that—hopefully very briefly—she was going to be mistress of this very beautiful house.

'Would you like something to drink?' Gideon offered as
she stood on the thick-pile carpet admiring the elegant yet
comfortable room.

'I hadn't better. I'll be driving later,' she declined.

A moment later she was staring at him in amazement
when, pausing to take something from the drawer of a small
antique table, he came over to her and, opening what she
now saw was a ring box, said, 'You'd better have this.'

She took the ring from him purely because, when he
pushed it at her, it seemed impolite not to take it. 'What is
it?'

'Your engagement ring.'

Her glance flew from the diamond solitaire up to his
steady grey gaze. 'I…' I don't want it, she had been going
to say, but they weren't doing this for her, or for either of
them, but to ensure that Violette had the best. 'Is it r-real?'
she asked—never had she met such a man for scattering
her wits. 'The diamond, I mean.'

'Would I give my fiancée anything less?' he mocked.

'I'll let you have it back,' she promised. 'After…
When…'

Gideon smiled; with just the two of them there, and with
no one to witness it, he smiled. 'An honest woman!' he
teased.

'Believe me, there are women like that in the world,' she
teasingly quoted one of his comments back at him.

'And I've just met one,' he said softly, admiring of her
honesty, his glance going from her lovely eyes, over her
exquisite bone structure and creamy skin, down to linger
on her sweetly curving mouth. Taking the ring from her,
he slid it gently home on her engagement finger.

Her legs seemed to go to jelly. With the greatest of difficulty, she dragged the practical side of her up from somewhere. 'Talking of suitcases,' she said, turning away, 'I've one very large one in my car.'

He laughed; she heard him. As if he enjoyed her, he gave a short laugh. Perhaps, if they both kept their sense of humour, they might not fare so badly together after all—be it longer than they presently anticipated.

'You didn't lock your car; I'll go and get your case in,' he said, and was off, leaving her to dwell on the fact that her legs had gone decidedly weak a second or two ago.

He was away some minutes and, by the time he returned, with no suitcase in sight, Ellena felt much more in one piece. 'I've taken your case up to your room,' he informed her. 'Your room' somehow made her feel that she belonged. 'And Mrs Morris tells me lunch is ready.'

Lunch was a superbly cooked meal and Gideon was good company throughout, Ellena discovered. 'That was delicious,' she said, as she finished the last of her home-made apple pie. 'I think I'm going to enjoy living here,' she added. He had been so totally charming, she didn't want to let her side down. Though, lest Gideon thought that she might be staking some claim, 'Temporarily,' she tacked on quickly. Gracious, he knew, and was interested in, much more sophisticated types, if he was thinking of anything of a *permanent* nature, and—good heavens, what was wrong with her?—she didn't want him to be interested in her! Perish such a thought!

Ellena did not visit Gideon's home again before her wedding day. She wore her engagement ring to work on Monday and, because she was terrified that the least little slip might endanger her hopes that she and Gideon would have custody of Violette, she was scared to tell even Andrea that love didn't enter into her engagement with Gideon.

'May I see you?' she asked Andrea when she arrived at

the office, hoping because of the respect she had for Andrea
that she wasn't going to have to tell her too many lies.

'Of course. Come in and close the door,' Andrea agreed
at once. 'Any news?' she asked as they both sat down.

Ellena knew Andrea meant Justine and Kit. 'None,' she
answered, and straight away got down to the reason for
wanting to see her. 'The thing is, I'd rather like to have a
couple of days off,' she began, for authenticity's sake realising that she'd better take Friday off as well.

'You're going back to Aust—' Andrea began, then, her
observant gaze catching sight of Ellena's left hand, she
stopped abruptly. 'You're engaged!' she exclaimed. 'I
didn't even know you were going steady! When did this
happen?' More questions seemed to be on the way when
Andrea suddenly stopped. 'Who is he?' she slowed down
to ask. 'And does he know how lucky he is?' she added
warmly.

'Oh, Andrea. I—He…' Ellena began helplessly, then
seemed to get the energy she needed to explain, 'It happened very quickly, but we—need each other.' It wasn't a
lie. Without each other, her chance and Gideon's chance of
being guardians to Violette were greatly reduced. 'Gideon
Langford and I—'

'Gideon Langford!' Andrea cut in, her surprise evident.
Quickly, though, she recovered. 'Of course, you met him
through your sister,' she said gently, assuming—something
which hadn't occurred to Ellena—that, through Justine and
Kit, she and Gideon had known each other some while!
Even perhaps that, having been much in each other's company of late, they had realised their love for each other. In
any event, there was nothing but a warm sincerity in her
tones when Andrea wished her well.

'The thing is, we see little point in waiting. We're—
um—getting married on Thursday. Just a small private ceremony because of…' She had no need to go on.

'Oh, my dear, I'm so pleased! I've worried so for you.

But with Gideon Langford to care for you.' She stopped there, as a rather unpalatable thought suddenly came to her. 'You're not leaving? You haven't come to give me your resignation?'

Relief washed over Ellena that this interview had gone far better than she had anticipated. She even managed to look happy as she replied, 'No, of course not. I love working. Love working here. I just want Thursday and Friday off, that's all.'

The first thing Ellena did when she went to her own office was to put through a call to her solicitors and cancel her appointment with Mr Ollerenshaw. Gideon seemed to have everything sorted—she could fault none of his, or his lawyers', logic.

She hurried home from work that evening, hoping against hope that a second card from Justine had arrived. But there was nothing in the post from Austria.

Quite unexpectedly, Gideon stopped by her flat at around seven. She thought she was glad to see him. 'Did you tell them you wouldn't be in Thursday?' he asked, standing in her kitchen with her while she made him a cup of coffee.

She flicked a glance to him, feeling amused that it didn't occur to him she'd have to *ask* for time off from her work. 'I did,' she answered, and felt just a tinge discomforted when she revealed, 'I thought I'd better have Friday off as well—er—for the look of the thing,' she added, glancing quickly from him.

Naturally, he caught on straight away. 'Would you like to go away on a honeymoon?' he enquired politely.

'No!' She knocked that idea firmly on the head.

'My charm must be slipping,' he drawled, and, for all she gave him a speaking look, she liked him when he grinned, especially when he confided, 'Funny thing. I've arranged to be absent from work, too, on Friday. Had time to pack anything else? I can take it with me if you've got another case ready.'

She did not see him on Tuesday, but he phoned on Wednesday evening, just as she was starting to panic about what she was on the eve of doing. 'I'm glad you rang!' she said without thinking.

'Problem?'

'Only with me,' she confessed. 'Are we doing the right thing? Getting married, I mean.'

There was a slight pause the other end, then he replied tautly, 'I don't think I'd ever forgive you if you stood me up.'

Was he joking? She couldn't tell. 'Jilted on the registry office steps,' she said lightly—as if anyone would *dare* to jilt him! 'I'm sorry,' she apologised, 'It's just—well, I suppose I'm getting the jitters and need a bit of reassurance.'

'So how about—divided, and single, we each have a very poor chance of having the right to guard one Violette Ellena Langford. United, and married, our chances of caring for that little girl are far better than the other claimants'.'

'So, put a carnation in your buttonhole,' she answered, and suddenly felt a whole heap better.

To her surprise, Ellena slept well that night. She was up early, though. They were marrying at three that afternoon. Since they could hardly leave after the marriage ceremony in two separate vehicles, Gideon had arranged for her to be picked up and driven to the registry office. On Monday morning Gideon would drive her to her flat, where she would pick up her car and go to her office. From there, on Monday evening, she would drive to her new home, Oakvale.

Save for the fact that nerves were again attacking her, everything went as planned. The chauffeur-driven limousine arrived and Ellena was certain by then that what she was doing was right. She felt nervous only because, well, as she told herself, it wasn't every day that a girl got married, or to such a man as Gideon. She was met by him at ten to three that afternoon.

He came close up to her and—purely because other people were about, she was sure—he murmured, 'I knew you were beautiful. Today you look sensational.' And, lightly, he touched his lips to hers.

What could she do? She smiled. Blow anyone watching—Gideon had made her feel good. He gave her roses, and then snapped one bloom off and put it in his buttonhole. She laughed.

He looked at her. 'It will be all right, I promise,' he whispered—and just then a camera flash went off, and she realised some of the press were there.

The ceremony went without a hitch—she had been afraid she might develop a stammer or, worse, lose her voice entirely. Their witnesses were a couple of directors from Gideon's firm who, possibly because they were aware of the tragedy that might have befallen his brother and her sister, were both compassionate and congratulatory, but in a controlled way.

Ellena and Gideon posed briefly for press photos after the ceremony, then she and the man she had just married were in his car, alone, and driving away. Ellena transferred her engagement ring from its temporary home on her right hand to pair it with her wedding band on the third finger of her left hand. She caught Gideon giving her a glance.

'That's two rings I owe you,' she commented lightly.

'You amaze me!' he declared.

There wasn't any answer to that. 'I know,' she said, and felt like smiling. His eyes were back on the road but, from the way the corner of his mouth twitched, she had an idea that he was suppressing a smile too.

Her smile went deep into hiding, however, when, on reaching his home, and having been warmly congratulated by both Mr and Mrs Morris, Gideon suggested that she might like to change.

Ellena hadn't thought about it, but guessed this was his way of saying he would show her where she would be

sleeping and where she could wash her hands. She went up
the wide staircase with him, a thought only then striking
her. Gideon had spoken of her room. Oh, heavens, did it
matter that Mrs Morris, his housekeeper, would soon know
that they would not be sharing a bed?

Ellena did not have long to worry about it, however,
because, moving to the right-hand side of the landing,
Gideon escorted her to a door, which he opened, and stood
back. Ellena went in.

It was a large airy bedroom, with a large double bed,
elegant furniture, ankle-deep cream carpet matching the
cream curtains. 'You'll be comfortable here, but if there's
anything you want to change, or need, remember that
you're mistress here now.'

'Oh, Gideon, how nice,' she said, thinking it very kind
of him, but if Justine came home soon she wouldn't have
time to change anything. Not that the decor needed changing anyway.

There were another two doors in the room, to the bathroom, she judged, and dressing room. Wrong, she discovered as, unbeknown to her, Gideon had been watching her.
'That's your bathroom,' he said, indicating one door, 'and
that,' he said, indicating the other, 'is the door to my room.'

'Your room!' Startled, she stared at him, her blue eyes
wide. 'There's no key!' she observed.

'Now don't panic. Just stay calm and listen,' Gideon
urged.

'You said this marriage wouldn't be con-con...'

'Just because I'm sleeping next door doesn't mean I'm
going to lustfully charge in and claim my conjugal rights!'

'You tell me what it means, then!' she flew heatedly.
'You must have half a dozen bedrooms you can use, or one
I could have either if...'

'Spare me from outraged virgins!' Gideon threw up a
prayer, while she would have liked to have thrown up a
hand—and hit him. 'See here, I've told you Mrs Morris's

loyalty is without question. What is questionable is the loyalty of any unknown newcomer to this household.'

'Newcomer?' Did he mean her? He couldn't, could he?

Apparently not. 'Nanny!' he reminded her. 'We have to have a nanny, don't we?'

Ellena calmed down somewhat. 'We do,' she agreed.

'A nanny who, whether we like it or not, may be alone in this part of the house at any time of the day while we're out of it.'

'You think she may pry into our sleeping arrangements?'

'Most probably not. But I'm not jeopardising my claim to guardianship of Kit's daughter by taking that risk. I've no intention of it getting back to Russell and his wife that the newly married couple sleep at opposite ends of the house.'

'You think Pamela would go so far as to question our nanny?' Ellena couldn't believe it! Although, recalling Pamela Langford…

'I doubt she'd do it personally, but she'd pay to have someone sniff round for any useful information.'

'It sounds incredible!'

'There's big money to be had—Pamela wants it,' Gideon said succinctly.

Ellena's thoughts went straight to the baby. Poor little love. She just couldn't leave her with that woman; she just couldn't. Justine couldn't have been thinking straight to have left Violette with Pamela to start with.

Suddenly, then, it seemed secondary to panic that Gideon might want to lustfully make a call on her—when clearly he did not. Indeed, he had never—apart from a couple of extremely light kisses when there was a chance they were being observed—made, done, or said anything to give her the smallest qualm about such a matter. And, in any case, he could as easily make a call on her via the main door to her room as the communicating door.

'I'm making a fuss about nothing, aren't I?' she apologised, feeling a little shamefaced.

'The fault is mine,' he took the blame handsomely. 'I'd intended to show you your room last Sunday, then got to thinking it might worry you and that perhaps it would be better to wait.' He looked at her from his steady grey eyes. 'You're not worried now?' he asked.

Having kicked up a fuss needlessly once, she was anxious not to make a fool of herself a second time. 'Not a bit!' she assured him stoutly.

'May I then suggest that while, naturally, the communicating door will remain closed at night—' Ellena felt a hint peeved—to hear him talk, anyone would think *his* honour was at stake—he should be so lucky! '—I'd appreciate, assuming you're the last one to leave for the office, if you'd open it, and leave it so during the day.'

'To show that…'

'While to sleep separately is perhaps not too unusual, it might be as well for us to be seen—should word escape—to have an…intimate…relationship.'

'Of course,' she quickly agreed.

'Good,' he said. 'Now, I'll leave you to settle in while I make a phone call. I've an idea Mrs Morris may have gone to town on our dinner this evening.'

Mrs Morris had made a wonderful meal, Ellena discovered, when that evening Gideon knocked on her door and they went down the stairs. As before, Gideon was a splendid host, talking on any subject but the one she was most interested in: their niece. He had said that once they had their marriage certificate things would move fast in that direction. So, what was happening?

Realising she was being impatient—for Heaven's sake, the ink was barely dry on that certificate yet—Ellena decided that tomorrow she and Gideon must have an in-depth talk about it. She had come close to upsetting him when she'd objected to his easy access to her room. Much better to leave it until the next day.

Ellena had no idea why she didn't want to upset Gideon twice in one day, but, looking across to him as the meal came to a close, she knew only that she preferred him in this friendly mood of companionship, than when he was looking as if he was about to get tough.

'That was wonderful,' she stated, and, placing her napkin on the table, she continued, 'Would it be all right if I went and thanked Mrs Morris? She must have worked awfully hard.'

'How sweet you are,' Gideon murmured, and, standing up, 'Come on, I'll go with you.' Ellena wasn't sure how she felt about 'sweet', though supposed it was preferable to sour.

It had seemed natural to Ellena to seek Mrs Morris out, but the housekeeper seemed delighted that she had troubled to do so. 'It was a pleasure,' Mrs Morris beamed at their thanks, and Ellena, with Gideon at her side, left her and went back to the main part of the house.

At the door of the drawing room, however, Ellena decided she would quite like to go up to her room. 'I think I'll leave you to it,' she offered pleasantly.

Gideon halted. 'Had enough of my company for one day?' he teased.

'That would be a first,' she laughed.

'You've got me all wrong!' he protested.

'You don't have women by the score? You don't subscribe to the love 'em and leave 'em school of thought?'

'I'll have you know, madam,' he countered, 'that I'm a happily married man.'

That 'happily' pleased her. 'Goodnight,' she said quickly.

He caught a hold of her hand, the teasing and banter suddenly gone from his eyes. 'Goodnight, Ellena,' he said softly, and, with no one there at all to observe, he bent down and gently kissed her lips. And, as he straightened, he looked deep into her warm, if perhaps slightly confused eyes, and added, 'Thank you for marrying me today.' Then he took a step back. 'I'll see you at breakfast,' he said.

Ellena turned away, her feet seeming to make automatically for the stairs. It seemed odd to her that she hadn't protested when he kissed her.

Though no odder, surely, she thought whimsically, than the fact that she should go to bed on her honeymoon night with her husband's words 'I'll see you at breakfast' ringing in her ears!

CHAPTER FOUR

ELLENA slept soundly that night. She'd heard Gideon moving about in the next-door room before sleep claimed her. But, though she had thought she would feel a little on edge, come night time, that he was close by in one bedroom while she lay in another, she had to admit that she'd felt more secure by his near presence than anything else!

She heard a noise, and realised that it was muffled sounds from next-door that had awakened her. She heard the soft thud of his door closing and, remembering Gideon's parting remark that he would see her at breakfast, realised she'd better get a move on.

Leaving her bed, Ellena quickly showered and dressed. She had little knowledge of what a bride might wear for breakfast on the first day of her honeymoon but, since she wasn't going to work that day, considered that tailored trousers and a light sweater would fit the bill.

From force of habit she made her bed, and was on her way out of the room when she suddenly remembered the communicating door. Oops, she was supposed to leave it open! She changed direction and, just in case Gideon had returned to his room while she was in the shower, she tapped lightly on the wood panelling.

No answer! She opened the door a little way, then thought, Stupid! and pushed it wide. Gideon's room, though large, was not as large as hers, she saw. Oh, now, wasn't that kind of him, to give her the larger room? True, it might not be for very long, but he needn't have... Her attention was drawn to his large double bed, as yet unmade, and a small gurgle of laughter erupted. She had played her part by opening the door wide, Gideon had played his by putting a decided dent in the pillow beside the one he had used.

Gideon was in conversation with Mrs Morris when Ellena entered the breakfast room, but he broke off, rising to his feet when he saw her. 'You made it while the coffee's still hot,' he greeted her, and Ellena, about to greet him back with a pleasant 'Good morning', halted just in time, feeling herself go a shade pink as she realised that in normal circumstances a bride would very probably already have given her husband a much less formal greeting.

She smiled at him instead. 'Good morning, Mrs Morris,' she addressed the housekeeper, and realised that Gideon wasn't the only one to have noticed her suddenly pinkened cheeks when the woman answered her greeting, her expression going dreamy and understanding.

Gideon was holding out a chair at the table for her. 'What are you having for breakfast?' he enquired solicitously.

She was glad to take the seat, and, as Gideon sat down beside her, Ellena answered, 'May I have some cereal and a banana, if there is one?' Mrs Morris went smilingly on her way to arrange it. But Ellena was still feeling a shade awkward. 'I never used to blush until I met you!' she laid the blame at his door.

'What did I say?' Gideon asked, but there was a light of mischief in his eyes when he added, 'Mrs Morris was positively enchanted.'

Ellena, for all she supposed she had instigated this conversation, had already had quite enough of it. 'What sort of thing do you normally do when you have a day off?' she enquired to change the subject. 'And don't answer that if you'd rather not!' she added quickly, as she realised that there was every good chance that he spent most of his free time wining, dining and—whatever—with the opposite sex.

He looked back at her as if she amused him—she wasn't very sure how she felt about that. 'Apart from a holiday now and then, I can't remember the last time I had a day off,' he answered.

'Diplomatic!' she murmured, her lips twitching.

'You really do have a wrong opinion of me,' he answered smoothly. And at that juncture, into that pleasant atmosphere, Mrs Morris came in bearing a tray with everything Ellena required.

She thanked her, and as the housekeeper left the breakfast room it suddenly came to Ellena what she wanted to do with her own day off. 'I don't suppose...' she began without thinking further—and stopped.

'You don't suppose?' Gideon encouraged.

'Forget it.' She shook her head. 'It's an enormous cheek.'

'Now I really *am* intrigued.'

Oh, help. She was making too much of it. Wishing that she had never opened her mouth, yet aware that Gideon was waiting, she felt forced to go on. 'Well, I—um—want to go to my flat to check if there's anything in the mail from Justine—only I haven't... My car's not here.'

'I'll drive you, of course...'

'Oh no, I didn't mean that!' Ellena exclaimed hurriedly. 'What I was going to ask, was that, if you aren't using your car yourself, if I may borrow it.'

Gideon stared at her in dumbfounded surprise. 'Oh, my stars, Ellena,' he said after a moment. 'You slay me!'

'I knew I shouldn't have asked!'

'Yes, you should,' he replied. 'It's because of our—arrangement—that you're without your vehicle for the moment. And, while it's true I do have some work in my study that I could be getting on with, my housekeeper is looking on us all misty-eyed and I just haven't the heart to shatter her illusions by shutting myself away and depriving myself of your company.'

'Your charm's back,' Ellena commented faintly.

Gideon stared at her. For an age, it seemed to her, he

just sat and stared at her. Then, 'Thank heavens for that,' he mocked, but was serious as he went on, 'How do you fancy incorporating your plans for the day with my plans for the day?' She had no idea what he meant, and looked at him as if trying to gauge what he intended.

'Give me a hint,' she suggested.

'How about first of all I show you my old nursery, followed by a trip to your flat, followed by a quick bite to eat somewhere, followed by a shopping spree for whatever you think is needed to modernise the nursery, ready for when we bring our niece home?'

'Oh, Gideon!' Ellena cried, and, her emotions wobbly of late, and touched by his thoughtfulness, she had a feeling she might break down in floods of tears at any moment. Which caused her to struggle desperately for something light to say. 'If I weren't married to you, I'd say you'd be quite a catch for somebody,' she managed.

Solemnly he stared back at her. 'You're not so bad yourself, Mrs Langford,' he replied—at which her fear of tears vanished and they both burst out laughing.

Half an hour later, they were inspecting the nursery quarters housed on the top floor. It consisted of a playroom, bedroom and kitchen and, like all the others in the house, the rooms were large, though empty of furniture. Ellena was glancing round the spotless bedroom, struck by its light and airy feel, when something else suddenly struck her.

'It's pink!' she exclaimed of the palest pink walls.

'True,' Gideon replied.

'You were all boys!'

'True,' he answered again.

'Your mother wanted a girl?'

'Probably. Although up until last Saturday the walls—and the furniture I moved out—were blue.'

Oh, Gideon! Was he special, or was he special? Feeling that the tears she had striven so hard not to shed might yet get the better of her, Ellena went and took a look out of the window. She swallowed hard. 'You've had it redecorated,' she said, and, turning, regained the control she needed. 'How long will it be, do you think, before we have Violette?' she asked.

'Soon,' Gideon promised. 'Trust me. Quite soon.'

She wanted him to be more specific, wanted to ask, how, why, and what was happening on the legal front. But, with the evidence before her, of the pale pink of the nursery, that Gideon had waited only to hear her say last Saturday that she would marry him before he'd straight away got the decorators in, she knew she could trust him. That 'quite soon' meant the first possible moment.

'In that case, it seems to me we'd better hurry and get some nursery furniture delivered as soon as we can.'

They delayed only for Gideon to show her the connecting self-contained apartment which the nanny would use, then they walked down to the landing below and to where their own bedrooms lay. His door came first; Ellena left him, and entered her own room.

She washed her hands and tidied her hair and, conscious the whole time of the open door between their two rooms, sorted through her wardrobe for the jacket she wanted.

'Ready?' Gideon strolled into her room. It seemed ridiculous to object.

'I'll just put my jacket on,' she answered evenly, and most oddly felt her insides go like jelly when he came over, took it from her and, after holding it up for her to put on, caught hold of her hair and pulled it out from her collar.

'Fascinating colour,' he commented. 'Blonde with streaks of gold. Is it natural?'

She took a few steps away from him, strangely still able to feel his fingers in her hair, warm against her neck. 'As a matter of fact, yes,' she answered. 'Though it's no wonder to me you know so much.' What he didn't know, he found out!

His lips twitched. 'Stop me if I ask too many questions,'

he invited, and, going to her bedroom door, he opened it. They left by that route.

Ellena was in a very sober frame of mind when they pulled up outside her flat. 'I shouldn't be long, but if you'd like to come up for a minute or two…' she offered.

He didn't answer but accepted by going with her into the building and up to her flat. Disappointment awaited her. There was nothing in the post apart from a couple of circulars.

'I didn't really expect anything,' she murmured, looking away from him. Though she guessed she wasn't making a very good job of hiding from him how wretched she felt not to have an alive-and-well communication from her sister when, as she turned from him, Gideon caught a hold of her.

Like a homing pigeon she went into his arms. A moment of weakness it might have been but for a brief while she obeyed the instinct to lean her head against his chest. She felt safe, secure, comforted—yet at the same time she had a funny sort of feeling inside, to be held close by him, wrapped in his firm strong arms.

'They'll be all right,' Gideon said to the top of her head. And because she knew he was hurting too, she could do nothing else but put her arms around him. 'We have to believe that, Ellena,' he murmured gently, and placed a light kiss on her hair.

She looked up, straight into a pair of direct and steady slate-grey eyes. And suddenly her unhappiness started to recede and she felt she wanted him to kiss her, to kiss her mouth. And, as they gazed at each other, she thought for one crazy moment that he was going to.

She took her arms from him, took a step back, common sense clamouring for a hearing. 'A fine pair of guardians we are,' she found her voice out of a breathless nowhere.

He let go of her. 'One half of us is beautiful,' he said.

'You've been looking in your mirror again,' she mocked

with a laugh. It was senseless that she felt instantly brighter because he thought her beautiful.

'Let's shop,' he decreed.

By mutual consent they decided it was too early for lunch, and that they would eat later. They shopped, and shopped—nothing was too good for the infant they hoped to soon have in their care. And yet, even while eating, drinking, playing and sleeping equipment began to mount up, Ellena found her thoughts returning again and again to that time at her flat earlier, to the haven of Gideon's arms, to the fact that she had wanted him to kiss her.

She and Justine had been on their own for so long now, and she'd had to be the one with the sensible head. So had it been purely that it was comforting to relax and let somebody else take charge for a change? But he wasn't taking charge, it was a joint thing. Grief, she'd been held by a man before, be it only in a warm-up embrace that had not gone much further—but she couldn't ever remember feeling this way before! What on earth was happening to her?

Nothing was happening to her, she decided very firmly. It was just that she was going through a very emotional time at the moment. Ellena tuned back in to the discussion Gideon was having with the salesman when she heard him say that he wanted the chest of drawers, the cot and its bedding, together with a whole host of other paraphernalia, delivered the next day.

'We're having Violette with us tomorrow?' Ellena asked him eagerly the first moment that they were alone.

'No,' Gideon straight away disabused her of that idea. 'I said soon, and I meant soon. I merely want to have the nursery ready to eliminate any ''You haven't so much as a cot for her to sleep in'' argument, when the time comes.'

'Did I mention before your ability to think streets in advance of anyone else?'

'I think you've just paid me a compliment.'

'Don't let it go to your head. I meant nothing personal by it.'

'My dear,' Gideon drawled, 'we don't have that sort of a marriage.'

So put me in my place, why don't you! Ellena fumed, wishing she hadn't spoken and not liking the arrogant devil after all. She was only trying to be friendly. 'What's the latest from your lawyers?' she asked snappily.

Gideon looked surprised. 'You're a sensitive soul, aren't you?' he questioned.

'Don't tell me that you, with all your research, have never come across a type like me!' She took refuge from bruised feelings in sarcasm, though she was aware of Gideon's steady and considering gaze on her for long seconds before he answered.

'Do you know, Ellena, I rather think I haven't. I knew before there was something different about you. Now I realise that you are not merely different—you're unique.'

She had no idea how she was meant to take his remark, whether to be pleased or offended. 'I'm certainly not as clever as you,' she admitted. 'You can tell a compliment from a mile off—I don't know whether I've just been insulted or complimented.'

'Would I insult my wife?' he asked solemnly.

She had an idea he was laughing at her. 'So what's with the lawyers?' she insisted.

'They're put on ice, for the moment,' he deigned to answer. 'It will be natural, should the worst have happened, that you and I as next of kin take the baby. But, until we know that for sure, and if you're willing, I'd like to hold back from taking court action to have her legally declared ours.' He was talking about adoption! He was talking as if, were the worst to have happened, they would take steps to legally adopt Violette! Ellena, while not wanting to look too far into the future, could only think with all her heart of Violette's well being.

'I'm willing,' she confirmed, and wanted to add the proviso providing they *had* Violette living with them at some early date. But, as Gideon had reminded her, he had said she *would* soon be with them, and that meant soon. She didn't want him to think of her as some carping female— though why she should want his good opinion defeated her.

She didn't care a light for his opinion of her, she decided promptly. Regardless of the facts that they had shopped well into lunchtime, and seemed to have bought up the store—their list of requirements now completed—Ellena decided he could lunch on his own.

'Actually, it seems senseless for you to drive me in on Monday when I'm near enough to my flat to go and collect my car now,' she informed him.

'You're proposing to drive home without me?' Gideon queried, and Ellena felt quite misty-eyed. How lovely that word 'home' sounded. How lovely that Gideon should refer to his house as her home. She took a steadying breath— grief, was she as sensitive as he suggested?

'Anything wrong with that?'

'I know this is your first honeymoon, my dear,' he drawled, 'and I know you've a definite lack of experience in the togetherness department, but have you considered, for a moment, our housekeeper's romantic sensibilities?'

It was utterly crackers, to Ellena's mind, not to pick up her car while she had the opportunity. And yet, so much might rest on their being seen together—on their supposedly being too much in love to want to be parted. 'How could I bear to be apart from you for so much as a moment?' she offered.

'So we'll eat.'

It was a late lunch, but it was a pleasant affair. They discussed many things of a non-personal nature, and that suited Ellena fine. She had always thought of herself as having a fairly even temperament, but, recalling how bruised she'd felt when Gideon had referred to their impersonal marriage, she had no wish to invite the bruised experience again.

Somehow, after that, the time simply flew. They returned to the home they now shared and when Ellena just could not resist going along to the nursery to mentally place the furniture that would be arriving tomorrow, she turned on a sound—and found Gideon had followed and was watching her.

'How did I know I'd find you here?' he asked.

She smiled at him, unable to remember a time when she hadn't liked him too well. 'I was just deciding where everything would go. Er, with your agreement,' she added hastily, lest he had views on the subject.

'I'll leave that entirely up to you,' he answered, and came to the purpose of why he had come looking for her. 'Mrs Morris wondered if you had any special likes and dislikes for dinner?'

'Oh, heavens. I'm still full from lunch!' Ellena exclaimed, only then realising that, as mistress of Oakvale, she had the responsibility of discussing menus with their housekeeper. 'I'd better go and have a word with her,' she decided. 'Then I'm going to walk off our last meal.' She had seen little of the surrounding countryside yet. 'Um— talking of togetherness...' he wanted togetherness, she'd give him togetherness '...you'd better come with me.'

Gideon gave her a startled look, then good humour was spreading across his features. 'What have I married?' he asked, amused.

'A bossy woman. Come on.'

Ellena spent a pleasant ten minutes or so with Mrs Morris, and had an extremely pleasant walk with Gideon. After which she went up to her room and closed the communicating door. Then she took a leisurely bath and, while still extremely anxious underneath about Justine and Kit, she felt better than she had in a long while.

Dinner with Gideon was a relaxed affair. He had an uncanny knack, though, of drawing from her matters which, while not in any way secret, she had always felt were private.

'Did you always want to be an accountant?' he asked at one juncture—and Ellena found she was telling him of her university plans before her parents had died, and how fortunate she regarded herself that Andrea had given her the chance to train with her. 'She's been wonderful,' Ellena went on. 'Always very understanding when things with Justine got a bit fraught.'

'Justine was a tearaway?'

'Understatement!' Ellena smiled.

'Out all hours?'

'That doesn't make her a wicked person!'

'Put your hackles down. We've already agreed that she and Kit are a pair well met.'

'Sorry,' she apologised, and Gideon smiled at her across the table.

'So, in between keeping an eye on her—which probably meant charging around in the middle of the night looking for her—and studying for your accountancy exams, you never had any time to get your own social life going.'

'Oh, it wasn't that bad!' she denied, not liking the idea that this man should think her as green as grass, never had a boyfriend, a dullard. 'I've had my moments too.'

'Boyfriends?'

'Of course.'

'Anyone special?'

Ellena shook her head, and, though it went against the grain, felt compelled to confess, 'I never went out with anyone long enough to find out.'

'A half a dozen times?' he suggested.

'More like two,' she had to admit. 'Then some crisis with Justine would crop up and I'd have to cancel. With Justine going from crisis to crisis I got fed up with breaking dates and decided I'd rather concentrate on my studies and her.'

'With Justine always coming first?'

'What can I tell you?' He had a brother she rather thought he'd drop everything for. 'But my sister wasn't always giving me headaches,' Ellena went on quickly. 'She was wild, certainly. Impetuous, unthinking, reckless—a living nightmare sometimes—those words all apply. But she was warm, loving, funny—and as honest as the day.' She paused, a most unpalatable truth she had never been able to shrug off getting to her again.

'What is it?' Gideon asked urgently. 'There's such pain in your eyes.'

'I'm sorry,' she apologised. 'I've tried telling myself that Justine's hormones must be still all over the place after having Violette, and they've caused her to act in a way totally alien to her. But she's so honest; I just know she wouldn't dream of flitting from a hotel without settling her account first. She just *wouldn't*—I *know* her!'

Gideon considered what she had said for a moment then, hormones aside, came up with another explanation. 'She may have thought Kit had settled the account.'

Ellena wanted to believe that. Not to believe it would mean that Justine and Kit had not left their hotel. That they had gone out that morning of the avalanche intending to return—only something had prevented them from returning. 'Justine was the one with the money,' she reminded him shakily.

Gideon had not forgotten but he was, it seemed, determined not to lose heart. 'If she's anywhere near as sensitive as her sister, I'd say she handed over some money rather than let Kit feel small.'

There had been plenty of time in which Justine could have used one of her credit cards to obtain some local currency, Ellena saw, currency which, without a doubt, she would most certainly have shared with Kit. But even while Ellena was musing on that, her heartbeat seemed to quicken at the gentle way Gideon was looking at her.

Abruptly, she changed the subject. 'So—um—how about you?' she questioned, striving hard for a bright note.

'Me?' he queried.

'I've told you all about my love-life, and, given I've only skated on its perimeters, fair's fair.'

'You're suggesting I tell you of my love-life?'

'Well, you needn't go into too many details,' she qualified hastily.

He laughed. She liked him. But then he shook his head. 'That,' he said sadly, 'I cannot do.'

She knew that she didn't want him to, but some devil was pushing her. 'Why not?' she insisted.

'It's the code,' he answered; his laughter was gone but his eyes were amused.

'What code?'

He looked at her. Looked at her as if he enjoyed doing so. Somehow, when her heart had started to jig about a bit, Ellena had managed to hold his gaze. 'Men—don't,' he informed her.

'Hound!' They both smiled.

Ellena lay in her bed that night giving herself a talking to. She owned that Gideon Langford was getting to her, that she found him stimulating, and that she enjoyed being in his company. But it would never do. He was entertaining her, was having her live in his home, indeed had gone so far as to marry her—purely as a smokescreen. But there was nothing personal in it—not that she wanted there to be, for goodness' sake—but it wouldn't hurt to remember that. It was just that it was in their mutual interests to be seen together. Ellena went to sleep that night, with the view that while she would play her part in this togetherness thing when anyone else was around, at other times she was going to keep out of Gideon's way. In the interests of self-preservation… Abruptly Ellena doubled back on her drowsy thoughts. Self-preservation? Gosh, she must be more tired than she had thought. What did she need self-preservation for?

She found she had no trouble in keeping out of Gideon's way over the next couple of days, however, for, regardless of Mrs Morris's romantic sensibilities, he seemed hardly ever to be around.

'You can borrow my car if you wish,' he offered at breakfast time the next morning.

Somehow that annoyed her. He could keep his magnanimous gestures! 'Thanks all the same, I hadn't planned to go anywhere today apart from the nursery.'

'Give me a shout when the furniture arrives—I'll be in my study.'

Ellena looked at him. She had an idea he had gone off her. Well, she wasn't so keen on him just then, either. 'I'll do that,' she answered coolly, and received a cool stare back—and that was about the sum total of their conversation.

She did not have to tell him when the furniture arrived. He heard the vehicle pull up. They had done well yesterday, she realised, when a pretty chest of drawers was carted into the nursery, followed by a cot and a padded highchair.

Gideon returned to the nursery once he'd seen the delivery men on their way. She again wanted to ask him *when*, but just then realised that she trusted him, and knew that when he said 'soon', no man would do it sooner.

'I don't remember you buying that!' he said when he saw the pretty smocked dress she was taking out of its tissue, ready to place it in the chest of drawers, once she'd given them a wipe out.

'You'll have to be quicker than that,' she returned lightly, and saw that it looked as if he was striving hard not to let his lips twitch.

He did not smile. In fact the rest of that day, and the whole of Sunday, seemed to be designated No Smiling Days.

Ellena was glad when Monday came around. She heard Gideon moving about very early and leapt out of bed and headed for the shower. He was giving her a lift in; it would be a fine start to the week if she kept him waiting!

As she had assumed, they left the house far earlier than she had planned to once she had her own wheels. They passed the journey in relative silence. But, on arriving at her flat, ever mindful of photographers, even though Ellena thought it most improbable that one of them would be stationed at her address, Gideon got out of the car and came to stand on the pavement with her.

She looked up at him, unsure about what happened now. He looked down, pinning her with those steady slate-grey eyes. 'Enjoy your day,' he bade her.

'You too,' she answered politely, and felt instantly all hot and bothered when he bent down and kissed her on the mouth.

She turned away. Perhaps, if they were still together in a month's time, his kisses would have been relegated to her cheeks. You're growing cynical, Ellena, go and get your car.

She was extremely busy at work that day, and she was glad it was so. Still, all the same, there were many times when Justine came into her head and, most unexpectedly, and many times, thoughts of the man she had married would arrive unbidden too—and require quite some moving.

Everyone at the office was most kind and, to her huge embarrassment, which she hoped she covered well, they had made a collection and presented her with a most beautiful cut-glass vase. There was also a bouquet of flowers to go with it.

Oh, what a sham it all was! A very necessary sham, she quieted her conscience a moment later. She wanted Violette. She was not, not, not going to leave her with that dreadful woman! And, having married in order to claim her, then if she had to be *happily* married, there'd be none happier.

She thanked everyone sincerely and escaped back to her office. She had only another unexpected hiccup to her day when one of Andrea's best clients came in to see her at the close of business, upset that, because he hadn't an appointment, Andrea was tied up and had passed him on to Ellena.

'It was only a small piece of advice I wanted,' Cliff Wilkinson protested. 'And you know how difficult it is for me to come and see her in normal office hours.'

'I know it isn't easy,' Ellena sympathised, aware that Cliff, who was nice, not bad looking and thirty-eight to Andrea's forty-two, was enamoured of her employer and had most probably called this late hoping to extend a business discussion into dinner. It had happened before, only Andrea, who didn't want to know, had invited Ellena along, as part of her training, to be an unwanted third guest. 'I'm sure that I can—' Ellena broke off—Cliff had spotted her bouquet.

'It's your birthday?' he guessed.

Oh, crumbs. She'd rather keep quiet. But any girl who'd married only last Thursday would, she felt sure, be keen to announce it from the rooftops. 'I—um—got married last week,' she revealed, feeling herself growing pink.

Cliff, like the nice person he was, forgot his disappointment that Andrea wasn't available to see him, and showed only delight at her news. 'Congratulations!' he exclaimed enthusiastically. 'Though it's your husband I should be congratulating.'

'Thank you,' she murmured, desperately wanting to change the subject, while at the same time wanting to play her role to perfection.

'I'm keeping you!' Cliff suddenly realised. 'You'll want to get off home. Of course you do.' He stood up. 'Perhaps you'll tell Mrs Keyte that I'll come back another day.'

Ellena protested that she'd be pleased to advise him on

his problem but he wouldn't hear of it. And, since she guessed it was more a problem he had invented so he could have a one-to-one with Andrea, Ellena did not press it.

She was delayed leaving the office and took some papers with her in her briefcase. But, late though she was, she drove first to her flat. The mail normally arrived some while after she had set out for work. There had been nothing there for her this morning; there was nothing there for her now. But she refused to be down-hearted and moved about her flat, wondering if she should make herself something to eat there, or go to her other home.

It was the thought that Mrs Morris might possibly be offended if she had gone to the trouble to prepare something for her that decided Ellena. This and her togetherness pact with Gideon Langford.

Her phone rang; she quickly answered it. 'Hello?' she said—talk of the devil!

'Do you intend coming home tonight?' Gideon questioned aggressively.

Who *did* he think he was? 'How could I stay away?' she answered sweetly—and put down the phone.

Ratfink! Perversely, she wanted to stay away another hour. However, thoughts of offending Mrs Morris neutralised her feelings.

Ellena drove to the home she now shared with Gideon—albeit temporarily—realising that he must have left his office early. Strange! Somehow she'd thought, without actually being aware of thinking it, in normal times he'd probably be the last one to leave the office.

A smile of merriment lit her mouth. No doubt he couldn't wait to get home that day. Togetherness; he couldn't possibly wait another moment to rush home to his bride. What a pity his bride wasn't there!

Ellena pulled up on the drive of Oakvale and, with no idea if there was anywhere special she had to garage her car, she paused only to pick up her briefcase, floral bouquet, shoulder bag and crystal vase, and left her vehicle where it was.

The front door opened before she rang the bell. Gideon stood there, tall, straight, sort of impatient—her heart started pounding a little erratically.

'Glad to see you. I'm laden.' She ignored her wayward emotions.

Gideon relieved her of her briefcase and stood back for her to enter. 'What's with the flowers?' he gritted when he saw the presentation bouquet.

'A present,' she said, and would have added an acid 'from an admirer', only just then she spotted Mrs Morris hovering in the hall. 'They made a collection at the office...' Her voice tailed off when, without more ado, Gideon took the flowers and the cut-glass vase from her hands and passed them over to his housekeeper.

'I've a present for you too,' he announced solemnly. 'At a guess, I'd say a ten to fourteen pound one.' And, while Ellena stared at him uncomprehending, 'It's waiting for you...' he broke off, his slate-grey eyes on hers '...up in the nursery.'

Ellena stared at him, caught Mrs Morris's beaming smile and—click! Her bag went down, and Ellena was haring up the stairs, up to the top floor. Along the landing she ran. She opened the nursery door.

A matronly woman with a wonderful homely face was standing in the nursery. In her arms, she held a baby. 'Violette!' Ellena cried huskily and, hurrying forward, took the baby from her.

How long she held the little scrap to her, crooning, cuddling, loving, she had no idea. But suddenly she became aware that Gideon was in the room too. She took her attention from the baby, and, her heart full, she said chokily, 'Thank you, Gideon. Oh, thank you.'

For long, silent moments he stared back at her, then he answered quietly, 'For you, my dear, anything.'

CHAPTER FIVE

So MANY questions rushed to Ellena's lips as she looked from the baby to Gideon. Discretion ruled the day. Later, perhaps at dinner when they were alone, she would have the opportunity to ask him how he had performed the miracle of wresting Violette from that avaricious woman, who had never looked like giving her up.

'For you, my dear, anything,' he'd said. Ellena knew he had only said it because there was another person there with them, and that they must still maintain a loving front. But, most peculiarly, in this happiest of moments, she felt she would not have minded had he truly meant it.

She gave her undivided attention to being reunited with her niece and learned that Marjorie Dale, the woman who had temporary charge of the nursery, had everything under control. Although Mrs Dale had her own home in the village, she would be sleeping at Oakvale that night in a next-door bedroom that was to be turned into a bed-sitting room.

Ellena wanted to protest that there was no need for Mrs Dale to sleep over, that she would use that room and be on hand should Violette not sleep through until morning. She held back. Gideon must have a lot to tell her; she would wait to hear it all before she made any decisions regarding her niece's care.

Meantime, when Gideon had disappeared, she cuddled and loved the baby some more, and only reluctantly gave her up when Gideon returned. 'Mrs Morris delayed dinner for you,' he hinted, and Ellena was torn between wanting to stay right where she was, yet at the same time wanting to put a half-dozen or more questions to Gideon—namely why hadn't he let her know Violette was there sooner. Reluctantly, she handed the baby over to Marjorie Dale.

'Have you eaten?' she thought to ask her.

'Yes, thank you, Mrs Langford,' the woman replied.

Ellena left the nursery. She felt awkward. Mrs Langford! Ellena Langford! Ellena Spencer Langford! Crikey! Suddenly she realised that Gideon was right there beside her. 'I'll just slip off and wash my hands,' she murmured when they reached the next landing. She halted momentarily, expecting him to go down the stairs. He didn't, but stood looking at her. Earlier that day she had drawn her gold spun blonde hair back from her face in a classic knot. She looked down at the dark trouser suit and white shirt she had worn all day. 'I won't change,' she told him, for no reason other than she thought she had kept Mrs Morris waiting long enough.

'It's amazing,' he answered.

He was still looking at her—she was lost to his meaning. 'What is?'

'That you've reached the age of twenty-two without some man making off with you.'

'You're saying I look all right?' Where had that imp of mischief come from?

'You're beautiful and you know it.'

'You can't blame a girl for fishing,' she grinned, and went on her way.

A quick wash of her hands later and she was heading down the stairs, wondering at this light-heartedness that had overtaken her. Was it purely because of the fact that Justine's daughter was now under the same roof? It couldn't be because, in contrast to the last two days, Gideon suddenly seemed light-hearted too, could it?

He was standing talking to Mrs Morris when she entered the dining room. 'I'm sorry to have kept you waiting,' Ellena apologised, unsure as to which of them she was apologising to.

Gideon pulled out her chair and Mrs Morris went on her way, looking every bit as if, in this instance of their new arrival, it didn't matter a scrap how long she had to delay dinner. Ellena had an idea that Violette Ellena Langford might end up being one very spoilt young lady.

'So?' she questioned, the moment she and Gideon sat down at the table. 'You obviously phoned me at my flat to tell me that you'd managed to bring Violette home.' His aggressively phrased, 'Do you intend coming home to-night?', had told her precisely nothing. But now there were more important matters to discuss here. 'So tell me, how, why, where?' she asked.

'You're pleased, obviously.'

'Never more so,' she replied. 'You said "soon" and I've kept hoping, but didn't like to keep asking in case you thought I was a nag.'

'That bothered you?' he questioned, an eyebrow going aloft.

Why had it bothered her that he might think her carping? She couldn't find an answer. 'Are you being annoying on purpose?' she questioned shortly.

His lips twitched. 'So, to start at the beginning. I rang Russell after our wedding last Thursday to apologise for not inviting him and his lady to it, and to tell him I wanted him to know before he read it in the papers the next day.'

Ellena remembered the press photographers at the registry office. 'Was he upset?' He was family after all. 'That you hadn't invited him?'

'He lives in his own world,' Gideon stated. 'But, while I felt pretty certain he'd remember to tell his wife that you and I were married—' more the object of the telephone call, Ellena realised '—I had a pleasant surprise when he told me they wouldn't have been able to come anyway because their nanny had walked out. In between coping with the incessant crying of an upset infant, Pamela had spent the day on the phone endeavouring to find a replacement nanny.'

'You should have told me!' was Ellena's first reaction.

'What—so you could be upset too?' he countered. Had he not told her of the nanny's departure because he'd thought better than to cause her upset over something she could do little about? He had called her sensitive—Ellena was beginning to think that Gideon was also far more sensitive than she had credited. 'I knew it would worry you,' he went on, 'but it seemed to me that the more exacting the little one became, the sooner my sister-in-law would have enough of her.'

'Was she unable to hire another nanny?'

'Hiring a nanny wasn't the problem. Getting one to stay was another matter. I rang Russell this morning to enquire how things were with the baby. Nanny number two had just walked out and Pamela was going up the wall. Time, I felt, to pay her a visit.'

'She handed Violette over just like that?' Ellena, remembering the hard-faced woman, could barely believe it.

'She put up a small show of resistance, but against our marriage certificate, her non-maternal instincts and her inability to cope with a fractious four-and-a-half-month-old, she folded when money changed hands.'

'You paid her!'

'I always knew I was going to have to—it was just a matter of timing. We had to be married—it would be a bonus if, as turned out, her nerves were frazzled.'

'I've said it before—you're clever, aren't you?'

'I like to think I've got everything covered,' he replied mock-modestly.

Her lips twitched. She concentrated on the matter in hand. 'You brought Violette back with you there and then?'

'I'd taken the precaution of calling on Marjorie Dale in the village first.'

'You took her with you?' she asked amazed.

'I thought of you, firstly, but felt it would be too distressing for you if the little one was still wailing and Pamela wouldn't hand her over. So I fitted the car baby seat you'd left in the nursery and took Marjorie Dale, hoping she'd be necessary—nothing would be lost if she wasn't,' he answered. 'Marjorie has always helped out here in one capacity or another. She's a widow with children at university. Apparently, as well as having majored in common sense, Marjorie positively adores babies.' His lips most definitely did twitch when he added, 'I thought her a most likely candidate to pass muster under your exacting requirements.'

'You make me sound like an ogre!'

'Not at all. I'm just aware of how very seriously you take your responsibilities to that little lady upstairs. Marjorie and the new qualified nanny who arrives tomorrow will between them ensure that our niece lacks for neither love nor attention.'

'Just a second!' he was racing on too fast! New nanny! Looking after Violette between them? 'When did the new nanny come in?'

'Didn't I say?' He knew darn well he hadn't! 'There was just time when we got back for me to interview Beverly Clark, most highly spoken of by the agency. She liked us, cooed over the infant, and passed the inspections by both Mrs Morris and Marjorie Dale. If you don't take to her, though,' he inserted, 'then we'll find somebody else.'

Ellena had started to grow a little annoyed that all this had taken place without him consulting her. But, in view of him being prepared to let Beverly Clark go if she wasn't happy about her, Ellena didn't think she could raise too much of an objection. 'You know that I intend to look after Violette myself at the weekends.'

'If that's what you want, you still can. But you do an exacting job too, remember. You may be glad to be able to hand her to someone else while you take a break. I believe tots like that can sometimes grizzle on endlessly with no cause whatsoever.'

All the time they'd been talking, they had been eating. Neither of them had bothered with a first course, and Ellena had a few minutes to think over everything that had been said when Mrs Morris came in and cleared their main course dishes. They were both having cheese and biscuits to finish.

'You've got everything worked out, by the look of it,' Ellena commented, once Mrs Morris had gone from the dining room.

'You don't sound very happy about it?'

'I should have liked to be consulted,' Ellena stated, but tacked on, as in all honesty she must, 'Though it's a fact I don't think I could have improved on anything you've done.'

Gideon looked at her for quite some moments, then, his eyes roving her dainty features, her perfect skin and her eyes, he stated quietly, 'You're so honest. Beautiful on the inside, as well as out.'

She blushed, she knew she did. She wanted to say something witty, something clever, sharp. But her wits seemed to have deserted her, and what she did say was a quiet, husky, 'Thank you.' But this would never do, and to counteract the sudden banging of her heart for no reason against her ribs, she asked politely, 'Do we get divorced now?'

His eyes were still on her, his look growing incredulous. 'My stars—you really are something else again!' he grunted. And if she wanted a blunt answer she soon had it, when he curtly told her, 'No, we do not get divorced now!'

'Pardon me for asking!' she snapped, and, refusing to be intimidated, she asked belligerently, 'Why not?'

'We haven't been married a week yet!' he retorted.

As if that was the end of the subject! 'What's that got to do with anything?' Ellena tossed back.

She had the heat drawn from her anger when, as they sat glaring at each other, Gideon's lips suddenly started to twitch. 'I'm enjoying the—rest—for one thing,' he drawled, and, while her sense of humour stirred at his reference to his having a break from his women friends—and all *that* entailed!—Ellena felt confusion, too, when she found herself staring at his mouth. He really had quite a divine sort of mouth. Grief! Rapidly she forced her glance away and saw he had been watching her. She refused to colour up again when, with those slate-grey eyes piercing hers, he went on, 'For another thing, in my view my sister-in-law gave in too easily. I don't trust her.'

'You think she'll try and get Violette back?' Ellena no longer felt amused.

'Give her a couple of days to get over the trauma of coping with a fretful infant and intractable nannies, and she'll be setting her devious mind to find some loophole.'

'You think she'll challenge you in court—even though you have—er—recompensed her!' Ellena gasped.

'That one has pound sterling signs stamped on her eyeballs—she'll try.'

'But she won't win?'

'Who could—against the two of us?'

'United we stand…' Ellena didn't finish, nor did she wish to consider a divorce any further. 'We stay married,' she agreed. She had eaten all she wanted. She got to her feet. 'I've a little work to do; I'll go up,' she said.

Gideon was on his feet too. 'I can put another desk in my study,' he offered.

'Now, isn't that kind!' Ellena replied in sincere amazement. 'But I shouldn't dream of disturbing you,' she declined. And added promptly, 'Goodnight, Gideon.'

She left him and went up the stairs. At their head she halted. Then, for all she guessed her niece must be asleep, she could not resist going up the extra flight to take a look at her.

Violette was safe, gorgeous and cherubic in sleep. Ellena whispered a goodnight to Marjorie Dale and returned to her own room to find that, from the evidence of her briefcase on her bed, Gideon had been to her room. A smile lit her face—with so much else happening, she had forgotten he had taken it from her when she had arrived home earlier.

She had meant to thank him the next morning but passed him in the hall on his way out to an early meeting when she went down to breakfast. True, she was delayed—she'd popped up to the nursery.

'Bye, my dear,' he said, and, putting an arm around her, he kissed her.

She didn't move. His kiss was for the benefit of Mrs Morris, who must be about. Ellena realised that even as she acknowledged that his kiss seemed to be a little longer than the others he had bestowed on her.

'Er—bye,' she answered, and, grateful that he knew nothing about the nonsense going on inside her, she watched him stride purposefully to the door.

When she did move and turn, Ellena saw no sign of the housekeeper, but knew without a doubt that sharp-eyed Gideon must have spotted her as she had gone from the kitchen to the breakfast room.

Ellena had her breakfast and, running a little late, dashed upstairs to collect her jacket and briefcase from her bedroom, and—by the skin of her teeth—remembered to open the communicating door wide. Gideon, she saw, had remembered to dent the other pillow.

A fortnight later, and opening the door between the two rooms had become a habit. As, too, a visit to the nursery each morning was a must. Beverly Clark was a super nanny, and Ellena knew she could not have chosen better herself. Beverly was a stocky, sensible female of around twenty-four, dedicated to her work and perfectly matched to work with Marjorie Dale. The two got on famously— but were pleased to allow Ellena some time with her niece.

So, on that front, Ellena could not have been more happy. But the day when Justine and Kit should have returned came and went, causing her more than a little anxiety. Gideon had been again to Kit's flat and had left a note for Kit to contact him immediately and most urgently on his return, but so far had heard nothing.

Ellena still returned to her own flat first thing every evening to check her mail, but there was never anything from her sister. She refused to give up hope and put all her energies into the knowledge that, if the fancy took Justine, she was as likely to stay away for three or four months as the month or so she had stated.

After her usual, disappointing mail-checking visit to her flat that Tuesday evening, Ellena drove home to Oakvale in a grave frame of mind. Gideon had mentioned at breakfast that he had a business dinner to attend that evening and would be late home; his only reason for telling her was, she well knew, so that she wouldn't look surprised should the housekeeper refer to it in any way.

Ellena left her briefcase on the landing when she went up to the nursery. 'How's this bundle of joy been today?' she asked Beverly, as the nanny placed the thriving mite into her arms.

'She has her moments, but, for the most part, she's a little gem,' Beverly replied, clearly won over by her young charge.

As was Mrs Morris, Ellena learned when she later went down to eat her solitary meal, for the housekeeper seemed to have only one topic of conversation these days, and that was the baby.

Most evenings Ellena spent some time in the nursery, playing with the baby, or helping out when there was anything left to do. If Violette was sleepy, and also for the way it looked, she would sometimes go back down to the drawing room, occasionally spending some time chatting to Gideon after dinner if he was around.

But that evening he wasn't there and after her meal Ellena experienced such a feeling of restlessness, of being unable to settle, that she returned upstairs. She paid a visit to the nursery, but Violette was asleep, and, not wanting to intrude on Beverly's time off, Ellena returned to her room.

She had some complicated corporation accounts in her briefcase, something she normally enjoyed, but she couldn't settle to that either. She got the work out anyway, and laid it on the medium-sized antique desk which had magically appeared in her room when she'd arrived home two weeks ago. Gideon, of course.

Her thoughts stayed with him, this man she had married—and would sooner or later divorce. He was excellent company. She wasn't missing him, was she? Was that why she was feeling so unsettled? What rot! For crying out loud, she rarely saw him, apart from at breakfast—and not always then. She went and closed the communicating door, remembering how twice last week he'd had early appointments, and had been off and away before she'd gone down the stairs. She saw him most evenings, though, at dinner. But he, like her, brought work home, and would more often than not take himself off to his study.

Ellena was still avoiding her desk like the plague a half-hour later. It was ridiculous—she owned it was—but something *was* unsettling her. In an attempt to get more relaxed she went and had a bath and changed into a non-sense of a nightdress Justine had given her last Christmas, and then donned the matching silk wrap.

Fifteen minutes later, and she was thoroughly into the work on her desk. She was deep into facts and figures when, having lost count of time, she was suddenly aware of the communicating door opening.

Her eyes widened as Gideon entered her room. Her mouth went dry. He was fully dressed—she wasn't! 'I didn't hear you knock.' She said the first thing that came into her head.

He looked tired, she thought. He smiled; it took his look of tiredness away. 'I'm afraid I more lightly rapped than knocked.' He clearly hadn't wanted the rest of the house to hear that he had to hammer on his wife's bedroom door to be let in. 'You were obviously absorbed and didn't hear.' He came over to where she was sitting and looked over her shoulder. 'Looks complicated,' he commented of her paper-work.

'It took me five years to get the hang of it,' she quipped, referring to her long apprenticeship. Unconsciously, she arched her neck, pulling her shoulders back to release the tension of sitting in one position for an age.

'Here, let me,' Gideon offered—and, before she could stop him, his long, sensitive fingers were massaging her neck and shoulders.

'I...' she went to protest, but his hands were marvellous. Wonderful wasn't stretching it! 'Oh!' she exclaimed softly, the warmth of his touch suddenly starting to make a muddle of her. She never wanted him to stop. She closed her eyes. She was being seduced—and she was enjoying it. 'That was good,' she attempted to end it when she felt she could speak without sounding husky. Her voice *was* husky.

She turned in her chair; his hands fell away. Her warm blue eyes met warm slate-grey ones. She had a dreadful notion that he knew how she was feeling. 'Don't strain your lovely eyes burning the midnight oil,' he remarked evenly.

'I'm nearly through,' she managed. 'Er—did you have a good dinner?' She was making conversation near midnight and in her nightie! Brain! Where's your brain, girl?

'Fair,' he answered. 'We got caught up in heavy business discussions afterwards.'

'Naturally,' she smiled.

His eyes fell to her lips. He seemed to lean forward. It was all in her imagination, she realised, because as she quickly veiled her eyes, she thought, ooh, he was going to kiss her, and just then she didn't seem to have the strength to tell him she was more interested in her calculator than his kisses! Instead Gideon ambled over to the door through which he had just come in. 'In line with our togetherness policy, of letting one half know what the other half is doing, I've a very early appointment tomorrow and will be on my way before you're down to breakfast.'

'Thanks very much for letting me know,' Ellena smiled; there was nothing wrong with her manners. She wished she could say the same about the female he had just awakened in her who, with very small encouragement from him, was feeling extremely wayward—not to say wanton!

It took her a long time to get to sleep that night, and when she awakened the next morning she was still feeling restless. She had a moment's respite when she went up to the nursery and observed again how her niece was positively blossoming under the devoted care she was receiving.

That feeling of being unsettled was back with her again when she sat eating a brief but solitary breakfast. In a way she was glad that Gideon had left early. Somehow, and she could still feel the intimate warm touch of his hands through the thin silk of her covering, she was still feeling very much confused by the way she had wanted him to continue to massage, caress... Oh, grief. She closed her mind to such thoughts and went to work.

It was useless to run away, though, she discovered. For around mid-morning Andrea came to see her and said Cliff Wilkinson had been on the phone saying he'd be in town in the early evening, and would she meet him for dinner when they could discuss a problem he was having.

'Oh, dear,' Ellena sympathised, aware Andrea had been badly hurt in her marriage and was just not interested in giving any other man a chance.

'Precisely! I shall have to go—I can't get out of this one,' Andrea said, plainly trying to keep her personal feelings separate from business. 'But I've told him, since his problem seems to be quite involved, that I would bring an associate along.'

'He didn't like that?' Ellena guessed.

'He huffed and puffed. But in the end he agreed—provided it's you I bring with me. I know that, technically speaking, you're still on your honeymoon—which, of course, if I read the man correctly, is why he specifically stated you and no one else...'

'Clearly thinking that there was no way I'd want to miss dinner with my husband.' Ellena put in, and, smiling, added, 'I'd be delighted to prove Mr Wilkinson wrong.'

'I'll make it up to you,' Andrea promised gratefully.

'No need,' Ellena assured her, and when Andrea had left knew that because of their togetherness she should ring Gideon and let him know she would be late home. But then she recalled his touch, the way she had felt—and she was confused again.

Good manners were prodding at her, though, so that in the end she dialled Oakvale and spoke with Mrs Morris, explaining that she would not be at dinner, and asked her to mention it to Mr Langford.

'I couldn't get him at his office or on his mobile,' she perjured her soul, then heard that Violette had given the housekeeper the most gorgeous smile when Mrs Morris popped into the nursery "just for a minute", and felt warmed at yet another indication that everyone was spoiling Violette dreadfully.

Having covered herself for dinner, however, Ellena found that thoughts of Gideon constantly came between her and her work that day. So much so, that she found she was running late.

It had been her intention to drive to her flat, check her post and from there drive to the smart hotel where Cliff Wilkinson was staying for their seven o'clock dinner appointment.

That was the first of her plans which went wrong. It was

an easy adjustment, though, to decide to pay a visit to her flat after dinner rather than before. Ellena was still at her desk at six when Andrea, who wasn't going home first either, came into her office looking green.

'Migraine,' she said faintly.

Ellena got her to the couch in the restroom, but could see that her boss was going nowhere but to her bed. 'I'll ring Cliff and cancel, then I'll drive you home,' Ellena took charge.

Only she found that, for all she was looking and feeling ghastly, Andrea was still able to make decisions. 'Don't cancel. He's important,' she decided.

Ellena didn't want to cause her any more hassle. 'I'll ring and tell him I'll be delayed,' she agreed soothingly. 'I'll take you home and…'

But Andrea had worked long and hard to get her business off the ground, and although in Ellena's book there was not the remotest chance that Cliff Wilkinson would go to another accountancy firm, Andrea stated the situation as she saw it. 'He's going to be offended that I'm not there—I'm not having him finishing with us because my representative turns up late.'

'You're not fit to drive!' Ellena argued.

'I couldn't if I tried!' Andrea agreed, going on to say she'd had these attacks before, she'd taken medication, and that a lie-down with the lights out for an hour or so would work wonders. 'By the time you're thinking of having coffee, I'll be home and in bed,' she assured her.

Contrary to her employer's opinion that Cliff Wilkinson would be offended that she wasn't there, once Ellena had assured him over dinner how genuine Andrea's migraine was, Cliff was more concerned than anything else.

'You say she's still at the office?'

'She should be coming out of it by now.'

'I'll go and see if she'll let me drive her home,' he promptly stated, and would have been off like a shot had

Ellena not been able to convince him that what Andrea needed just then was utter quiet and darkness.

'She's promised me that in the event this attack doesn't soon clear, she'll call a taxi,' Ellena assured him—and was still assuring him when their first course arrived.

It took until the main course for them to get down to business, and Ellena became engrossed in his plan to extend some of his development to the London area.

By the pudding stage they were deep into discussion, with Ellena pointing out a financial aspect which, for all his business acumen, Cliff hadn't seemed to have thought of. 'Now I know why I need accountants,' he smiled, and Ellena smiled back—but, on glancing away, she looked up—staggeringly—straight into a pair of slate-grey eyes!

At that moment she felt that her heart would stop. Gideon! What was he doing here? There was, however, no time for her to think further. Goodness, he was looking furious about something! And, oh, help, he was coming over to their table!

Ellena had lost track completely of what Cliff Wilkinson was saying, and stared mesmerised as Gideon, not interested in being introduced, apparently, stopped at their table and, his pleasant tone much at variance with the hostility she saw in his steel-grey scrutiny, smiled. 'Hello, darling,' he greeted her, going on smoothly, 'Sorry I missed you at breakfast. I've something on, so can't stay, but I'll see you at home later.' With that, and without the smallest acknowledgment to her dinner partner, he turned abruptly about—and was gone.

Ellena was still feeling floored when she became aware that Cliff had just said something. She stared at him. 'Was that your husband?' he asked, and Ellena rapidly came to.

'I'm sorry. I would have introduced you, only…'

'Only he was in something of a hurry,' Cliff said soothingly.

Ellena didn't want soothing. Having got her second

wind, she was starting to get angry. She hadn't misunderstood the hostility in Gideon's eyes, she knew she hadn't,
nor his fury either. Who did he think he was? Did he think
he was the only one allowed business dinners?

'I shouldn't have insisted that you come,' Cliff was going on.

Oh, grief, he was starting to sound guilty. 'Yes, you
should. And I'm very happy to be of assistance,' she
smiled. But she started to have some very dark thoughts
about Gideon Langford, husband and swine!

'And I've enjoyed your company,' Cliff replied handsomely. 'But now I think I've taken up enough of your
time. You must be longing to get back to your home and
new husband.'

She'd trained for five years for this! To be sent home
because she had some 'loving' man in the background. Like
hell she'd go home! But their business was as near complete as made no difference. So she smiled and chatted—
and hoped to see Gideon Langford on her way crossing the
foyer, so she could give him a swift, hard kick on the shins.
However, of the man she had married there was no sign.

Outside the hotel Cliff Wilkinson escorted her to her car.
'Thank you for a very pleasant dinner,' Ellena said, shaking
hands with him. 'If you need to know anything further, I'll
be very pleased to help.'

By the time she arrived at her flat, Cliff Wilkinson was
long gone from her mind. What right had Gideon Langford
to be mad at her? She'd done nothing wrong!

Her spirits dipped when she saw there was nothing in
her post from Justine—but she refused to lose heart. She
turned her thoughts on Andrea and wondered about phoning her. If her medication was working, though, she could
be tucked up in bed and fast asleep. Ellena decided against
it—and Gideon Langford, never absent for long, was back
in her mind.

How dared he? She gave quite some angry thought to

staying the night at her flat, and was still angry when she decided against it. Apart from anything else, should Pamela Langford have her scouts about, there was still their to-getherness to consider.

It was approaching midnight when, having worked her-self up into a fine state, Ellena pulled up at Oakvale. Who did he think he was? she fumed again as she quietly entered the house. For all his smiling mouth, it was a slur on her professionalism to have him stand there glaring at her while she was dining with a client.

She climbed the stairs and went silently along the landing to her room. She wasn't having it; she wasn't! She shrugged out of her suit jacket, going to her wardrobe for a hanger. First thing tomorrow, at breakfast, she would tell Mr Furious-for-no-reason-Langford where he got off.

She hung up her jacket. First thing tomorrow she'd… She heard the sound of a door opening—she swung round! She wasn't going to have to wait until tomorrow! Framed in the open communicating door, Gideon stood there. Being furious, if his expression was anything to go by, was not her sole right.

She attempted to get in first, but he beat her to it. 'Where the hell have you been?' he demanded.

He wasn't wearing a watch. In fact, if his bare legs and what she could see of his bare chest were anything to go by, he wasn't wearing anything at all very much underneath the black towelling robe he had on.

'You know where I've been!' she snapped, dragging her eyes from the dark exposed hair on his chest.

'Till this hour?' he snarled aggressively, coming away from the doorway and further into her room.

She nearly reminded him that she was twenty-two, not sixteen, but she fell back on sarcasm instead. 'What hap-pened to "Hello, darling"?' What in creation had *he* got to be mad about?

He ignored her question. 'We had an agreement!' he rapped. 'No cosy twosomes with the opposite sex.'

'Cosy twosome!' she exploded. 'He was a client!'

'Huh!' Gideon grunted, clearly not believing her. She could have hit him.

'We were discussing business!'

'It looked like it!'

'We were having a business dinner!' Why the Dickens was she bothering to explain? It was his jugular that should be gone for, not hers!

'From where I was standing, another half-hour and you'd have been *eating* each other!'

'How dare you?' She might have said more, but a look of such fury came over his expression that her words dried in her throat as he came forward, and she backed away.

'That's where you've been, isn't it?' he demanded. 'To your flat. To...' Enraged, he grabbed her wrists. 'While I've...'

'Don't talk rot!' she yelled. 'And don't judge me by your own over-sexed standards!'

'Over-sexed!' Gideon let go of her wrists as though her skin burned him. Then he shook his head, as if not quite believing any of this.

Ellena took the opportunity to get in quickly before he could draw breath. 'I went to my flat, yes—but alone.' And, enraged with herself suddenly, she continued, 'Why the devil am I explaining any of this to you? You're the one in the wrong, not me!'—and saw straight away that Gideon hadn't taken very kindly to that.

'Me!' he roared. 'I'm not the one who's out half the night playing the field.'

'Playing the field!' Oh, she so nearly hit him then. 'Listen, you!' she snapped furiously. 'If Cliff Wilkinson is interested in anybody, it's my boss, not me. My boss, incidentally, who was scheduled to come with us, only she got flattened by a migraine attack at almost the last—' Ellena broke off—she was explaining! Dammit, she was explaining, when she should be going for his throat! 'Don't you ever do anything like that again!' she told him off well and truly.

Much did it bother him! He didn't bat an eyelid but was instantly and aggressively firing at her, 'You couldn't ring? You couldn't let me know in advance that—'

She was not going to have blame put at her door—she was not. 'I rang Mrs Morris!' she cut him off short.

Those slate-grey glistening hard eyes narrowed. 'You're not married to Mrs Morris!' he snarled icily.

'With luck, I won't be married to you for much longer!' she hurled back.

His look went from icy to arctic. 'We're stuck with each other and you know it!' he clipped curtly, and it was obvious to Ellena from his remark that he was more than a little fed up with their arrangement. 'You do anything to jeopardise my claim to my brother's child, and—' He broke off when Ellena, her fury abruptly departing, was left feeling defeated suddenly, left feeling most unexpectedly dangerously close to tears. Hurriedly she turned her back on him.

'I...' She tried to speak, but was too full of emotion and found she needed all her strength to battle to regain control. She'd just die if she broke down in tears while Gideon was there.

She was still striving for control and wishing the Gideon would go back to his own room and leave her when, to prove that he was still right behind her, his hands came to her shoulders.

She could feel his touch, warm, firm but oddly gentle, through the cream silk of her blouse. He turned her to face him. She didn't want to look at him, but seemed compelled to. From unhappy blue eyes she looked up, fully expecting to see him tough and aggressive but, to her surprise, she could see not an atom of aggressiveness about him—and, even more surprisingly, there was nothing in his steady gaze but understanding.

'You've been so brave,' he said softly. She shook her head, denying, wanting to tell him that he was the rock she leaned on.

'No,' she whispered, their argument, its cause, suddenly meaning nothing. Gideon still had his hands on her shoulders as, instinctively, she put her hands on his waist.

She tried to smile. It was a poor effort. Gideon bent his head, and kissed her. It was a gentle yet lingering meeting of mouths. His arms came about her. She put her arms about him, and as their kiss broke she laid her head against him for a few moments.

Then she looked up into warm slate-grey eyes. Gently, tenderly, slowly, with their arms still about each other, they kissed again. And, as that dreamlike kiss ended, Ellena looked up at Gideon once more. All her anxieties seemed to vanish while she was in his arms and she felt she wanted to stay there for ever. But—this would never do.

She stepped back, her arms falling away from him. Gideon's hands were now at her waist. 'Goodnight,' she said huskily.

'Will you be all right?' he asked.

'Yes. Fine,' she answered.

He searched into her eyes for perhaps ten seconds longer. Then, 'Goodnight, my dear,' he said, and left her.

CHAPTER SIX

ELLENA awakened on Thursday morning and without conscious thought touched her fingers to her lips. Never had she known a kiss as gentle. Giving, comforting—little short of wonderful.

A sound in the next-door room brought her fully awake. It was Thursday, a work day, she hadn't time to lay here dreaming. Swiftly she left her bed and headed for the shower. Yet—dreaming aside—she could not remove the feel of those tender kisses from her mind.

They weren't supposed to kiss, she and Gideon, not like that! And certainly not at all when it was not for the benefit of anyone watching, but just for the solace of each other. Oh, help, what was happening?

Ellena knew that they should not have kissed, but yet—it had seemed so right. They were both in their own way, and privately, quite desperately trying not to believe that the worst had happened to their siblings. But it had only taken a mention of his brother's child—her sister's child—for her to fold.

Ellena left her shower and got dressed, knowing that their gently exchanged kisses had been a warm consoling of each other, no more. Just an attempt to soothe their inner disquiet.

But, having fairly logically disposed of any questions that had been aroused by the fact she had felt she had wanted to stay in his arms for ever, Ellena recalled how she had flown at him to start with. Had that been her, normally quiet, calm and even-tempered yelling at him? Heavens above, she was starting not to recognise herself!

Abruptly, wearing a blue suit and crisp white shirt,

Ellena left her room. She was halfway down the stairs, though, when she suddenly started to feel all churned up inside at the thought of seeing Gideon again.

She swallowed hard on nerves she didn't know she had and made herself go on. She went briskly, matter-of-factly, into the breakfast room. Gideon was already there. He lowered the paper he was reading. Quickly she went to her usual seat.

There was no sign of the housekeeper. 'Good morning,' Ellena greeted him primly.

Gideon did not take up his paper again but put it from him and studied her for a moment, before, to her dismay, he said sincerely, 'I was out of order last night. I apologise that...'

'You're apologising for those kisses we—' She broke off. They were kisses she wanted to remember—she felt bitterly let down that he was saying sorry about the comfort given and received.

But—she'd got it wrong! And, it seemed, Gideon was annoyed that she could think the way she had. 'You expect me to apologise for something that was warm, and spontaneous—and beautiful?' he demanded sharply.

He'd thought that too! She didn't care that he was cross with her. 'You know, Langford, if you tried really hard, I could quite get to like you,' she answered mischievously.

Gideon stared at her, his glance going to her mouth tugging up at the corners. His own lips started to twitch—and Mrs Morris came in. He was still looking at Ellena when he stood up. 'Bye, sweetheart,' he murmured, planted a husbandly kiss on her cheek and, picking up his paper, he went.

Went, leaving Ellena wondering about this new person inside her who had stirred into life since knowing him. The person, the imp who, without her volition said things like '...if you tried really hard, I could quite get to like you'.

Ellena passed a few pleasantries with the housekeeper,

but when a little later she left the breakfast room herself and started up the stairs, she suddenly started to wonder about something else. Every morning, on leaving her room, she would, without fail, go up to the nursery. This morning, with thoughts of Gideon Langford so much in her head, her visit to the nursery had gone completely from her mind!

Having rectified that omission, Ellena drove to work in a pensive mood. Cool it! sprang to mind. Gideon was taking up too much time in her head of late. Their marriage had nothing to do with feelings for each other, but was a necessity for their own ends, and she must remember that. Quite why she was giving herself this lecture, Ellena was unsure. She should not have to remind herself that the sole and only reason she and Gideon had gone through that marriage ceremony was in order to ensure that—should it come to it—some judge would consider they, with their joint family tie to Violette, would be a better choice to be her guardians than Russell and his avaricious wife.

Determining that never again would she put her arms around Gideon and enjoy the strength of his arms about her—and kissing when no one else was around was *definitely* out—Ellena parked her car and went to the offices of A. Keyte and Company.

Her first port of call, however, was not her own office. 'How are you feeling?' she asked Andrea when she dropped in to see her.

'As good as new,' Andrea answered, and indeed looked it.

'Is it convenient for you to hear my report about my meeting with Cliff last night?' Ellena asked.

'No need.'

'No need?' Why was Andrea looking what Ellena could only think of as a little bashful?

'Well actually, Cliff showed up here last night.'

Ellena was intrigued. She went and took a seat near

Andrea's desk. She wanted to hear more. 'He came here after I had dinner with him? You were still here?'

Andrea nodded. 'I was feeling heaps better by that time and was down in the car park and about to drive home when Cliff turned up.' Ellena was absorbed. Andrea went on. 'Anyhow, despite my arguments, he said I still looked a degree under, and insisted on tailing me home.'

'What a nice man he is,' Ellena commented.

'That wasn't what I was thinking when, every time I looked in my rear view mirror, there he was. Although...' Andrea hesitated for a moment or two, and Ellena thought she wasn't going to say any more. But, all at once, she started to confide, 'Although, when we left the bright lights behind, it suddenly started to be comforting to have Cliff's headlights in my rear view mirror. And, by the time we got to my place, yes, I confess it, I had started to think myself what an extremely nice person he was. And then, as we both got out of our cars, it seemed the height of churlishness when he was miles away from his hotel to give him a curt goodnight and leave him standing there.'

'You invited him in?'

'And was staggered when he insisted I put my feet up while he made me some sandwiches and something to drink. I'm amazed that a man could be so kind!'

Gideon was kind, Ellena found herself thinking when she went along to her own office. Grief! Stop thinking about him! Get on with some work, do!

Ellena went home that night still determined to cool it. Fat chance! Gideon seemed to have something on his mind and, while courteous to her in every way, he seemed to be too preoccupied with his own thoughts to want to chat. Fine, that suited her perfectly!

'I've an appointment in an hour,' he deigned to inform her at the end of their meal.

Business, I trust! 'I'll say goodnight, then,' she returned

as coolly as she got, and, getting to her feet, she headed for the door.

She had some work she could be doing. Feeling perverse, she went and spent some time in the nursery. Beverly was on duty that night and Violette was awake with no sign of going to sleep. Ellena was able to play with her for some while.

Ellena saw very little of Gideon in the next few days. They shared meals together but neither of them was very chatty, and the meals invariably ended with Gideon going to his study and Ellena going to the nursery.

The weekend passed in that fashion and on Monday Ellena drove to her office and owned to feeling extremely down. She tried to lose herself in her work, but couldn't. She gave up trying when, at three that afternoon, her phone rang, and she heard the all-masculine tones of the man who was taking up far too much space in her thoughts.

'Ellena?'

She recognised his voice at once.

'Gideon?'

'I've just had a call from home.' Home. What a lovely sound that was.

But, 'What's wrong?' she questioned urgently, instantly all attention.

'Nothing at all,' he straight away calmed her fears. 'Other than, as you know, Beverly's having an extended weekend off, and Marjorie Dale has just phoned to say her daughter has come home from university, upset about something or other and in need of a little tender loving care.'

'Marjorie wants some time off?' Ellena guessed.

'I've told her to take as long as she needs—she says she's sure to be back tomorrow. Meanwhile she'd had a word with Mrs Morris, who's said she can cope quite well on her own, but...'

He didn't have to finish. 'I'll go home now,' Ellena told him.

'You're lovely,' he said softly, and she felt warmed as much by the fact that it seemed there was a thaw in the coolness between them, as by his comment.

Nonsense! 'Goodbye!' she said crisply, and put the phone down and went in search of Andrea.

Ellena spent a delightful time with Violette, who was at her charming best. She was still in the nursery when, around seven that evening, Gideon came home and came up to see how she was faring.

'You seem to be coping,' he observed.

'A piece of cake,' she answered casually. 'Er—I forgot to mention to Mrs Morris... Would you mind telling her that I won't be dining downstairs?'

'I'll bring your meal up to the nursery,' he offered, not exactly weeping, she noted, that he was to be deprived of her company at dinner. 'I could have my meal up here with you,' he offered after a moment.

A smile beamed inside her suddenly. She at once denied it. 'You don't think that's carrying togetherness a little too far?' she queried coolly.

'I merely thought I might spend some time with my niece,' he replied, his chilly tone beating her offhandedness hollow—and then he ambled out.

That puts you in your place! Oh, what she would have given to thumb her nose at his back. Thaw, my foot! Her inner smile had died, but she wouldn't let him get to her; she wouldn't.

She smiled prettily at him when he delivered her tray, and thanked him nicely. No way was he going to know that his smallest remark had the power to hurt her.

'Oh, by the way...' she said just as he was leaving. He halted and favoured her with an aloof look, and Ellena almost told him to forget it. But, knowing him, he'd only want to know, 'Forget what?' and that would make too big an issue of it. 'I could do with some male muscle around half-nine, tennish.'

His aloof look disappeared. 'I'm intrigued,' he drawled when she hesitated to tell him why.

Beverly had a lovely self-contained apartment on this floor, but it was private. As was the large bed-sitting room which was allocated to Marjorie Dale. And, while there was an exceptionally good baby alarm which was plugged into the room of whoever was on duty, and Ellena could easily have transferred it to her own, she had not the smallest intention of doing so. Just as she had not the smallest intention of leaving the small mite to sleep on this floor all on her own tonight. And, since it was going to take quite some of Gideon's valuable time from his work in his study to have her double bed moved up to this floor, the answer was obvious.

But, feeling he would think her over-protective, Ellena grew belligerent, and let him know she was not going to take any nonsense when she informed him, 'Violette will be out of her cot for her last feed around that time. I'd like her cot dismantled and carried downstairs.'

Gideon seemed only a little less intrigued. 'Presumably, madam,' he mocked, letting her know he wasn't very good at taking orders—she had never supposed he was—'you'll want it reassembling elsewhere?'

'You know where my bedroom is, I believe,' she answered crisply.

And could have thumped him when he muttered something that sounded suspiciously like, 'Now, there's an invitation!' But his expression was bland when he went on to question, 'You're intending the infant should sleep in your room tonight?'

Ellena sensed trouble. 'You can put her cot in your room if you prefer,' she replied sweetly. But, brooking no argument, she told him fiercely, 'There's no way the little one is going to sleep up here on her own!'

He stared at her flashing blue eyes. 'You're a dragon!' he accused.

'No, I'm not!' she denied.

He smiled suddenly—her heart flipped crazily. She wanted to smile back. 'Did you fight your sister's battles like this?' he wanted to know.

Tears sprang to her eyes. She looked away. Who else in the space of moments could have her laughing and crying? 'Clear off!' she ordered.

'And we haven't been married a month!' he sighed—but went. And Ellena no longer felt like crying, but wanted to laugh.

Beverly had told her that Violette slept all through the night now. By the time she had the baby settled and asleep in her room, Ellena was ready to sleep the night through herself. A tiny scrap Violette might be, but it was amazing how much energy was required to cope with all her needs.

So why, if she was so tired, couldn't she sleep? Ellena lay in her bed willing sleep to come. But it evaded her. She tried to make her mind a blank, but all she kept thinking of was Gideon. Tough, cool, sharp—smiling. Hateful, icy, aloof—charming. Who else did she know who could so easily change her mood? No one. His grin, his laugh—oh, drat the man!

She had heard him come up the stairs, making as little noise as he could, in view of the baby in the next-door bedroom. He'd have been asleep for ages by now! Were it not for her infant guest, Ellena felt she would have put her light on and read a chapter from a book or something. Her only option was to lie there.

It was around three o'clock when she finally drifted off into a deep, exhausted sleep. But only to be dragged rudely half awake at half past three by a light in the room—which *she* hadn't left on.

'Ellena!' She came a little further awake to hear her

name spoken. 'Come on, wake up!' the male voice urged. 'It's been crying, and it's wet!'

Ellena came fully awake. She opened her eyes fully. Gideon was in her room, the centre light was on and he had Violette in his arms. Poor love, how long had she been crying and she hadn't heard her? Instinctively she wanted to go and take charge. She controlled the instinct. He wanted to spend more time with his niece. Let him!

'Change her, then,' she said prettily, and, closing her eyes, snuggled down.

'Aw, come on, Ellena!' he pleaded.

Beg! She opened her eyes again. He was robe-clad, as she'd seen him once before—and didn't look at all comfortable as he awkwardly held the damp bundle. 'Ask me nicely,' she suggested, all huge eyes and innocent.

'Please!' he said.

Ellena was considering his request when the matter was settled for her. The baby started to cry—and instinct could no longer be denied. In a flash she had whipped her bedclothes back.

She saw Gideon's glance leave her face and go to the thin, almost transparent material of her nightdress, her pink-tipped breasts seeming to momentarily fascinate him. A small squeak of a sound escaped her as she rapidly whipped the sheet over her again.

Gideon was the first to speak, his glance back on her face again, easing her embarrassment as he offered, 'Can I do anything to help?'

'You can shut your eyes for a start!' she snapped, and had chance to get herself together when he presented her with his back. 'Give her to me,' she said when, out of bed and decently robe-clad, she was ready to take charge.

It took all of a half-hour to get the baby attended to. To his credit, Gideon just didn't return to his own room and leave her to it, but did all the fetching and carrying Ellena needed from the nursery. And when Violette was once

more comfortable and nodding off to sleep, he held the
baby while Ellena tidied away and washed her hands.

'Bliss,' Ellena whispered, the infant back in her cot again
and looking positively angelic. They stepped away from her
cot and, the communicating door open, Ellena switched on
her bedside table lamp and went and snapped off the main
bedroom light switch. There was still ample light coming
from a lamp in Gideon's room. She felt sensitive to him
for some reason, and quietly apologised, 'I'm sorry Violette
woke you.' A hard worker herself, she was very much
aware of how tired he must be. 'I didn't hear her crying.'

'I thought all women had an inbuilt baby alarm,' he replied softly.

'Mine must be on the blink,' she whispered lightly, and
prepared to wish him goodnight—only somehow he came
nearer to go to his room, and since she was still by the light
switch and the communicating door, they somehow seemed
to bump into each other.

He automatically put out a hand to save her from a stum-
ble—his touch electric! 'Ellena!' he murmured—she wasn't
sure that she didn't breathe his name, too. What she was
sure about was that she didn't mind one tiny bit when, as
if compelled, Gideon started to draw her to him.

Gently they kissed and instantly she felt her heart ease.
His strong arms came around her thinly clad body, and he
held her to him. Ellena's arms seemed to go round him of
their own accord. Gideon broke his kiss and looked down
into her bemused face.

His head came down again, his lips once more on her
own. Yet, something different was there. His kiss was gentle still, but something—was happening—and Ellena welcomed it.

Gideon's arms about her grew firmer; he moved her with
him through the doorway and into his room. And suddenly
the tenor of his kisses was changing. While still giving, his
lips were also demanding.

Ellena was happy to give. At least, she thought she was. There was no thought in her head telling her to back away, at any rate, so taken up was she in the thrill, the passion of his kisses. She had no notion that they were moving, subtly moving, towards his bed. Again and again they kissed, and then Gideon was gently moving her to lie down.

He did not leave her, but lay down with her, his body next to hers, his wonderful hand caressing her shoulders, his kisses to her throat making her want to arch herself closer to him.

Ellena followed her instincts and pressed herself against him. She heard a kind of a groan escape him, and started to feel nervous that, just as Gideon had ignited a fire within her, she seemed to have power to do something to him too.

His hand caressed to the firm fullness of her breasts. 'Gideon!' she breathed—and pulled away while she had a modicum of strength.

Immediately he removed his hand from her breast. 'Am I going too fast for you, sweetheart?' he asked softly.

It was the endearment that did it! He had called her sweetheart before, but only so Mrs Morris should hear and think them head over heels in love. 'I—I don't think this is a very good idea,' Ellena gasped, struggling to sit up.

There was one terribly tense moment when she thought Gideon might not let her go. But let her go he did—and then she half wished he hadn't. 'Up to now, your manners have been impeccable,' he grunted.

'It's not done to feel yes but say no?' she queried.

He gave a short bark of laughter. 'At least you're not denying what you feel,' he commented. After the way she had clung to him she didn't see how she could! Anyhow, she had an idea he had sufficient knowledge about women to know exactly how she was feeling. 'Just denying me,' he added—but, she noted, not sounding very unhappy about it.

He got off the bed and reached down and helped her off

it. 'Are you going to forgive me my appallingly bad manners?' she asked.

'Never,' he replied.

Briefly, they kissed. His hands tightened on her waist.
He gave her a small push. It was what she needed.

'Goodnight,' she said, and swiftly left him, hoping that,
though he knew all about women, he had no idea of how
she yearned to be with him always.

There were not many hours to go before she got up and
started her day. She spent them in wonder at this all-
consuming love for Gideon that had come to her unsought,
and also in earnestly hoping that she could get through this
marriage and divorce without him ever discovering the
depth of her feeling for him.

How she had come to fall in love with him she had no
idea. She supposed, thinking back, that something had
started to stir in her that day he had called at her flat and
had spoken of marriage. She had thought he meant marriage to someone else and, she easily recalled, she hadn't
liked it.

Ellena felt torn in two: she loved Gideon, but he didn't
love her, and would probably die laughing at the very idea.
She tried to find rest in sleep. She had just nodded off when
Violette decided that she wanted to start her day. Ellena
went over to the cot, picked Violette up and hugged the
lovely, precious bundle to her.

Ellena was late getting to her office—she would have
been surprised if she'd been on time! She was busy with
Violette so didn't get down to breakfast until after Gideon
had left for his office. He had poked his head round the
communicating door to tell her he was off—Ellena, feeling
decidedly pink about the ears, had kept her head bent and
doubly concentrated on the baby.

'I—may be late this evening,' he'd remarked.

'Fine,' she'd answered, loving him with all of her being.
He had gone and she'd taken the baby with her to the

window and watched, catching a glimpse of his good-looking face as he'd steered his car to the front of the house and had gone down the drive.

She was still at the window with Violette when she saw Marjorie Dale hurrying up the drive. Beverly was due back this afternoon. Everything was getting back to normal—though since her discovery of her love for Gideon, Ellena felt things would never be normal for her again.

'Are you sure you should be here?' she asked Marjorie Dale before she handed Violette over. 'Your daughter…'

'She's fine,' Marjorie beamed. 'Hannah's a home-loving girl and felt in the need of a bit of reassurance. I've just seen her off now, but she'll be home again in no time when her university term ends. She wanted some of her mum's cooking and a cuddle to keep her going until then.'

What a lovely family they must be, Ellena mused. For all she had been late in, she sat staring out of her office window, her thoughts on anything but her work. Marjorie had said she'd get Ted Morris to give her a hand with taking the cot up to the nursery… Ellena wanted Justine home, home safe. Wanted her family back. Ellena took heart when she recalled how Gideon had once warmed her by saying that she was family. How generous of him to say that—the thought of marrying had not occurred to him then. How kind he… Gideon was back in her head.

She'd had a late start, she was tired, and Gideon kept coming between her and her work. Ellena was still trying to catch up when Andrea popped in and a business discussion followed, during which Andrea revealed that one of the small and discreet out-of-the-way hotels they did some work for had been in touch and were anxious to have some of their books back.

'I was working on that account only half an hour ago,' Ellena smiled, and, since the hotel was on the way to her flat, she offered, 'I'll drop them in if you like.'

'They're a bit short-staffed, or they'd send someone over.'

'No problem,' Ellena assured her.

Nor was it. That was, delivering the books and having a small and friendly conversation with the pleasant woman who did the hotel's books amongst a dozen other jobs, was no problem. What was a problem, though, a most infuriating one, was that, having left the book-keeper's office, briefcase in hand, Ellena walked back through the hotel and, in the open lounge area on her left, saw the man she was married to sitting in deep and absorbed conversation with a most stunning brunette!

Barely able to believe her eyes, Ellena stopped dead in her tracks. This wasn't the kind of hotel Gideon would normally use; she would swear to it! So what was he doing in this out-of-the-way, small but discreet type of establishment? Ellena reckoned she knew full well what he was doing there, and such a feeling of fury and sickness engulfed her at that moment that she was barely conscious of what she was doing.

'I may be late this evening,' he'd said. Now she knew why! What she should do, Ellena knew full well, was to get out of there before Gideon turned round and saw her. No chance! Besides, Gideon was so taken up with what the brunette was saying, Ellena reckoned that the ceiling could fall in about his ears and he'd never notice it.

And that made her angrier than ever. But it was the sick feeling in the pit of her stomach that was her prime motivator as, sick beyond bearing, Ellena took a left turn into the lounge area.

Gideon looked startled to see her. Well, he would, wouldn't he? He thought she was miles away, playing happy families! He rose to his feet; tall, good-looking, and he was a swine—a swine, swine, swine, and she loved, loved, loved him.

'Hello, darling,' Ellena smiled, ignoring his companion—to hell with manners! 'I'm in something of a rush,' she beamed at his surprised countenance. 'I couldn't get you at the office, but, if you see Nanny before I'm home, would you remind her that our baby alarm isn't working?' That would settle his hash! Explain that, Daddy!

She was out of there before he had chance to draw breath. Not that he was likely to introduce the brunette!

Ellena was in her flat before she had cooled down sufficiently to start to be appalled by what she had just done! Oh, no, she hadn't, had she? The fact that there was still no communication from her sister had taken some of her steam away but, as the minutes after that slowly ticked away, Ellena owned that what she'd done had been totally crass.

Only then, when anger had departed, leaving only that sick feeling in its wake, did she realise what it was that had motivated her back there at that hotel, what that sick feeling was. She had been jealous! Unthinking, unseeing, acting on pure, blind, outraged jealousy. Oh, Lord—now what?

Well, she couldn't return to Oakvale, that was for sure. She thought of Violette. Well, not for a while anyhow. But she wouldn't be surprised if it had gone midnight when Gideon came home. And, cringe though she might, there didn't seem any good reason why—when, because of the baby, she was going to return anyway—she shouldn't go home now.

This love she bore Gideon had turned her world upside down. Never had she known she was capable of acting as she had. She'd have said she hadn't a jealous bone in her body—but look at her!

Ellena set out for Oakvale, unsure quite when the house had become home, and the flat she had always considered home had become 'the flat', but she had more serious things on her mind during that drive. What in creation was she going to say to Gideon the next time she saw him?

As she had anticipated, and she was sat on thorns until

she knew for sure, Gideon had not arrived home yet. Ellena went through all the motions of appearing as if everything was normal. She went up to the nursery and spent some time with Violette and Beverly, asking everyday questions about the baby's welfare, about Beverly's welfare. She left the nursery to go to the dining room, even managing to eat some of her meal and appear as if none of it was about to choke her.

But, when she retired to her room that night, she was still no further forward with regard to what sort of an excuse she could give to Gideon—and she did not mistake that he would come looking for one, because of her jealous outburst.

It was about eleven o'clock when she showered and got into her night things and calculated that since she wouldn't see Gideon until the morning she'd better use these in-between hours to think up something. Whatever happened, he must never know that jealousy had been the root cause.

It was too late now to wish that she hadn't done it. She had an idea that Gideon admired her honesty, and she valued his good opinion. But what honesty was there in telling him, in front of a stranger, that their mechanical baby alarm was broken when it wasn't? When it was only his reference last night to the female, built-in baby alarm system—hers had manifestly failed to go off—that had brought forth her outright lie.

At eleven-fifteen, and in utter desperation to forget that she had been jealous for an instant, Ellena went back over conversations, events and happenings—and, at last, felt she had something which might wash to explain her behaviour.

He'd done something similar to her, if she remembered rightly. That night she'd had dinner with Cliff Wilkinson to discuss business, Gideon had been furious because he thought she'd broken their agreement and was out on a date. Well—couldn't she claim the same thing?

In Gideon's case, of course, it *was* a girlfriend, *and* a

date. Obviously he was still concerned that his sister-in-law might have her spies about—hence the small, out-of-the-way hotel. Dastardly rat!

Gideon had once suggested that she'd be hell on earth once she got going—well, she couldn't argue that. Never would she have believed she could have acted the way she had tonight—oh, what had he thought? What was he thinking?

She was still sitting up in bed hugging her knees—what point was there in lying down when sleep was light years away?—when suddenly, into the silence of the night, she heard his car coming up the drive. Hastily she put out her bedside lamp. The light from his headlights swept her room. Oh, grief!

She heard him quietly enter the house. Perhaps he'd go and make himself a cup of coffee in the kitchen or something? But no. She heard him coming up the stairs—and realised she was barely breathing, which was ridiculous, she owned, because she wasn't going to see him that night. That communicating door would stay closed until just before she left for work in the morning, when *she* opened it.

With her ears tuned to the direction of that communicating door—just in case—Ellena had the shock of her life when, not having bothered to go into his own room first, Gideon came along the landing and entered hers.

'Oh!' she exclaimed in utter shock, her heart threatening to leap out of her body when, without so much as a by-your-leave, Gideon came in and switched on her bedroom light.

'Forgive the intrusion,' he apologised—oh, heavens, had there been a faint emphasis on that word 'intrusion'? 'I spotted your light on a minute or so ago—I didn't think you'd be asleep yet.' And, having taken away any excuse she had to protest, he stared at her for some long seconds, and then quietly said, 'Would you mind telling me what all that was about back at that hotel tonight?'

Oh, help! What had she planned to say? She couldn't remember! Ellena all at once became conscious of her flimsy attire and pulled the covers closer around her—she was still sitting and stayed that way, knowing she would feel far more vulnerable than she was already if she lay down.

'It's your prerogative, is it?' she somehow found the wit to challenge. He'd done something similar—that was it! 'Your *tête à tête* wasn't over dinner, though no doubt dinner followed.' Stop it, stop it, you're starting to sound jealous! 'Forgive my fib about the baby alarm,' she ploughed on—*attack, attack*—'I just wanted to establish that we both play by the same rules.'

'You think I was out—partying?'

'Whatever you like to call it,' she offered sarcastically.

'You're wrong!'

And the moon was made of Gorgonzola! 'Go on, tell me—you were putting Violette's name down for Cheltenham Ladies' College!'

Gideon moved away from the door, came nearer to her bed and stood looking down at her. Ellena didn't think she liked that very much. 'No,' he answered, his eyes scanning her face.

He made her nervous—help her, somebody! *Attack.* 'No?' she tossed back at him, anything rather than he should discover how dear he was to her, how very much she loved him, how green-eyed and sick she'd been to see him with the stunning brunette. Ellena got her second wind. 'Well, stap me, Sir Percy,' she taunted, 'if she wasn't your girlfriend—and it was *you* who stipulated we have no friends of the opposite sex, I believe, then...' She hesitated. He was still standing over her and she *was* feeling vulnerable. 'Then—oh, I know,' she went on, refusing to be browbeaten, 'it must have been our divorce lawyer.'

Oh, heck, what had she said? Up until that point she had been unable to read anything in Gideon's expression, save that he seemed determined to get to the bottom of her behaviour. But, at her last remark, his face darkened—and she could not mistake that he was exceedingly angry.

'You can forget *that*!' he snarled, so angry that he snaked out an arm, his right hand taking a hold of one of her wrists as if to underline his decree. 'I haven't…'

'Let go of me!' Ellena exploded in sudden panic. 'I don't care what you have or haven't. If…'

'Then you damn well should. This is about…'

'I know quite well what it's about!' She refused to let him dictate the terms. She might love the man with an intensity that had shaken her, but no way was she going to stay quiet and let him steamroller her. 'It's about you not needing as much "rest"—if you'll pardon the euphemism—as you thought. Well let me tell you something, Langford, if…'

'You don't know what you're talking about!'

'I may not have your superior brain, but I play fair!'

'What the hell do you mean by that?'

'Just that if I—um—abstain as part of our agreement, then it's unfair that…'

'How can you abstain from something which you've never tried?' he wanted to know, his fury all at once seeming to ebb, mockery taking its place.

There was no answer to that. 'You're still holding my wrist,' she complained.

His answer was to reach down and take hold of her other one. And, thus manacled, she glared at him. Much good did it do her! 'You were saying?' he mocked—and she wanted to hit him.

Wanted to hit him—and hold him. Oh, Gideon—she felt helpless. 'You're hurting me!' she stretched the truth a mile—and gained nothing, for Gideon did not let go his hold on her, which was what she had been after. But, coming to sit on the side of her bed, he gently brought her wrists to his mouth, and, one after the other, he kissed them.

Her heartbeat was already in overdrive. He had to let her go; he had to! Just a simple kiss to her wrists; just the fact of his lips against her skin seemed to be scrambling her brain power. 'Okay, so you've kissed and made it better—now go to bed,' she ordered, with what strength she had left.

Gideon stared at her for some moments, then with the very devil suddenly appearing in his eyes, he replied, 'Not until you kiss me, and make *me* better for the hurt you inflicted.'

She loved the way his mouth curved up at the corners, as if caught by some amusement. 'I never touched you!' she denied.

'You hurt my feelings.'

'How?'

'You accused me, unfairly, of breaking our no dating agreement.'

'She, the beautiful brunette, she wasn't—er—a rest cure?'

'You're a cheeky baggage,' Gideon informed her. But added what she wanted to know. 'It was—business of sorts—trust me.'

Ellena's heart instantly lightened. She wanted to believe him. In that moment of having him with her, of his seeming so sincere, she wanted to give him the benefit of the doubt.

'You win,' she smiled. 'Take it that I've kissed you better.'

'Oh, Ellena Langford—what do you take me for?' he reproached her, and while she was wallowing in bliss because he'd called her Ellena Langford—albeit that Langford was now her name—Gideon, still holding her wrists, pulled her gently to him and placed his mouth over hers.

And Ellena, her heart racing, knew that she should pull back. Knew it as soon as Gideon broke that kiss—but, somehow, she just could not. Nor, it seemed, could Gideon.

Their lips met again, unhurried, gentle still. And again they gently broke apart. 'G-goodnight,' she said—but seemed too transfixed to move backwards.

'Goodnight,' he replied, moved but a fraction away— and then, with a strangled kind of groan, took her in his arms.

Ellena went willingly, his touch, the feel of him as she put her arms about him, sending all logical thought fleeing. Gideon kissed her, drawing the very soul from her. She kissed him back and was enrapt, enchanted.

'Little love,' he called her, and she was floating.

She wanted to cry his name, but his mouth was over hers again. She wanted to get closer to him and stretched towards him, mindless of where the bedclothes were. She felt the warmth of him, felt burned by it, was enflamed by him.

Gently his hands caressed her back, his touch through her thin covering sending her into further raptures of delight. He held her yielding body to him—oh, utter bliss!

His hands caressed her shoulders as he kissed her and drew her very soul from her. She was vaguely aware that at some time his jacket and tie had been disposed of, and as he tenderly lay her down and came to lie down beside her, their feet entwined and Ellena realised that he had parted with his shoes and socks also.

'Sweet Ellena,' he breathed, his fingers in her hair, his body so close to hers. 'Sweet, sweet, Ellena.'

Her bones went to liquid. She melted under his touch as the caress of his fingers moved over her face, her throat. 'Gideon,' she whispered shyly, and loved him when he looked understandingly into her eyes, those wonderful direct slate-grey eyes seeming to say, Trust me.

And trust him she did. Tenderly he kissed her throat, her shoulders; he was aware, it seemed, of her every shy reaction. 'Don't be alarmed,' he soothed when his caressing fingers moved the thin strap of her nightdress down her arm.

'I'm not,' she smiled, and basked in his smile of encouragement which came a moment before he bent his head and traced gentle kisses from her shoulder to her breast.

Though she did clutch onto him when he captured her naked breast in his mouth. But the fire he had ignited started to burn out of control when, with his mouth, he moulded the swell of her creamy breast and its hardened pink tip, and she wanted more.

'Gideon,' she called his name.

He kissed her breast, and, raising his head, he smiled, 'Are you all right?' he asked softly, when she felt sure he must know that she was.

'Oh, yes,' she breathed and—for her, extremely bold— she confessed, 'I want to kiss you too.'

His look was gentle, understanding completely as he discarded his shirt. It was an utter joy to her to feel his naked chest beneath her hands. Side by side they lay together. She bent her head and kissed his nipples.

She looked up and was about to tell him that she loved him—only he kissed her. A kiss that demanded, received, and then gave so much. Ellena was lost in the wonder of it all.

Then their kiss broke. And, with shock, she realised that she hadn't a stitch on. 'What happened to my nightdress?' she questioned on a strangled gasp of sound—and Gideon grinned.

'Sweet love, you wriggled just a little—and I helped.'

She loved his grin but, shy again suddenly—and how she could be defeated her—she stayed close to him. Then discovered that somehow he had managed to remove his trousers. 'Did I...?' she questioned, as her bare legs mingled with his.

'I managed that by myself,' he murmured, and all was silent for a while then, as they kissed deeply.

Ellena felt his hands caressing her skin, and sighed with love and longing when with gentle fingers he caressed her breasts. She wanted to call his name again—but felt too full of love and longing to speak.

He raised his head, his eyes resting on her nakedness. 'You're so, so beautiful,' he breathed.

'Oh, Gideon,' she whispered—and, shyness getting the better of her, she rolled onto her side and against him, hiding her curves from his view. For some long moments they stayed like that, Gideon understanding of her reticence and not pushing her at a faster pace than she was happy with.

Together, breast against naked breast, legs entwined, feet caressing, they looked at each other. He kissed her, a tender, giving, small kiss. He held her in his arms, one hand straying to gently stroke the rich contour of her left buttock.

'Are you going to be mine?' he smiled down at her.

Her heart was near bursting with happiness. 'I—I want to be,' she answered nervously. 'But...'

'But?' he questioned, that hand on her behind stilling, warm and wonderful. She wanted to tell him that she didn't know how things went from here, that she was frightened that he might be disappointed that she didn't know very much. Well, she knew nothing, if it came to that. 'You're not going to go all bad-mannered on me again, are you?' he softly teased.

And Ellena so wished that he hadn't. Because it brought back memories of last night. And it was just as if, like last night, he had called her sweetheart again. 'Sweetheart'— that meant nothing to him. As this, their lovemaking, meant nothing to him—whereas it meant the whole world to her.

She kissed him, knowing that was getting in the way of feeling. She wanted to give and give, to be his—but 'sweetheart', his insincere 'sweetheart' was pounding in her head.

'What's wrong?' Of course, as she might have known, Gideon straight away sensed that something was very much amiss.

She took her arms from him. 'You're going to hate me,' she said chokily—and hated *him* when, lightning-sharp on the uptake, it seemed it was beneath him to attempt to persuade her against her wishes.

Though his voice was far from even, when, rolling away from her, he grunted, 'May I suggest that the next time you feel like committing yourself—sweetheart—you have your timing checked!'

And, with that word 'sweetheart' hanging so powerfully in the air as Gideon left her bed, Ellena felt it was beneath *her* to change her mind and, as her body still demanded, attempt to persuade him to stay.

CHAPTER SEVEN

NEVER had a night seemed so long! Out of sheer exhaustion Ellena realised she must have slept at some time, but she was awake long before dawn, and was again fretful.

Gideon had swallowed the explanation she had given him for her behaviour in that hotel last night. And, by now knowing something of the man he was, she had accepted, and trusted him, when he'd assured her that he and the brunette were discussing some business.

Jealousy tried again to get a grip—Ellena ousted it. She must believe him. Trust him—which was not why she was wide awake and fretful. She had kissed him and, from the love she bore him, had wanted to make love with him. And he, Gideon, had kissed her and had wanted to make love, only—he did not love her. He felt something physical for her, yes, but it was not love.

And she wanted him to love her—but she might just as well cry for the moon. Because he did not, and was never going to, love her. And so much for guarding her secret—she was terrified that in her responses to him last night she had given away something of how very much she loved him.

Ellena came out of the mental torment of her thoughts when she heard the muffled sound of movement coming from the next-door room. By the sound of it, Gideon couldn't sleep either.

To get up and start her day didn't seem a bad idea. At least it would give her something to do, something else to think about.

As if... Gideon was in her head the whole time she was in the shower, and all she had achieved when she was dressed was to realise that she would have time to spare—time to spend with Gideon over breakfast!

Grief, no! She had no idea how she was going to face him, much less spend a leisurely breakfast with him! She could, she suddenly realised, leave without breakfast. Cowardly perhaps, but might she not feel better able to face him when she'd had a day away from home, conversing with other people, putting in a day's work…?

Ellena knew she wasn't fooling anyone but herself. The way she was feeling now, she was never going to feel any better. She waited three minutes after she heard Gideon leave his room, then went and opened the communicating door. Then, briefcase in hand, she went up to the nursery. Gideon sometimes had to leave home earlier than usual— she didn't see why she shouldn't, too.

Beverly and Violette were busy starting their day, and Ellena guessed she would be interfering with routine if she stayed too long. Even so, she only left the nursery when she judged that Gideon would be deeply absorbed with his newspaper. For the look of the thing, she would have to pop her head round the breakfast room door.

It should have been easy. So why did she feel all trembly inside and little short of a nervous wreck as she approached the breakfast room door? She swallowed hard and, wanting to go in any direction but the one in which she was going— she entered.

'Good morning!' she said brightly to his raised newspaper and, recalling how last night she had lain naked in his arms, felt herself go scarlet—oh, why did she remember that now! Gideon lowered his paper, his gaze taking in her flushed face. A gentle smile began to take shape on his mouth. Ellena rushed on. 'I want an early start,' she explained, waving her briefcase in his general direction. 'Pending file, overflowing!' she explained—and would have got out of there—only Gideon was on his feet and was starting to come over to the doorway where she stood.

'Ellena, about last night…' he began—and she nearly died. Did he *have* to?

'Tell you what, Gideon,' she managed, still somehow holding her bright tone, 'you promise never to do that again, and I'll…' she was backing out of the door as she spoke '…and I'll promise not to go where—er—I've never been before.' With that she turned and, as if her pending file was the most important thing on her mind, rushed out to her car.

Gideon was in her head all the way to her office. '…about last night…' he'd started to say. What had he been going to add? 'I'd like you to forget it'? 'Never do that again'? 'Whose bed shall we try next time'? Grief, there wasn't going to be a next time. She'd take jolly good care of that. And, anyhow, after the two times—once in his bed, once in hers—when matters had started to get out of hand and she had politely declined, was it likely Gideon would want to bother a third time?

Ellena's pending file was as she'd left it, empty save for information she was waiting on and could not take action without. Even so, she intended to have a far better day today than she'd had yesterday.

An intention that abruptly got away from her. Indeed, it went straight out of her head when, just after ten that morning, her office door opened. When her visitor did not at first speak, she dragged her eyes away from her computer—and nearly fainted with shock.

'Gideon!' she gasped, the computer instantly forgotten, her mind in a spin. Apart from anything else—how had he got past reception? Why hadn't Lucy warned her? Irrelevant! 'What are you…?' Ellena's voice faded. He looked stern, serious. Her mind started to race—so much for her dashing away from the house that morning. There was no escape. Gideon had seen her love for him—he'd come to bluntly tell her…

'May I?' He took hold of a chair and, bringing it close

to where she was sitting, he sat down next to her. And while she was desperately striving to summon up some sort of a defence, Gideon went on to make her extremely agitated, when he started, 'Last night…'

'Last night,' she echoed as firmly as she was able, and while she was searching for something else to add Gideon continued, and she discovered that a defence was not needed.

'Last night at that hotel,' he went on—and she wished that she had not interrupted him.

Jealousy, that cursed, wretched emotion which she wanted no trade with, but which since its introduction would not, it seemed, leave her alone, was picking at her again. 'You weren't there on business?' she queried coolly, memory of the lovely brunette burning bright in her mind's eye. But—Ellena was puzzled—why would Gideon come to her office looking so serious just to tell her he'd lied last night?

'It was business—of sorts, as I said,' he answered.

'She—the lady you were with—' Ellena's tone was off hand—he'd never know the effort it cost '—she was more—er—friend than business connection?'

Gideon shook his head and, those serious slate-grey eyes holding hers, he said quietly, 'Ellena, my dear, Mrs Turner is a private detective.'

Ellena's eyes shot wide, his quiet, 'my dear' startling enough without the rest of it. 'A private detective!' she exclaimed, her mind darting off in all directions. Pamela Langford was having them watched, as he'd intimated she might? 'A private detective looking like that?' she exclaimed out loud, her question regarding Pamela getting lost under her feeling of shock.

'I thought they were all long raincoats and headscarves too,' Gideon agreed. 'I suppose, in some cases, Mrs Turner being the opposite of what one would expect might achieve better results. But that's beside the point,' he went on, the sternness of his expression relenting for a moment. 'I've had a highly recommended detective agency working for me from the beginning.'

Ellena strove hard to keep up. '*You* employed a detective agency—not Pamela?'

She guessed her confusion must be showing, for it was quickly and quietly that Gideon explained, 'I wasn't ready to believe that my brother was dead.' Ellena was instantly all attention now—nothing else mattered.

'You said you'd employed this agency from the beginning?' she questioned tautly, knowing that he would employ only the best.

'From the first.'

'And?' There was more—there had to be if this was the reason Gideon had come to her place of work to seek her out!

'At first nothing. Then a detective stationed in Austria found someone who'd seen a couple answering to Kit and Justine's descriptions having drinks in a bar with another couple, the night before the avalanche struck.' Ellena's mouth went dry. 'Time passed and no more news came through, but I insisted the detective stayed there, stayed to ask questions. Then someone was found who belatedly remembered seeing four people looking like the same quartet in a car heading south the next morning, the morning of the avalanche.'

It wasn't much to go on. Indeed, it could be absolutely nothing to go on; Ellena saw that. But she latched on and refused to let go of the fact that Gideon wouldn't be here with her now telling her this much if it wasn't relevant to something. 'Is that all?' she questioned huskily, refusing to believe that it was. Not now!

'For an age it was—though I've received scrappy bits of information which amounted to nothing. Then last evening I was between meetings when I took a call on my car phone from Mrs Turner, who'd just landed after a case conference

in Spain.' Spain! 'She indicated she might have something
of interest to report.'

Ellena felt her colour draining away. 'You met at…'

'I was on my way to a meeting in connection with a
takeover we're planning. But that could wait. This was far
more urgent. I said I'd like to see her straight away, and
she suggested the mutually convenient hotel where you saw
us.'

Oh, grief, what a pain he must have thought her—rattling
on about the baby alarm! But, as Gideon had himself intimated, this was more important than any of that. 'What did
Mrs Turner have to say?' she asked hurriedly.

'She started by saying that the trail had gone cold, but
that they'd an excellent man in Austria who daily called at
the hotel my brother and your sister were staying in, and
that he'd made friends with the staff.'

'And?' Ellena asked again.

'And, in so doing, learned of an inconsequential happening concerning a ''Mrs Pender'', who telephoned from
Spain having apparently left the hotel without settling her
account. The view was that some other poor hotelier had
been left nursing an unpaid account because ''Señora
Pender'' had never stayed at his hotel. But the detective
thought it worth a mention when he phoned through with
his daily report.'

Ellena could hardly speak. 'You think it was Justine?'
she questioned hoarsely. 'You think it was her phoning
from Spain?'

'Mrs Pender—Miss Spencer? A long shot but, to a foreign ear, during a bad telephone connection from Spain to
Austria? Not forgetting you were certain your sister would
never leave a hotel without paying her account.'

'She wouldn't! I know her.' Ellena's mind raced on. 'It
could be that she thought Kit had paid, and he thought that
Justine had.'

'And that when she discovered differently, she phoned the hotel straight away,' Gideon finished for her.

'You believe it, don't you?' Ellena questioned tensely.

Gideon stared into her strained tense and ashen face. 'I'm—starting to,' he said slowly. 'I had another telephone call from Mrs Turner a short while ago.'

Her mouth went dry again. 'You've an address—a phone number?'

'Neither,' he said at once. And, before revealing what his phone call had been about, he warned, 'Now don't hope for too much. Mrs Turner rang a minute before I left my office to come here to tell me she'd just received information that a man by the name of Langford is on a flight from Barcelona.'

Ellena stared at him. 'Kit's on—a plane—now!'

'It may not be him, so neither of us must hope for too much, but...'

'Neither of us?' she questioned chokily.

Gideon looked at her steadily. 'He's not travelling alone,' he said succinctly.

She so desperately wanted to believe it was Kit and Justine, but Gideon had said that neither of them must hope for too much. How could she not? 'This man—his travelling c-companion—is female?' she questioned.

'She is,' Gideon confirmed.

'What time are they due?' she asked, unsurprised to find that they had both left their chairs and were now standing.

'I'm on my way to the airport now,' he answered, adding quietly, 'I came to collect you.'

'Oh, Gideon!' she whispered shakenly, and it somehow seemed totally natural that they should for a moment go into each other's arms—that they should support each other in this moment of extreme stress.

She felt him place a light kiss in her hair, then he was taking her by the arms. 'Come on, love,' he said gruffly.

By the time they reached the airport Ellena was in a

dreadful state of anxiety. She barely remembered leaving the office. She had a vague memory of seeing Andrea, of Gideon introducing himself and alluding to her ashen face, explaining that his wife wasn't well and that he was taking her home. It passed her by that this hardly explained to Andrea what he was doing at the office to begin with.

Ellena was barely aware of the drive to the airport either. Though she did recall almost asking him why he hadn't thought to tell her any of what he knew before. Then she also recalled that the only chance he'd had to tell her anything about his meeting with Mrs Turner had been when he'd come to her room late last night. Perhaps it had been his intention to discuss it with her then—only they'd kissed and—oh, grief! She wasn't likely to remind him of that!

The wait for the Barcelona flight seemed endless. 'It may not be Kit and Justine,' Gideon warned when they saw from the arrivals board that the plane had landed.

'I know,' she agreed, as another interminable wait ensued and she mentally followed the passengers through passport control, baggage reclaim and customs.

The first of them started to come into the arrivals hall, and she found she was hanging onto Gideon's left hand as if it were a lifeline. Yet she couldn't let go.

Then she saw them! Justine and Kit were yards away, arms around each other, as happy and unconcerned as ever they were. Ellena realised that some kind of sound must have escaped her. Because, although Gideon had spotted the errant pair too, he pulled her against him for a moment.

'All right?' he queried.

'Never better now,' she said, and thought that this must be one of her happiest moments when the man she loved looked down at her and, taking out his snowy white handkerchief, gently wiped away a stray tear she didn't know had escaped.

It then became urgent for both of them to get to their relatives and touch and feel, and just be heartily overjoyed, when they could have been forgiven if they'd accepted that they would never see the pair again.

'Ellena-Ellen! Fancy seeing you here!' Justine exclaimed, in high spirits, but obviously glad to be home as the two hugged each other. 'Have you got your car? We left ours at h—' She broke off, suddenly realising that Kit had been greeting a man unknown to her.

'Gideon, you don't know my fiancée,' Kit was saying, and while Ellena was getting used to the fact that it seemed her nutcase of a sister was now engaged to the father of her child, Justine was shaking hands with Gideon and asking how come he and her sister were at the airport to meet them.

There was a lot Gideon could have said and, now that the agony of not knowing if they were alive or dead was over, he could have been forgiven for finding release by reprimanding the pair of them for what they had put Ellena and himself through. But, since both Kit and Justine appeared blithely unaware of the fear endured in their absence, Ellena felt that she had never loved Gideon more when, with a glance to her, he answered mildly, 'It's a long story. We were a little worried about Violette, so you could say we joined forces to look after her.'

'She's all right?' Justine questioned a touch frantically. 'My baby's all…?'

'She's fine,' Gideon assured her. 'She's being very well looked after at Oakvale…'

'She's at your home?' Kit chipped in. 'What happened at Pamela's? Every time we phoned she said the baby was blooming. She…'

'You phoned Russell's wife?' Gideon questioned grimly.

'Like every week,' Kit answered—and, with a grin to his fiancée, continued, 'It would have been every day just lately, if Justine could have got to a phone—came over all mumsie, didn't you, love?'

Justine hit him, and they all laughed together. The four

of them made a general move towards the airport car park—and Ellena, overjoyed to the point of tears to see her dear sister again, at the same time coped with fresh shock when Justine revealed she had been about to telephone her too, one time, after she'd rung Pamela. 'Only Pamela told me you'd only just left after one of your regular visits to see Violette—so I knew you wouldn't be back at the flat yet, even if I did ring to say hi.'

The four of them were in Gideon's car on their way to Oakvale. Justine and Kit were extremely excited at the prospect of seeing their daughter again and taking her to their home while Ellena struggled with the fact that Pamela Langford had known Justine and Kit were alive!

All this time, while she and Gideon—each in their own way—were going quietly demented, Pamela had known that Justine and Kit were safe and well! All this while she and Gideon had been through their own private hell need-lessly!

Hard-nosed! It was little short of criminal! Not only had she lied about Ellena's regular visits to see Violette, Pamela had even made out that she was still looking after the baby!

Gideon had felt that she had given Violette up too eas-ily—now they realised why! Pamela had known for a while that Justine and Kit would be coming back, doing away with the necessity of a guardian for their child, and there-fore there was nothing to be financially gained by trying to get Violette back. Criminal—she had been downright wicked!

'We've decided to get married!' Kit's announcement cut through Ellena's thoughts.

Though, before she could find the words to offer her congratulations, she heard Gideon offer drily, 'While it goes without saying, Kit, that you're a very lucky man—what brought this on?'

Both Justine and Kit laughed, though it was Kit who,

suddenly serious, replied, 'Justine gave me one hell of a shock, that's what!'

'I—er—went a bit broody,' Justine explained. 'We were in Austria when we bumped into some friends of Kit's who were driving to France the next day. So we went too, and had a whale of a time. Then Nick's father wanted his boat sailing down from Marseilles to Gibraltar, and Nick said he could do with some extra crew. Anyhow, it seemed a good idea at the time—to volunteer, I mean—only, then I started to get a terrible longing to see Violette, to be with her. But I didn't like to tell Kit and spoil his fun.'

'And I thought, when Justine went in for long silences, that she'd gone off me. It took me about a week to pluck up courage to ask what I'd done wrong.'

'And he looked so hurt—I just had to tell him it wasn't his fault, but mine, and that I was just homesick for Violette, and wanted to be a proper mother.'

'And that was when I knew I wanted to be a proper father—a married one, but only to Violette's mother.'

There did not seem to be much more to say after that. 'Congratulations,' Ellena smiled, and the rest of the journey seemed to be taken up with talk of the baby, of the wedding which would take place as soon as Justine and Kit found a house to buy.

Though Justine did remember to thank Ellena and Gideon for looking after their offspring. 'I expect the neighbours complained when you took Violette to your flat to live,' she opined to Ellena. 'How clever of you to contact Gideon. I had an idea you disapproved of my farming her out on Pamela in the first place.'

'Some aunts are like that,' Ellena answered. Violette was obviously the centre of Justine's universe just then, and, while it pleased her that her sister's maternal instinct had finally arrived, Ellena saw no point in telling Justine about the avalanche, of which she clearly knew nothing. Nor about the other matter, which of course Justine knew nothing about either—that she and Gideon had gone through a marriage ceremony in order to safeguard Violette's security, caring and happiness.

Gideon must be seeing things the same way, Ellena realised, for he was saying nothing on the subject either. In fact, given that Justine and Kit were babbling away, there was little room left for other conversation, so he was saying scarcely anything at all.

'May I go and find Violette?' Justine asked when they pulled up at Oakvale—and was first out of the car.

'Of course.' Gideon smiled. And to his brother, 'You know where the nursery is.'

Ellena stared after them as, hand in hand, Justine and Kit took off. She got out of the car and went to follow them, but was startled when Gideon, placing a hand on her arm, stopped her.

She halted, looking at him, and loved him so much. 'Happy?' he asked.

She nodded. 'Relieved, oh, so very relieved,' she said. 'You?' she asked.

'Torn between a desire to give Kit a manly hug and box his ears for what the inconsiderate pair have put us through.'

She knew the feeling. 'When was it ever any different?' she smiled and, as he let go her arm, they walked side by side into the house—where peace had ceased to reign.

'Isn't she gorgeous?' Justine cried from the first landing, Violette in her arms, Beverly hovering nearby. 'Can we go home now?' Justine, it appeared, wanted her baby and Kit to herself, and was not the least interested in lunch or any sort of refreshment. Gideon took charge.

In no time at all, he had interviewed Beverly, who was about to lose her charge. Then, between them, he, Kit, Ellena and Beverly were carrying a whole mountain of baby equipment out to Gideon's car.

'There's no room for Ellena!' Justine objected when, the

car boot full, other bits and pieces took up the available space inside.

'I shan't need any,' Ellena smiled, and, as it suddenly dawned on her, 'There's no reason why I should come too!'

'Will I be all right?' Justine asked, as if suddenly nervous that she might have forgotten how to care for Violette.

'It's like riding a bike,' Ellena promised.

And, reassured, Justine beamed, 'See you, then—and thanks. Thanks, Beverly.' Then she gave all her attention to the little darling she had so yearned to see.

'Bye, Ellena—we'll be in touch,' Kit said, getting into the front passenger seat.

Ellena stepped back, and Gideon, his large car full to capacity, paused before he got into the driver's seat. 'I'll see you when I get back,' he said, those direct slate-grey eyes steady on her blue ones.

And all at once Ellena felt shy, tongue-tied. 'Drive carefully—Uncle,' she said—and wanted to die from sheer mortification because he might think her remark was as ridiculous as she felt it to be.

She stood with Beverly and waved them goodbye. On turning and heading back into the house, the superb nanny declared, 'I'd better go and tidy up the nursery and pack.'

'I'm sorry,' Ellena apologised.

'Oh, don't be,' Beverly smiled. 'I've loved working here, being here, but I won't have a problem being redundant—I'll soon get something else. And your husband has been most generous with my severance pay.'

They went up the stairs together in pleasant conversation and parted when Beverly carried on up to the next landing. Ellena went along to her own room and went to stare out of her bedroom window.

She loved the view of lawns and shrubs and trees. She, like Beverly, loved being here. She... Oh! Suddenly, painfully, screaming out of a dark unwanted somewhere, Ellena only then realised that Beverly wasn't the only one who was redundant! That—with Violette gone—there was no earthly reason for her and Gideon to remain married. With a sick feeling hitting her, Ellena all at once realised that her marriage was over!

Swiftly on the heels of that thought came another dreadful realisation—that she too must be expected to pack and be on her way! Oh, good heavens, what on earth was she doing daydreaming out of the window, thinking of how much she loved it here at Oakvale, Gideon's home! He had said 'I'll see you when I get back' but wasn't that his way of saying, I won't expect to see you when I get back?

Ellena realised that her love for Gideon might have made her over-sensitive where he was concerned. But, while she had seen an extremely kind side of him which gave a small percentage of doubt that he had meant anything at all by his parting remark, there was absolutely no denying that Justine and Kit's arrival home most definitely spelt the end of her marriage to Gideon.

Her pride gave her a kick-start when Ellena saw that the odds were Gideon would not expect to see her there when he returned. Come to that, this being a working day, he might not return at all but could well go straight from Kit's to his office. Ellena, her car still at her office, rang for a taxi.

With a heavy heart she left her room and went to say goodbye to Beverly and to wish her well in the future. Then, having been unsure whether to pack and go, or whether to return for her belongings when Gideon had explained matters to his staff—and, of course, come back when she knew he would not be around—she started to feel edgy. She was growing more and more convinced that Gideon would wait only to unload his car at Kit's flat, and he would then go straight to his office. But, just in case he did plan to return straight away to Oakvale, Ellena decided to leave now.

She still felt emotional about Justine and Kit's safe return. Loving Gideon the way she did, she just didn't feel up to discussing their divorce arrangements just yet.

She went to the drawing room to wait for her taxi. She would ring Gideon, perhaps come for her things at the weekend. By then she would be emotionally stronger— more able to cope. Yes, it would be far better to contact him over the phone, when she wouldn't see his dear face, far better to discuss their divorce never having the chance to see him again, when he would not be able to see the sadness in her eyes that might, in an unguarded moment, be there. Never was he to know how deeply she loved him.

Gideon, and the fact that she would never probably see him again, was very much on her mind on the taxi ride to her flat. Her heart was somewhere down in her boots when she suddenly remembered that Justine and Kit intended to marry. She would see Gideon at their wedding, she realised. Though, by then, since their siblings didn't appear to be in any particular hurry to wed, Ellena was hopeful that she would have perfected a friendly—if perhaps just a trifle offhand—technique when next she saw Gideon.

She supposed that at some time Justine and Kit would get to hear that she and Gideon had married and why. That was another area she must guard, to make sure that Justine, so close to her in some ways, picked up not the slightest hint that she had come away from this marriage so achingly heart-sore.

For a brief while Ellena thought of Justine and Kit, and how the two of them now seemed a little more grown up. Ready to take on the responsibilities of marriage and a family life. Ellena realised that she must take a back seat in Justine's life. She would always be there for her; that went without saying. But Justine had Kit now, and both of them were ready to commit to each other.

By the time the taxi dropped her off at her flat—some-how returning to her office just did not figure in her list of priorities—Gideon was back in her head—where he was to stay. For no matter how much she decided to think positively, to think of her future, of the endless possibilities, sights to see, things to do and hear, she always seemed to come back to thinking about Gideon.

Think positively, she asserted to herself yet again. Then the phone, which had been silent for so long, started to ring. Gideon! Oh, stop it! It would be Justine... Ellena picked up the phone.

'Hello,' she said lightly.

'You didn't go back to your office, then?'

Gideon! Her heart started to hammer, adrenalin rushed. 'Did you?' she managed.

'I said I'd see you when I got back,' he reminded her evenly.

'Oh, sorry, I must have misunderstood.'

He could have taken her up on that—she was glad that he didn't. Though she owned to being completely thrown when, after a moment or two of saying nothing, he abruptly asked, 'When are you coming home?'

'Er...' Words failed her. Home! Hope started to soar high. 'I'm—not.' She quietened ridiculous hope.

The pause that followed was electric. Then Gideon commented, 'Your belongings are here.'

And Ellena fell to earth with a bump—all too obviously, now that they had no reason to stay married, he didn't want her belongings cluttering up his home.

'I was going to ring you and suggest I come over at the weekend to collect them—I'd have brought everything with me today,' she went on to explain, 'only I wasn't sure how you wanted Mr and Mrs Morris told, or Marjorie and...'

'The weekend will be fine,' Gideon cut through her lengthy explanation, and while Ellena's spirits sank lower and lower she knew all too plainly that she had read the situation correctly: he wanted her bedroom cleared. Because, quietly, he put down his phone.

Well! Goodbye to you, too! Who did he think he was?

she fumed indignantly. Not even the courtesy of, 'It's been nice knowing you', did she get! Well, could he go sky-diving without a parachute!

She wiped at her damp eyes—she wouldn't cry over him; she wouldn't. Instead she busied herself tidying an already tidy flat, and dusted everywhere. Then she went and took a shower and washed and dried her hair.

Having donned a pair of jeans, she had just finished buttoning up a crisp white overshirt when her doorbell sounded. Gideon! Don't be ridiculous! Her start of alarm was flattened by deadly dull common sense. She went to answer the door, beginning to feel guilty that she hadn't rung Andrea to tell her about the safe return of Justine and Kit. If memory served, Andrea had an appointment with a company out this way later today. She wouldn't put it past Andrea to stop by to see if she was feeling any better.

Ellena had the door unlatched, and was about to open it, when suddenly and alarmingly it hit her that Andrea fully believed her to be no longer living at her flat, but at Oakvale with Gideon!

It wouldn't be him—why on earth would it be? But, too late now, the door was ajar. She pulled it open—and felt colour rush to her face. She dug her nails into her palms, desperate for control.

'Hello,' she said brightly. 'I didn't expect to see you before the weekend!' And not even then if she couldn't control her emotions better than this—she was inwardly trembling!

Gideon stared at her, his expression unsmiling. 'You and I, Mrs Langford,' he said after some moments of tough scrutiny, 'have some unfinished business.'

That 'Mrs Langford' told her all she needed to know. Gideon, never a man to let the grass grow—ever a man to get things done—had come to talk about their divorce!

She came away from the door. 'You'd better come in,' she invited.

CHAPTER EIGHT

'WOULD you like something to eat? Have you had lunch?' Ellena asked, leading the way into the sitting room. Keep calm, civilised. For heaven's sake, theirs wasn't a proper marriage, never had been, was never meant to be; so there was no need for recriminations or apportioning blame at its ending.

'I've more important things on my mind than food,' Gideon declined her offer shortly.

He looked serious, she saw. In fact, quite grim. 'Er— take a seat,' she invited, holding back the urge to offer him coffee. She needed those few moments alone, by herself, moments in which to get herself together—but there was no guarantee that he wouldn't follow her to the kitchen. Gideon walked over to an easy chair, but waited until she was seated on her sofa first before he sat down. 'Did Justine and Kit get settled in all right?' Ellena asked politely after some desperate moments of trying to find something natural to say. Oh, heavens! There was a determined sort of glint in Gideon's eyes.

'I don't know,' he answered, those eyes holding hers, 'I didn't stay around that long.'

'You went straight back to Oakvale?' By all means, let's keep this polite.

He nodded. 'Where you weren't!' he commented succinctly.

Why should she feel a need to swallow? Because he was so dear to her, that was why. She loved him so much. But it was time to sever all ties with him, time to stop pussy-footing around. 'It's a great day—Justine and Kit coming home,' she remarked. 'Though there was no need for you to come here in person—our lawyers can sort out the details of our annulment, and…'

'You don't think we should discuss it a little first?' Gideon cut in grimly.

Ellena stared at him in some surprise. What was there to discuss? 'You want alimony?'

His lips twitched briefly, no more. 'I once called you a cheeky baggage,' he recalled.

'You bring out the best in me!' she said off the top of her head, and found she couldn't keep her eyes off his wonderful mouth, the mouth that had wrung from her such an ardent response of which she had never dreamed herself capable.

'Sex aside…' Gideon remarked, and while she dragged her gaze from his mouth she was having forty fits inside that he had so easily hopped on to her wavelength. '…we married, you and I, from a cold necessity. But, Ellena, my dear—' his voice softened '—I like to think we found a—friendship—if you like, a warmth…' he seemed to be selecting his words very carefully '…that rules out a cold and impersonal divorce.'

Her blue eyes were fastened on his now. They would divorce, naturally they would. Gideon was not saying that the divorce was ruled out—just that, from where he saw it, it would not be cold and impersonal.

She smiled; she just had to. Gideon had as good as stated that he felt a warmth and a friendship for her. 'You've been a good friend,' she acknowledged, 'there for me when I needed a shoulder.'

'It was mutual,' he answered.

'I helped you—during the long, painful waiting?'

'It was a comfort to hold you in my arms,' Gideon confessed. But proceeded to shake her rigid when, quite deliberately she felt, he added, 'That was, initially. Later I found there were many times when I just wanted to take you in my arms, and hold you.'

Ellena blinked, her eyes growing wide. 'For our—er—mutual strength—comfort?' she sought clarification.

Gideon studied her attentive expression. 'Partly,' he agreed. 'But more, I think, because I could barely help myself.'

She coughed lightly; her heart was hammering away. Don't be ridiculous! She shouldn't read anything at all into what Gideon was saying. 'Sex aside,' she tried to quip, 'you…'

'You're a desirable woman, you know that,' he stated. 'But I don't think sex had a great deal to do with those moments when I had to make myself turn from you. Those moments when I had to resolve to keep away from you, to shut myself in my study.'

Ellena took a shaky breath. She knew he liked honesty, but she wasn't sure that she was up to taking much more of this without giving something of her feelings away.

Pride was a wonderful ally. 'So that was why I gained the impression you'd gone off me—that first weekend we were married,' she attempted to tease lightly.

'I'm encouraged that you noticed my absence,' Gideon answered, far too astutely for Ellena, causing her to realise that she was going to have to watch every word while this divorce conversation lasted. She opted then not to answer at all, for fear that she might reveal even a fraction of her feelings for him, sealing her lips—that was, unless she absolutely had to answer him. 'You're not going all cool and uppity on me, are you?' My heavens, was there ever a man who was not letting go!

'When did I ever do that?' Ellena felt that was a safe enough reply.

'Hopefully only when you, like me, felt it might be an idea to back off.'

'You're talking in riddles.' She denied to herself that she had ever, for a single moment, thought, Cool it, Ellena, or that he was taking up too much time in her head.

'So I'll go back to the beginning,' he decreed, when she would far rather that he wouldn't. 'You were really suffering on that plane ride out to Austria.'

'We both were,' her tongue disobeyed the embargo she had placed on it not to speak another word.

'And when we reached our destination the news was not good,' he went on. 'Which, fear being the animal it is, had both of us trying to hold down on the aggression that it triggered.'

'I let go of mine in that hotel room where Justine and Kit had been staying,' she recalled.

'And apologised at once,' Gideon took up, having instant recall, it seemed.

'You suggested I might call you by your first name,' she was right there with him.

'When actually what I felt, when you looked at me with those beautiful but unhappy blue eyes, was an absurd urge to cradle you in my arms.'

'Did you?' she exclaimed, astonished.

'Nothing sexual,' he assured her.

He didn't have to. 'I know,' she said, and felt she was going all to pieces again when he smiled gently at her.

'You've a lovely mind,' he murmured.

Ellena didn't know about that. What she did know was that Gideon talking this way, about her beautiful eyes and lovely mind—without that softening in his expression— was making it not a scrap easier for her to hide how much his every word and look affected her.

'You—er—were going to go back to the beginning,' she reminded him, desperate to keep the discussion impersonal—but realising too late that she hadn't wanted him to go back to the beginning either. She owned up to herself that just having him here muddled her thinking.

'I still am,' he assured her, and resumed, 'So we returned to England, and I soon discovered that you couldn't care less that Kit, or his heiress, would shortly be quite wealthy, and that the only reason you wanted guardianship of his and your sister's infant was for love of the child.'

Oh, grief, was Gideon saying that he—liked her? Ellena felt that he was—or was that all part of her being muddle-headed? 'You wanted Violette too,' she reminded him, feeling a need to take the conversation away from herself. 'You were prepared to marry to get her,' she added, though she wasn't terribly sure why she had added that, except she was feeling decidedly jumpy and was still anxious to have their talk moved away from herself; this astute man she had married might see too much.

'All very true,' he agreed evenly. 'I'd already worked out, before I consulted my lawyers, that I'd be better placed to win guardianship of Kit's offspring if I was married rather than single.'

'Should I feel honoured that you chose me?' Oh, Ellena, watch that tongue, do! She forced a smile. 'You must know quite a few other females who'd be willing—' She broke off when she saw Gideon start to smile.

'You were almost on your way to flattering me,' he observed with a charm which sank her.

'Well, you're not *all* bad,' was the best she could manage. 'So—um—you'd realised you'd better marry?' she prompted. Far better, she realised, to encourage him to talk than to converse herself when her tongue was proving so unwary.

'Reluctant though I was, it was an obvious solution,' he owned. 'The problem, as I saw it then, was—since I wanted to be certain I could as easily get myself unmarried—who did I know who would go along with it?'

'You realised Ellena Spencer would be easy to get rid of?' Ellena inserted—and inwardly cringed at the tart note that had crept into her voice. Oh, buck up, do! Any minute now, if she didn't watch her step, Gideon was going to realise that she was taking all this much too personally— already he was looking at her sharply.

Ellena gave an inner sigh of relief, though, when it seemed he had not noticed the acid in her tone, for quite pleasantly he acknowledged, 'You were the infant's aunt, and because of your love of your sister and the babe, you were as determined as me to have her. The decision was as good as made for me. And it should,' he went on, after a moment or two of just looking steadily at her, 'have been as simple, and as easy, as that.'

She stared at him, her blue eyes fixed on his slate-grey ones. She still felt jumpy, nervy. But there was a question begging to be asked here. 'Only—it wasn't?' she asked.

'It wasn't,' Gideon agreed. 'Logically, it was the obvious solution. But…' He paused, and then, again deliberately, added slowly, 'I discovered there's little room for logic when the emotions became involved.'

Her heart leapt—what was he saying? Idiot—idiot! He was saying that in a very short space of time he had gone from not knowing so much that his niece existed, to caring for Violette. His emotions weren't involved with *you*, Ellena berated herself, and strove hard to keep her voice even when, since it seemed Gideon was waiting to hear what she thought of his last remark, she forced a smile and conceded 'It would be a hard heart who couldn't be won over by one of Violette's smiles.'

'The young lady has a way with her,' he concurred—though he caused Ellena no small agitation to her heart when he corrected, 'Though it was more her aunt I was referring to.'

'Oh,' she said. There was no answer to that but—oh, foolish love—she wanted to hear more. 'Er—you mean—um—last night, when we—er—um—kissed?' Ellena's heartbeat quietened down as she realised that there was nothing to get very excited about. It was, after all, despite his remark about 'Sex aside', nothing but the physical desire that had sparked between them to which he was referring, with his comment about 'emotions involved'. Wonderful though those minutes in his arms had been.

'I mean last night,' he confirmed, flattening any of her wayward hopes—but only to arouse them again a second later when he quietly added, 'I mean, everything.'

Everything! Sorely did she wish she knew what he meant by 'everything'. 'You're obviously referring to our—um—Violette's very early alarm call yesterday when—er—things started to get out of hand the first time,' she managed to finish the sentence she had embarked upon.

'I don't know about getting out of hand,' Gideon grunted. 'It seems to me more that, of late, things between you and me have been growing more and more impossible.'

She had to admit he was right. From starting with an occasional kiss on the cheek when someone else was around, twice yesterday they had kissed when no one else was around, and had been extremely unrestrained. 'Well, you have been "resting" for rather a long while now,' she reminded him, wondering where the heck—when she was as tense as could be—that imp of mischief had come from.

'Sometimes, madam,' Gideon observed, 'I see the very devil in your eyes.' As long as that was all he saw! 'But this,' he went on, his expression suddenly extremely serious, 'is about you and me—and…'

'And our divorce,' Ellena finished for him—and at once saw him go from extremely serious to extremely angry.

'To hell with a divorce!' he snarled. 'You're married to me, Ellena Langford, and that's the way you'll stay!'

She stared at him in amazement. What had brought this on? But, while she might love what he said, she disliked very much the tone in which he said it. 'And to hell with you!' she erupted, both of them now angrily on their feet at the same time. 'We married for a specific reason; that reason has now gone! *We split!*' she informed him, glaring at him, loving him, desperately wanting him to cradle her in his arms, as he'd revealed he had wanted to that first night in Austria. But she was not prepared to be spoken to like that by any man—a girl had her pride! 'First thing tomorrow, I shall see my lawyers about getting this marriage annulled.'

'Impossible!' he rapped.

'Why impossible?' she flared.

'Because, by first thing tomorrow, this marriage will be consummated, and...'

Ellena was on her way to the door. 'Against my will! That's also grounds for divorce!' she exploded, not very certain of her facts, but panicking and ready to bluff it out.

She was about to open her door to show him out when Gideon, an angry Gideon, caught hold of her and spun her round. He seemed about to let forth a stream of something which she knew in advance that she would not like. Then, suddenly, all his fury vanished.

In an instant, perhaps seeing a flicker of fear in her eyes, all anger went from him. 'Oh, love,' he groaned, 'I wouldn't use force.'

What could she do? He sounded so anguished, and called her 'love'—Ellena just melted. As if they both needed a salve from the violence of their five-second spat, Gideon's arms came around her, and Ellena went into his embrace and put her arms around him.

'You probably wouldn't have to,' she whispered, remembering how last night she had wanted to be his.

She felt his kiss in her hair. 'One of the things I've always loved about you is your honesty,' he said softly.

Ellena felt near to tears. She swallowed hard. Then raised her head from his chest. 'Our—discussion seems to have lost its way,' she said.

'My fault,' he accepted. 'I've so much I wanted to say to you. And—perhaps because this is all so new to me—it doesn't seem to be coming out the right way.' He looked down into her warm blue eyes. 'I'd like to try again,' he requested.

Ellena stared up into his warm grey eyes. She didn't know what he wanted to try again. All she knew then was that pride no longer mattered. She wanted to hear him out. If during the time when they talked of a divorce—which for some reason he didn't seem to want at the moment—some of her love for him showed, then it no longer mattered. Ellena felt she knew enough of the man to know that, albeit that it might be unwanted, Gideon would treat her love kindly.

'Shall we go and sit down again?' she invited him to try again. She was still in his arms but, until he took them from her, she seemed powerless to move.

'May I kiss you?' he asked, something which, but for that harsh word 'force' still floating in the air, she guessed he would not have sought permission for. He truly was more sensitive than he let anyone see.

Her answer was to stretch up. Gideon's head came down and gently he kissed her—a kiss of such sweetness, almost love, she thought, that she felt quite choked that a man could be so tender.

She moved in his arms, her heart full. His arms fell away. 'Are you sure you wouldn't like something to eat, a coffee?' she enquired, desperately striving for some sort of normality. How could she ever have imagined that there was almost love in his kiss? She had better get her head together—and fast.

'Nothing, thanks,' he refused, but as she went to resume her seat on the sofa, 'You won't object if I sit here?' he asked. She shook her head, nerves biting when he came and shared the sofa with her.

'Do I take it that you—object—to our marriage being ended at the moment?' she asked, doing her utmost to stay calm—detached, if possible.

'Most decidedly, I do,' he confirmed.

'There has to be a reason?' she hinted.

'I could give you a dozen, but there's only one that matters.'

Her brain took off. 'Something to do with business?'

'No!' he denied emphatically. But, with a wry look to her, 'Lord knows how your mind works! We're talking about *us*, not business.'

Us? how wonderful that one word was. With difficulty—how easily he could scramble her thinking—Ellena got her head back together. 'You—make it sound—personal,' she said haltingly.

Gideon scrutinised her face for long moments. 'You don't think the fact that we're talking of our marriage, the fact of you being my wife, makes it personal?'

Ellena felt a lump in her throat, and was drowning in the beauty of hearing him call her 'my wife'. Oh, how dear he was, her husband. 'Well, if you put it like that,' she did her poor best to reply. And, gaining a little emotional strength, 'So why, Mr Langford, do you personally not want us to get unmarried at the moment?'

'You haven't guessed?'

She wanted to say something sharp like, I've lost my crystal ball, but she could not. There was just something in Gideon's expression, a warmth, a tenseness—could it be—a nervousness?—that flattened anything but her sensitivity to him.

Wordlessly, she shook her head. Then, huskily, she found her voice. 'I'd like to know,' she dared—and observed he looked more tense than ever.

But she it was who was tense and nervous when, after long, long moments of just looking at her, Gideon, as if under a great deal of strain, quietly revealed, 'My dear Mrs Langford, I have to tell you—when falling in love is not something I do—that I seem to have fallen in love with you.'

Ellena stared. Blinked, and stared at him. It was the last thing she'd expected to hear. That most wonderful sentence totally astonishing. 'Seem?' was the best she could manage, her voice cracking, not sounding like her voice at all. 'When?'

He ignored both questions, but sounded extremely unsure as he asked, 'You don't—mind?'

Mind! Were she able to believe him, she would be ecstatic. Though, when had he ever told her a lie? Oh, my... She swallowed, had the wildest urge to throw herself into his arms. But she loved him with all she had—which made it just too incredible that he should feel the same way about her!

'I—er—wouldn't mind hearing more about it,' she gave him the most encouragement she could manage.

'Is caution part of your accountant's training?'

'This isn't about business,' she tossed back at him. But, seeing that he still seemed under a great deal of strain, she relented a little. 'How much more encouragement do you want?' she asked, and again asked, 'When?'

'When did I start to fall in love with you?' Her misbehaving heart did a cartwheel; a few more comments like that and she didn't see how she would be able to stop herself from throwing her arms around him! 'As near as I can tell, and you've been in my head so much just lately, interrupting my work, my sleep...'

'You too!' she gasped.

'It's the same for you?' he questioned as quick as a flash, grasping a hold of her arms, seeming about to bring her closer. She wasn't ready!

'Forget I said that!' she backtracked fast.

'Not a chance!' he replied. But, when seconds passed and it seemed she was determined not to say another word, he reluctantly took his hands from her arms. Then he caught a hold of her hands instead, as if resolved that she was not going to move away from him until he had told her what she wanted to know, and had heard from her what he dearly wanted to know. 'On thinking it over and over, I've realised that I must have started to feel something different for you way back in Austria when, with Kit so much on my mind, I experienced that urge to cradle and comfort you. Then a few days later, when I rang you after you'd agreed to marry me, and I thought you'd been crying, I experienced a most definite pang. I didn't like at all the idea of you crying alone.'

'I discovered some time ago how sensitive you are,' Ellena said softly.

'Rot,' he denied. 'Well, perhaps where you're concerned,' he allowed. She smiled, and it seemed as though he would kiss her. Wanting to meet him halfway, Ellena pulled back instead. If he kissed her, she'd be lost, she knew she would, and, because it was so incredible that he might love her, she just *had* to hear more first. Gideon pulled back too, though he threatened, 'When I do kiss you, you're going to beg for mercy.'

'Never!' the imp who had recently come to live inside her body replied.

Gideon grinned, and her heart flipped. Oh, how she loved him. 'So,' he continued after some moments, serious again, 'there was I, denying that it mattered to any degree that you cried alone. Then the next time I rang you it was to hear you were getting cold feet about marrying me, and I told you I didn't think I'd forgive you if you stood me up—only to later realise, though barely knowing why then, that I somehow needed to have you in my life.'

Oh, how wonderful that sounded. 'Er—you didn't perhaps think your needing me in your life had something to do with you wanting to guard Kit's baby?'

'I was trying hard to be truthful with myself.'

'And me—will you be truthful to me?' she asked, purely because she had to.

'Especially truthful to you,' he answered sincerely. She smiled her thanks and, maybe because he was a man in a hurry to hear how matters were with her, and where he

stood, he went on, 'So there we were, married, platoni-
cally—only there was I, constantly holding back on the
urge to take you in my arms.'

'You—er—gave in sometimes,' she remembered.

'And didn't at so many others. You told me once that
my charm was back—and I had such a near-irresistible urge
to kiss you. But knew at once that I must not. We hadn't
been married twenty-four hours and I felt you might feel
you were in a vulnerable position.'

'That was thoughtful!'

Gideon's smile came out again. 'I confess I was feeling
a touch vulnerable myself then.'

'You—were—um—starting to feel something for me,
you said.'

'It was there, and getting more deeply entrenched. Which
is why, of course, after we'd called here—that day we went
nursery shopping—I so nearly kissed you again...'

'I wanted you to,' Ellena clearly remembered.

'Stay honest with me, my darling,' he breathed—and her
bones melted again.

'I'll try,' she replied softly, and was truly starting to believe that—fantastic though it was—Gideon did, as he'd
said, care for her. 'Go on,' she invited.

He gave her hands a gentle, but heartening squeeze. 'So
there was I, wanting to hold you, only realising then that
it was not just because we comforted each other when our
spirits were low, but also because I somehow liked the feel
of you in my arms. Anyhow, it was around then that I gave
myself a talking-to on the fact that if I didn't watch my
step I could end up in real trouble.'

'How?'

'I could, my dear, have found myself married for real.'

So much for wanting him to be truthful with her! 'That
can easily be remedied,' pride insisted she should inform
him.

'And you call *me* sensitive!'

Ellena had the grace to feel ashamed. 'Pardon me for interrupting!' she apologised—with a trace less acid.

Gideon said something that sounded like 'enchantress', but resumed: 'I then decided I'd better cool things—only, after a bleak weekend of keeping out of your way I drove you here to pick up your car on the Monday, and just had to give in to the urge to kiss you as we parted.'

'It wasn't because you thought there might be photographers around!'

He shook his head. 'You were getting to me in a big way. Later that day I went and collected Violette and could hardly wait for you to get home—which, even then, I thought was odd, because I wanted the infant for me, not you. It was only later that—having coped with my first experience of jealousy when you came home carrying a huge floral bouquet—as you held the baby in your arms, I experienced such a wonderful feeling of joy at seeing such happiness in your face as you thanked me. I answered, ''For you, my dear, anything.'' Then I realised it was true, that I would do anything for you.'

'Oh, Gideon…' she whispered.

And he smiled a loving smile as he told her, 'It was only a short step from there and I was starting to forget that it was only because of the baby we were together. I enjoyed having you living in my home; my heart lifted when you walked into a room; I enjoyed seeing you there, eating with you, hearing you laugh.' Ellena sat staring at him in wonder that it had been like that for him. 'Also wanting to comfort you when fear that you may have lost your beloved sister got too much for you.'

'Oh, Gideon,' she sighed tremulously.

'Do tell me you love me,' he urged. Ellena opened her mouth to speak, but was so choked, no sound came. Tenderly Gideon laid a butterfly kiss on her cheek. 'Do I have to tell you more about the effect you have on me? Of how heartily glad I was to hear your car on the drive the day I brought Violette home. The…'

'You'd phoned me here…'

'And asked if you intended coming home—and you snapped "How could I stay away?"—which left me deciding to be nicer to you.'

'Really? "What's with the flowers?"' she reminded him of his greeting when she had arrived.

'I've told you—I was jealous!' She smiled; she loved him so. He had been jealous? Unbelievable, wonderfully unbelievable! 'So,' he said, 'what have you got to tell me?' I love you, she wanted to tell him, only he let go her hands and caught a hold of her arms again. 'Your eyes tell me you do, but my darling, I so need to hear you say it.'

'You—um—suspect that I do?'

He shook his head. 'Never in my life have I felt so all at sea about anything. Sometimes I've thought I've seen a little fondness for me in your smile—others, I felt you didn't give a damn about me. Yet were it not for that detective, Mrs Turner, giving me the unsolicited information, "Now there's a lady in love", when you barged into our conversation in that hotel last night, I doubt I'd have this much confidence to reveal my feelings for you.'

'Mrs Turner said that I…!' Ellena gasped.

Gideon nodded. 'Which made me wonder how good a detective she was. To my mind she was completely wrong. Only, this morning, when she phoned with the news that Kit was possibly on a plane on his way home—the agency she works for living up to its excellent reputation—I began to consider that they were definitely in the business of employing somebody who was extremely astute in all aspects.' He paused, and took a long-drawn breath. 'So tell me, Ellena, was she right?' he demanded.

Ellena, looking at him, seeing that for all he must know how she felt about him—or she would never have let him get this far—seeing the look of strain still there in his dear face, suddenly folded. 'Who said to be jealous was your sole privilege?' she asked him softly.

'Darling!' He leaned forward and gently kissed her. 'Say it!' he urged. 'Put me out of my misery one way or the other. Say it.'

'Do you think I'm the sort of girl who'd go into a man's bedroom if I didn't love him?' she asked softly.

'God! I said you'd be hell on earth... *Say it!*'

She laughed; it was a joyous sound. 'I—love you,' she said.

She felt his grip on her arms tighten. 'And again, so I can believe it!'

'I love you, I love you, I love you!' she said—and knew he believed her, for the next she knew she was wrapped in his arms and he was raining adoring kisses down on her face.

For long, long minutes they held each other, and kissed each other, and just looked at each other, both too full for words. Then Gideon was kissing her again and telling her once more of his love.

'I'm having the same trouble you had in believing it,' Ellena whispered.

'But you do?' He kissed her.

She smiled. 'Oh, but I do,' she answered huskily—and was kissed again. And held tightly to his heart for ageless, wondrous seconds.

Then Gideon was pulling back to gaze adoringly into her loving upturned face. 'Never do I ever want to live again through an experience like the panicky uncertainty of these last few hours,' he said throatily.

Ellena moved to gently kiss him. 'Has it been so awful?' she asked softly.

'Nightmarish is understating it!'

'Not knowing if you would see Kit again—if it was truly him on that plane?'

'Not knowing, but having to face, if it was Kit, that I stood to *lose you*!'

Her breath sucked in on a gasp. 'Because there'd no longer be any need for you and I to join forces to protect Violette.'

'Exactly.'

'You thought of it *then*!' Ellena exclaimed.

'As you must have done.'

She shook her head. 'Not until after you'd gone to take Justine and Kit home did it dawn on me that my role as guardian—er—um—wife—was over. I was feeling a bit emotional, and not up to—er—discussing our divorce,' she owned.

'You really do love me,' Gideon said softly, as if still taking it in.

'Has it truly been so nightmarish?'

'Horrendous! One way and another I've been in hell ever since I've known how very deeply I'm in love with you.'

'I'm sorry,' she apologised lovingly.

'Which is why you're going to explain why you've given me such a hard time,' Gideon announced, but paused to give her a long, lingering kiss before he drew back to growl, 'Explain yourself, woman.'

Ellena laughed in pure delight. 'You're wonderful,' she told him, and absolutely loved being able to be this open with him. 'Er—where do you want me to start?'

'When did you know of your feelings for me?' he suggested without having to think about it.

'Um—I suppose, if I'm truthful…'

'I'll accept noting less,' he interrupted, taking a moment out to place a whisper of a kiss on her nose.

'Well, thinking back, I don't think I liked it too well when the day after we came back from Austria you came to see me and started talking about if you were married—and I thought you might be going to get married.'

'That was before I got around to suggesting that you and

I should join matrimonial forces. You started to care for me then?'

He was wonderful; he seemed really eager to know. Ellena's heart swelled with her love for him. Though she had to shake her head and tell him, 'It wasn't anything as definite, as clear as that—just a feeling.'

'Go on,' he urged, much in the same way as she had done.

'Oh, I don't know,' she smiled. 'We married, and seemed to be getting on so well, that I started to get wary and decided to keep out of your way.'

'Self-preservation.'

'Are you always going to be able to read my mind?'

'I hope so,' he grinned, making her heart somersault. 'More, please,' he requested.

'Then—the night Violette arrived—so much for my notion of self-preservation—I remember feeling light-hearted and had to wonder if it was because you seemed light-hearted too.'

'You took your mood from my mood?'

'Must have.'

'That was the same night you niggled me by impudently asking if we now got divorced.'

'You didn't seem to go much on the idea,' she recalled, that impudence he had spoken of there again in her eyes.

'Why would I? You were starting to get under my skin. That was the night I suggested putting a desk in my study for you—you declined, saying you wouldn't dream of disturbing me—having no idea how much you were disturbing me already. And that was before I accepted that there was no way I was going to let you go if I could help it.'

'Oh, Gideon,' she sighed, his words utter bliss.

'I've got to kiss you—then you must tell more,' he breathed—and kissed her not once, but twice.

'You expect me to concentrate after that?' She emerged pink about her cheeks.

He grinned. 'Try,' he suggested mercilessly. 'I want to hear all your thoughts and feelings. While part of me feels I've known you for ever, that there was never a time when I wasn't in love with you, there's another part of me that needs to know so much more about you, my beautiful Ellena.'

She sighed happily, and then concentrated really hard—but, instead of telling him anything, she found she was asking, 'That night, that night last week when you came home late from your business dinner, when you came into my room—it—er—wasn't in your mind to kiss me, was it?'

Gideon's mouth picked up at the corners. 'Not to start with. Having kissed you a couple of weeks before on my way out—knowing you'd think it was because Mrs Morris was around—I…'

'I remember that—we were in the hall. Mrs Morris wasn't…!' she gasped.

'She was nowhere near,' he confessed, not looking the slightest ashamed of himself. 'I kissed you purely because I was glad to see you, found that I didn't want to leave you, but, having done so, I realised that I was getting too attracted to you—and, since forward thinking decreed that was a no-no, I tried my level best to distance myself from you.'

Amazement mingled with pleasure because Gideon was being so wonderfully open with her, trusting in her love, revealing to her his innermost thoughts. 'I love you,' she said, purely because she had to, and was drawn up against his heart as he once more placed his mouth over hers.

'Keep telling me,' he insisted.

'Don't you believe me?'

'It's so utterly fantastic,' he answered jubilantly, and for long minutes was content to just hold her in his arms. Then he was saying ruefully, 'So there I was, thinking I might distance myself from you.'

'You couldn't?' she smiled impishly.

'Not always. There were times when I just couldn't resist your company. Which is why, lonesome for a sight of you, I came to your room that night and found you still working at your desk.'

'You came to tell me you would be away early the next morning,' Ellena remembered.

'And, for my sins, had to get up extra early so you wouldn't see that excuse for the lie it was.'

'It wasn't!' she gasped, and just had to burst out laughing. 'You lying toad!' she laughed. 'You wonderful, wonderful lying toad!' She pulled back to look at him and loved that he seemed to be enjoying her laughter, for his expression was clearly delighted.

'I hadn't seen you all day—I was missing you,' Gideon excused as her laughter faded.

'You—massaged my neck and shoulders,' she remembered. 'Er—did you have any idea of the—um—emotions you awakened in me that night?'

'Oh, sweet love,' Gideon said softly. 'I'm afraid I did suspect that you were not physically immune to me—just as you knew, I think, how very badly I wanted to kiss you.'

She sighed in pleasure. 'I thought you were going to, but then thought I'd got it wrong when you didn't.'

'Sweet Ellena, you got it absolutely right. I,' he went on to confess, 'got it absolutely wrong the next evening when, with you on my mind for most of that day, I'd just left a hotel conference room—and couldn't believe my eyes when through the glass doors of the dining room I saw you smiling happily at some good-looking swain as you ate your dinner.'

'You were jealous!' she gasped.

'I was furious! Damn that for a tale! I barely realised what I was doing when I charged through those doors, intent only on letting your good-looking escort know that you lived with me.'

'You *were* jealous!' she laughed.

'Wretched woman!' he becalled her. 'So I was jealous,' he admitted. 'As jealous as hell. I've never before known such a gut-tearing murderous emotion.'

Ellena was instantly contrite. 'I'm sorry. I should have phoned you to tell you about it in advance—only, well, I was still quite confused about what you'd made me feel the night before.'

'You say the most fantastic things,' he teased.

She looked away, shy for a brief moment. 'We had a row when I got home,' she recalled dreamily.

'Why wouldn't we?' he acknowledged. 'It was around midnight when you got home, and I'd been pacing the floor, alternating between concern for your safety and fury—jealousy blinding me to what I knew of you.'

'We did kiss and make up,' she reminded him.

'Oh, that we did,' he smiled.

'It seemed so right,' Ellena smiled back.

'It was,' he agreed. 'But I found you were so much on my mind, rarely out of my head, that I feared everything was getting out of hand. I felt I should calm the situation down—my study became my prison.'

'Serves you right,' she teased lovingly.

'It did too. Within a very few days we were having staffing problems and you were covering for them by having Violette sleep in your room. Which rather defeated the object,' *he* teased, 'when said infant started hollering—and you slept straight through it.'

'It was your fault,' she blamed him cheerfully. 'Thoughts of you kept me awake half the night! I'd only just dropped off when you were waking me up, a helpless male with a damp baby in your arms.'

'Remind me to get you for that!' he threatened. 'Though it's a fact I was wide awake with you on my mind when the little one started yelling. Did I mention, by the way, that you look adorable in sleep, with your hair all tousled and a beautiful tint of pink on your skin?'

'Oh, Gideon,' she murmured, and they kissed.

'Oh, my darling, I love you so much,' he breathed. And kissed her again, but pulled back to ask, 'When did you know for sure that you loved me?'

'In the early hours of yesterday morning,' she answered without hesitation. 'We got Violette settled to sleep again. And somehow started to make love—and I just knew. I no longer had to wonder why it was that you kept me sleepless. It was just—there. I knew I was in love with you.'

'Oh, sweet, sweet Ellena,' he breathed, and softly asked, 'Was that after you heartlessly informed me that you didn't think our making love was a very good idea?'

'I didn't mean to be heartless,' she said at once. But, remembering everything about that night, and with the honesty which Gideon appreciated, she mentioned slowly, 'I don't think I've ever felt so sensitive as I did at that particular time.'

'Entirely understandable, my little love,' Gideon murmured.

'You called me sweetheart,' she reminded him. 'Only you'd done it before—but for Mrs Morris's benefit—you'd meant nothing by it. And...'

'Oh, darling—in your highly sensitive state you thought I meant nothing by the endearment then?' Gideon cut in tenderly. 'You thought our lovemaking meant nothing to me! Sweet love,' he added gently, 'I loved you then, as I love you now.'

They kissed away any traces of pain or anguish. 'I'm sorry,' she apologised lovingly as they pulled back to look at each other.

'What for?' he teased, clearly having forgiven her for every one of her misdeeds.

'For being as outraged and jealous as you, for one thing,' she smiled.

'This I want to hear,' he encouraged.

'Last night—at that hotel,' she reminded him.

'Yes?' he quite plainly wanted more.

'I'd popped in to return some books they wanted—they're clients,' she inserted. 'And there are you, absolutely totally absorbed with a beautiful brunette... Need I go on?'

'The detective saw at once what I failed to see,' Gideon answered, cheerfully reminiscent.

'She saw I was in love with you,' Ellena agreed, confessing, 'I was appalled by my behaviour afterwards.'

'And I didn't know where the devil I was,' he owned. 'All the while I was wondering, dismissing, and hoping, that Mrs Turner had got it right when she stated ''Now there's a lady in love'', clearly meaning in love with me. At the same time I was trying to keep a lid on the hope she had given me about that phone call from Spain to the hotel in Austria from Señora Pender.'

'You intended to tell me about it when you came home and came to my room, didn't you?'

'There were so many reasons why I came to your room last night,' he owned. 'With Mrs Turner being certain you loved me, it was a splendid excuse—it wouldn't wait until morning—to try and find out how you felt personally about me. Also, I'd kept to myself the information I had that a couple answering Kit and Justine's description had left the area before the avalanche had struck. It had seemed to me too cruel to raise your hopes on anything so vague when the ski resort must have hundreds of couples who would fit the same description. But this time, backed by your absolute faith that Justine would never leave a hotel bill unpaid, I felt I had to share this latest news with you.'

'But—you didn't,' she teased. With both Justine and Kit now safe—not to mention that the man she loved incredibly loved her back—Ellena had no trouble in feeling lighthearted.

'I was nervous,' Gideon admitted. 'Afraid of tripping

over my words, and not knowing what to do first—tell you of the news from Austria, or try to find out if there was a chance that our detective might have got it right and you did care for me. You were not,' he accused, 'at all as I would imagine you would be—if you loved me.'

'Well—er—not to start with,' she agreed, feeling a shade pink about the cheeks. 'But I didn't know then that you loved me. If I remember rightly, you weren't too lover-like yourself to start with.'

'Why would I be? I'd come to your room with a head and heart full of matters that wouldn't wait until morning, and there you were sounding more as though you hated me than loved me. And if that wasn't enough, when I came home filled with hope, you had the colossal nerve to start talking divorce lawyers!'

'You—er—did seem a bit angry about that,' she murmured demurely.

'Wretch! I was furious!' Gideon admitted wryly.

'We did kiss and make each other better,' Ellena reminded him quickly.

'What was better about you so beautifully sending me away to my own bed?' he demanded mock-severely.

'I—was—um—frightened you'd think me gauche, might be disappointed that I didn't know very much,' Ellena confessed—and could only wonder at the tenderness for her that came over his expression.

'Oh, little love, your innocence is precious, didn't you know that?' he murmured gently. And, finding himself at fault, not her, he said, 'I should have been more understanding.'

'Don't say that! You were. You were understanding! You were wonderful. Only…'

'Only?' he encouraged.

'Only you referred to the night before when you asked was I going to go all bad-mannered on you again? And…'

'Oh, love, my sensitive love—and you remembered I'd

called you sweetheart the previous evening, and you believed again our lovemaking meant nothing to me.'

'You called me sweetheart once more on your way out.'

'Oh, little darling! Are you going to forgive me my sins?'

'Every one of them,' she smiled, and tenderly they kissed.

'What a woman you are!' he murmured adoringly, when after their tender kiss they drew apart and just looked lovingly at each other. 'Is it any wonder you come between me and my work, me and my sleep?'

'You were awake early this morning—I heard you moving about.'

'You were awake too?' Ellena gave a small nod, and Gideon cradled her into his shoulder. 'How could I sleep with so much going on in my head? I'd hoped to have some kind of a conversation with you this morning, even imagined that you might feel a little shy of me. I was all ready to put you at your ease. But no, even though you blushed scarlet, you didn't give me the chance to try and make things easier. You appeared to let me know you hadn't given me so much as another thought; in you breezed to the breakfast room as bright as a button, not interested in breakfast, and certainly not seeming to give a damn about me in your rush to get to your infernal pending file.'

'It would seem that love makes liars of us all,' she confessed, and apologised, 'It was the only way I could think of facing you after… Anyhow, it wasn't long before I saw you again.' She smiled. 'You came to my office to take me to the airport.'

'That was one hell of a wait!'

'I wouldn't argue that,' Ellena replied. 'Can you imagine Pamela withholding the information that Justine had been in touch!'

'I should have realised what she was up to—but just didn't,' Gideon replied. 'It's just so unthinkable that anyone wouldn't have the common decency to pass that information on, that I never for a moment gave the notion a thought. She couldn't have told Russell either.'

'He'd have phoned?'

'Straight away. He may wear blinkers where his wife is concerned, but he knew I'd been worried.' For a moment, a whisper of bleakness crossed his expression, and Ellena knew that while she had kept her feelings and fears that she might never see Justine again bottled up and hidden, so, too, had Gideon.

'They're safe,' she said gently, and smiled at him. 'It's all over now,' she added softly.

'It isn't—is it?' Gideon asked, his expression serious, something new there in his question.

'I—don't think I'm with you?'

'Us!' he said distinctly. 'I mean us, Ellena.'

Us! Suddenly her heart was once more thundering against her ribs. She swallowed, and took a gulp of breath. 'What are you saying, Gideon?' she asked.

'I'm saying that, having said I would see you at Oakvale, I never dreamed you wouldn't be there when I got back. I'm saying that I was only a little relieved when I checked your wardrobes and found that your clothes were still there.'

'You rang and said the weekend would be fine for me to come and pick them up.'

'There was no way, sweet love, I was going to leave it until the weekend before I saw you again,' he smiled, and, placing a tender kiss on one corner of her mouth, 'Darling Ellena, the house is empty without you there.'

It was no use, she had to swallow again. 'You—um— could only have been there for a couple of minutes before you left Oakvale to come here,' she managed huskily.

'The ache for you, the fear in me that you wouldn't want to come back, was such that it was as though you had been away months.'

'You—want me to come back?' she whispered.

'My darling, I love you. You can't begin to know how much. Nor know how terrified I've been, and am, that my worst fears may be confirmed, and that you will not want to return. That you may, God forbid, want our marriage to be over.'

Ellena stared at him, her lovely eyes huge in her face. 'Are you saying—that—er—you don't?' she whispered.

'Sweet, sweet love,' he murmured. 'That's what I thought I'd been telling you all this while. That I love and adore you, and that I want you and I—us—to stay married—permanently.'

'Oh!' she exclaimed, her heartbeats racing, emotional tears of the moment not far away, making it impossible for her to say more.

'Will you, my darling?' Gideon asked, his tone growing urgent. 'Will you? Do you love me enough to come with me, and live with me, and be my wife?'

Ellena had to swallow one more time before she could speak. 'Oh, Gideon,' she answered chokily, 'I love you enough.'

She felt his arms tighten around her. 'You'll stay married to me—never to divorce?'

Unbelievably, he still sounded unsure! 'Oh, Gideon, don't you know? I love you so much—I never want to be apart from you.'

His exclamation was lost as he held her close to him, his face in her hair—and for long moments they stayed like that. Then he was getting to his feet, bringing her to her feet, standing there with his arms still around her.

'Are you ready, then, wife, to come home?' he asked gruffly.

Ellena beamed a smile at him, thoroughly enchanted. 'Yes, husband, I am,' she whispered rapturously.

There was time for just one more kiss before they went.

Catherine George was born in Wales, and early on developed a passion for reading which eventually fuelled her compulsion to write. Marriage to an engineer led to nine years in Brazil, but on his later travels the education of her son and daughter kept her in the UK. And instead of constant reading to pass her lonely evenings she began to write the first of her romantic novels. When not writing and reading she loves to cook, listen to opera, browse in antiques shops and walk the Labrador.

Look out for Catherine George's wonderful novel: CITY CINDERELLA Coming in April in Modern Romance™

THE BABY CLAIM
by
Catherine George

CHAPTER ONE

WHEN she was certain the balcony was empty Joscelyn Hunter hid behind one of its pillars and let her smiling mask slip. For what seemed like hours she'd laughed and chatted and circulated like the perfect guest. But enough was enough. It had been a test to come to the party alone tonight. But Anna was her oldest friend. Missing her engagement celebrations had never been an option.

The breeze was cool, and Joss shivered as it found her bare arms. Soon she could make some excuse and go—where? Home to the empty flat? She stared malevolently at the view, lost in angry reverie, until at last a slight cough alerted her to unwanted company. Joss turned with bad grace, to see a tall man with a glass in either hand.

'I watched you steal away.' The stranger held out one of the glasses. 'Something told me you might be glad of this.'

Because there was no way she could snap at one of Anna's guests and tell him to get lost, Joss muttered perfunctory thanks and accepted the drink.

'Would you rather I left you to your solitude?' said the man, after a long silence.

Joss looked up into his face. A long way up, which was a novelty. 'You've as much right to look at Hyde Park as me,' she said, shrugging.

'I'll take that as a no.' He touched his glass to hers. 'What shall we drink to?'

'The happy pair?'

He echoed her toast, but barely tasted his wine.

'You don't care for champagne?' she asked politely.

'No. Do you?'

She shook her head. 'Secretly I detest the stuff.'

'Your secret's safe with me,' he assured her.

Joss relaxed against the pillar, surprised to find she rather welcomed the man's company after all. It was certainly preferable to her own. 'Are you one of Hugh's friends?'

'No.' He shrugged rangy shoulders. 'I'm a friend of a friend. Who dragged me along.'

She looked him up and down, amused. 'You're a bit on the large side to be dragged anywhere. Why were you unwilling?'

'I'm no party animal. But the friend disapproves of my social life. Or lack of it.' He leaned comfortably on the other side of the pillar. 'All work and no play is bad for me, he tells me. With monotonous frequency. So once in a while I give in and let him have his way. Don't drink that if you'd rather not,' he added.

'I've been on mineral water so far. Maybe a dose of champagne will improve my mood.' She drank the wine down like medicine.

Her companion nodded slowly. 'I see.'

She tilted her head to look at him. 'You see what, exactly?'

'I've been watching you for some time. Noting your body language.'

She stared up at him in mock alarm. 'What did it say?'

'That something's not right with your world.'

'So you came charging to my aid with medicinal champagne.' She shook her head in pretend admiration. 'Do you often play Good Samaritan?'

'No. Never.'

'Then why now?'

He leaned closer. 'Various reasons. But mainly because I'm—curious.'

'About what, in particular?'

'The mood behind the smiles.'

'I'd hoped I was concealing that,' Joss said gruffly, and turned away to stare across the park.

'No one else noticed,' he assured her.

'I hope you're right. The last thing Anna needs is a spectre at the feast.'

'Anna's a friend of yours?'

'Oldest and closest. But too euphoric tonight to notice anything amiss.'

Her large companion moved until his dark sleeve brushed her arm, and to her astonishment Joss felt a flicker of reaction, as though he'd actually touched her.

'Do you live with Anna?' he asked.

'No, I don't,' she said flatly, and shivered.

'You're cold,' he said quickly. 'Perhaps you should go in.'

'Not yet. But you go, if you want.'

'Do you want me to?'

'Not if you'd prefer to stay,' she said indifferently, but hoped he would. In the dim light all she could make out was the man's impressive height, topped by a strong-featured face under thick dark hair. But what she could see she liked very much.

'Take this.' He shrugged out of his jacket and draped it round her shoulders, enveloping her in a warm aura of healthy male spiked with spice and citrus. 'Otherwise you might get pneumonia in that dress,' he said, his voice a tone deeper.

Joss gave a laugh rendered slightly breathless by the intimacy of the gesture. 'You don't approve of my dress?'

'No.'

'Why not?'

'If you were mine I wouldn't let you out in it.'

Joss gave him a sub-zero stare. 'Really!'

'I'm not famous for tact,' he said, lips twitching. 'You asked a question and I answered it.'

'True,' she acknowledged, and thawed a little. 'The dress was very expensive, in honour of the occasion. I like it.'

'So do I!'

The dress was an ankle-length tube of black crêpe de Chine, edged with lace at the hem and across the breasts, held up by fragile straps and side-slit to the knee. Joss looked down at herself, then shot an amused look at her companion. 'But you don't approve?'

'No.'

'And I was so sure I looked good in it,' she said with mock regret.

'Every man present thinks you look sensational,' he assured her.

'Except you.'

'*Especially* me. But it's a very ambiguous dress.'

Joss found she was enjoying herself. 'A strange word to describe a frock.'

His deep-throated chuckle vibrated right through the fine bespoke suiting, sending a trickle of reaction down her bare spine.

'It may be a party dress to you,' he went on, 'but to me it smacks of the bedroom.'

Her chin lifted. 'I assure you it's not a nightgown. I don't sleep in this kind of thing.'

'Which makes me even more curious about what you do—or don't—sleep in,' he said softly, sending a second trickle down her spine to join the first.

'We shouldn't be having this conversation,' she said brusquely.

'Why?'

'We've never met before.'

'Then let's introduce ourselves.' He took her hand in a hard, warm clasp. 'Tell me your name.'

Joss stared down at their hands, amazed to find herself flustered by his touch. 'Let's not get into names,' she said, after a moment. 'I don't want to be me tonight. Just call me—Eve.'

'Then I'll be Adam.' He shook her hand formally. 'The party's almost over. Take pity on a lonely stranger, Miss Eve, and have supper with me.'

Joss gave him a very straight look. 'I thought you came with a friend.'

'I did. He won't mind.' He bent his head to look in her eyes. 'What was your original plan for the evening?'

Joss turned back to the view. 'Originally I did have a date for tonight,' she admitted shortly. 'But it fell through. Which accounts for the lack of party spirit. Consequently—Adam—I don't much fancy bright lights and a restaurant.'

'Then I'll get a meal sent up to my room here,' he said promptly, and grinned at the incensed look she shot at him. 'All I offer—and expect—is dinner, Eve.'

'If I say yes to a meal in your room,' she said bluntly, 'you might expect a lot more than that.'

'I was watching you long before you vanished out here,' he reminded her. 'I know you're not the archetypal party girl out for a good time.'

'Do you?' Joss detached her hand and gave him his jacket. 'But you have the advantage, Adam. If you watched me earlier you obviously know what I look like. I haven't even seen your face properly yet.'

He shrugged into his jacket, then moved to the centre of the balcony. From the room inside a shaft of light fell on a strong face with an aquiline nose and a wide, firmly clenched mouth. His cheekbones were high, the eyes slanted, one heavy dark eyebrow raised towards his thick, springing hair as he bore her scrutiny.

'Well?' he said dryly. 'Will I pass?'

With flying colours, she decided. 'All right—Adam. I'd like to have supper with you,' she said quickly, before she could change her mind. 'But *not* in your room.'

He smiled wryly. 'Then tell me which restaurant you prefer and I'll arrange it.'

Just like that. Joss eyed him curiously, in no doubt that if this man asked for a table no restaurant, however sought after, would refuse him. She thought it over for a moment, then gave him a straight look. 'As you've gathered, I'm not in party mood. But we could have supper at my place—if you like.'

His lips twitched. 'Can you cook?'

'I offered supper, not haute cuisine,' she retorted.

He laughed, then moved into her shadowy corner to take her hand. 'I'm delighted to accept your invitation, Miss Eve.'

The charge of electricity from his touch hinted at danger she chose to ignore in her present reckless mood. 'Let's go, then,' Joss said briskly. 'But not together. You first.'

He nodded. 'Allow a discreet interval for me to thank your friends. I'll have the car waiting at the main entrance in twenty minutes.'

When she was alone Joss leaned on the balcony for a while, almost convinced she'd imagined the encounter. But a furtive peep through the curtains showed her new acquaintance dominating the group clustered round Anna and Hugh. Very nice indeed, thought Joss, reassured, and much too tall to be a figment of anyone's imagination. She waited until he'd gone, then emerged from her hiding place and joined Anna and Hugh.

'We were about to send a search party for you, Joss,' said Anna indignantly. 'Where on earth have you been?'

'Communing with nature on a discreet balcony,' said Joss demurely.

'Alone?' asked Hugh, grinning.

'Of course not.' She batted her eyelashes at him. 'Anyway, must dash—supper for two awaits. Thanks for a lovely party. See you soon.' Joss hugged Anna, kissed Hugh's cheek, then did the rounds, saying her goodbyes, made a detour to tidy herself up in a cloakroom, and at last took the lift down to the foyer, where a man in hotel livery ushered her outside to a waiting car.

'You're late,' growled an impatient voice as she slid into the passenger seat.

'Sorry. Couldn't get away.' Joss gave him her address with sudden reluctance, hoping this wasn't a colossal mistake.

'I'd begun to think you'd changed your mind,' said Adam as he drove away.

He was very nearly right. 'If so I would have sent a message,' she said crisply.

'Ah. A woman of principle!'

'I try to be.' Joss turned a long look on the forceful profile, and saw the wide mouth twist a little.

'I hear you, Eve, loud and clear.'

'Good. What happened to the friend, by the way?'

'When told I was dining with a ravishing lady he sent me on my way with his blessing.'

Joss laughed. 'You're obviously very *old* friends.'

'We've known each other all our lives.'

'Like Anna and me.' She sighed. 'I just hope Hugh makes her happy.'

'Is there any reason why he shouldn't?'

'None that I know of. I like him very much.'

'Then it's marriage itself you distrust?'

'Not exactly. But Anna is so certain they'll live happily ever after. And all too often people don't.'

'Leave your friend to her quite obviously besotted fiancé and concentrate on yourself, Eve.'

'Thanks for the advice,' she said tartly, and made polite small talk until they arrived at a modern apartment building sitting in surprising harmony with its Victorian Notting Hill neighbours.

Adam parked the car, then followed Joss into one of the lifts in the rather stark, functional foyer.

'I live on the sixth floor,' she said, feeling a definite qualm as the door closed to pen her in the small space with her large escort.

Adam frowned down at her. 'You're not comfortable with this, are you?'

'Not entirely,' she admitted.

He shrugged. 'In which case I'll just see you safely to your door and fade into the night.'

Joss felt sudden remorse. 'Certainly not,' she said firmly. 'I invited you to supper so I'll provide it.' She looked at him questioningly. 'Would you really have left me at my door?'

'If you'd wanted that, yes. But with great reluctance.' He pressed her hand in reassurance. 'I keep my word, Eve.'

'If I didn't believe that I wouldn't have invited you here,' she assured him.

Inside the flat, Joss led her visitor past her closed bedroom door and switched on lights as she took him along

a narrow hall into a sitting room with tall windows looking out over communal gardens. The room was large,
with free-standing shelves crammed with books, and a
pair of brass lamps perched precariously on the top shelf.
Otherwise there was only a small sofa and a large floor
cushion.

'Please sit down,' said Joss. Half empty or not, the
room looked a lot smaller than usual with her visitor
standing like a lighthouse in the middle of it. 'Supper's
no problem because I did some shopping today. But I
wasn't expecting company so all I can offer you in the
way of a drink is red wine—or possibly some whisky.'

'Wine sounds good.' Adam let himself down on the
sofa, and stretched out his endless legs. 'If it's red it
should breathe, so I'll wait until the meal. Can I help?'

Joss shook her head, chuckling. 'No room for giants
in my kitchen. I'll open the wine first, then throw a meal
together. Shan't be long.'

As she worked swiftly Joss decided she liked the look
of her unexpected guest very much. Not handsome, exactly, but the navy blue eyes, dark hair and chiselled
features appealed to her strongly. So did the air of confidence he wore as casually as his Savile Row suit. She
tossed a green salad with oil and vinegar, carved a cold
roast chicken, sliced and buttered an entire small loaf,
and put a hunk of cheese on a plate. She shared the
chicken salad between two dinner plates on a forty-sixty
basis, put them on a tray with silver, napkins and glasses,
added the bread, cheese and wine, and a bowl of fruit,
then went back to the sitting room and put the tray on
the floor.

Her guest swung round from his absorption in her
bookshelves to smile at her. 'A wide range of literature,'
he commented.

'My main extravagance. Do sit down again.' She smiled in apology as she poured the wine. 'I'm afraid it's a picnic. You may live to regret not having your hotel dinner.'

'I doubt it.' Adam received his plate with approval. 'What could possibly be better than this?' He looked up, the indigo eyes holding hers. 'Thank you, Eve.'

'My pleasure,' she said lightly, then curled up on the floor cushion to eat her own meal, realising this was the truth. After resigning herself to a solitary evening, probably not even bothering to eat at all, the present circumstances were a vast improvement.

'For me,' said Adam, raising his glass to her in toast, 'it's a pleasure—and a privilege—I never anticipated when I first set eyes on you tonight.'

'When was that?'

'The moment I arrived. You stood out from the crowd.'

'Because I'm tall,' said Joss, resigned. 'But how on earth did I come to miss someone of your dimensions?'

'We were late. And it was the hair I noticed, not your height. You had your back to me, but you were facing a mirror. I could see that narrow face of yours framed in it, and wondered why the eyes were at such odds with the smiling mouth. The contradiction intrigued me.'

'I'm glad I didn't know,' said Joss with feeling. 'Rather like being caught on Candid Camera. I hope I was behaving myself?'

'Of course you were. The perfect guest.' Adam helped himself to more bread. 'But I could tell you weren't in party mood. I was surprised—and impressed—that you stuck it out so long.'

'So you saw me disappear,' said Joss thoughtfully.

He nodded. 'At which point inspiration struck. At worst, I reasoned, you would send me packing.'

'And at best?'

'The privilege of talking to you.' He gave her a direct look. 'My imagination never got as far as this.'

'Chicken salad and questionable claret?' she said flippantly.

'Exactly. Now, tell me why you asked me back here tonight.'

Joss shot him a warning look. 'Certainly not to share my bed.'

'I thought we'd sorted that out already,' he said impatiently. 'Listen to me, Eve. In basic terms, I swear I won't leap on you the moment we've finished supper, or at any other time—is that blunt enough for you?'

Blunt and very reassuring, decided Joss. 'Yes. Thank you.'

He eyed her searchingly. 'You've obviously had bad experiences in the past in this kind of situation?'

She shook her head. 'I never invite men here for supper.' Which was true enough.

He frowned. 'Never?'

'Never.'

'Then why me?'

'Because you were in the right place at the right time,' she said candidly. 'I was in need of company tonight, and you offered yours.'

Adam leaned forward, one of the heavy brows raised. 'You mean I happened to be nearest, that any man would have done?'

'Certainly not,' she snapped, and jumped up. 'You were kind. I liked that. But, best of all, you're *very* tall.'

He looked amused. 'Is height a vital requirement?'

'No. But for me it's a definite plan. I'm five feet ten, with a passion for high heels.'

Adam laughed as he refilled their glasses, and took very little persuading to finish off the bread and cheese. She offered him the fruit bowl. 'Have one of these to go with it.'

His lips twitched as he took a shiny red apple. 'Very appropriate, Eve. Will my life change for ever after one taste?'

'Try it and see.' Joss smiled and sank down to her cushion again as his strong white teeth crunched into the apple. 'Sorry there wasn't any pudding.'

'This is all a man could ask for. Company included,' he added. 'Do you feel better now?'

'Yes. I haven't been eating well lately.'

'I didn't mean the food.'

'I know. And since you ask, yes, I do feel better.'

'Good.' Adam finished everything on his plate and put it on the tray. 'Shall I take this out to your kitchen for you?'

She shook her head. 'Leave it. I'll see to it later.'

'Much later.' He looked at her steadily. 'I've no intention of leaving yet.'

Joss was glad of it. The last thing she wanted right now was solitude.

'I've respected the veto on names,' he went on, 'but is it against the rules to ask what you do with your life?'

Joss decided against telling him she was a journalist. That might give too much away. For tonight she would just be romantic, mysterious Eve. 'I'm—in publishing.'

'Fiction?'

'No. Fact.' Joss settled herself more comfortably. 'How about you?'

'Construction.'

Joss was struck by a mental picture of suntanned muscles and heavy loads of bricks. 'It obviously pays,' she
commented, eyeing his clothes.

'If you mean the suit,' he said, straight-faced. 'It's the
one I keep for parties and funerals. My Sunday best.'

'Is it really?'

'Absolutely.' His eyes roved over her tawny blonde
bob, the wide-spaced eyes, the faint suggestion of tilt to
the nose. His gaze lingered for a moment on the full
curves of her mouth, then continued down until it reached
her black silk pumps. 'I don't think you bought any of
that in a chainstore, either.'

'True. I felt Anna's engagement party deserved something special.' Her eyes clouded. 'And when I bought it
I was in belligerent mood.'

'Is this something to do with the dinner date that fell
through?'

Joss smiled bleakly. 'In a way.'

'But there's a lot more.'

'Oh, yes.' Her eyes glittered angrily. 'A whole lot
more.'

'Would it help to tell me about it?'

Joss frowned, taken aback.

'It's easier to confide in strangers,' he pointed out.

'I see. I confide my pathetic little story, you offer me
a shoulder to cry on, then off you go into the night and
we never meet again?' She smiled. 'I think I saw the
movie.'

'I'd prefer to alter the script a little,' he said, chuckling.
'But whatever you tell me will be in strictest confidence.'

'Like confessing to a priest?'

Adam shook his head. 'Wrong casting.'

She nodded, looking at him objectively. 'You're right.
You don't suit the role.'

'But I'm a superb listener,' he assured her.

'And you're curious?'

'Interested, certainly.'

Joss gazed at him for a moment, weakening by the second in her need to talk to someone. Anna would have been her normal choice, but that, like staying away from the engagement party, had been out of the question. At least until Anna's celebrations were over and the new, yawning gap in Joscelyn Hunter's life could no longer be hidden.

'Are you sure about this?' she asked.

Adam nodded decisively. 'I want to know what was behind the Oscar-winning performance tonight.'

Joss gave him a wry little smile and took the plunge. 'I used to share this flat with my fiancé. A few weeks ago he walked out on me.'

CHAPTER TWO

Joss had made an all-out effort to get home early for once. She'd rushed through the door, laden down with groceries for a celebration dinner. And almost fallen over the luggage in the hall.

As she'd stared Peter Sadler had rushed from the bedroom, his face the picture of guilt. 'You're home early!' he accused.

Joss nodded coolly. 'And you're obviously not pleased to see me. Is there a problem?'

'Yes, you could say that.' He took the grocery bag from her. 'I'll put this in the kitchen. Would you like some tea?'

Joss stood tense with foreboding, watching as Peter filled a kettle and put teabags in a pot. 'So what *is* the problem? And why the suitcases? Are you going somewhere for the firm?'

'No.' He turned to look at her, a truculent look on his fair, good-looking face. 'I've resigned.'

She stared incredulously. '*Resigned?* Why?'

'I got in first, before they could fire me.'

Joss shook her head in disbelief. 'This is terribly sudden, Peter! If you were that worried they'd fire you why didn't you talk to me about it?'

'When?' he threw at her in sudden anger. 'You're never here.'

'That's an exaggeration,' she snapped. 'We share a bed, remember? You could have given me a hint on one

19

of the rare occasions you stayed awake long enough to say goodnight.'

'You know I need my sleep,' he said sullenly. 'And lately there's been precious little to stay awake for. We haven't made love for weeks. You lust for your job more than you ever did for me.'

Joss felt as though her entire world was disintegrating. 'You've obviously been building up to this for a long time. I've been blind.' She thrust an unsteady hand through her hair. 'I know you've been very quiet lately, but I thought that was for a different reason.'

'What other reason?' he said blankly, adding salt to the wound. 'All I could think of lately were my plans for the new riverside complex.' His mouth twisted. 'In case you're interested, Athena turned them down.'

Joss stared at him in horrified sympathy. 'Peter—I'm so sorry! I know how hard you worked.' She frowned. 'But it isn't the end of the world, surely?'

'Of mine, with this particular firm of architects, it most definitely *is*.' Peter shrugged his shoulders moodily. 'Not that it matters. I was never cut out for corporate cut and thrust, Joss. I only took the job in the first place because you pushed me into it. I'm going back to the family firm. Where I belong,' he added as the crowning touch. He glanced at his watch, then caught her eye and flushed. 'I'm in no rush, Joss,' he said quickly. 'I can catch a later train.'

'Don't alter your arrangements on my account!' She stood with arms folded. 'I assume this means it's all over between us?'

Peter swallowed convulsively. 'I suppose it does.'

'You *suppose*?'

'I left you a letter, Joss,' he said hurriedly. 'It explains everything.'

'How thoughtful.' She eyed him with scorn. 'So if I'd come home at the usual time I would have found the bird flown?'

'I thought it would be easier that way,' he muttered, and handed her a cup of tea.

Joss slammed it down on a shelf. 'Easier for you, certainly, Peter.'

He shrugged sulkily. 'All right. Easier for me. Look, Joss, things haven't been right between us for a long time.' He squared his slim shoulders and looked her in the eye. 'If you want the truth, I'm just not happy with you anymore. You're older than me, more ambitious, you earn more money—hell, you're even taller than me. You—you diminish me, Joss. I can't take it any longer.'

'I see.' Joss's eyes burned angrily in her pale face. 'So that's it? The past year means nothing at all to you?'

'Is it only a year?' he said with unconscious cruelty. 'I thought it was longer than that. Anyway, I'm sorry it had to end like this. A pity you came home before I could—'

'Sneak away?' she said scathingly.

'Don't Joss! Let's part friends—please,' he pleaded, and put his hand on her arm.

She flung it away, suddenly unable to bear his touch. 'Just take your things and go, Peter. A pity my timing was wrong. You could have got away scot-free.'

He stepped back in quick offence. 'So why *were* you early?'

Joss clenched her teeth. 'I just felt like it. Goodbye, Peter.'

He moved towards her, arms outstretched, but backed away in a hurry as he met the look in her eyes. 'Goodbye, then, Joss. I—I wish things could have been different. If I'd won the Athena job—'

'I would still be older than you—and taller.' Her mouth twisted. 'I never dreamed it mattered so much.'

'In the beginning it didn't,' he muttered.

Joss locked militant eyes with his. 'Peter, tell me the truth. You owe me that much.'

He frowned. 'I *have* told the truth. Hell, I thought I'd even been a bit over the top with it. I never meant to come out with all that stuff about your age—and the height and so on.'

She shrugged impatiently. 'Never mind all that. Just tell me if there's someone else.'

'Another woman? Lord, no,' said Peter, with unmistakable candour. 'You've always been more woman than I can really handle, Joss. Never had any time—or energy—for anyone else.'

Joss looked across at Adam, taking comfort from the fierce look of distaste in his eyes. 'Oddly enough, that was the last straw. I lost it completely, made a terrible scene, threw my ring at him and sent him packing. Then I rang a removal firm and arranged to ship most of his belongings to his parents.' Her mouth twisted. 'Which is why I'm a bit lacking in home comforts. All the furniture was Peter's, but I've kept the sofa and the bed until—until I buy replacements.'

Adam gave her a probing look. 'You've kept all this secret?'

'Yes. No one knows yet, other than you.'

'Not even your parents?'

'I don't have any now. And I just couldn't spoil things for Anna before the party. I told her Peter was away on a course and couldn't come. She lives in Warwickshire, so it was easy to keep it from her for a while.'

'No wonder you weren't in party mood,' he said dryly.

She pulled a face. 'One way and another the party was a bit hard to take. Eventually the effort to sparkle was too much, so I spotted that deserted little balcony and vanished for a bit.'

Adam smiled a little. 'In the circumstances I'm surprised you were so polite when I joined you.'

Joss smiled back guiltily. 'My first reaction was to snarl and tell you to get lost. But after a while I was glad of your company. It kept me from wallowing in self-pity. It was gallant of you to come to my rescue.'

Adam shook his head. 'I'm no knight in shining armour, Eve. If the damsel in distress had been less pleasing to the eye I might have felt the same sympathy, but I doubt I'd have done anything about it.'

'An honest man!'

'I try to be. I watched your every move from the moment I first saw you. When you did your vanishing trick I seized the moment, grabbed two glasses of champagne and followed you outside.'

Her eyes danced. 'What would you have done if a vengeful husband had come after you?'

'Beaten a hasty retreat.' He grinned. 'I steer clear of husbands, vengeful or otherwise. I prefer my women unattached.'

'Your women?' Joss repeated.

'A figure of speech.'

Her eyes narrowed suddenly. 'Are *you* unattached, by the way?'

'Yes,' he said with emphasis. 'Otherwise this wouldn't be happening.'

'Would you like some coffee?' she said unevenly, very much aware that something *was* happening.

'Is that a polite way of asking me to go?'

Joss gave him a long, considering look. 'No,' she said quietly. 'Not if you'd like to stay awhile.'

'You know I would. And I don't want any more coffee,' he said deliberately. 'Shall I tell you what I do want?'

'No—please,' said Joss swiftly. 'Before Peter and I began to live together we'd been exclusive to each other for a fair time. I'm out of practice at this sort of thing.'

'What "sort of thing" do you think this is?' he asked, amused.

'More to the point, what do *you* think it is?'

'A simple desire to get to know you. How about you?'

Joss thought about it, fairly sure that 'simple' was the last word to describe her guest. 'I asked you here for a meal because I was depressed and angry, and you were kind and—'

'A lot taller than you,' he finished for her, and Joss laughed, suddenly more at ease.

'You're taller than most people!'

'I've never had more cause to be thankful for it than right now,' he assured her. 'So, mysterious Eve, come and sit beside me and hold my hand.'

'Ah, but if I give you my hand will you want more than that?'

'Yes,' he said bluntly. 'I'm male, and normal. But where women are concerned I don't take, Eve, only accept.'

'In that case...' Joss moved from her cushion to sit beside him on the sofa, discovering that the space left by his large frame was only just enough to accommodate her. 'A tight fit,' she said breathlessly.

Adam shifted slightly to give her more room, and took her hand in his. 'You were right,' he said after a moment.

'Just holding your hand isn't enough. Go back to your cushion.'

'Just how much else did you have in mind?' Joss asked very bluntly.

For answer Adam slid his arm round her. 'Only this.'

Joss laid her head against his shoulder, reassured, and the hard arm pulled her closer. It was new, and morale-boosting, to feel small and fragile in a man's embrace. She leaned against him, feeling safe and protected, his warmth soothing the anger and hurt of Peter's abrupt departure from her life.

'Why the sigh?' he asked.

'I was thinking how strange it was to be here like this with a man I'd never met until a few hours ago.'

'But you're no longer afraid of me,' he commented.

'I wasn't *afraid* of you,' she said indignantly, turning her face up to his.

He smiled down into her eyes. 'Nervous, then?'

'Yes.' She smiled back.

'Are you nervous now?'

'No.'

'So how *do* you feel?'

'Comfortable.'

His crack of laughter disarmed her completely. 'Not very flattering.'

'For me, tonight, it's the most flattering compliment I could pay you,' she said with feeling.

He raised the hand he was holding to his lips, and kissed it. 'If it's any consolation, I think the absconding fiancé's a complete idiot. But I'm grateful to him.'

'Why?'

'If he hadn't left I wouldn't be here.'

'True.' Joss yawned suddenly. 'Sorry,' she said with contrition. 'I haven't slept much lately.'

Adam smoothed her head down against his shoulder again. 'Relax,' he whispered in her ear, and Joss closed her eyes, melting against him pliantly.

She woke from a doze to find herself in Adam's arms *en route* to her bedroom. He bent slightly to open the door, then laid her on the bed and stood looking down at her.

'Goodnight, Eve,' he whispered, and bent to kiss her cheek.

Joss deliberately tilted her head so that the kiss landed squarely on her mouth, and suddenly the overwhelming need to feel whole and normal and desirable again obliterated caution. 'Don't go,' she said unsteadily. 'Don't leave me. Just for tonight. Please?'

Joss stared up in entreaty into the taut face, saw him close his eyes and clench his fists for an instant. Then he let out an unsteady breath, sat down on the bed and lifted her onto his lap, his forehead against hers.

'This wasn't meant to happen, Eve.'

'Don't you want me?' she said desolately.

'You know damn well I do!' he growled.

'Then show me.'

He locked his arms round her, pressing light, tantalising kisses at the corners of her mouth, but the contact ignited heat which rose in them both so quickly he was soon kissing her with a hunger which showed beyond all doubt how much he wanted her. She kissed him back, exulting in the desire she could feel vibrating through his body as he pulled her hard against him. Their kisses grew wilder, open-mouthed, tongues caressing as his hands sought breasts which rose taut with invitation in response. His breath rasped in his broad chest as he pulled away slightly to shrug off his jacket and tear his tie loose. Joss burrowed her face against him, her seeking hands undoing shirt buttons to find smooth skin hot to the touch. Darts of fire shot through her as she felt him hard and ready beneath her thighs, then he stood her on her feet and Joss backed away from him, her eyes locked with his in the semi-darkness. Slowly she slid the dress down her body, deliberate in her intention to inflame. She stepped out of the pooled silk and lace, then bent slowly to detach black silk suspenders from sheer dark stockings, and in triumph heard the hiss of his breath before he seized her, his mouth hard on hers as he dispensed with their remaining garments. At last he lifted her high in his arms, his eyes blazing with such need she shivered in excitement, and hid her hot face against his throat as he laid her on the bed.

'Are you sure?' he said harshly, in the moment before the question was too late. Joss nodded vehemently and stretched up her arms, pulling him down to her, and he stretched his long body beside her and slid his hands down her back to smooth her against him, their hearts thudding in perfect unison at the contact. Joss made a small, choked sound of protest as he put her away a little, then gasped in delight as he began to kiss every curve and hollow of her tall, slender body. The relentless, controlled caresses kindled slow fire along every nerve until Joss was in such an unashamed state of arousal that he abandoned the control, his hands and mouth so demanding they took her to dizzying heights of response. She surged against him, her fingers digging into the taut muscles of his broad shoulders, and he raised himself on his hands, his arms throbbing with the desire surging through his body. He asked a brief, urgent question and she shook her head wildly, and at last his body took possession of hers with a thrust of pure sensation, and she gasped, overwhelmed by fiery, rhythmic pleasure which mounted in increasing levels of intensity until white-hot culmination engulfed them both.

'What does one say in these circumstances?' she panted afterwards, when his arms had slackened slightly.

'What do you usually say?' Adam said hoarsely.

'Goodnight, I suppose.'

He raised his head to peer down into her face. 'Is that what you want *me* to say?'

'No.' Her eyes fell. 'Unless you want to go now.'

He kissed her hard. 'No, I don't want to go. I want to stay here, holding you in my arms all night, and maybe pinching myself from time to time to make sure this is real.'

'I feel like that,' she confessed. 'Shocked, too.'

'Shocked at what we did?'

'No,' she said dryly. 'I know about the birds and the bees.'

He laughed and kissed her again more gently, running the tip of his tongue over her lips. 'So what are you shocked about?'

'That I could have actually begged you to make love to me.' Joss bit her lip. 'I've never done that before.'

'I'm sure you haven't,' he said, his broad chest vibrating with laughter.

'I'm glad you find it so amusing!'

'Extraordinary, not amusing,' he assured her huskily. 'If you hadn't asked me to make love to you it's possible I might have found the strength to kiss you goodnight and leave, but I seriously doubt it. I wanted you from the moment I first saw your reflection in the mirror tonight.'

'Are you saying that to make me feel better?'

Adam smiled down into her eyes. 'No. It's the simple truth.'

Joss sighed with satisfaction, her mouth curving in a

smile he bent to kiss, taking his time over it. When she could speak she put a finger on his lips. 'You've achieved something rather wonderful tonight.'

'Don't I know it!'

'Not that,' she said impatiently, then smiled. 'Well, yes, that too, because it *was* wonderful. But the *way* you made love to me healed my poor, battered ego.'

'What way?' he asked, frowning.

'As though you were starving and I was food.' Joss blushed in the semi-darkness as he chuckled and ran his hands down the curve of her hips.

'That's it exactly,' he assured her. 'For me the entire evening was one long build-up of foreplay. Before I'd kissed this mouth, or caressed these exquisite breasts, all I could think of was this—and this—'

Adam matched caresses to his words with such skill desire swiftly engulfed them again, sending them in another breathtaking, headlong rush towards ecstasy.

CHAPTER THREE

AT SOME time in the night Joss was aware of hands pulling the covers over her, of a warm, hard mouth on hers for an instant, and a whispered goodnight in her ear, then she slept again until daylight brought her back to earth with a bump.

For a moment, as bright sunlight poured across the bed, she wondered if she'd dreamed the prolonged, sensual fantasy of the night.

But one look at the wild disorder of the bed told her it had all been blazingly real. A violent tremor ran through Joss at the thought of it. She breathed in deeply, pushed back the tangled covers and got out, raked tousled hair out of her eyes, restored a couple of pillows to their rightful place, then pulled on a dressing gown and ventured into the hall to make sure Adam had gone. When she found she was alone in the flat, Joss let out a deep, shaky breath. She hugged her arms across her chest, her face on fire at the memory of her utter abandon in the dark. She knew people who indulged in one-night stands without turning a hair. But it just wasn't her style. Last night had been a first on several counts. Living and sleeping with the man she'd expected to share her life with for ever had been no preparation for the bliss experienced in the arms of a total stranger.

There are names for women like you, Joss told herself darkly, and went off to run a hot bath. She lay in it for a long time, deep in thought, devoutly thankful that no one had actually seen her with Adam. If she were careful enough last night could remain a secret. She was unlikely to bump into her mystery lover again, whoever he was. Not that his identity mattered. Overpoweringly attractive he might be, but after her recent exit from the frying pan she had no intention of tumbling straight into the fire again, with Adam or anyone else. Joss got out of the bath, wincing as certain muscles protested in ways that brought colour to her face to think of them. She dressed hurriedly, and went into the kitchen, then stopped dead as she saw the note propped against the kettle.

Eve, it's damnably hard to tear myself away, but you might prefer to be alone when you wake. I'm out of the country for a few days. I'll ring when I get back. Adam.

Heat surged inside Joss. Shaken by the sheer, physical force of it, she fought hard against temptation. Last night, she told herself fiercely, had happened solely because Peter had left her devastated. Adam had restored her faith in herself quite miraculously. Their glorious night together had been a fitting climax to part of her life. But now it was time to get on with the rest of it. Besides, if she saw Adam again there would be no more mystery. Hard facts would be required about names and careers. So if he rang she would no longer be here. There had been a strong, sudden magic about last night. But magic couldn't be expected to last, or even happen twice. Joss hugged her arms across her chest to steady her thudding heart. Adam was a man of powerful charisma, and in her vulnerable state his passionate lovemaking had provided a quite wonderful salve for her bruised self-esteem. The Eve part of her longed to see him again. But realistic Joss knew that what seemed so irresistibly romantic in the

hours of darkness might seem very different if they met
again in the harsh light of day.

Early next morning Joss was packed and ready when the
removal firm came to take her belongings away. One of
the sub-editors on the *Post* had been searching for a flat
in Notting Hill for months. After Peter's departure Joss
had neither wanted nor could afford to live in the flat
alone, and so had asked Nick Holt if he and Carrie fan-
cied exchanging their flat in Acton for hers. The Holts
had jumped at the chance, and the exchange was carried
out at top speed. The new address was less fashionable,
but the flat was in good repair, carried a much smaller
price tag, and had no memories of Peter—or Adam—to
haunt it.

The removal men had finished loading her belongings
into the service lift and Joss was about to leave when a
youth came hurrying towards her, holding a florist's box.

'Miss Eve?' he asked.

Joss opened her mouth to say no, then flushed and said
yes.

'These are for you, then. They should have arrived
earlier—bit of a problem with the greenery.'

Joss thanked him, and gave him a tip. The box held a
sheaf of yellow roses on a bed of leaves. Fig leaves, she
realised, her heart hammering. *'From Adam'*, said the
card, and Joss buried her face in the blooms, suddenly
engulfed in the memory of a hard, possessive body taut
with desire, of skilled, caressing hands and gratifying,
devouring kisses… She shivered, eyes tightly shut for a
moment, then took in a deep, steadying breath, blotting
out the memory by sheer strength of will. Then she
closed the door and locked away a year of her life.

Her new home occupied the upper floor of an

Edwardian house in a picturesque terrace of identical
houses in varying states of restoration and repair. It was
much smaller than the flat in Notting Hill, but it would
need less furniture, had a separate front door and private
stairs, a forecourt to park the car, and, best of all, left
Joss in possession of a sizeable sum of money. Part of
this would go to Peter, to cover his half of the deposit
on the expensive Notting Hill flat he'd insisted on, due
to its superior architecture and fashionable address. But
Joss had paid off the mortgage.

   Once the removal men had gone Joss telephoned for a
pizza, then rang Anna to give her the new phone number.

   'I wish I could be there to help,' said Anna. 'Has Peter
taken time off to give you a hand?'

   'No,' said Joss, taking a deep breath. 'Look, Anna, are
you busy? I've got something to tell you.'

   Joss put the phone down later, feeling drained. Anna
had blown her top, said a great many uncomplimentary
things about Peter Sadler, congratulated Joss on being rid
of such a poisonous rat, then offered to drive up to
London that minute to provide a shoulder for her friend
to cry on.

   Joss had refused affectionately. 'I'll soon get used to
being single again. I'll be fine. Don't worry, Anna.'

   'I do worry,' said her friend stormily. 'Hugh was right.
He never liked Peter. Anyway, did you enjoy the party?'

   'Of course I did. By the way, who was that very tall
man I saw with you when people were leaving?'

   'Which one? I hadn't met half of Hugh's friends before.'

   'I think this one was more a friend of a friend.'

   'Shall I ask Hugh?'

   'No, don't bother. Anyway, I must go. My lunch has
arrived.'

Once she'd eaten her pizza, Joss locked up and went shopping for furniture. She ordered a comfortable sofa and pair of tables to hold her lamps, chose a restored brass bed, and arranged for delivery. Then she turned her attention to food. Her unexpected guest had demolished all the provisions bought to tide her over the move. Which was hardly surprising. There was a lot of him to keep fuelled. Joss thrust groceries in a basket at random, controlling a shiver at another memory of Adam's naked body. Making love with him, she told herself trenchantly, had happened purely because he'd materialised in her life at a time when she desperately needed to feel wanted and desirable again. And though Adam had fulfilled the need, with success so spectacular it overshadowed anything experienced with Peter, she had no intention of seeing him again.

When she got back to the flat Joss put the food away in the new fridge, then collected some tools together and began putting up her bookshelves, allowing herself to admit, at last, that her relationship with Peter had been foundering for some time. He had been all too accurate about their love-life, if she were brutally honest. It had been non-existent on a physical plane for a long time, and his failure to win the Athena contract had merely given him the excuse to break their engagement. But not the bottle to do it face to face. His dismay had been almost laughable when she'd turned up before he could sneak away.

At first Joss had been consumed with hurt and anger. Then fiercely grateful for the work which filled her life. She worked long, irregular hours as a freelance journalist, and regularly filled in for staff on holiday, or sick, or away on special assignments. Her free time had rarely coincided with Peter's, something he'd fiercely resented.

And there'd also been the burning question of a family. She had been adamant about waiting until he earned enough money for her to work less, and do more from home. And though he'd said he was agreeable Peter had obviously lied. As she should have realised. Everything Peter wanted he wanted right now.

Her eyes hardened. In the unlikely event that she ever considered a relationship with a man again she would make sure their aims were mutual. Her experience with Peter had taught her a salutary lesson. Any man in her future must fit certain requirements. He would be older, for a start, equally ambitious, and so successful in his own career he wouldn't resent hers. Joss smiled cynically. If such a paragon existed he was certain to be married anyway, to a stunningly beautiful woman who was a perfect wife and mother and ran her own thriving business while helping with the children's homework and producing cordon bleu dinners for twelve.

Joscelyn Hunter's interest in journalism had first begun when she'd edited the school magazine, which had fired her with such enthusiasm she'd found a job working at weekends and as holiday relief on the local morning paper. She'd started out as a messenger, then progressed to researcher, and soon begun bombarding the editor with so many stories and features he'd eventually accepted one, and she'd never looked back. She had been in her element mixing with journalists, so interested in all aspects of the job she'd made contacts which had won her a full-time job on the same paper, after she had a degree in modern languages and a year's post-graduate course in journalism under her belt.

At first Joss had loved her job, and with undiminished enthusiasm had covered law courts, local government, industry, the arts and a variety of local events. She'd interviewed a wide range of people, from local members of parliament, county councillors, businessmen, victims of tragedy, to schoolchildren and celebrities of all kinds. But after three years or so Joss had begun to feel inhibited by parochial bias. She'd lusted after a job on a national paper, and in her spare time had regularly submitted features to London dailies. When her efforts had begun to be accepted she'd taken the plunge and left for the capital, where her experience, coupled with the right qualifications and a willingness to work long, irregular hours, had won her jobs as a freelance, doing shiftwork on some of the national dailies.

Joss had set off for London with her father's blessing and a small legacy left by her mother. But soon afterwards the Reverend George Hunter had died, shortly before his retirement, leaving a grief-stricken Joss without a base in the Warwickshire village of her birth, other than her constant welcome from Anna's family. But her visits to the Herricks had been few and far between since her relationship with Peter, who had never fitted in with them. Now he was gone she could please herself, and would definitely drive down to Glebe House for lunch one day soon, Joss decided, preferably on one of the Sundays likely to drag a bit from now on.

Once she was settled in the new flat Joss steeled herself to forget Adam—and Peter—and soon found she quite enjoyed living alone. Her job absorbed most of her time, as usual, but now she could suit herself about what time she finished, with no reproaches when she got home, late and tired, to someone expecting her to cook supper and iron shirts. There were definite advantages to being single again.

As a change from reporting on press conferences, demonstrations, or whatever event the news editor wanted covered, one day Joss was told to dig out information about ancestral homes hired out by their owners for corporate entertaining, and spent time consulting with the *Daily Post* library and electronic database to discover which aristocratic personalities and properties were likely to be most newsworthy.

'We've got some mail for you,' said Carrie Holt, when Joss was poring over her findings with a lunchtime sandwich. 'And a message on the machine when we got home last night.' She handed over a bundle of junk mail and a slip of paper. 'How are you settling in at the flat?'

'Very well,' said Joss with satisfaction. 'How about you and Notting Hill?'

'I love it. I don't know how you could bear to leave the place, Joss.' Carrie bit her lip. 'Sorry. I'm a tactless cow. I suppose it was painful once Peter left.'

The message Carrie gave her was brief. *'I'm back. Ring me at this number. Adam.'*

Joss wanted to. Badly. But if she did ring him, Adam, like any man with blood in his veins, would expect to take up where he'd left off. Half of her wanted that so much it made her shake in her shoes, but the other half wouldn't hear of it. Peter's treatment had left her so vulnerable it would be madness to plunge into a new relationship. Her mood had been abnormally emotional with Adam that magical night. But she was back to normal now. And normal didn't include making mad, passionate love with strangers.

But when her phone rang late that night Joss felt oddly disappointed when she found it was just Anna, checking up on her.

'Are you pining, Joss?'

'No way. Too busy.'

'Is everything spick and span at the new place?'

'Hardly! I've only just got delivery of the new furniture, so the place is a mess. Who do you think I am, Superwoman?'

'Leave it all where it is and come down to stay with us instead.'

Joss was deeply tempted. 'I'd just love to, but the place is a shambles, Anna. I really must soldier on,' she said with regret. 'I'll come down as soon as I'm a bit straighter.'

'I'll keep on until you do,' threatened Anna, then went on to talk of wedding plans, and afterwards asked what Joss was up to at work, her interest caught when she heard about the article on ancestral homes.

'One of Hugh's old schoolfriends does that. He was at the party. Francis something. I'll tell Hugh to give him a call.'

Next day Joss spent a morning on the phone, setting up interviews with the owners of various ancestral piles she'd decided on for her article, then settled down to one of the more mundane tasks of the freelance journalist, and began sifting through a pile of regional newspapers looking for stories that could be followed up on a national basis. When her phone rang Joss was heartily glad to be interrupted.

'Miss Hunter?' asked a light, attractive male voice. 'My name's Francis Legh. Hugh Wakefield rang last night, asked me to get in touch. What can I do for you?'

Hugh's old schoolfriend, Joss learned, was only too pleased to be part of her story on corporate entertaining.

'Publicity of the right kind never goes amiss,' he assured her.

'Would it be possible for me to see you this week?' asked Joss hopefully. 'Where exactly do you live?'

'Deep in the wilds of Dorset. Do you know the area?'

'Not very well, but if you give me the address I'll find you.'

'I don't suppose you could possibly come on Sunday, Miss Hunter?' he asked. 'We're having some fancy electronics installed during the week. On the other hand,' he added suddenly, 'it's colossal cheek to ask you to give up your time on a weekend—'

'Not at all. I'd be glad to,' said Joss quickly. 'What time shall I come?'

'Midday,' he said promptly. 'I'll give you lunch.'

The news editor buttonholed her shortly afterwards, with the news that Charlotte Tracy, who covered all the smart events of the season, had rung in to say she was going home early from Ascot with flu.

'Flu in June,' said Jack Ormond bitterly. 'How the hell did she manage that? Anyway, Joss, it means you'll have to cover Ladies' Day at the races tomorrow. Thank goodness you can handle a camera—you know the happy-snappy kind of thing Charlotte turns in.'

'You bet,' she said with enthusiasm. But no way was she going to Ascot in her normal working gear of trouser suit and T-shirt. She was due at Harrods later, to interview a movie star at a book signing. Afterwards she would dash along the road to Harvey Nichols, splurge on an outfit for Anna's wedding and wear it to Ascot first.

After her chat with the actress Joss rang in her brief report to accompany the glamour shot waiting to go with it, then spent an hour on choosing a bronze silk suit and large, flattering hat in creamy translucent straw. It's for Anna, she reminded herself, wincing as she signed the credit card slip.

For once the British summer turned up trumps and favoured Ladies' Day with glorious sunshine. Joss found a good place in the crowd at the rail in front of Tattersalls to watch the procession of carriages bearing the Queen and various members of the royal family, and afterwards wandered among the elegant crowds, murmuring discreetly into her little machine, pausing now and then to photograph a particularly adventurous creation. It was the outlandish which made news, and Joss snapped away at towering feathered confections and precarious architectural fantasies, glad for once of her height as she jostled to get a clear shot.

Towards the end of the afternoon Joss had seen quite enough hats to last her for life, and decided to take one last shot of the horses in the starting gate instead, then leave to beat the rush. Before she could get her shot in focus someone jostled her elbow, and instead of a row of snorting horseflesh she found she was looking through the viewfinder at the top half of a man who towered above the crowd. Joss stood rooted to the spot, her heart thumping at the discovery that Adam looked even better by daylight in morning coat and top hat, an opinion obviously shared by the woman gazing up at him raptly from under the brim of a sensational feathered creation. On impulse Joss snapped the striking pair, then pushed her way through the crowd before she was spotted, all her pleasure in the day gone. Seen in daylight, in all the glory of formal Ascot wear, Adam was even more impressive than she remembered. No wonder she'd wanted him to make love to her. But so did his beautiful companion by the look on her face. The pair of them had been obviously engrossed in each other. Joss drove back to London in a black mood, and snarled irritably at the wolf-whistles and lip-smacking which greeted her finery when she plunged back into the usual frenzy at the *Post*.

For most of the next day Joss found it hard to put

Adam and his lady from her mind. How smug she had been, she fumed bitterly, about her virtue in avoiding another meeting. So smug she had no right to such irrational, mortifying jealousy. But because of it Friday seemed interminable, and when it was over at last Joss did her best to put Adam from her mind by spending a couple of lively, unwinding hours over a meal in a wine bar with a bunch of fellow journalists before she finally went home.

'Joss,' said Carrie Holt's indignant voice on the answer-machine. '*Two* messages tonight. One from Peter and another from this mysterious Adam person. For pity's sake give the men in your life your new number.'

Joss bit her lip. The Holts had every right to be annoyed. She would drop a line to Peter and tell him she'd moved, and not to get in touch again. Adam she would ring right now. She tapped in the number, then sat, tense, on the edge of the bed while she waited for him to answer. But the only response was a terse recorded message stating his number and a request for the caller's identity. For a moment Joss was so shattered by disappointment she couldn't speak. Then she pulled herself together and said coldly,

'This is Eve. I've moved from the flat in Notting Hill. To make an entirely new start. In every way,' she added with emphasis. 'Thank you for the beautiful roses, and for your—your kindness that night. Goodbye.'

When Joss reached Dorchester on Sunday, she skirted it, as directed, and after a few miles turned off on a minor road which took her straight into the rolling, deeply cleft terrain familiar to fans of Thomas Hardy novels. With time to spare she drove slowly, to appreciate her surroundings, but eventually spotted a sign for Eastlegh Hall, home of Francis Legh, who, she'd discovered from research beforehand, was the ninth Baron Morville to live there. Joss turned in through a pair of beautiful gates and drove along a carriageway that wound through tree-dotted parkland for a considerable distance before approaching a rise crowned by Eastlegh Hall, which gleamed in pale, Palladian splendour in the sun.

Hugh's friend would have very little trouble letting this beauty out for conferences, or anything else, thought Joss, impressed. She walked up a flight of shallow stone steps to the terrace, and crossed to the pillared portico, where large doors stood open, giving a view of a lofty hall with a pair of carved chests and a pedestal holding an urn overflowing with fresh flowers. She lifted the ornate knocker on one of the doors, then waited on the threshold, admiring the burnished dark wood of the graceful double staircase, and eventually a slim, well-dressed woman emerged from a door at the back of the hall and came hurrying towards her.

'Miss Hunter? Lord Morville apologises for being held up. He suggests I show you over the house while you're waiting. I'm Elizabeth Wilcox, the housekeeper.'

'How do you do?' Joss smiled warmly. 'Thank you. I'd like that very much.'

'We'll just take a quick tour,' said Mrs Wilcox. 'Lord Morville will show you the rest after lunch.'

Joss followed her guide through a series of beautiful rooms hung with paintings, a formal drawing room with pale yellow walls and gilt and damask furniture, a double-cube salon, a ballroom with a painted ceiling, and a dining room with sweeping velvet curtains, swagged and tasselled in gold, and a table long enough to seat thirty at a push. The grand staircase led to a long gallery hung with more paintings, and formal bedrooms with four-posters.

'Few stately homes are able to offer overnight facilities of the type available at Eastlegh. We even have central heating in some parts,' added Mrs Wilcox proudly. 'Installed by Lord Morville's American grandmother.'

'It's all very impressive, and so well kept,' said Joss with respect.

'Thank you. I'm lucky to have a good team.' The housekeeper smiled, gratified, then looked at her watch. 'Now I'll show you how to get to the farm.'

'Farm?' said Joss, surprised.

The other woman smiled regretfully. 'Lord Morville no longer lives in the house. He moved into Home Farm when his father died.'

Following the housekeeper's directions, Joss drove past a formal knot garden and skirted a maze, then drove along a carriageway through woodland until a large house with barleystick chimneys came into view above box hedges which enclosed its gardens in privacy. Joss parked the car, then opened a tall wrought-iron gate and followed a paved path through beds filled with roses. Before she could knock on the massive oak door it was flung open by a fair, smiling man in jeans and checked shirt.

'Lord Morville?' Joss smiled. 'I'm Joscelyn Hunter.'

'Francis, please,' he said quickly, holding out his hand, grey eyes friendly in a long, attractive face easily recognisable from some of the portraits in the Hall. 'Sorry I wasn't on hand when you arrived, Miss Hunter. We were sorting out a problem with the latest booking.'

Wondering if the 'we' meant Lady Morville was on hand, she smiled, liking him on sight. 'I'm usually Joss.'

'Then Joss it shall be.' He led the way through a square, stone-flagged hall into a sitting room with panelled walls, comfortable chintz-covered furniture and a massive stone fireplace. He waved her to a chair, then crossed to a tray of drinks. 'What can I give you?'

'Something long, cold and non-alcoholic, please,' said Joss, smiling, pleased that the long journey had dictated her choice of clothes. Her fawn linen trousers and plain white shirt were in perfect keeping with her casually dressed host.

'I thought we'd have lunch first,' he said, handing her a tall ice-filled glass. 'Then we can go back to the house and you can ask what questions you like. Or you can ask some now.'

'I was surprised to find you don't actually live at Eastlegh,' said Joss. 'Did you find it strange, moving to a much smaller house?'

'Not in the least.' He grinned. 'When I was young I was never allowed in the state rooms anyway, and the bedrooms here are a damn sight more comfortable than my old room over at the house.'

He looked up as a young woman came into the room. 'Ah, Sarah, this is Miss Hunter from the *Daily Post*.'

Sarah was composed and dark-haired, and oddly familiar, with a swift, charming smile. 'Hello. I'm Sarah Wilcox.'

Not Lady Morville, then. Joss smiled and took the proffered hand. 'Hello. I assume I've just met your mother.'

'Yes. She loves showing Eastlegh off to visitors.'

'Between them the Wilcox family run my life,' said Francis. 'Elizabeth is housekeeper, as you already know. Her husband Alan acts as butler when necessary, and helps me run the estate, and their frighteningly well-qualified daughter here is my House Manager and executive right hand.' He turned to Sarah with a coaxing smile. 'Change your mind. Have lunch with us.'

CATHERINE GEORGE 45

'I'd love to,' she said regretfully, 'but I promised to share the family roast for once. I've heated Mrs Wyatt's soup for you. The vegetable flan is in the warming oven, and the rest is just salad, cold beef and cheese.'

'What would I do without you, Sarah?' he said warmly.

She smiled at him serenely, and turned to Joss. 'Francis will give you my extension number, so if you need any further information just ring me and I'll provide it.'

'A lot better than I can,' said Francis wryly.

Joss thanked her, then watched thoughtfully as Francis escorted his attractive right hand from the room. Sarah Wilcox might not be Lady Morville, but it was plain to the onlooker, if not to His Lordship, that she would like to be.

When Francis got back he topped up Joss's glass and told her Mrs Wyatt was the lady who looked after him during the week. 'I fend for myself on weekends, but when Sarah heard you were coming for lunch she insisted on organising it. Very efficient lady, young Sarah.'

'A very attractive one, too,' said Joss.

Francis looked blank. 'Sarah? Yes,' he said, surprised. 'I suppose she is.'

'Is this actually a working farm?' asked Joss.

'Not any more. I won't bore you with politics, but we gave up farming a few years ago as no longer feasible. But we do a roaring trade in shrubs and bedding plants, and every type of herb imaginable—and people come from miles around to buy Sam's organic vegetables.'

'Who's Sam?'

'Used to be head gardener at one time, officially now retired. But he still terrorises the groundstaff here. When I was a schoolboy I don't know who frightened me more,

Sam or my father. Ah, good.' Francis opened one of the windows and leaned out. 'Hurry it up, Dan, I'm hungry.' He turned back to Joss with a smile. 'I persuaded a friend of mine to join us for lunch. Let's go straight to the table.'

The dining room was across the hall, with more panelling, and a table set for three with a posy of flowers for centrepiece.

'Courtesy of Sarah?' asked Joss, then her smile congealed on her face as a man loomed in the doorway, ducking his head to enter the room. Instead of a formal suit he wore jeans and a thin dark blue shirt, but there was no mistaking his identity. Or the face which hardened to a mask at the sight of her.

'Perfect timing, Dan,' said Francis, grinning. 'Let me introduce Miss Joscelyn Hunter—Joss to her friends, she tells me. Joss, this is Daniel Armstrong.' He looked from one rigid face to the other, his eyes gleaming with curiosity. 'Ah! You two know each other already.'

CHAPTER FOUR

'WE'VE met,' agreed Dan Armstrong tightly. 'How are you—Miss Hunter?'

'Very well.' She smiled brightly, wondering if he could hear her heart banging against her ribs.

His eyes held hers relentlessly. 'Francis told me a journalist was coming to do an article on Eastlegh. Quite a surprise to discover it's you. What paper do you work for?'

'I freelance, but in this instance I'm working for the *Daily Post*.'

'The article Joss is doing will provide some welcome publicity,' said Francis, and waved Dan to a chair. 'Stop towering over us and sit down.' He fetched a tureen of soup from a hotplate and set it in front of Joss. 'Will you do the honours?'

Joss sent up a silent prayer of entreaty, and managed to fill three bowls without spilling a single drop of steaming vegetable soup, something she was rather proud of with a slanted, hostile gaze fixed on her throughout the operation.

'I gather you've moved to a new flat,' Dan observed as she passed him his bowl.

So he'd received her message. 'Yes.' She smiled at Francis. 'I'd been living in a flat in Notting Hill, but I moved recently. My new address is less smart, but a lot cheaper.'

'You forgot to mention the move last time we met,' said Dan without inflection.

'Did I?' said Joss casually. 'Some friends at the *Post* bought it.'

'Have you known each other long?' said Francis with interest. 'Dan's never mentioned you.'

'No, not long,' said Joss, her eyes on her soup.

'Unlike Dan and me,' said her host. 'We've known each other all our lives.'

'Really?' Joss looked up in polite enquiry. 'Do you still live in this part of the world, Mr Armstrong?'

'Not any more.' His eyes met hers head-on. 'But I was born in a cottage on the Eastlegh estate. My father was head gardener here until recently.'

'He still is in all but name,' said Francis, grinning. 'Dan's father is Sam Armstrong, the despot I was talking about earlier.'

Dan stiffened visibly. 'I'm surprised my family is of such interest.'

'Joss is interested in all aspects of Eastlegh for her article,' said Francis, looking down his nose. 'Your father's name came up due to his famous vegetables, Dan. He's as much part of Eastlegh as I am. You have a problem with that?'

Dan threw up a hand like a fencer, giving his friend a wry smile. 'No, milord, so get off your high horse.' He looked at Joss. 'But if you plan to mention my father in your article, Miss Hunter, I strongly advise asking his permission first.'

'I second that,' said Francis with feeling. 'All right for you two; you won't be here when he reads it. I will.'

'If he makes a fuss just look down your nose like that and remind him you're Lord Morville,' advised Dan dryly.

'Fat lot of use that would be! You know damn well

that as far as Sam's concerned my father was Lord
Morville, and that's that.'

'Don't worry, I never write anything without the subject's permission,' said Joss hastily. 'If Mr Armstrong
objects I won't mention him.'

'No!' said both men, with such force Joss stared in
surprise.

'If you leave my father out of anything written about
Eastlegh he'll make Francis's life a misery,' said Dan,
smiling at her for the first time.

'Then of course I won't,' Joss assured them.

To her surprise both men got up, with the ease of long
habit: Dan to take the plates, and Francis to serve the
main course.

He grinned at her blank look. 'Did you expect a foot-
man behind every chair?'

She smiled wryly. 'No, but I didn't expect you to wait
on me in person.'

'Not much choice these days.' Francis shrugged. 'My
problem is common among my breed. Asset-rich and
cash-poor.'

'May I quote you on that?' she asked.

'Of course,' said Francis cheerfully, slicing a vegetable
tart. He served Joss deftly, and offered a platter of rare
roast beef. 'Can I tempt you?'

Joss refused, her appetite diminished by the presence
of the man she must now think of as Daniel Armstrong.
And think of him she would. She'd been a panicking fool
to believe the magic of that night would vanish by daylight. Meeting him again only confirmed her reaction at
Ascot. If he wanted to take up where he left off she would
have no objection at all. But it was depressingly obvious
that he had no such intention.

'You're very quiet, Miss Hunter,' he commented, startling her. 'For a journalist,' he added.

'Now then, Dan,' warned Francis. 'Don't get on your hobby horse.'

'He means I shun the attentions of the press,' said Dan, looking her in the eye.

'Dan tends to be a bit of a recluse,' explained Francis. 'Which is an odd trait for someone of his particular calling.'

'What exactly do you do, Mr Armstrong?' asked Joss, remembering his mention of construction work. And the picture it had conjured up.

'He's a property developer,' said Francis, grinning. 'He knocks down beautiful old buildings and puts up modern monstrosities in their place.'

'I don't knock them all down,' said Dan, unmoved.

'True. You work miracles on some of them,' conceded Francis. 'Dan and I went into banking together originally,' he informed Joss. 'We were good at it, made a bit of money with some fancy investments in the eighties. Then my father died, I had to come back to Eastlegh, and Dan started up his property company.'

'This is strictly off the record, Miss Hunter,' said Dan quickly, his eyes spearing hers. 'If I read an article on the theme of ''gardener's son makes success in property world,'' I'll sue.'

'My mission concerns Lord Morville and Eastlegh,' said Joss loftily. 'Not,' she added, 'that you *could* sue, if it's the truth.'

'Got you there, old son,' chortled Francis, and rose to his feet. 'You stay and entertain Joss, Dan. I'll make coffee.'

When they were alone Dan got up and began transferring dishes from table to sideboard.

'Do you need any help?' asked Joss politely.

'No.' He sat down again, eyeing her with undisguised animosity. 'So, Joscelyn Hunter. This is an unexpected pleasure. For me, at least. Obviously not for you.'

'Why not?'

'You know damn well. Your message came over loud and clear!' He leaned forward, no longer troubling to hide his hostility now there was no one to see. 'It does damn all for a man's ego to be used like a bloody gigolo,' he said in a harsh undertone. 'And found wanting at that. When did you move?'

'The following day,' she said, fighting the urge to cower in her seat.

'So why keep me in the dark?' he demanded.

'Isn't it obvious? After—afterwards I was hideously embarrassed.' Her eyes fell before the hard glitter in his. 'It's not a habit of mine to behave like that.'

'Credit me with enough intelligence to know that. Look at me!' he ordered.

Joss raised her eyes reluctantly.

'The maidenly panic is unnecessary,' he said abrasively. 'It was *you* who asked me to make love to you, remember.'

'Which is the whole point!' she said with sudden passion. 'In the cold light of day I couldn't believe I'd done that. I just couldn't cope with meeting you face to face again.'

'Afraid I'd haul you off to bed the minute you opened the door?'

Her mouth compressed. 'Of course not,' she muttered.

He sat back, looking irritatingly relaxed. 'Or maybe I didn't come up to scratch as replacement for the absconding lover.' He shrugged negligently. 'Not that it matters. I don't aspire to the role.'

His words acted like a stomach punch. 'Then there's no harm done,' Joss snapped.

'By the way, I saw you at Ascot, fleetingly,' he said, startling her. 'As soon as I could I came after you, but you took off faster than the winner of the three-thirty. And vanished again. Did you see me?'

'No,' she lied huskily. 'I was working—' She looked up in relief, deeply grateful for the interruption when Francis backed into the room with a tray.

'Sorry I took so long,' he apologised. 'Hope you two managed to entertain each other?'

'Of course,' said Dan blandly. 'It's a long time since I enjoyed such an entertaining lunch. Thanks, Francis. Excellent meal, as always.'

'When I go up to his place he gets food sent in,' said Francis, pushing the tray towards Joss. 'We make sure he gets some home cooking when he honours us with a visit.'

Joss poured coffee with a gratifyingly steady hand, then smiled at Francis, pointedly ignoring his friend. 'When we've finished this could we make a start?'

Dan pushed his untouched cup aside and jumped to his feet, his eyes cold. 'I must go. It's been very interesting to meet you again, Miss Hunter. Goodbye.'

'Goodbye,' she said politely.

Francis excused himself to see his friend out, then rejoined Joss, looking perplexed. 'You two obviously don't get on very well.'

Remembering how spectacularly well they'd got on in one instance, Joss forced a smile. 'Maybe he didn't take kindly to breaking bread with a journalist.'

'Possibly,' conceded Francis, unconvinced.

Alone in a cloakroom at the back of the hall, Joss ran cold water on her wrists until she'd cooled down. Meeting the man she now knew to be Dan Armstrong had given her such a shock she'd failed to adjust to it right through lunch. Neither man had commented, but the food left on her plate must have given Dan *some* satisfaction, if he recalled the other meal they'd shared. She ground her teeth in frustration, then repaired her face, brushed her hair into place, and went to rejoin Francis.

Once they were in Eastlegh Hall together Joss soon discovered a shrewd, businesslike streak beneath the easy charm of its owner. Francis Legh, ninth Baron Morville, obviously loved his home with a passion. He was deliberately offhand when describing the fashionable Palladian façade one of his ancestors had thrown up around the original Tudor building, but unashamedly impassioned about his determination to hang on to his home, even if it meant moving out of it to do so.

'It costs so much to open it to the public it's better business to offer the entire house to corporations, banks or television companies who want it exclusive to themselves for whatever period their funds run to,' he informed her. 'Here, due to my darling Yankee grandma, we have relatively modern plumbing and heating, and some comfortably furnished bedrooms as well as the formal stateroom variety. The package I offer includes a room, dinner, plus early-morning tea and breakfast, supervised by Alan Wilcox in butler mode to impress.'

'With far more privacy than possible at a hotel,' said Joss, nodding.

'Exactly.' Francis led the way through a door opening off the ballroom. 'This used to be a music room. It's still a bit untidy, due to the alterations I mentioned. I've put in a new sound system, and at the touch of a button a screen descends from the ceiling.'

'I'm impressed,' Joss assured him. 'If I send a photographer down during the week, would you allow some pictures?'

'Of course—but only if I can vet them first,' he added quickly, and grinned. 'I sound like Dan.' He shot a searching look in her direction. 'Talking of Dan, why don't you like him?'

Joss shrugged. 'It's he who objects to me.'

'Because you're a journalist?'

'Your friend can tell you that better than I can,' she said tartly, then smiled at him in apology. 'Sorry. Didn't mean to be rude, Lord Morville.'

'My name's Francis,' he said gently. 'If you've seen all you want here perhaps you'd like a stroll outside. It's a beautiful afternoon.'

'Thank you, I'd like that very much.'

The present Lord Morville of Eastlegh so obviously loved every stick and stone and blade of grass of his property that Joss warmed to him more and more as they strolled through the afternoon sunshine. Eventually they left the gardens behind and made for the hothouses, where plants and shrubs were sold to the public.

'That's the house where Dan was born,' said Francis, pointing. 'Used to be a tied cottage, but Sam Armstrong owns it now.'

'You sold it to him?' said Joss, surprised. 'I thought people like you—' She halted, embarrassed.

'You thought that people like me hang onto every possible bit of land and property they possess,' he finished for her. 'They do. So do I, tooth and nail. But in this one instance I yielded to powerful persuasion.' He waved a hand towards the people milling round the hothouses. 'Sunday's a busy day at the nursery. The groundstaff sell Sam's produce there for him. Would you like to meet him?'

'Very much,' said Joss promptly.

But when they reached the cottage she hesitated.

'On the other hand I don't want to intrude. Your friend might disapprove if I barge into his father's house uninvited.'

'He won't disapprove of *me*,' said Francis, with the assurance of his pedigree. 'Besides, I mentioned it to Dan when he was leaving.'

The Armstrong home was very different from Joss's expectations. Tied cottage by name, in actual fact it was a house, and a surprisingly sizeable one. Her preconceived idea of thatch and roses round the door was a long way from the reality of a house built on a smaller scale than Home Farm, but otherwise identical in age and architecture.

The man who answered Francis's knock was older than Joss had expected, but instantly recognisable. The height and hawk-like features were the same. But the hair was white, and the lined face below it weathered to a hue much darker than his son's. Sam Armstrong wore a formal white shirt and tie with comfortable old corduroys and a fawn cardigan, and nodded, unsurprised, at the sight of them.

'Good afternoon to you both. Dan said you were coming over.'

'Hello, Sam,' said Francis cheerfully. 'Hope we're not disturbing you. This is Miss Joscelyn Hunter, a journalist from the *Daily Post*. She's come to do a piece on Eastlegh, so I said she couldn't possibly leave without talking to you.'

'How do you do, Mr Armstrong?' said Joss, holding out her hand.

It was clasped for an instant of contact with a rough, workworn palm. The shrewd blue eyes looked her over, then Sam Armstrong nodded, and stood aside to usher them into a cool, dark hall. 'Come in and have some tea.'

A small table under the window in the sitting room was laid with fine china and a dish of buttered scones. Dan stood erect by the fireplace, his body language stating very clearly that he was there on sufferance.

'You go and make the tea, Dan,' ordered his father. 'The kettle's on the boil.'

Stiff-backed, Dan excused himself and went out to do his parent's bidding, very much aware, by his rigid expression, that Joss was entertained by his role of dutiful son.

'Sit down, Miss Hunter,' said Sam.

Francis held out a dining chair for Joss, then perched himself on the stone window ledge and gave Joss time to examine her surroundings by engaging Sam in a conversation centred on asparagus. Two vast leather chairs flanked the fireplace in a room furnished with good, solid wood pieces very much in keeping with the home of a family which had served the masters of Eastlegh Hall for generations. Until Dan had broken the pattern.

'So you're going to do a piece about Eastlegh, Miss Hunter?' said Sam Armstrong.

Dan appeared with a teapot and set it down on the tray in front of Joss. 'My father doesn't approve of letting the Hall out to strangers, Miss Hunter.'

'Lord Morville wouldn't have liked it,' said the old man bluntly.

His son shot him a warning look. 'Lord Morville, Father, is taking tea with us at this moment.'

Sam Armstrong looked discomfited for a moment. 'I meant no offence,' he said gruffly.

'None taken, Sam,' Francis assured him, and helped

himself to a scone. 'Besides, you know that death duties gave me no choice.'

'I know, I know,' said Sam grudgingly. 'Will you pour the tea, miss?'

Joss complied, finding it no easier to fill cups than soup bowls with Dan looking on. He handed tea to Francis and his father, then took his own to the fireplace and stood there, listening in silence as Joss began to ask questions she soon found were superfluous. Sam was only too glad of an audience for his anecdotes.

He settled back in his chair, letting his tea cool. 'My forebears were reivers in the Borders—moss troopers, as they were called—'

'Cattle rustlers, actually,' interrupted Dan, and won himself a glare from his parent.

'My grandfather, Adam Armstrong,' resumed Sam, unaware of the name's impact on Joss, 'came down here looking for work. He was given a job in the stables, and eventually became head coachman.'

Adam Armstrong's son, Daniel, had preferred work with plants and soil to horses, and had worked his way up to the job of head gardener, a post taken over in time by Sam, his own son.

'Armstrongs have lived in this house for three generations,' Sam went on bitterly, 'but not any more. *My* son prefers London.'

'And I live in Home Farm instead of at the Hall,' put in Francis, aware that Dan was silently seething. 'Times change, Sam. We change with them or we go under.'

Sam turned to Joss. 'I watched these two run wild, miss. Master Francis—Lord Morville—lost his mother when he was a little lad, so he used to come here to my wife for cakes and spoiling—and bandaging up, often as not. They were always up to mischief, these two.'

'I don't think Miss Hunter needs to hear all this, Father,' said Dan stiffly.

'Why not? She must be wondering why the gardener's son is so pally with Lord Morville of Eastlegh,' said Sam, unmoved. He smiled at Joss. 'They went to different schools and different colleges, but it never made much difference.'

'Lacking any brothers of our own, we made do with each other,' said Francis matter-of-factly.

'Which is why I can't understand why the pair of you don't get married and start families of your own,' said Sam irritably.

'You may be retired, Father, but Francis is still Lord Morville. You just can't say things like that to him. And you forget you're in the presence of a journalist,' Dan reminded him. 'The absence of wives might start her wondering about our sexual preferences—'

'Speak for yourself, Dan!' said Francis heatedly.

'And remember there's a lady in the room,' thundered Sam.

Dan shrugged. 'Miss Hunter's a journalist,' he said flatly, making the implication very plain.

Joss swallowed the insult, and looked at Dan levelly. 'Don't worry, Mr Armstrong. I don't write a gossip column. My article centres on the ancestral homes I'm featuring and the commercial facilities offered by their owners. Other than your father, I'm more likely to bring in people like Sarah Wilcox than property developers with no relevance to the subject.'

'Actually, that's not true—' began Francis, then halted at the ferocious scowl Dan turned on him.

Joss got up, bringing Sam and Francis to their feet. 'Thanks for the tea, Mr Armstrong, and for sparing time to talk to me. It's been fascinating. I'll let Lord Morville know when the article's due to appear.' She shook Sam's hand, then turned to Dan. 'Goodbye, again.'

'Goodbye,' he said, looking down at her. He held out his hand. 'Perhaps we'll meet again.'

Joss put her hand in his for the barest instant, aware that Francis was looking on with undisguised interest. 'Perhaps,' she agreed.

Sam Armstrong went with Joss to the door, but Dan called Francis back for a moment, talking to him in urgent undertone. Wildly curious to know what Dan was saying to his friend, Joss duly admired the garden instead of trying to listen, thanked Sam Armstrong again, then walked back to Eastlegh Hall with Francis.

'Do you have enough for your article?' he asked as they reached her car.

Joss nodded. 'I certainly do. You've got a good thing going here. Thank you for letting me see it, and for giving me lunch.'

Francis fished out his wallet and took out a card. 'If you need more information contact me here at the Hall or at Home Farm. Sarah will find me if I'm missing.'

'Thank you. I'll let you know about the photographer.' Joss put the card in her handbag and held out her hand. 'Goodbye.'

He took it in his. 'And just in case I need it could I have your home number and address?'

Joss hunted in her bag and handed him a card, then got in the car and, with a final smile and wave, drove back through the parkland of Eastlegh Hall and made for the road to Dorchester. She made no effort to hurry, preferring to enjoy the beautiful summer evening at leisure rather than hurtle back to London. At one stage she stopped off for coffee at an inn roofed in the thatch typical of the area, and sat outside to drink it while she recovered from the shock of meeting Daniel Armstrong. A pity she'd left such a cold message on his phone. Not that it mattered. He'd obviously washed his hands of her when he'd found she'd moved. Nor, thought Joss, trying to be fair, could she blame him. He obviously felt he'd been tried and found wanting. Which was so far from the truth it was ludicrous. But she could never tell him that now.

As Joss neared London later the traffic was heavy, and after the strain of the day she was tired by the time she parked her car on the forecourt outside the house. She switched off the ignition, then gave a screech of fright as her door was yanked open.

'Where the devil have you been?' said Dan Armstrong irritably. 'You took your time.'

CHAPTER FIVE

HER heart hammering at the sight of him, Joss got out of the car, slammed the door shut, locked it, then turned hostile eyes up to his face. 'You told Lord Morville to ask for my address,' she accused.

He shrugged. 'It was unlikely you'd give it to *me*.'

Joss glared at him, secretly cursing him for catching her with a shiny face and windblown hair. 'So why are you here?'

'I was just passing.' The slanted navy blue eyes gleamed with a smile which set her teeth on edge.

'Very amusing,' snapped Joss, and put her key in the door, then turned to face him. 'I'm tired, so I'll say good-night.'

'Not so fast—I want to talk to you,' he said imperiously. 'It won't take long. Ask me in. Or we can have the conversation out here in the street. Your choice.'

Since Daniel Armstrong so very obviously meant what he said, Joss gave in. 'Oh, very well.' She unlocked the door and led the way up the stairs that led directly into her new sitting room.

'I like this better than the other place,' said Dan, looking round him in approval. 'Sound investment.'

'Ah,' said Joss tartly. 'There speaks the property developer.'

Dan stood at the window, looking down at the street. 'You make those sound like dirty words.' He turned to look at her. 'Francis was joking. If I do knock buildings down they're derelict eyesores. And the others I put up in their place are always sympathetic to their environment.'

'How interesting,' said Joss politely, hoping he couldn't tell how deeply she was affected simply by being alone with him again. And by the way his sheer presence dominated the room. She gestured at the boxes of books waiting for transfer to the shelves she'd put up. 'I'm afraid I'm not very tidy yet. And I've bought only the basic requirements, like this sofa and—and so on, but at least it's all my own. Won't you sit down?'

But Dan wasn't looking at the room. 'You look just as good in trousers as the sexy black dress,' he said, startling her.

'Thank you,' she said, swallowing. 'Can I give you a drink, or some coffee?'

'Aren't you curious to know why I came chasing after you?' he asked, moving closer.

Joss backed away. 'To vent your anger about my disappearing act?' she said curtly, annoyed because she felt flustered.

'I did that in Home Farm while Francis was making coffee.' He smiled slowly. 'Have you any idea how I felt when I found you sitting at his dining table?'

She nodded. 'Similar to my own reaction, I imagine—'

'I doubt it.' Dan moved nearer, and this time Joss stood her ground. 'I couldn't believe my eyes. For the first time in our long association I could have blacked Lord Morville's eye.'

'Why?' she demanded, half knowing the answer, yet afraid to believe it.

'Because it was a shock to find my elusive Eve in the last place I expected,' he said, his voice deepening. 'I was jealous. An emotion unknown to me before today.'

Joss cleared her throat, feeling breathless. 'I'd never

have known. You were so damn hostile you put me off my lunch.'

'I noticed!' His smile was so smug she wanted to hit him. 'It gave me great satisfaction to watch you pushing food round your plate.'

'Why?'

Dan took her hand and led her to the new sofa, which was larger and much better suited to his proportions than the old one. 'Sit down while I explain.'

Wishing her funds had run to a matching chair, Joss sat, leaving as much space as possible for her unexpected guest. 'Explain what?' she asked coolly.

'The night we met you were smarting over your treatment at your defecting lover's hands.' His eyes locked with hers. 'Am I right?'

Joss nodded. 'Yes. You know that. Otherwise—'

Dan nodded swiftly. 'Otherwise you wouldn't have let me drive you home, let alone asked me to make love to you. Not,' he added, with a crooked smile, 'that I needed persuasion. But up to that point I'd actually deluded myself I could leave you on that bed and steal virtuously into the night.'

·'I knew that all along. Which is why I was so shameless. But suddenly I needed my belief in myself as a woman restored.' She held his eyes. 'I'd never asked a man to make love to me before, and don't foresee doing it again. Ever.'

Dan nodded soberly. 'I realise that. But picture my feelings when I found you'd vanished. And the owner of your old flat flatly refused to give me your new address.'

'Nick was acting on instructions,' said Joss, biting her lip.

'Another slap in the face.' He took her hand. 'I came

back from my trip expecting to come courting, Joss—
sounds naive now.'

'Not to me,' she said quietly.

'Then why the hell did you hide from me?'

'I was sure I'd be exchanging the frying pan for the
fire. I gave you entirely the wrong impression about the
real Joscelyn Hunter.' She gave him a wry smile. 'I may
be a supposedly hard-nosed journalist, but underneath it
all I'm still my father's daughter.'

'What was he like?' asked Dan with interest.

'Kind, humorous, supportive. Dad was the vicar of a
large country parish in Warwickshire, and brought me up
single-handed. My mother died when I was little.'

'So you're the product of lone parent upbringing, like
Francis?'

Joss nodded. 'Mrs Herrick—Anna's mother—always
treated me like a second daughter, but I used to envy
girls who had mothers of their own. Which is part of the
reason, in the end, why Peter Sadler left me.'

He frowned blankly. 'Run that past me again?'

'He wanted children right now. I didn't.'

'Why not?'

'I wanted to wait until our joint finances let me work
from home. Being motherless myself, I was determined
to be on hand for my child and do my job at the same
time. The best of both worlds.' She eyed him challengingly. 'But, confidentially, I'm not sure I'm the maternal
type. I don't drool over other people's babies. And I love
my job the way it is. I was perfectly happy to wait.'

Dan nodded. 'I can appreciate that. Fatherhood doesn't
appeal to me in the slightest. It does to Francis, but in
his case it's only natural. He wants an heir for Eastlegh.
But I applaud your honesty—Joss.' He smiled wryly.

'Your name doesn't exactly trip from the tongue yet. I still think of you as Eve.'

'You must have thought I was a total airhead, insisting on assumed names!'

He shook his head. 'I never doubted your intelligence. And *my* name wasn't assumed. I was christened Daniel Adam Francis Armstrong.'

'Of course—Adam after your great-grandfather. But why Francis?'

'All the first-born Morvilles are Francis. Old Lord Morville was my godfather, and insisted I took the name as well.'

'So you even share a name with Francis—did you cut each other's wrists and swear a blood oath, too?'

'Of course we did.' Dan nodded matter-of-factly, and held out a sinewy wrist where a slight scar was just visible. 'Before Francis went away to school.'

'Did you miss him when he went?'

'Damn right I did,' said Dan tersely. 'But to return to the subject of motherhood, did your lover jilt you for your lack of enthusiasm?'

Joss winced. 'It was part of it, I suppose. He'd been growing steadily more morose for weeks, which I took to be displeasure on the subject coupled with problems with his current project. But actually it was a lot more basic than that.' She shrugged. 'He just didn't want me anymore.'

'I do,' said Dan casually.

Joss sat very still, her heart thumping so loudly it seemed certain he could hear it.

'Did you hear what I said?'

'Yes.'

'You look stunned.'

'I feel stunned.'

'Why?' He leaned back, looking so relaxed Joss felt resentful.

'For one thing,' she began, pulling herself together, 'today, at lunch, you said you had no ambitions to fill the vacancy in my life.'

'I lied. I was still seething over your treatment, Miss Hunter.' He shrugged. 'I was furious when I came back from my travels to find you'd vanished.'

'I've explained about that.'

'Yes. Convinced I'd demand a repeat performance the moment I laid eyes on you.' He shook his head. 'Not likely, anyway, Joss. That kind of experience rarely happens twice.'

'True,' she said lightly, and got up. 'But I'm glad we did meet again.'

Dan rose slowly to his feet. 'Why?' he demanded.

'Because it gave me the opportunity to explain.' And because meeting him again made it plain her instincts had been faultless, after all.

'When I said that night could never be repeated,' Dan said deliberately, 'I meant the assumed names and the emotional state you were in.'

'I see.'

'I don't think you do.' Dan took her hand and drew her closer. 'I propose we backtrack a little. Get to know each other and go on from there.'

She looked at him steadily. 'That sounds very businesslike.'

'Then I'm putting on a good act.' His eyes glittered suddenly. 'To be blunt, I want to pick you up and take you to bed right now. But even if you were willing I wouldn't try.'

Joss stared at him, her eyes asking the question she couldn't bring herself to utter.

Dan smiled, and put out a hand to touch her cheek. 'If I did you'd be convinced that was all I wanted. And it isn't. Not by a long way.' He raised a sardonic eyebrow. 'Or is your opinion the same now we've seen each other in the light of day?'

'What opinion?'

'The one that sent you running for cover.'

'No,' she said honestly.

Dan frowned. 'Does that mean I pass muster after all, even now you know who I am?'

'Yes.'

'Does journalism train you to be monosyllabic?'

She scowled at him. 'It trains me in a lot of things, one of which is the ability to see both sides of an argument. Which means I can appreciate how you felt when I went missing. But try to put yourself in my shoes. My trust in men isn't exactly rock-solid these days.'

Dan looked at her levelly. 'You can trust *me*.'

Joss went over to her desk, took a snapshot from a drawer, and held it behind her back as she returned to him. 'If,' she began with care, 'we did become friends, is there anyone who might object to the arrangement?'

Dan frowned. 'A woman?'

For answer Joss held out the photograph of Dan at Ascot with his beautiful befeathered companion.

He took it, staring at it in surprise. 'Where did you get this?'

'I took it myself.'

'Then you *did* see me that day. Why the hell didn't you speak to me?' he demanded.

Joss shrugged. 'You were too involved with your companion.'

He tapped the photograph irritably. 'The Honourable Mrs Denby Hayter, to be precise. Otherwise Serena, cousin of our mutual friend Lord Morville, and incorrigible flirt all her life. Which is how long I've known her.' Dan advanced on her belligerently. 'So. Was Serena the reason for your second disappearing act?'

'Partly, yes.'

'Only part.' He seized her by the elbows, pulling her on tiptoe. 'Tell me. Was the other part because I disappointed you in bed?'

'No,' snapped Joss, trying to break free. 'You were wonderful, amazing, utterly unsurpassed in my experience—if you like I'll write a piece lauding your sexual prowess and publish it on the front page of the *Post*.'

For a moment Dan looked ready to shake her until her teeth rattled, then to Joss's relief he began to laugh and let her go.

'So you thought I was involved with Serena,' he said, grinning. 'Were you jealous?'

'Of course not,' she said scornfully. 'For all I knew the lady could have been your wife.'

'I told you I was unattached.'

'You wouldn't be the first to lie on the subject!'

'My father brought me up to tell the truth at all times,' said Dan virtuously, then his smile faded. 'It's getting late. I should go.'

Desperate for him to stay, Joss said the first thing that came into her head. 'Would you like a drink first?'

'No.' He moved closer. 'All I want is this.' He let out a deep, unsteady breath, then pulled her into his arms and kissed her mouth.

Joss didn't even try to resist. Whatever components made up Daniel Armstrong's chemical formula they reacted so instantly with her own that her response brought his arms round her like bands of steel.

'I didn't intend this,' he muttered against her mouth.

'You said that last time,' she muttered back.

'Then I won't talk any more!' Instead he kissed her with a demand her body welcomed with such ardour that Joss trembled in his arms, her tongue meeting his in an invitation he acknowledged by picking her up. 'Where's your bed?' he demanded hoarsely.

Joss stiffened. 'No!'

Dan set her on her feet so suddenly she staggered. They stood staring at each other, breath tearing through their chests.

'I apologise,' panted Dan raggedly.

Joss inclined her head in silent acknowledgement, unable to speak.

'And now, of course,' he said bitterly, 'you're convinced you were right.'

'No,' she said unsteadily. 'I know you didn't come here tonight just to—to—'

'Prove your suspicions correct.'

Joss smiled faintly. 'I was going to say to make love to me.'

'If,' he said tightly, 'we could talk about something else I might possibly stop wanting to do that.'

'Would you like a drink?' she said quickly.

His smile was wry. 'Black coffee?'

Joss went off to the kitchen alone, in desperate need of time to recover. What was it about this man? she thought despairingly. One touch of his hands and she melted like butter. And in a way she'd never been prone to before, with Peter or anyone else.

'Joss,' Dan said soberly, when she rejoined him. 'Let's start again.'

'Where, exactly?'

'From somewhere before I touched you.' His eyes met

hers. 'As must be painfully obvious, I can't allow myself to do that.'

She flushed, then busied herself with pouring coffee. 'Which is deeply flattering from my point of view. And reassuring.'

'Reassuring?'

'It convinces me I didn't go totally insane that night.' She handed him his coffee. 'But it does tend to make sensible conversation difficult.'

He grinned. 'At least you didn't throw me out.'

Joss looked him up and down. 'Somehow I can't see myself managing that single-handed. Besides...' She bit her lip.

'Besides what?' he prompted.

'I wasn't exactly fighting you off.'

'That honesty of yours again.'

She smiled wryly. 'Like you, I had early training in such matters.'

Dan drank his coffee quickly, then got to his feet. 'I'm off to Scotland in the morning, until Friday, unfortunately. But next Saturday I'll return your hospitality—on neutral territory. Just tell me which restaurant you prefer.'

'I haven't said I'm free next Saturday.'

Dan bent down to take her hand and pulled her to her feet. 'If you're not, cancel,' he ordered.

Her immediate instinct was to refuse. But some deep-hidden instinct responded quite shamelessly to such high-handedness. 'All right,' she said after a while.

'Where?' he demanded.

'I'll think about it—and fax my choice to you.'

Dan laughed, and raised her hand to his lips. 'This morning I had no idea what lay in store for me at Eastlegh.'

'Neither did I!' she said with feeling.

'If you had, would you have cancelled?'

'Certainly not. I was working, remember.' She looked up at him, very conscious of the hard hand still holding hers. 'How about you?'

'No way,' he said promptly, then spoilt it by reminding her that a visit to his parent had been his motive. 'Filial respect and all that,' he added virtuously.

Joss laughed, and tried to remove her hand, but Dan held onto it.

'I want to kiss you,' he said abruptly.

Because every one of her hormones was urging her to let him, Joss was well aware of it. 'Unwise,' she said reluctantly.

'And are you always wise?' he asked, his voice deepening to a note which dried her mouth.

'No,' she said unevenly. 'As you well know—' The rest of her words were smothered as his mouth made nonsense of her defences.

Joss gave herself up to the strength and barely controlled passion of his embrace, the heat and desire in his taut body arousing hers in a way no other man had ever been able to. Then she stopped thinking about other men, or about anything at all, as Dan sat her on the edge of the sofa and knelt between her parted knees to undo her shirt. With unsteady hands he freed her breasts to his lips and grazing teeth, stroking her covered thighs with caressing fingers which brought her rapidly to an arousal equal to his own. This time there was no mention of bed. By unspoken consent they sank to the floor, upsetting the coffee tray with a crash neither of them even noticed in their frantic haste to shed each other's clothes, their wild caresses rousing each other to such a state of frenzy their mating was short, but shatteringly sweet, the magic as powerful as before.

Afterwards, it was a long time before either of them stirred. Dan raised his head at last and looked down at Joss's flushed face and kissed the beads of moisture away from her upper lip.

'You're a dangerous lady,' he said hoarsely. 'I've never lost it like that before.'

Joss opened a considering eye. 'Tactless to mention "before" right now,' she pointed out, and Dan grinned.

'Point taken.' His grin widened as he spotted various garments scattered among broken china and spilt sugar from the coffee tray. 'Not that I've ever been in this particular situation with a woman before.'

Joss detached herself sufficiently to look and shuddered. 'What a *mess*!' She struggled to get up but Dan prevented her, looking down at her in a way which drove all thoughts of clearing up from her mind.

'Are you going to make love to me again?' she asked bluntly.

Dan's silent laugh vibrated against her breasts. 'Since you ask, yes. Why?'

'This floor is hard.'

'When I asked about bed last time it put an end to proceedings,' he reminded her, his lazy, skilful hands making sure this was unlikely a second time.

'My bedroom's at the end of the hall,' gasped Joss, and Dan pulled her to her feet, kissed her, then scooped her up in his arms and carried her to bed.

It was the early hours of morning before Dan forced himself to break away. 'I must get home,' he said without enthusiasm. 'I haven't even packed yet.'

'Do you want a shower before you go?' said Joss, yawning, then raised an eyebrow at the sudden gleam in his eyes. 'What?'

'Have one with me,' he said, kissing a bare toe.

The shower took a long time, and ended in more love-making and then another shower, so that dawn had over-taken them before Dan was finally ready to go.

'This time,' he said sternly, from the foot of the bed, 'don't steal away in the morning without telling me.'

Joss shook her head, and pulled the covers up to her chin. 'Nowhere to go.'

Dan took a wallet from his back pocket and fished out a card. 'You can reach me at either number if you need me.'

Joss took the card and held it to the lamp to read it, her face suddenly blank with astonishment. 'Is *this* your company?'

'Yes. It's relatively small as yet, but expanding fast. I promise you, Athena will soon be one of the biggest names in property development. Why do you ask?'

Joss gave him a very odd little smile. 'Peter Sadler's an architect. He worked for one of the firms who tendered for your riverside development. You turned his plans down.'

Dan eyed her challengingly. 'Does it make a differ-ence?'

'To what, exactly?'

'To a relationship between us.' He strode round the bed to sit beside her.

Joss shook her head. 'Why should it? You chose the best tender for the job; Peter's effort didn't come up to scratch. End of story.'

Dan took her in his arms and held her close. 'No,' he said against her hair. 'Not the end. For us it's just begin-ning.' He put her away from him and looked down into her flushed face. 'Though if I'd met you beforehand I'd have thrown Sadler's plans out without looking at them.

He had his chance with you and blew it. Do you still mind about that?'

Joss considered for a moment, then answered with her usual candour. 'No. Not after meeting up with you again.'

Dan smoothed her hair back from her face. 'In that case, Miss Hunter, am I going too fast if I demand exclusive rights on your free time from now on?'

Joss looked at him thoughtfully. 'I enjoy socialising with other journalists—male and female—for a meal or a drink after work sometimes.'

'Done,' he said promptly. 'But keep the male company in the plural.'

'And I work very irregular hours,' she reminded him. 'With Peter that was always a bone of contention. I can never guarantee to be in the right place at the right time.'

'Neither can I,' he said, then took her breath away. 'Move in with me, Joss. That way we can at least spend whatever free time we've got together.'

Joss shook her head firmly. 'It's too soon for that, Dan. I'm still recovering from my last relationship. Let's get to know each other better first. For the moment I rather like living alone again.'

Dan looked down at her in silence, then a wry smile curved his mouth. 'It can't be soon enough for me, but I'll wait—but only for a while, Joss. On the journey to Scotland I'll think up ways to make you change your mind.'

'Have you lived with a woman before?' she asked bluntly.

'No. Unless you count a flat shared with both sexes in my student days.' Dan shrugged. 'But that was just accommodation. You're the first woman I've asked to share on a one-to-one basis.'

'Really?' She wreathed her hands behind his head,

bringing his mouth to hers for a kiss that quickly threatened to get out of hand again.

'If I don't go now,' said Dan thickly, 'I'll miss the plane.' He straightened, his smile crooked as he looked down at her. 'I'll give you breathing space, Joscelyn Hunter. But not much. Why waste time apart when we could be together?'

CHAPTER SIX

WHILE Dan was away on his travels Joss threw herself into her work with a zest which had been missing since Peter's departure. Colleagues noticed, and teased, but Joss refused to give details. For the moment her new, fledgling relationship with Daniel Armstrong was a secret she hugged to herself, unable to discuss it with anyone except Anna, who approved heartily, particularly since Dan was a friend of a friend of Hugh.

Until her broken engagement Joss had been utterly sure of her goals in life, confident that she was liked and even respected by her colleagues, and loved by Peter Sadler. But she had been wrong about the last, and in the recesses of her mind a little seed of insecurity refused to wither and die. Until she was officially living with Dan Armstrong she would keep their relationship private. But in the meantime, when her training overcame her reluctance to pry, she did some in-depth research on the man who'd made such a success of Athena.

Because Daniel Armstrong shunned publicity, Joss discovered little more about him than she already knew, other than his phenomenal success. She read a lot about his aim to provide buildings which blended with their environment, but the only photographs were shots of Dan at race-meetings, or in the financial section, with none of him on the town with beautiful women. Dan had obviously been truthful when he'd told her he was no party animal.

To her great satisfaction Dan rang Joss every night,

and always ended the conversation by reminding her that her breathing space was one day less.

'Have you missed me?' he demanded, towards the end of the week.

'Yes.'

'How much?'

'A lot. Yet this time last week I thought we'd never meet again.'

'That, Joscelyn Hunter, was never a possibility. I would have found you eventually, even if I'd had to hire someone to do it for me.'

'Would you really have done that?'

'Damn right I would.'

She paused. 'Was it just because we were so good in bed together?'

Dan's chuckle sent the familiar trickle down her spine. 'I would be lying if I said it wasn't part of it, but there's a whole lot more than that. So get yourself in the mood to move as quickly as you can. Patience isn't my strongest point.'

The week was a particularly busy one, for which Joss was grateful. Even so the days seemed to go by far more slowly than usual, and Saturday refused to come quickly. It was useless to tell herself to stop it, that she was a mature, level-headed woman. One, moreover, who only recently had expected to marry Peter Sadler. Was this purely a rebound thing? On Friday night Joss shook her head at her reflection in the mirror. If she were totally honest—and it was her honesty that Dan particularly admired—it was a good thing she hadn't met him before Peter's departure. Otherwise she might have been the one who'd left Peter, rather than the other way round. Shaken by this discovery, Joss faced the truth. The persistence which she brought both to her job and her private life had made her fight to keep her relationship with Peter alive long after it had shown unmistakable signs of faltering. When Peter finally left her pride had taken the beating, not her heart.

Joss took a quick shower and went to bed early with a book, too restless to watch television. But instead of reading she kept scowling at the telephone beside her bed, willing it to ring. She stretched out in the bed, clasping her hands behind her head, and stared at the ceiling. Living alone had lost its attraction very quickly. Dan's fault entirely. He was such a big man in every way that his absence left a space impossible to fill. But moving in with him was a risky proposition. Relationships changed. As she knew. After a while Dan might want out, just as Peter had. She'd known Peter for years, and her time with Dan could be measured in hours, but she had a strong suspicion that recovering from a break-up with Dan would be a lot less easy. Maybe not even possible.

Joss gave up trying to sleep in favour of tea and a book. When she was on her way to the kitchen the doorbell rang, and her heart leapt. Joss ran to the door, picked up the receiver and spoke into it, her heart thudding as she heard Dan's voice.

'I couldn't wait until tomorrow,' he said tersely.

Joss pressed the buzzer for answer, and a minute later Dan came bounding up the stairs to snatch her up into his arms and kiss her until her head was reeling. When he released her at last, he grinned down at her striped nightshirt. 'So that's what you wear to bed.'

Joss laughed, secretly glorying in his impatience to see her. 'You mean you came round here at this time of night just to find out what I wear to bed?'

'No. I came,' he said very deliberately, 'because I couldn't wait another minute to hold you in my arms.'

'Good,' said Joss, her matter-of-fact tone at odds with the tattoo her heart was beating under the cotton. 'Are you hungry?'

Dan picked her up and sat down on the sofa, settling her comfortably on his lap. 'Not for food. I ate on the plane.' He smoothed her head against his shoulder and let out a deep sigh of satisfaction. 'So, tell me about your week, Miss Hot-Shot Journalist.'

Joss obliged, telling him about the various assignments she'd been given, of the photographs taken at Eastlegh, and, in the end, confessed that she'd done some research into the career of Daniel Armstrong, founder of Athena Developments. She raised her face to look at him. 'Do you mind?'

He shook his head. 'No. Because you told me about it. The women in my past rarely considered candour important. You, my darling, are different.'

Elated by the endearment, Joss ran a hand along his jaw. 'You need a shave,' she said huskily.

'I need a lot of things,' he said, grinning down at her.

She frowned at him in mock disapproval. 'You might have rung first. I could have had a visitor.'

Dan's eyes narrowed menacingly. 'Another man?'

'Of course not! I was thinking of Anna. Or I could have been hosting the occasional get-together with some fellow journalists—female variety.' Joss freed herself from his arms and sat upright, her eyes steady on his. 'Listen, Dan. There were men in my life before Peter Sadler. But only one at a time. And no one since. Except you. I thought you might have taken that for granted after—after last weekend.'

'Pax!' Dan pulled her down into his arms, rubbing his cheek against her hair. 'I apologise—humbly.'

'You, *humble*?' Joss snorted inelegantly.

'Yes,' he said flatly. 'I never knew what jealousy meant before you, Joss. All the time I was trying to bring canny, hard-headed Scots round to my way of thinking I kept wondering what you were doing, and who you were doing it with. Your face kept getting between me and the matter in hand.'

'I'm flattered.' Joss slid her arms round him under his jacket. 'But bear with me, Dan. Let's go on seeing each other for a while before I burn my boats.'

Dan tipped her face up to his. 'Don't you fancy living with me?'

'Of course I do. A lot. But I'm not normally the type to throw caution to the winds. Nor,' she added, 'are you the type of man to respect me if I did.'

'True,' he conceded. 'All right. You win. I won't push. For the moment, anyway. So where do you want to go tomorrow?'

'The forecast is good.' Joss smiled at him coaxingly. 'Could we just go somewhere and walk in the fresh air?'

'No restaurants or smart nightspots?' he mocked, tracing a fingertip over her bottom lip. 'A pearl among women!'

'You don't care for that kind of thing, according to my research.'

'I don't. I would very much enjoy walking with you.' He looked at her for a moment. 'I live near Kew Gardens. We can walk there, then I could feed you at my place afterwards. Perhaps it might tempt you to move sooner.'

Joss nodded. 'Sounds good. I'd like that.'

'Done,' said Dan, and yawned widely. 'Sorry.' He stood up with her in his arms, then set her on her feet. 'Time I was off.'

She stared at him blankly.

He smiled. 'You obviously thought I meant to stay the

night. Which, of course, I would very much prefer to driving back to Kew. For obvious reasons. But if I stay you'll be convinced that bed was all I came for. And it wasn't.'

Joss was assailed by a variety of emotions, elation and disappointment battling for supremacy as she followed Dan down to the door. At the foot of the stairs he took her in his arms and kissed her.

'Sleep well. I'll collect you in the morning.'

'But I can drive myself to Kew—'

'No. I'll come for you,' he said flatly, then kissed her again. 'Aren't you proud of me?' he said against her lips. 'Awestruck by my restraint?'

'Absolutely,' she agreed, and kissed him lingeringly to show her admiration.

'That's not fair,' Dan said hoarsely, but he kissed her again at length before he finally made it through the door, leaving Joss to wander back upstairs in a daze of happiness.

That night marked the beginning of a relationship which very swiftly became such a vital part of Joss's life it effectively blotted out her time with Peter Sadler. Sometimes it was hard to remember she'd shared her life with anyone other than Daniel Adam Francis Armstrong. They saw each other as much as their various lifestyles allowed, and when Joss was obliged to cancel at the last minute, due to the demands of her job, the only objections raised by Dan were his opposition to her continued residence in Acton.

'I'm tired of having you with me in small doses,' he said, late one hot, starlit Sunday night. 'If you lived here we would at least come home to each other. Actual time spent together is a very small percentage of our acquaintance, Miss Hunter. Too damn small. I want more. A lot more.'

They were lying together on a wicker chaise longue in the walled courtyard behind Dan's home in Kew. The house was large and very private behind tall, dense hedges in a quiet side-road that could have been in the country instead of near the famous gardens. Joss adored everything about the house. She had been trying to bring herself to leave for the past half-hour, knowing what Dan's reaction would be. Every time they parted his arguments grew more persuasive.

'I'll put the flat on the market tomorrow,' she said suddenly, and said no more for some time as Dan seized her in his arms and kissed her by way of demonstrating his triumph at her surrender.

'You mean that?' he said eventually.

Joss nodded, too breathless even to say yes.

'Why now?' he demanded. 'I've been persuading—'

'Bullying,' she corrected.

'I've been persuading you for weeks,' he went on, shaking her slightly. 'What's so special about tonight?'

'Because in a minute I've got to drive back to Acton, and I don't want to.'

'At last,' he said smugly. 'The lady admits she hates the thought of leaving me.'

'Oh, it's not you,' lied Joss shamelessly. 'It's the house.'

'Witch!' His voice deepened to the note which always melted her bones. 'As long as you come and share it with me I'll try not to be jealous of it.' He laughed. 'Listen to me! I never imagined a woman lived who could change me so much.' He tipped her face up to his. 'Tell me the truth. Were you jealous when you saw me with Serena at Ascot?'

'Horribly. Which is why I ran away. I couldn't bear the sight of you together.'

Dan kissed her hard by way of appreciation. 'As a matter of interest, did you feel jealous where Sadler was concerned?'

Joss thought about it for a moment. 'No,' she said, surprised. 'Never. Nor about anyone else, either. I've always disapproved of jealousy.'

'Including mine?'

'No.' She smiled up at him. 'I like that a lot. Very ego-boosting.'

He laughed, and pulled her bodily into his lap. 'I know other ways to boost your ego. Want me to demonstrate?'

'No,' she said firmly. 'Otherwise I'll never leave.'

'I know!'

'Dan, please, I've got work tomorrow; it's time I went—' Joss stopped mid-sentence. 'I was going to say time I went home,' she said, looking up into his eyes. 'But from the day you brought me here your house feels like home. Not the flat.'

'Then move in with me tomorrow,' he said urgently. 'To hell with the flat. Let an estate agent sell it for you.'

Joss was sorely tempted, but in the end she shook her head. 'Don't be angry with me, Dan, but I'd like to stay there until it's sold. Organise it myself. I need to be in control of my own life. It's a big step from living alone to dependence on you for the roof over my head.'

Dan looked down at her in silence for a moment. 'Joss,' he said slowly, 'it's a house, not a cage. And you'll have your own key. And live your life the way you want to. The only difference will be sharing your spare time, and my bed, with me. I did mention that bed was part of the arrangement?' he added.

'Why else do you think I'm moving in?' she said, smiling provocatively as she jumped up.

He leapt to his feet and took her in his arms, laughing. 'Do I take that as a compliment?'

'You certainly do,' she assured him, and held up her face for his kiss.

For the next week Joss spent any spare time left over from Dan and her job in cleaning and polishing the flat to maximum allure for potential buyers. The estate agent she contacted was optimistic about a quick sale, and, having burnt her boats, Joss called Anna to tell her about the move.

'Well, hello,' said Anna, when Joss rang. 'I thought maybe you'd emigrated.'

'Sorry, love. I've been a bit busy lately.'

'This Dan of yours must be really something. Bring him down to see us so the Herricks—and Hugh, of course—can make sure he's good enough for you.'

'Sorry,' said Joss, laughing. 'It's too late for that.'

'Why?'

'For your ears only, Anna, I'm head over heels in love with him,' Joss blurted, putting the truth into words for the first time. 'In fact the moment I've sold the flat I'm moving into his house in Kew.'

'I thought you might,' said Anna jubilantly. 'Oh, Joss, I'm so happy for you. And very glad you've recovered from Peter. By the way, I met him outside his father's office in Stratford the other day.'

'How was he?'

'Very much on the defensive with me, as usual. But he asked about you, so I took great pleasure in telling him about your relationship with Dan Armstrong. But never mind Peter. Come down to lunch one Sunday.

Mother misses you. So do I. Bring Daniel to the lions' den. We won't eat him.'

'You couldn't,' chuckled Joss. 'He's too big.'

'Seriously, Joss, we'd love to see you. Will he come?'

'I'll ask him, and let you know. But thank your mother for me and give her my love, your father, too. And tell Hugh the article on Eastlegh Hall was a great success. Lord Morville—Francis—is a charmer.'

'So Hugh says. But if your Dan is a friend of his, how come Hugh doesn't know him?'

Joss explained, promised to drive down to Warwickshire with Dan as soon as possible, then rang off and took advantage of a rare early night alone.

Because Dan was tied up with problems about his riverside complex Joss showed several people round the immaculate flat during mid-week evenings. Afterwards the agent told her there was a lot of interest in the property, but she could sell it at once if she were willing to drop the price a trifle. Joss wouldn't hear of it. She wanted the full asking price as a nest-egg, and eventually one of the prospective purchasers agreed to pay the full amount as long as they could move in as soon as possible.

'I've done it!' said Joss in triumph when Dan rang later that night. 'I've sold the flat.'

'Already?' He whistled. 'Did you give way on the price?'

'No way.'

'Good! So when are you moving in with me?'

'As soon as I exchange contracts,' she promised. 'The purchasers want immediate possession.'

'So do I!' he said, the note in his voice as tactile as a caress.

'I'll drive to Kew as early as I can on Friday evening,' she promised breathlessly.

'That's forty-eight hours away,' he said gloomily. 'I hate Thursdays.'

'Since I met you I'm not keen on them either, but it's my job, Dan.'

'I know, I know. Make sure you get off early on Friday.' His voice deepened. 'I'm impatient to have you here with me all the time.'

'I'll still have to work late.'

'But afterwards you'll come home to me, my darling.'

Joss went to bed smiling, her happiness complete except for one tiny flaw. Dan made it very plain at all times that he respected her intelligence, and liked being with her whatever they were doing, quite apart from their physical rapport and the shameless amount of time they spent in bed. But he'd never said a word about love. He just found it hard to express his feelings, she assured herself. She could understand that. Up to now she'd been the same. But recently it had taken every ounce of self-control she possessed not to express her own feelings when they made love.

Thursday was even more hectic than usual, and it was very late by the time Joss got back to Acton. She unlocked the door and climbed the stairs wearily, longing for a hot bath and some beauty sleep in preparation for seeing Dan next day. While she was exchanging her clothes for a towelling robe the doorbell rang, and she smiled radiantly, forgetting her fatigue. So Dan hadn't been able to wait after all. She ran to lift the receiver.

'Impatient man!' she said lovingly. 'Come up.'

But the man who came through the door at the foot of the stairs was slim and fair, and half the size of Daniel Armstrong. As he ran up towards her the triumphant smile on Peter Sadler's face made Joss want to slap it.

'What are you doing here?' she said furiously. 'How did you find out my address?'

'I met Anna recently. She let slip that you lived in Acton, and because the Holts now live in our place I made an educated guess,' he said airily.

'I'm sorry you went to the trouble,' she said curtly, 'because you can't stay. I'm tired and I want to get to bed.'

He pushed back a lock of fair hair, eyeing her narrowly. 'You've changed, Joss. You've grown hard.'

She stood with arms folded, her eyes implacable on his fair, good-looking face, secretly astonished that she'd once imagined her happiness depended on him.

'I would have got in touch before, but you wouldn't answer my messages,' he said, moving nearer. 'When you wrote you didn't give your address, so I couldn't even thank you for sending the furniture back, or the cheque.'

'If you've come to do that now, fine,' snapped Joss. 'But right now I need to get to bed.'

'Not yet. Joss, listen to me. I made a mistake,' he said, astonishing her. 'I want you back.'

She stared at him blankly. 'You must be joking!'

Peter's eyes narrowed dangerously. 'Not a thing to joke about. After the Athena rejection things got out of proportion for a while. But I've had time to reconsider—'

'So have I,' said Joss quickly. 'And you were right, Peter. I have changed. When you left I made a new life. And I much prefer it to the old one. There's no place in it for you.'

His eyes narrowed in sudden malevolence. 'So you're telling me you feel nothing for me?'

'You did a great hatchet job on my feelings,' she re-

minded him coldly. 'Now I think of you—when I think
of you at all—as part of a growing-up process.'

'I'd hardly describe it like that, Joss,' he sneered.
'You're thirty-two years old.'

'True,' she said unmoved. 'I wasted a lot of time on
you.'

Peter moved like lightning, seizing her by the elbows.
'I could *make* you want me again!'

'Oh, *please*,' said Joss, deliberately bored—something
she regretted as Peter dragged her close with a show of
strength which took her by surprise. He ground his mouth
against hers and, enraged, Joss tried to break free. But
one of Peter's stylish boots landed on her bare foot, and
she let out a choked cry of pain as they collapsed on the
sofa in a writhing mass of arms and legs. Peter Sadler
was slim, but wiry, and in his present mood Joss found
she was no match for him. He flattened himself on top
of her, one hand cruelly tight in her hair as he smothered
her protests with his mouth, the other pushing the robe
away to get at her breasts. Joss shuddered with distaste,
bracing herself to break free. Then Peter raised his head
and smiled in pure triumph, and she gave a gasp of horror
as she saw Dan at the head of the stairs, staring at them
in disbelief. Joss clutched her robe together, reaching out
a hand in entreaty, but with a look which stabbed her to
the heart Dan turned his back and left as silently as he'd
arrived.

Peter got to his feet at once, holding out his hand to
Joss as politely as though the assault of a minute before
had never happened.

'Get out!' she spat.

'Certainly,' he said, smoothing his hair. 'Sorry I
was rough.'

'I should call the police,' she said bitterly.

'Not much point in that, Joss.' He smiled blandly. 'I didn't rape you.'

Joss shook with rage, wanting to throw him out bodily so she could run after Dan. But Dan, she realised hopelessly, would be well on his way to Kew by now.

'*Why*, Peter?' she flung at him, tightening the belt on her robe.

'I had my reasons,' he said enigmatically, and looked at his watch. 'From a personal point of view my visit has been a great success. But time I was off.' He went to the head of the stairs, then gave her a smile which clenched her hands into claws. 'I'm so sorry your visitor got the wrong impression.'

'No, you're not,' Joss stalked towards him with menace, feeling fierce satisfaction as he backed away, the smile suddenly wiped from his face. 'Get out of my life, Peter. And this time stay out.'

Peter looked at her for a moment, opened his mouth to say something, then thought better of it as he met the look in her eyes, and ran downstairs without a word. After the door had clicked shut behind him Joss felt cold with reaction. Shivering, she clutched her arms across her chest, eyeing the phone with longing. But Dan wouldn't be home yet. And what she had to say was impossible to leave as a message. To pass the time, and get warm again, she soaked in a bath as hot as she could bear, desperate to remove the soiled feeling left by Peter's hands. The hands whose caresses she had once welcomed. Joss ground her teeth in angry frustration, able to recognise, now she had time to think, that Peter's assault had been punitive, and nothing at all to do with love, or even sex. But why was he punishing her? He was the one who'd walked out.

Joss ran water over her head for a long time in the

urge to feel clean, but at last swathed a towel round her head, wrapped herself in another, then went to the phone to ring Dan and found the red light glowing. She pressed the button, then stood in disbelief, listening to the message Dan had left while she'd washed her hair.

'I'm glad you're not there,' he said, in a tone which tore her to pieces. 'If you intended ringing me with explanations, don't. It's finished between us. Nothing you can say will make any difference.'

Joss rang his number just the same, convinced that she could make him understand if he'd only listen. But the only response was his recorded message.

'Dan, pick up the phone,' she said unevenly. 'Please listen to me. I can explain. *Please!*' She rang again, several times during the next hour, and at last, disgusted with herself for pleading, Joss gave up and went to bed, to lie awake in dry-eyed misery too intense for tears.

Early next morning Joss rang Dan again, but with the same result. Then she rang his office, and was told by his personal assistant that Mr Armstrong had given instructions that he was unavailable to Miss Hunter, or any other reporter. At least, she thought dully, he'd added the face-saving bit about reporters. After an hour of coming to terms with unwelcome reality, Joss rang the estate agent and told him she no longer wished to sell. And at work, when told she looked like death, she lied about an oncoming cold and got through the day as best she could.

When she got home she rang Anna, to say, as flippantly as possible, that she wouldn't be bringing Dan down after all, but if the Herricks would put up with a very depressed guest, she would take them up on their offer of Sunday lunch.

'Dan walked out on me,' Joss said baldly.

'Oh, Joss, no!' said Anna, horrified. 'Drive down in

the morning and stay the weekend. Hugh's gone off on a cricket tour, so come and be cosseted.'

At first Joss demurred, unable to quench a little flicker of hope that Dan might have a change of heart and contact her. But in the end she accepted Anna's invitation, grateful for an alternative to a weekend spent alone in the flat. Only a short time ago she'd expected to spend it in Dan's company, in Dan's arms, in Dan's bed. Something which, he'd made very clear, would never happen again.

CHAPTER SEVEN

Joss felt her heart lift when she saw Anna, clad in the inevitable jodhpurs and riding boots, wild dark hair blowing in the breeze as she came running from the open door of Glebe House.

'I took Goodfellow out for a ride first thing,' said Anna. 'Haven't had time to change.' She hugged Joss close, then held her at arm's length. 'Heavens, you look ghastly. Mother and Dad have tactfully taken themselves off to a flower show, so we're on our own for a bit. You can cry as much as you like.'

'No crying,' said Joss firmly, returning the hug.

'Want to tell me about it?' said Anna as they went inside. 'We'll have lunch first; you can take your things upstairs later.'

The big kitchen, with its old-fashioned cupboards and big square table, was so hearteningly familiar and unchanged that Joss gave a sigh of pleasure. 'It's so good to be here. Thanks for letting me come.'

Anna gave her a withering look as she took a napkin from a plate of sandwiches. 'It wasn't a case of "letting," Joss. I've been trying to get you down here for ages. I only wish it had been under happier circumstances. Come on, sit down. Do you want tea, coffee, or something alcoholic and mind-numbing?'

Joss grinned. 'Tea. I draw the line at breathing gin fumes over your mother.'

'That's better,' approved Anna as she made tea. 'Nice to see you can still smile.' She sat down and fixed Joss

92

with a commanding hazel eye. 'Right. Tell me what happened.'

Joss gave a short, succinct account of Peter's visit, and apart from the odd exclamation Anna managed to keep from interrupting until the end.

'You should have reported him to the police,' she said, and bit into a sandwich as though it were Peter Sadler's jugular.

'What could I have said?' said Joss. 'He didn't rape me—in fact, looking back on it, I know he never intended that. He just wanted to frighten and humiliate me, for some reason. Which is rich. He was the one who walked out.'

'Hmm,' said Anna, unconvinced. 'Couldn't you have charged him with bodily harm, or something?'

'The harm he did wasn't physical,' said Joss bitterly.

'But surely if you explained to Dan Armstrong he'd believe you?'

'He wouldn't answer the phone at home, and when I rang his office his secretary told me he was permanently unavailable to Miss Hunter.'

'Ouch!' said Anna, and nudged the plate of sandwiches nearer. 'Eat one. Just to please me,' she coaxed.

Joss did her best, but the food stuck in her throat. 'I just don't seem to feel hungry lately,' she said apologetically.

'No wonder!' Anna poured tea, and handed a cup to Joss. 'You haven't known this Dan Armstrong long,' she went on. 'Will it be very hard to get over him?'

'At the moment it seems impossible. But I'll do it. Eventually.' Joss managed a smile. 'Journalists are persistent beasts, remember?'

Her friend eyed her thoughtfully. 'Have you given up all idea of knocking the truth into the man's head?'

Joss lifted her chin belligerently. 'I did my bit of pleading, Anna, and hated it. No way am I doing it again.'

The weekend with the Herricks did Joss a lot of good. She was able to face work with more zest the following week, even though it became obvious, as days went by, that Dan had meant what he said. With all hope finally quenched, Joss buckled down to reshaping her life, and because it was holiday season there was no shortage of work to pass the time. In the evenings she reverted to having a meal after work with other journalists, and sometimes went on to a film or the theatre, no matter how tired she was. And the dreaded *longueurs* of the weekends were filled by sub-editing work for whichever Sunday paper required her services.

Some nights she fell into bed too exhausted even to mourn her ill-fated passion for Dan Armstrong. Because passion, she assured herself bitterly, was all it had been. She had been—and still was—deeply in love with him, but on Dan's side the relationship had obviously been purely physical. But she was no teenager, mourning the death of calf-love. She was thirty-two years old, with sufficient maturity to prevent Daniel Adam Francis Armstrong from ruining her life. He had spoiled her for the company of other men, it was true. But that would pass. Time, and her own determination, would make sure it did. But her fine resolutions failed to damp down the rush of hope every time her phone rang. Or to prevent intense disappointment when her caller was never Dan.

To Joss's surprise Francis Legh rang her one evening, to tell her he was bringing Sarah Wilcox up to an auction next day and wondered if Joss could spare an hour to have lunch with them. She made a hasty mental rearrangement of her itinerary for the next day and accepted with pleasure.

'I know that something went wrong between you and Dan.' Francis went on, startling her. 'If you'd rather we didn't mention him we won't.'

'It makes no difference to me,' she lied airily.

'Really?'

Joss sighed. 'No, *not* really. Not yet, anyway. But I'm working on it. Thank you for the invitation, Francis, but bear with me if I'm not punctual to the minute.'

Joss looked thoughtful after she'd put the phone down. Lord Morville was a very subtle man, she decided. With Sarah along there was no ambiguity about his invitation—or his intention. Not that she had any aspirations where Francis was concerned. He was charming, friendly, good-looking in a well-bred kind of way, but though she liked him very much he paled into insignificance compared with Dan. In which case, Joss told herself viciously, it was time to stop comparing men with Dan Armstrong and from now on just view them on their own merits.

Next day it was hot and sunny, and Joss wore a dress bought to celebrate moving in with Dan. Sleeveless, V-necked, in a powder-pink knitted fabric fragile as cobwebs, the dress clung rather more than she'd remembered, but it was flattering and she felt good in it as she walked into the restaurant she'd read so much about in the reviews. At the mention of Lord Morville Joss was ushered to a table where Francis jumped up, hand outstretched, as she approached.

'Joss, you made it.'

To her surprise he kissed her on both cheeks, then turned to the young woman smiling at them from a chair by the window.

'You remember Joss, darling?'

'Hello,' said Sarah Wilcox warmly. 'Nice to see you again.'

Joss took the chair Francis held out for her, and after conventional greetings looked from one face to the other with a questioning smile. 'Is there something a journalist should know? Or are the hearts and flowers strictly off the record?'

'Off the record, for the time being,' said Sarah, flushing.

'Haven't asked her father yet,' said Francis, beckoning the wine waiter.

'So why am I playing gooseberry?' asked Joss.

'I proposed on the way up in the train this morning,' said Francis, grinning. 'No one knows yet—I haven't even given Sarah a ring—' He broke off to go into a discussion about the choice of wine, and when menus were put in front of them sat back in his seat, looking very pleased with himself.

'Congratulations to you both,' said Joss sincerely, quelling a dart of pain. 'I hope—no, I *know* you'll be very happy.'

'Thank you,' said Sarah, and gave her a very straight look. 'Something tells me you're not surprised.'

Joss tapped her nose. 'My instincts are rarely wrong. I suspected as much the day I visited Eastlegh.'

'Talking of which, Sam Armstrong took quite a fancy to you,' said Francis. 'He approved of the article you wrote. So do I—heartily. Business is twice as brisk since it appeared. This lunch is by way of a small token of appreciation.'

'That's very nice of you.' Joss smiled warmly. 'The photographs turned out so well my editor decided on Eastlegh as the main thrust of the article.'

Francis had placed her with her back to the room. When Sarah looked up with a smile of welcome a few minutes later Joss felt the hairs rise on the back of her neck, like an animal scenting danger.

Francis sprang to his feet, hand outstretched. 'Hello, Dan, better late than never. Help us celebrate.'

For a moment time seemed suspended. Dan took one look at Joss and obviously wanted to turn on his heel and walk out. But good manners and his genuine attachment to Francis and Sarah prevailed. He took his friend's hand and shook it, eyeing him in enquiry.

'Celebrate?'

'I've just persuaded Sarah to marry me. And I've sold another manorial title.'

Because every nerve in Joss's body was hypersensitive to Dan's slightest reaction she could have sworn that his first gut reaction was relief. Then he went round the table to kiss Sarah, and at last greeted Joss, with a courtesy which chilled her to the bone.

To the onlooker it was an ordinary lunch party, with four people enjoying the food and each other's company, but to Joss it was a particularly refined form of torture. Not by a flicker of an eyelash did Dan portray the slightest hostility towards her. He was, if anything, far more pleasant to her than on the day at Eastlegh. Yet the experience was worse. Sheer determination made Joss eat some of the exquisite food and drink a sip or two of the celebratory champagne. But Dan said nothing directly to Joss, nor she to him, and only Francis's skill as a host kept the conversational ball in the air as he discussed plans for a party at Eastlegh to celebrate the engagement in proper style.

'You'll come, Joss, of course,' he said.

'Thank you,' she said, surprised. 'I'll look forward to it.'

'You too, Dan,' said Francis, and gave his friend a straight look. 'Wasn't it on a similar occasion that you met Joss?'

'Yes, it was,' said Dan briefly, and changed the subject. 'So which of your extraneous titles did you sell off today?'

'I've heard about this,' said Joss, her interest caught. 'Was that the auction you came up for?'

Sarah nodded. 'Quite a few manorial titles went under the hammer today. Ours did particularly well,' she added, eyes sparkling. 'Every time the price went up I totted up more lead for the Eastlegh roof.'

'That's my girl,' said Francis lovingly, and raised the hand he held to his lips.

'What did you do with the money I paid for mine?' said Dan.

Joss stared at him. Daniel Armstrong had actually paid money to Francis so he could add Lord of some Manor to his credentials? In her astonishment she barely heard Francis talking about unromantic plumbing repairs. Dan caught the look in her eye and smiled sardonically.

'Thinking up a new headline, Joss? ''Gardener's son aspires to Lord of the Manor status''?'

She shook her head. 'One of my colleagues followed the sale of manorial titles some time ago.'

'But I didn't feature in it,' he pointed out. 'No one knows about mine.'

'Nor would have done today, if you hadn't mentioned it,' said Francis, eyeing him narrowly.

Dan shrugged. 'It's not a dark secret.'

'Well, no but—'

'As Joss says,' interrupted Dan firmly, 'it's old news.'

Joss got up, looking pointedly at her watch, and the men rose with her. 'Talking of news, I'd better get back to it. Thursday's a busy day for me.' She noted a pulse throbbing at the corner of Dan's mouth, and rejoiced. Mention of Thursday had struck a chord his impervious mask couldn't hide.

'It's time we were all away,' said Francis, helping Sarah from her chair, and to Joss's dismay the four of them left the restaurant together. She had desperately wanted to leave first, and leave alone at that, due to an unpleasant feeling she put down to an overdose of stress.

'Can we give you a lift, Joss?' said Sarah.

To Joss, the heat of the day seemed intense after the cool room inside. She shook her head, meaning to say something about a taxi, then gasped as the earth shifted beneath her feet. Great spots of light danced in front of her eyes, and Dan leapt to catch her as she fell.

When Joss came to she was lying on a sofa in the restaurant's powder room, with Sarah bending over her anxiously.

'How do you feel?'

'What happened?' Joss struggled to sit up and Sarah sat beside her, supporting her with a comforting arm.

'You fainted.'

Joss groaned. 'I never faint! I hardly drank anything, either.'

'I know. Maybe it was something you ate. Drink this.' Sarah handed her a glass of water and Joss drank thirstily, then gave Sarah a rueful smile.

'Sorry I messed up your celebration.'

'You didn't,' said Sarah firmly, and smiled. 'Nothing could do that.'

'You really love Francis, don't you?' said Joss, mopping her forehead with the tissue Sarah gave her.

'From the moment I first saw him, though he never seemed to notice me. But recently he started looking at me with new eyes, as though he'd never seen me before.'

'I'm very glad for you both,' said Joss with complete truth. 'Now I really must get back to work.' And against Sarah's advice she got carefully to her feet, splashed cold water on her ashen face, applied lipstick with an unsteady hand, then smiled valiantly. 'Right. I'm ready.'

'You look ghastly, Joss,' said Sarah with concern.

'People keep telling me that lately. Very bad for my ego.'

After assuring the various members of staff that she was fully recovered, Joss went outside with Sarah, to find Dan still waiting with Francis.

'How do you feel?' asked Francis anxiously. 'I've got a taxi waiting. We'll get you home right away.'

'I can't do that,' protested Joss. 'I'm due back at work.'

'Don't be an idiot, Joss,' said Dan tersely. 'You look like a ghost. You're obviously coming down with something.'

Secretly Joss felt quite terrible, and in the face of three opposing arguments ran out of strength to argue. 'Oh, very well,' she said wearily, and let Francis hand her into the cab.

'Sarah, move Joss to the middle,' instructed Dan. 'We'd better sit either side of her, in case she keels over again.'

Joss made no attempt to join in the conversation on the journey back to Acton. She felt muzzy, and oddly detached, and the voices of the others came and went in a very confusing way. When the car stopped Sarah and Francis jumped out, but Dan told the driver to wait for a moment before taking them on to Waterloo.

He took Joss by the arm, and looked at Francis. 'I'll see her inside.'

Francis put a restraining hand on Sarah's arm. 'All right, Dan. Ring me later.'

Dan nodded briefly, and asked Joss for her key. He unlocked the door, said goodbye to the others, picked Joss up and carried her inside, kicking the door shut behind him. And Joss, by this time almost totally unaware of what was going on, only registered where she was when her head met the cool comfort of her own pillow. She subsided gratefully, then shot upright, holding her head.

'Must ring Jack Ormond,' she muttered, but Dan pushed her back against the pillows, his large hands surprisingly gentle.

'I'll ring him,' he said firmly. 'Stay where you are.'

Convinced by this time that she was coming down with flu at the very least, Joss did as he said, feeling so ill she had no attention to spare for the fact that Dan was actually here in the flat, where she'd longed for him so much.

'What did Jack say?' she asked, when he came back.

'"If you're infectious stay home until you're not,"' he quoted tersely, and frowned down at her. 'I should have let Sarah stay.'

'Did she want to?'

'Yes. But Francis took her off.'

'Maybe he didn't want her to catch whatever I've got.' She turned her head into the pillow. 'The same applies to you. You'd better go.'

'Do you want me to go?'

In a more normal state of health Joss would have been ecstatic if he'd stayed. But she had a growing conviction

that any minute now she was going to lose her lunch.
'Yes, I do. Right now,' she added with sudden urgency.

Dan's face went rigid. He turned on his heel, then
paused in the doorway. 'Isn't there someone I could ring
to come and take care of you?'

'I'll ring Anna later,' said Joss, swallowing hard. She
began to breathe rapidly. 'Go away. *Please.*'

Dan went precipitately, after giving her a look which
acted like a green light on her digestive system. He was
barely out of the flat before Joss bolted to the bathroom
and surrendered to the sickness, which went on for so
long she was shaking and cold by the time it was over.
With trembling hands she washed her face, then undressed, pulled on a nightshirt and forced herself to go
to the kitchen for a bottle of mineral water and a glass.
At last she crawled under the covers and surrendered un-
conditionally to whatever bug was making her feel so ill.

It was dark when Joss woke. She rolled over to look
at the clock and found it was after two in the morning.
Wonderful, she thought morosely. Now she had a whole
night to get through. But to her surprise she found she
was hungry. The first thing on the agenda was food. After
a visit to the bathroom she went to the kitchen, made tea
and toast, curled up on the sofa with the tray beside her,
and settled down to watch late-night television until it
was time to get up. She stared at the screen with brooding
eyes. Now she was feeling better she could have kicked
herself for wasting the opportunity to talk to Dan. Not
that the occasion had been tailor-made for discussion.
After making a spectacle of herself at a very expensive
restaurant she couldn't have borne throwing up in front
of Dan as an encore.

And now, thought Joss despairingly, she'd told him to
go away. So things were back to square one again. She

sighed heavily, wriggled deeper into the cushions and tried to think of some other way to see Dan. Maybe she could ask Francis…

When Joss surfaced again she found it was her usual time to get up. And once she'd confirmed, surprised, that she felt normal, she decided she might as well go to work. After a quick shower, she put on her customary white T-shirt and trouser suit, navy linen now in deference to summer, and decided her stomach bug had been one of the lightning, twenty-four-hour variety.

'Joss?' said the news editor, when she reported in. 'I thought you were at death's door.'

'I was for a while,' she said, pulling a face. 'But I'm fine now. What's on for today?'

He gave her a wolfish look. 'The man who rang in to say you were ill yesterday insisted on speaking to me personally. Said his name was Armstrong. Is he, by any strange, wonderful chance, the Armstrong behind Athena?'

Her heart sank. 'Yes,' she admitted unwillingly.

Jack smiled. 'Rumour has it you're involved with him.'

She shook her head. 'Not any more.'

'But you know him well?'

Joss had doubts about that. 'I know him, yes.'

'Dammit, Joss, if he was in your flat when you were ill yesterday you must know him *fairly* well.'

'What's this about, Jack?' she demanded.

'There's a row raging between conservationists and developers over buildings along the Thames. Dan Armstrong is in the front line with the latest Athena development. For once he might welcome the chance to air his point of view. Contact him.'

'No way!' Joss shuddered at the thought of it. 'He doesn't like reporters. Never gives interviews—'

'Precisely!' Jack's eyes fixed on Joss without mercy. 'This could be very good for you careerwise.'

Joss stared him out for a moment, then heaved a sigh. 'Oh, all right. I'll try. But I'm warning you, Jack, I'm not the best person for the job. My relationship with him is over.'

'Oh, yeah?' Jack gave her another of his unsettling smiles. 'He sounded hellish worried when he rang yesterday.'

'Probably afraid of catching my bug!'

With a view to grasping the nettle, Joss dialled the Athena offices the moment she got back to her desk, expecting Dan's assistant to give her the same message as before. But this time, to her astonishment, Joss was put straight through to the man himself.

'Joss? Are you worse?' Dan demanded.

'No, I'm better today. This isn't a personal call.' She breathed in deeply. 'Look, Dan, don't slam the phone down. This isn't my idea—'

'What are you talking about?'

'Jack Ormond wants me to interview you. I told him it was out of the question,' she went on quickly, almost gabbling in her rush to get the conversation over. 'He assumed, because you rang yesterday when I was ill, that we were still—'

'Lovers?' said Dan abrasively.

'Friends,' she corrected. 'I told him we weren't, but he insisted I contact you about your row with the conservationists, to see if you'd like the opportunity to air your views.'

'All right.'

'I'm sorry?' said Joss blankly.

'I said, yes. You can have your interview. When do you want it?'

Joss pulled herself together and told him journalists always want stories yesterday.

'You can have half an hour at seven-thirty tonight.'

'Thank you,' she said faintly.

'Come to the front entrance and tell Security you're expected.'

'Right.' Feeling dazed, Joss went to report her success to the news editor.

On the strength of the coming confrontation with Dan, Joss wheedled her hairdresser into fitting her in at lunch-time on a busy Friday instead of her usual monthly slot, and on the way back afterwards bought a silk camisole to replace her T-shirt, and a pair of very expensive navy linen shoes with four-inch heels as an extra boost. Joss had conducted interviews with every kind of celebrity that caught the public fancy, but this particular interview, she well knew, would be more important and emotionally difficult than all the others rolled into one.

When she arrived at the Athena building just before seven-thirty Joss found it was smaller than she'd expected, and, though modern, blended so well with its surroundings it was a good advertisement for the skill and success of its owner. Squaring her shoulder, Joss pushed open the glass doors, her new heels clicking satisfactorily on the marble floor as she crossed to the desk. She gave her name, and with a pleasant smile the security man escorted her to the lift and pressed the button for the top floor.

'Mr Armstrong is in the office at the end,' he informed her.

When the lift stopped Joss girded herself mentally for battle, then walked along a corridor lined with deserted offices. She knocked on the closed door at the end, took in a deep breath, then in response to Dan's command opened the door and walked in.

CHAPTER EIGHT

THE office was vast, with a panoramic view of the Thames on both sides. Daniel Armstrong rose from behind a large, cluttered desk as she went in, and drew himself up to his full, intimidating height. But courtesy of the new shoes Joss was only a few inches shorter, and stood as erect as he, her eyes unwavering as he motioned her to the chair in front of the desk. Joss sat down with composure, taking mental notes as she looked at the room. The walls were entirely of glass, with the view for sole ornament. The desk was modern and functional, as was the leather sofa along one side of the room, and the entire office was in such stark contrast to the conventional comfort of the house in Kew it was hard to believe the same man inhabited both environments. Dan was wearing a dark city suit with a plain white shirt and rather flamboyant tie, as usual, but fatigue smudged the slanted eyes fixed on her face.

'How are you feeling?' he asked as he resumed his seat. 'I'm surprised you were able to work today. You looked like death when I left yesterday afternoon.'

'I felt it,' Joss agreed. 'But I woke up this morning feeling so much better it seemed pointless to stay at home.'

'Nothing comes between you and the job, of course. I hope this Jack Ormond appreciates your enthusiasm,' he said without inflection, and leaned back in his seat.

'I doubt it,' she said bitterly, and looked at him in appeal. 'I didn't want to do this, Dan.'

He smiled mirthlessly. 'I'm sure you didn't.'

'I never thought for a moment you'd agree.' She met his eyes. 'Why did you?'

He shrugged. 'I might have refused, as usual, if we hadn't met again yesterday.'

'Which doesn't answer my question.'

His eyes hardened. 'There's something I need to know.'

Joss sat very still. 'What is it?'

Dan's mouth tightened. 'Why the hell did you ask me to come round so urgently that night?'

She stared at him blankly. 'I didn't. It was Thursday. I wasn't expecting you.'

'Think back,' he said harshly. 'I was out of the office until late that day. I got back to an urgent message saying that Miss Hunter needed to see me immediately.'

'I didn't leave the message, Dan,' she said flatly. 'Whoever took it got it wrong.'

He raised an eyebrow. 'You expect me to believe that?'

'Yes. I do.' Joss lifted her chin. 'You always approved of my honesty, Dan. Besides, why should I lie?'

'It's a question I've asked myself a hundred times.' Dan's mouth twisted. 'In the circumstances I was surely the last person you wanted to walk in on you—'

'Actually, you're wrong about that.'

He raised a disbelieving eyebrow. 'You surprise me. Unless you wanted an audience for your reunion with the former lover. I assume that's who it was?'

'It was Peter, yes. He rang the bell, I thought it was you, and—'

'Spare me the rest,' he shot at her. 'I saw what happened for myself, heard the little choking noises you were making, heard you saying ''please'' over and over again as he made love to you—'

'Peter wasn't making *love* to me,' said Joss, incensed. 'He was assaulting me. Couldn't you tell that we were fighting? I was begging him to stop. What you saw was punishment on his part.'

'It didn't look like it,' he threw back at her. 'Not that it matters. If you'd told me about it later it's just possible I might have been able to forget. But because I saw for myself—' He shrugged, his mouth twisting bitterly. 'I just can't blot the scene from my mind.'

The last little flicker of hope died inside Joss. 'So why did you agree to an interview?' she asked quietly.

Dan stared down at the pen he was rolling between his fingers. 'It's a gesture on my part. To give you the interview all the other journalists hound me for.' He looked up. 'I can't blot *you* from my memory, either, Joss. So because of what we had together I decided to give you the exclusive your editor wants.'

The silence lengthened until tension stretched between them to breaking point.

'Payment for services rendered,' Joss said dully. 'An interview instead of a roll of notes left on the dressing table.'

Dan flinched as though she'd struck him, and Joss flung up a hand to silence his reply. 'My gut reaction is to storm out of here and tell you to stuff your interview, Mr Armstrong. But I can't afford the luxury. There are lots of talented people out there after my kind of job. So let's get on with it, shall we?' She put her tape recorder on the desk, pressed the button and smiled encouragingly. 'Tell me, Mr Armstrong, how will conservationist opposition affect the plans for your riverside development?'

Half an hour later Joss pressed the 'stop' button and

put the recorder in her handbag, then got up. 'Thank you very much for seeing me.'

He came round the desk towards her. 'Did you get everything you wanted?'

I want a whole lot more than a stupid interview, raged Joss inwardly. 'Oh, yes,' she said politely. 'More than I'd hoped, in fact.'

The sudden, molten look in Dan's eyes sent her backing away hurriedly.

'I'm glad you got what you wanted,' he growled, advancing on her. 'I wish I could say the same.'

'Keep your distance,' she snapped, eyes flashing. 'You can't say I disgust you one minute, then fancy a spot of fun and games the next.'

His light in his eyes snuffed out abruptly. 'I apologise.'

'For what, exactly?'

'For everything that's happened since we met!' he said in sudden rage. 'Starting with my crass stupidity in following you out on that balcony.'

Joss turned blindly and opened the door, stumbling a little in the new shoes in her hurry to get away, and Dan reached for her and caught her in his arms, his mouth descending towards hers. Then he pushed her away again so violently she stumbled again, and flung a hand out against the wall to right herself.

'It's no good,' Dan said in hoarse anguish. 'I can still see the man's hands on your body, his mouth devouring yours—'

Joss could stand no more. With a choked sound of despair she fled along the corridor to the waiting lift, feeling safe only when she was locked away inside it on her way down to the foyer.

Joss had intended to go to a house-warming one of her friends on Production was hosting, but by the time she got home it was late, and after the meeting with Dan she was in no mood for partying. She rang up to plead the stomach bug as an excuse, then got out her laptop and typed up the article to release the emotions she'd kept under control in Dan's office. When she'd polished it she switched on her mobile phone and transmitted the article to the *Post*. Afterwards, suddenly remembering she'd eaten nothing all day, Joss scrambled some eggs, then after supper had a bath and went to bed to watch television from the comfort of stacked pillows, determined to get a good night's sleep, for once, in preparation for her Saturday stint on the *Sunday Globe*.

It was well after midnight when Joss got home the following evening, utterly exhausted. She was so tired she fell into bed the moment she'd brushed her teeth, and it was next morning before she bothered to see if there were any messages. When she heard Dan's voice on the machine her stomach gave a great heave, and before she could listen to what he had to say she was forced to make a run for the bathroom. Return of the killer stomach bug, she thought wretchedly, and washed her sweating face swiftly so she could get back to the phone.

'Joss, it's Dan,' said the message. 'You looked so pale last night I was concerned. But if you're out presumably you're better.'

No, I'm not better, she thought, enraged. Nor was I out on the town. I was working like a slave to pay for haircuts and expensive shoes to impress a man who can't forgive me for something which wasn't my fault. But that's it. No more. As you once said so emphatically, Daniel Armstrong, it's finished.

Pride and hard work were poor bedfellows as the summer wore on, with an August so hot Joss found sleeping even more difficult than usual. The article about Dan had been well received by Jack Ormond, and as a result Joss was given more assignments than usual in the time leading up to the week she was taking off to stay at Glebe House for Anna's wedding. She was grateful for the work, which helped a little in her effort to forget the interview with Dan. But when she was alone at night his parting words still burned in her mind like acid. So much so that Joss made no response to his message, and refused to pick up the phone when he rang again to congratulate her on the article. She stood rigid, hands clenched at her side as she listened to Dan's voice thanking her for an accurate and informative piece of writing. He paused, as though he knew she was listening, but with superhuman effort she kept from snatching up the receiver to answer him. The vivid memory of her own fruitless, pleading messages steeled Joss in her resolve.

As the sweltering August dragged by she was eventually forced to face up to a truth so shattering it almost changed her mind about contacting Dan. But only fleetingly. And by then it was time for Anna's wedding. Burying her panic deep, Joss locked up the flat and fled the city to drive off to leafy Warwickshire, and the sanctuary of Glebe House.

'Your friend Francis went to Hugh's stag party,' said Anna, as they lazed in ancient deck chairs in the garden after dinner.

'Really?' Joss chuckled. 'Did Hugh get home in one piece?'

'Yes. Hungover, I gather, but with nothing broken or missing. I laid down the law beforehand. I insist on a bridegroom in mint condition.' She pushed back her mass of curls and eyed Joss closely. 'Heard from Dan since?'

'Yes.'

'And?'

'I didn't pick up the phone.'

'But you still care.'

'Oh, yes,' said Joss wearily. 'I still care.'

'Will you spit and scratch if I say you look fragile, Joss?'

'No. I know very well I look like a hag. It's too hot to sleep in London.' Joss smiled reassuringly. 'But I'll be fine by tomorrow, I promise. Is Francis coming to the wedding, by the way?'

'Yes. And bringing his new fiancée. The eligible Baron's engagement must have saddened the hearts of Dorset debs. What's Sarah like?'

It was restful to chat comfortably in a place which held only memories of childhood. And later, in the familiar narrow bed the Herricks always kept ready for Joss, for the first time in weeks she slept well, and woke so late she found Anna smiling down at her, ready to share the breakfast she'd brought up on a tray.

'Hey!' said Joss, struggling to sit up. She pushed the hair from her eyes and looked at her watch in astonishment. 'It can't be ten!'

'Certainly is. I took Goodfellow out for a ride, then asked Mother for breakfast for two. She was all for cooking eggs, bacon, and everything else in the fridge, but I whittled her down to tea, toast and her celebrated marmalade. OK?'

'Perfect.'' Joss grinned at her windblown friend. 'But it's brides who get breakfast in bed, not guests.'

'You can cart the tray up on the big day, then.'

The week rushed by in wedding preparations, with little time for introspection. But at the rehearsal it was a bittersweet experience for Joss to stand in the church where her father had delivered so many witty sermons. And afterwards, over dinner with the bridegroom and his parents, just to watch Hugh with Anna gave Joss's heart a painful wrench as she contemplated a future without Dan.

But Anna's wedding was too special an occasion to allow private turbulence to intrude on it. Determined that nothing should mar the day, Joss kept her smile firmly in place, and sat with Francis and Sarah and some of Hugh's farming friends for the wedding breakfast in the flower-filled marquee on the lawn, and later on, when Anna and Hugh left on the first stage of their honeymoon, she joined in with the rest to pelt the bridal car with confetti, then accepted with gratitude when Francis and Sarah insisted she had a snack with them in the village inn.

'We thought you might feel a bit flat at this stage,' said Sarah, when Francis was buying drinks at the bar.

'I do, a bit. It's the end of a chapter for Anna and me.' Joss changed the subject quickly. 'So when's *your* wedding?'

Sarah smiled wryly. 'We haven't even had the engagement party yet! Francis is determined to celebrate it at Eastlegh, but it's difficult finding a suitable date that isn't wanted by some company or other.'

'Which is wonderful,' said Joss warmly, and smiled as Francis set three glasses down on the table. 'I hear business is brisk at Eastlegh.'

'Long may it last!' He sat down close to Sarah with a sigh of satisfaction. 'This was a great idea of yours, Joss. A bed for the night here is a better idea than flogging all the way back to Dorset.' He gave her a searching look. 'How are you? Really?'

'I'm fine.'

'You gave us a fright that day at the restaurant,' said Sarah with feeling.

'I frightened myself,' said Joss wryly.

'And Dan,' added Francis.

She shrugged. 'He got over it.'

'I doubt that. Dan's not a happy man these days.' Francis exchanged a look with Sarah. 'Are we allowed to ask what went wrong?'

Joss smoothed the lapel of her silk jacket, avoiding the keen grey eyes. 'He walked in on me when a surprise visitor was getting over-familiar. Against my will, as it happens, but Dan refuses to believe that.' She shrugged philosophically. 'Let's talk about something else.'

It was still early when Sarah and Francis walked Joss back to Glebe House.

'When we finally set a date for our party, will you come, Joss?' asked Francis.

'Will Dan be there?' she asked bluntly.

'He'll be invited.'

'Then I won't—' Joss breathed in sharply, then clutched at Sarah as the starlit night spun round.

Sarah put an arm round her swiftly. 'Joss, shall Francis carry you up to the house?'

'No!' Joss breathed in deeply. 'Please—I'm not ill.'

'I think you're pregnant,' said Sarah baldly, and Francis gave a smothered exclamation, and seized Joss's cold hand in his.

'My God—is this true?'

Joss let out a deep, unsteady breath. 'I'm afraid it is.'

CHAPTER NINE

FRANCIS let out a whistle. 'And Dan doesn't know! Are you going to tell him?'

'No *way*.' Joss shuddered at the thought.

'But you must!' said Sarah urgently.

Joss shook her head. 'Fatherhood, he once told me, is definitely not on his agenda. In any case, Dan would never believe the child was his.'

'Because of the incident you mentioned?' asked Francis gently.

'Not exactly.' Joss shivered. 'I met Dan only a short time after breaking up with someone else. How could I expect him to believe me?'

'I think he has the right to know,' said Francis decisively. 'If Sarah were having my child I'd be furious if she didn't tell me.'

'The situation's different, darling,' Sarah pointed out.

'I still think Dan should know—' Francis halted midsentence. 'Forgive me, Joss,' he said in sudden contrition. 'It's none of our business.'

'Nothing to forgive. In a way it's a relief to tell someone.' She sighed. 'I couldn't tell Anna, or her mother, before the wedding.'

'What are you going to do?' asked Francis, sounding worried.

'I carry on with my job as long as possible, then hire a nanny afterwards and get back to work. No maternity leave in my kind of job. Nor am I the first lone parent in the world.' Joss kissed them both suddenly. 'Now go back to the pub—and go to bed. Make the most of your time away from Eastlegh.'

'Percipient lady,' said Francis, chuckling, and gave her a hug. 'Sarah won't even move in to Home Farm with me until we tie the knot.'

'We'll keep in touch,' promised Sarah, kissing Joss. 'Please don't feel you're alone in this.'

They saw Joss to the door of Glebe House, thanked the tired Herricks for inviting them to the wedding, then walked down the drive together, waving as they turned through the gates.

'What a charming pair,' said Mrs Herrick, and turned to her husband with a smile. 'Robert, do you think you could make some tea? Joss and I are going to collapse in a heap and indulge in wedding talk.'

'In which case,' he said with a twinkle, 'I'll provide the tea, then smoke a cigar in the garden while I assess damage to the lawn.'

Mrs Herrick chatted about her pleasure in the happy day, then, once her husband had brought in a tea-tray, she filled two cups, sat back in her chair and smiled at Joss.

'You can undo your jacket and be comfortable now, dear. I assume you bought the suit some time ago. How far along are you?'

Joss stared at her in blank dismay. 'Is it written on my forehead? Sarah Wilcox guessed, too.'

'I can't answer for Sarah, but I'm familiar with the signs. Your bust measurement may be bigger, but your face is far too thin. I've had my suspicions all week, Joss.' She smiled affectionately. 'But of course you couldn't tell Anna.'

'No. Not before the wedding, anyway.' Joss undid her jacket with a sigh of relief. 'Thank goodness for that. I moved the jacket buttons to ease the fit. I thought of buying something else, but I'll have to count the pennies from now on.'

'Is Peter Sadler the father?' said Mrs Herrick bluntly.

'No. It's someone I met the night of Anna's engagement party.'

'Does he know?'

Joss shook her head. 'It's my fault I got pregnant. I'd rather soldier on alone.'

'It's your choice about the baby's father, Joss.' Mrs Herrick eyed her sternly. 'However, when your father was ill I promised him we'd take care of you. And we will.'

Anna's mother meant what she said. She rang Joss regularly, with sensible advice, and other regular phone calls came from Sarah and Francis, and, after her return from the Seychelles, from Anna herself.

After the first shock of discovery Anna agreed with Francis, and left Hugh for a night to tell Joss so in person. Dan, she said trenchantly, had the right to know. But Joss was adamant. The mere thought of telling Dan gave her nightmares.

Eventually it was impossible to keep her condition secret, though workwise it made very little difference. She carried on with her job in much the same way as usual, finding she could cope well enough now she was over the dizzy spells and nausea of the initial stage of the pregnancy. But it was October before Joss received the promised invitation to the party at Eastlegh.

'Thanks for asking me, Sarah, but I can't come,' she said adamantly. 'My condition is pretty obvious now. All I lack is a scarlet A on my front.'

'Anna and Hugh are coming,' said Sarah, ignoring her.

'And if you're worried about meeting Dan he's in the States on that date. Probably on purpose. It's not a good idea to drive,' she warned, 'so come by train and put up for the night at Home Farm.'

'Which is a stone's throw from Dan's father's house! Thank Francis very much for the suggestion, but no way am I coming to your party.'

But in the end Joss gave in, because she was tired of the relentless hectoring she'd received on all sides, not least from Anna.

'Oh, all right, all right, I'll come,' she said impatiently at last. 'But I don't have anything to wear. Where can I buy a silk tent?'

'You're not that big. Anyway, Mother's buying the dress,' said Anna, silencing her. 'And if you think you can refuse my mother, Joscelyn Hunter, you're a better woman than me. She's knitting little white things, too.'

Joss wanted to bang her head on the wall. 'Anna, I just hate all this. I always wanted a baby some day. You know that. But not now—not this way.'

'Of course I know,' said Anna in swift sympathy. 'So stop being so damned independent and let us help. We worry.'

Joss took a train from Waterloo on the day of the party, and gazed through the carriage window in pensive mood. Though wild horses wouldn't have dragged the truth from her, she'd changed her mind about telling Dan. A routine scan at the hospital had shown her a little moving entity on the monitor, and Joss had stared at it in wonder, and received a copy of the ultrasound in a state of shock. From that moment on, no matter how often she'd dismissed the change as pure hormonal imbalance, nothing could alter the truth. She was carrying a real live baby born of her love for Daniel Armstrong. Because however hard she tried she couldn't stop loving him, and still missed him so badly that, unknown to her nagging mentors she'd picked up the phone several times to give him the unwanted news. But her courage had always deserted her at the crucial moment.

Francis met her at the station in a battered old Range Rover, and kissed her on both cheeks before lifting her up into the passenger seat. 'You look blooming, Joss.'

'Burgeoning, you mean,' she said dryly. 'You know I didn't want to come.'

'I could hardly fail to! But Sarah's a determined lady.' He chuckled. 'As you probably guessed, she'd decided to marry me long before it dawned on me that she was the perfect wife.'

'I knew that the day you gave me lunch at Home Farm.'

'Talking of which, have you changed your mind about telling Dan?'

Joss shook her head, unable to admit that she had.

Francis changed the subject tactfully, telling her that the Wakefields were waiting for her at Home Farm. 'They wanted to fetch you, but I had to go into Dorchester. Besides,' he added, 'I wanted a word in private before the party.'

When they drove past the brightly lit splendour of Eastlegh Hall to Home Farm, Anna and Hugh came hurrying out to the car, and Francis excused himself to rush off to his room.

'You two show Joss where she's to sleep. I must be ready and waiting with Sarah in the glad rags when the first guests arrive. Anna will give you some tea, Joss, then Hugh will drive you over to the Hall.'

'I can walk that far,' protested Joss.

'Not tonight,' said Hugh firmly. 'You get off, Francis; we'll see to the little mother here.'

'Hugh, for heaven's sake,' Anna remonstrated, but Joss laughed.

'I don't mind. I prefer people to talk about it naturally—makes me feel less like the whore of Babylon.'

'Who the devil was she?' said Hugh, laughing. 'Come on, wife. Give Joss some tea and buns, then bundle her into her party dress at top speed.'

'Bundle being the word,' said Joss ruefully.

Half an hour later she gave a last flick of mascara to her lashes, brushed more colour onto her bottom lip, then eyed herself with reasonable satisfaction in the mirror in one of the Home Farm guest rooms. Now that expensive haircuts were deleted from her budget her hair hung to the shoulders of her dress. She eyed herself wryly. The long, filmy sleeves, and deep, pearl-embroidered neckline could have belonged to any formal dress, but the generous folds of midnight-blue chiffon couldn't quite conceal the bulge where her once-trim waist had been. Joss patted it tenderly, hung pearl drops from her ears, and slid her feet into the navy linen shoes bought to impress Dan at the interview. Four-inch heels were frowned on for mothers-to-be, she thought guiltily, so she would just have to sit down as much as possible. But just for tonight she wanted to show that, far from being embarrassed by it, she was proud of approaching motherhood.

Once she was enveloped in the laughter and music inside Eastlegh Hall Joss enjoyed the party far more than she'd expected. With Hugh and Anna never far away, she circulated among the other guests very happily after the first welcoming hugs and kisses from Sarah and Francis, and after talking to some of the latter's neighbours for a while renewed her acquaintance with

Elizabeth Wilcox, who was full of praise for the article Joss had written on Eastlegh's corporate entertainment venture and called her husband over to add his own appreciation.

The party was a success from the word go, but by the time she'd eaten a delicious supper Joss was feeling the effects of unaccustomed socialising, and her feet were beginning to ache badly in the ridiculous heels. After telling Anna where she was going, Joss slipped out onto the terrace for some badly needed fresh air, her eye on one of the ornamental stone benches some former Morville had brought back from Italy after the Grand Tour. With a sigh of relief she sank onto the cold seat and eased off the shoes, thankful that the autumn night was mild enough to sit in comfort for a few minutes.

By the light of the full moon Home Farm and the Armstrong cottage were plainly visible in the distance. Joss sighed. She had disciplined herself to avoid thinking too much about Dan lately, but here, in these surroundings, it was impossible. She knew Dan had won his battle about the riverside development, but otherwise had had no news of him. She stared out into the moonlit night, wondering what Dan was doing in the States. And who he was doing it with. Then Joss heard footsteps on the stone flags, and bent hurriedly to thrust her feet into the crippling shoes. She looked up with a bright smile, prepared to make excuses for her sudden yearning for solitude. Then her eyes widened in shock as she saw a tall, unmistakable figure standing with a glass in each hand. Joss blinked, feeling as though she'd pressed a replay button on a video recorder. Barring one important detail, the scene was almost identical to their first meeting.

'Hello, Joss. I was told you were out here,' said Dan quietly.

Joss pinned the smile firmly back in place. 'Daniel Armstrong, no less. For a moment I thought I was seeing things.'

'Back in the same movie,' he agreed.

'Something like that. Why aren't you in America?'

'Why should I be?'

'Sarah told me you were.'

The sudden silence was all the more marked for the sounds of laughter and conviviality in the background.

'For probably the only time in her life Sarah was telling lies,' said Dan. 'I assume,' he added carefully, 'that if you'd known I was here you wouldn't have come.'

'Probably not,' she said lightly. 'Though I found it hard to believe you'd miss your oldest friend's celebration. Are you pleased that he's marrying Sarah?'

'Of course I am. I've been expecting it for years.'

Joss smiled. 'Francis must have been the last one to realise they were made for each other.'

Dan shrugged. 'Not everyone falls in love at first sight.'

'No,' said Joss, her face suddenly shadowed. 'Outside of fiction very few, probably.' She braced herself, nerving herself up for confrontation. Showtime. No point in dragging it out. 'Is one of those glasses for me?' she asked, and moved forward into the light to take one.

Dan took an incredulous look and dropped one of the glasses on the stone flags.

'Joss?' cried Anna, rushing out with Hugh. 'I heard a crash. Are you all right?'

'Yes. I'm fine. You remember Dan Armstrong, of course?' said Joss with composure.

The three of them muttered automatic greetings, but when Joss moved closer Dan shoved the glass in his hand at Hugh and leapt forward, hands outstretched to keep her back. 'Don't move; there's glass everywhere.'

'I'll get someone,' said Hugh, and whisked a reluctant Anna away, leaving a deafening silence behind them.

'What's known as a pregnant pause,' said Joss at last, deliberately flippant.

'How can you treat it so lightly?' he demanded bitterly, then broke off with a curse as two of Elizabeth Wilcox's team hurried outside to clear up the broken glass. He seized Joss by the hand. 'It's hot inside—fancy a walk in the moonlight?' he said urgently, winning indulgent smiles from the women who'd known him all his life.

'Lovely,' lied Joss, and let him lead her down the steps, doing her best to ignore the crippling shoes.

'Why are you limping?' he demanded as they reached the gravelled terrace below.

'My feet hurt.'

'I suppose you're tottering on six-inch heels as usual,' he said irritably.

'Four-inch tonight.'

'Rather stupid in your condition.'

'My condition is my own concern,' she snapped, wincing as his grasp threatened to cut off her circulation.

'Surely it's also the concern of the man involved!'

'Not in this case.'

'You haven't told him?'

'No.'

'Why the hell not?'

Joss spotted a bench at the edge of the knot garden. 'Can we sit, please? Otherwise I may never walk again.'

Dan made for the bench in silence, then sat beside her, studying her face in the moonlight. 'Is Sadler the father?' he asked at last.

'Certainly not,' said Joss, eyeing his clenched fists.

'Then is it mine, for God's sake?' he demanded, as though the words were torn from him.

'Of course it is,' said Joss, and turned her head to look at him.

'Is this the truth?' he asked hoarsely.

'Yes. And nothing but the truth, so help me God. Whether you believe it or not is up to you, of course.' Joss smiled comfortingly. 'But don't worry, Dan. Even if you do believe me I'm not asking you to do anything about it.'

'Don't be so stupid,' he roared at her.

'For heaven's sake,' she said irritably. 'You'll have Hugh charging to the rescue if you bellow like that.'

Dan controlled himself with obvious effort. 'Is this the reason for your phone calls after—'

'After you found me in what you took to be *flagrante* with Peter Sadler,' she said with composure. 'As a matter of fact, no. I didn't know then.'

'When did you find out?'

'My embarrassing faint at the restaurant that day was the start of it. I kept feeling so weird from time to time after that I eventually saw a doctor.'

'Surely you had an idea what was wrong!'

'No. The usual indications were conspicuous by their presence, not their absence. It happens sometimes, apparently.' Joss shrugged philosophically. 'And I mistook my lack of appetite and so on for something else entirely.'

'What do you mean?'

She laughed scornfully. 'Use your imagination, Daniel Armstrong. I was in seventh heaven about to set up house with you, then *wham*. You dumped me, wouldn't answer my calls, refused to have anything to do with me. Your attitude was a pretty effective appetite depressant.'

'I did call you, after the interview. More than once.'
He looked down into her face. 'Were you always out
when I rang?'

'No. I heard you every time.'

'And refused to pick up the phone.' His mouth twisted.
'Was revenge sweet?'

'Yes,' Joss said frankly. 'It was.' She got to her feet,
wincing. 'Time we returned to the festivities.'

Dan leapt up, and seized her hands. 'We can't leave
things like this. When's the child due?'

'In early spring.'

Dan held her hands wide, staring down at the curve
filling out her dress. 'That first night, you told me there
was no danger of this.'

She detached her hands, and began to walk. 'I'd forgotten that I gave up on birth-control after Peter walked
out. I only started again after your reappearance in my
life. Not quite soon enough, unfortunately.'

'Unfortunate indeed,' he agreed, pacing beside her. 'I
remember your views on motherhood only too well.'

'Yours on fatherhood were even more negative,' she
said tartly. 'Is it any wonder I didn't tell you I was pregnant?'

'I had a right to know.'

'So everyone keeps telling me.'

Dan halted in his tracks, holding her by the shoulders.
'So everyone knows I'm your child's father except me?'

'Only the people who matter.'

'And I don't!' he said bitterly.

Joss removed his hands. 'Last time we met you said
you couldn't bear to touch me. How on earth did you
expect me to tell you I was carrying your child?'

'If you'd answered my calls you'd know I'd got over
that,' he said gruffly, as they resumed walking.

'You knew where I lived, Dan,' she pointed out.

'I've driven round more than once,' he said savagely, astonishing her. 'I was parked along your street one night, waiting, when you arrived home with two other women. The next time you never arrived at all. I found out later from Francis that you were in Warwickshire with Anna. Then I went to the States. When I came back Francis said you were coming to the party, so I thought I'd wait, bide my time until you felt less bitter towards me. But I was held up at Athena and arrived late tonight, at which point Francis told me you were out on the terrace. So I decided to try a rerun of our first meeting.'

'And got the shock of your life!'

He nodded grimly. 'Why the hell didn't Francis warn me?'

'He feels—quite rightly—that it isn't his business.' Joss caught sight of Anna and Hugh coming towards them. 'Time to join the party again. Francis must be about to make the formal announcement. After which,' she added, wincing as she stumbled, 'I'm going back to Home Farm to bed. I'm tired.'

Dan held her arm in an iron grip. 'How did you travel down? I hope you didn't drive yourself in your con—'

'If you mention the word ''condition'' I'll scream,' she informed him. 'I came by train.'

'Then I'll drive you back,' he said promptly.

'No, thanks. I prefer the train.'

Secretly Joss felt rather crestfallen when Dan said no more, and because Hugh and Anna came hurrying to herd them back to the Hall for the big moment she had no more private conversation with him until she'd kissed Sarah and Francis goodnight, and it was time to leave for Home Farm.

'I'll see you tomorrow,' Dan stated, after Hugh had gone to fetch the car.

With Anna's eyes on them Joss couldn't bring herself to object. 'Goodnight, then,' she said politely.

Dan took his leave of them both with punctilious courtesy, and handed Joss into Hugh's car as though she were a time bomb about to explode, something Anna commented on with great satisfaction once the car moved off.

'How did he react?' she demanded.

'Stunned disbelief. You saw the smashed glass,' said Joss, yawning. 'Gosh, I'm tired.'

'You'd better let us drive you home tomorrow,' said Anna. 'A train journey on top of tonight is a very bad idea.'

'Certainly not; it's miles out of your way,' said Joss firmly. 'I like travelling by train.'

Rather to her surprise Joss slept very well that night, and woke only when Anna came rushing in to announce that Dan was downstairs, demanding her presence.

'At this hour? Demanding?' said Joss, scowling as she struggled to sit up.

'More or less. Imperious bloke, isn't he?'

'He'll just have to wait.' Joss swung her feet to the floor, then breathed in sharply, biting her lip.

'What's the matter?' asked Anna in alarm.

Joss pointed to two hugely swollen ankles and feet, and sighed despairingly. 'The price of vanity.'

'I *told* you not to wear those shoes!'

'But I did. And now I can't wear any shoes at all.' Joss stood up with difficulty, muttering something rude under her breath. 'Now what do I do!'

'Have a bath. Maybe the swelling will go down.'

'Good idea. Tell Dan he's in for a long wait.'

But neither a bath, nor the quantities of cold water Joss

poured over them afterwards, did anything to reduce the size of her feet. In the end she gave up, pulled on black jersey trousers with a drawstring waist, and a large Cambridge-blue sweater bought in the men's department of her favourite chainstore, then brushed her hair swiftly as a peremptory hand beat a tattoo on the door.

'Joss?' called Dan. 'Are you all right?'

Joss hobbled painfully across the room and opened the door. Dan stood outside on the landing, looking so good in faded old jeans and an indigo shirt she felt a leap of unwanted response.

'Good morning,' he said, eyeing her feet.

'If you say a word about silly shoes I'll punch you in the nose,' said Joss fiercely.

He looked up, smiling crookedly. 'You and whose army, Joscelyn Hunter?'

She tucked a strand of hair behind her ear, glaring at him.

'I came to deliver an invitation,' he said, surprising her.

'Invitation?'

'From my father. He liked the piece you did about Eastlegh. Asked if you'd have coffee with him this morning.'

Joss stared at him in surprise, then gestured at her front. 'Does he know about this?'

'No.'

Joss shook her head vigorously. 'Then please explain that I can't come due to my feet.'

'I brought the car. I can carry you downstairs and drive you over,' said Dan, and eyed the swollen feet, frowning. 'Do you have any socks?'

'Yes. But they won't go on. And I refuse to go anywhere barefoot *and* pregnant,' she snapped, her colour rising.

Anna came hurrying up the stairs, with Hugh behind her. 'How are the feet?'

'Large as life, unfortunately.'

Dan shot a glance at Hugh. 'Could you lend her a pair of socks?'

'Of course.' Hugh grinned. 'What colour do you fancy, Joss?'

'Size is the priority, not colour, Hugh Wakefield,' she said tartly, red to the roots of her hair as the other three gazed at the offending extremities. 'Could everyone stop that, please?'

Anna took her arm. 'Sit down while *I* choose the socks. Afterwards you can carry her downstairs, Dan.'

'There's no need for that,' said Joss explosively, then proved herself wrong when her progress to the nearest chair resembled a walk over hot coals.

'How do you feel? Other than the feet,' asked Dan, when they were alone.

Joss glared at him. 'Just dandy.'

'No more fainting?'

'No.'

His eyes dropped to the bulge. 'Is the baby fine too?'

'Yes. I've got a snapshot to prove it. An ultrasound photograph,' she added hurriedly at the look on his face. 'If you'll hand me that bag over there I'll show you.'

When Joss handed the copy over Dan studied it in awe. 'Do you know what sex it is?'

Joss shook her head. 'No. I preferred to wait.'

Anna came hurrying in, brandishing a pair of large black socks. 'Thank goodness Hugh has enormous feet. Try these.' She knelt in front of Joss and drew the socks gently over the swollen feet. Joss nodded.

'Fine.'

Dan bent and picked her up. 'I'll carry you down to the car.'

'Car?' said Anna. 'She's not leaving until after lunch.'

'I'm taking her to have coffee with my father,' said Dan rather breathlessly, descending the stairs with care. 'It's all right,' he told Anna over Joss's head when they reached the hall. 'I'll look after her.'

'Don't keep her long. She hasn't had any breakfast,' said Anna anxiously, as she went with them to the door.

'When did I ever eat breakfast!' said Joss.

'Then it's time you started,' grunted Dan in disapproval. 'Don't worry, Anna. I'll see she gets something to eat.'

'I don't want this,' said Joss mutinously, once they were on the way to his father's cottage.

'No. I don't suppose you do. But my father obviously took a fancy to you. Not,' added Dan, 'something he does very often.'

Joss sighed despondently. 'He'll probably change his mind when he sees I'm pregnant.'

Dan gave a bark of mirthless laughter. 'Why the hell should he do that?'

She flushed irritably. 'Does he know any single mothers?'

'Francis employs two of them. My father's unlikely to go into shock at the sight of you.'

Sam Armstrong came out of the house as the car stopped. His weathered face wore a welcoming look as he opened the car door. 'Come in, Miss Hunter.' He offered her his hand, and Joss took it, her heart in her throat as the keen old eyes took in the unmistakable bulge.

'Father, I'll have to carry Joss into the house,' Dan warned. 'She can't get any shoes on.'

Sam Armstrong stood back, his face unreadable as he watched his son scoop Joss from her seat. .

'Best bring her in front of the fire, Dan,' he said without comment. 'It's a bit nippy this morning.'

Dan deposited Joss in one of the leather armchairs drawn up to the fire in the familiar sitting room. 'I'll make the coffee,' he said swiftly. 'Joss hasn't had any breakfast.'

'Slice some bread, then,' said Sam, seating himself in the other chair. 'Bring it in and I'll toast it in front of the fire.' He reached under his chair, pulled out a footstool and pushed it near Joss. 'Put your feet on that, my dear.'

'Thank you. It's lovely. Was it your wife's?' asked Joss, admiring the stool's finely worked tapestry cover.

'Yes—she was clever with a needle.' Sam grimaced. 'Now it's mine. I get the odd bit of gout.'

'And doesn't take his pills,' said Dan, bringing in a platter of bread. 'I'll bring butter with the coffee.'

Now the initial ordeal was over Joss felt oddly comfortable alone with Sam Armstrong, watching with pleasure as he held slices of bread over the flames with a copper toasting fork. 'I haven't had proper toast since I left home,' she remarked.

Sam turned to look at her. 'Dan says your father was a vicar.'

Joss nodded. 'I miss him a lot. Especially now,' she added, patting her front.

'I hear you were seeing a lot of Dan, then there was some kind of quarrel,' said Sam, going on with his task.

'Yes.'

'Is my son the father of your child?' asked Sam bluntly, taking Joss's breath away.

'Yes, I am,' said Dan, dumping a coffee tray on the

table. He shot a look at Joss. 'Are you all right? Your colour went for a moment.'

'My house guest just did a little dance,' she said breathlessly.

Dan filled a coffee cup and handed it to her, then hunkered down in front of the fire to butter two slices of bread. He handed her the plate, then looked at his father. 'No comment?' he demanded.

Sam Armstrong gave his son a piercing look. 'Joscelyn tells me her father's dead. So I'll speak for him. In my day it was simple. If a girl got pregnant the baby's father married her.'

'Which is precisely what I'm going to do—now I've finally been informed,' said Dan with emphasis, and returned his father's look. 'And not because *you* think I should, either. I decided that the moment I discovered Joss was pregnant.'

'And when was that?' demanded Sam.

'Last night,' said Joss, deciding to put her oar in. 'But you must realise that the decision isn't up to Dan, Mr Armstrong. It's up to me. And I don't want to get married.'

The disapproval in the two pairs of identical blue eyes was almost amusing. Joss smiled gently. 'I prefer to manage on my own.'

Dan got to his feet, looming over her with such menace Joss exerted considerable self-control not to cower in her chair. 'Don't be silly,' he said coldly. 'We'll get married as soon as I can arrange it.'

'We will not!' Her eyes flashed dangerously. 'Not so long ago you couldn't bear the sight of me.'

'That's not true,' he said, his voice dangerously quiet. 'And this is no place to discuss it. But get this straight. When I decide I want something, I get it.'

Sam stared at his son in disbelief. 'Are you mad, boy? That's no way to make a proposal of marriage.'

'You keep out of it, Father,' his son shot at him.

'He wasn't proposing, Mr Armstrong,' said Joss scornfully. 'He was acquiring a property. Buying a wife, just as he bought his title.'

Sam stared at her blankly. 'What title?'

'She means the manorial title I bought from Francis,' said Dan impatiently.

Sam wagged a finger at Joss. 'Now you listen, young lady. Young Francis—Lord Morville, I mean—owes a lot to my son.'

'Father!' warned Dan. 'Keep out of this.'

Sam rose to his feet with effort, then straightened to look his son in the eye. 'I'll go in the kitchen and see to the meal. While I'm out talk to the girl like a human being. She's not a board meeting.'

After he'd gone the only sound in the room was the crackling of flames from the fire. Joss went on eating her toast, hungry despite the tension in the air, and determined that if anyone was going to break the silence it would be Dan. He took his father's chair, leaned forward with hands clasped loosely between his knees, gazing into the flames for a while. At last he cleared his throat, turned to look at her, and said, 'Joss, let's start again. Will you—?'

CHAPTER TEN

SUDDENLY the door flew open and Francis came in like a whirlwind, halting Dan mid-sentence. 'Why the devil can't you bend that stiff neck of yours, Dan, and tell Joss the simple truth?'

Dan leapt to his feet, glaring at him. 'And why the devil can't you mind your own business?'

'This *is* my business,' drawled Francis, suddenly very much the ninth Baron Morville. He stared Dan out, then turned to Joss. 'Forgive me. How are you this morning? Anna tells me you find walking difficult.'

'A self-inflicted problem, alas.' Joss managed a smile.

'What are you doing here, anyway?' demanded Dan, looking like thunder.

'Anna told me you'd brought Joss here so I came over to see how she was. On the way in your father told me you were being pig-headed about telling her the truth.'

'Did he, by God?' said Dan, striding to the door.

'Dan,' said Joss sharply. 'Come back here. Stop behaving like a barbarian.'

He turned to stare at her in such blank shock that Francis began to laugh.

'I think you've met your match, old son.' He put out a hand in appeal. 'Look at it from my point of view. I insist Joss knows the facts.'

Dan's face relaxed slightly. 'Then of course I've no choice—milord.'

'Pack it in, Dan,' said Francis irritably. 'And for

heaven's sake sit down. I can't talk with you looming over me.'

When Dan took his father's chair again Francis perched himself on the arm.

'As I told you once before, Joss,' he began, 'like a lot of my kind I'm perpetually short of funds when it comes to the upkeep of Eastlegh. And Dan, in his own way, is just as attached to the place as I am. So he continually thinks up ways for me to acquire money to keep it going.'

Dan, Francis went on, had asked to buy the gardener's tied cottage, plus some land to grow vegetables, thus giving Sam Armstrong a home he could call his own at last, and at the same time providing an infusion of cash for Eastlegh. Then later, when the auctioning of manorial titles gained in popularity, Dan had hit on the idea of buying one of Francis's extraneous titles to add to the deeds of a local manor house his company had restored, again a two-way benefit, as this had doubled the asking price of the finished property.

'But the real brainwave came when Dan asked if he could hire Eastlegh for a weekend conference Athena was hosting,' added Francis.

'Lord Morville, of course,' said Dan dryly, 'was all for letting me have the place for free.'

'But Dan stipulated a business transaction or nothing doing. And thus,' finished Francis with a hint of drama, 'was born the now flourishing Eastlegh corporate entertainment business.'

'Was it your idea for Francis to move into Home Farm, Dan?' asked Joss.

'No, that was mine,' said Francis. 'It was obvious that I'd have more to offer if I could hire out the entire house. I love Eastlegh, but's a big place to rattle round in on my own.' He smiled. 'So now you know, Joss. Dan never had the slightest desire to be lord of anyone's manor.'

Dan gave her a sardonic look. 'My motive, as always, was profit.'

'So, Joss, does all this make you better disposed to marrying Dan?' asked Francis, then winced as a hard hand clamped on his arm like a vice.

'I'd be grateful for just a *few* minutes' privacy to make my own proposals,' said Dan with sarcasm, 'so do me a favour—take my father off to admire his beloved garden, and give me ten minutes alone with Joss.'

'Yes, of course,' said Francis hastily, jumping to his feet. He bent to kiss Joss, grinned at Dan, then went from the room as quickly as he'd arrived.

'It seems I owe you an apology,' said Joss unwillingly.

Dan shrugged. 'Not really.'

'Though you deliberately mentioned the title at lunch that day to mislead me,' she said, eyes kindling.

He snorted. 'I thought you couldn't stay meek and mild for long!'

Joss glared at her swollen feet in frustration, yearning to jump up and follow Francis from the room.

'One way and another,' he said, reading her mind with ease, 'this time you can't perform your famous vanishing trick.'

'No,' she said shortly. 'In which case you can pour me another cup of coffee.'

Dan obliged in silence, then sat down again, a determined look in his eye. 'As I was saying before His Lordship interrupted us, we'd better get married, Joss.'

She gazed at him in silence for so long Dan began to frown. 'No,' she said at last.

He stared at her, incensed. 'What do you mean, no?'

'The opposite of yes.'

'You're enjoying yourself,' he said angrily. 'Look, Joss, I know I hurt you—'

'You certainly did,' she agreed. 'But don't worry, I've got over that now.' Her eyes clashed with his. 'I'm good at getting over things.'

The irritation drained from his face, taking the animation with it. 'In which case,' he went on after a tense pause, 'if I suggested a marriage in form only, for the sake of our child, would you at least agree to that?'

'A marriage of convenience?' said Joss, taking great pleasure in watching Dan's struggle to control his temper. 'How delightfully archaic. Like a Regency romance.'

'You obviously find all this hilarious,' he said harshly. 'I happen to think it's a bloody serious situation.'

'So do I,' she assured him, and shifted a little in her seat. The second cup of coffee had been a mistake. 'I'm afraid,' she said reluctantly, 'I need your assistance.'

'What's the matter?' he demanded, leaping to his feet.

She sighed. 'Unlike heroines in Regency romances, I need to go to the bathroom. I hope your father's got one on the ground floor.'

Dan's lips twitched. 'So do I. You weigh a ton these days.'

'Your proposal technique could do with polish,' she flashed at him, and put her hands flat on the arms of the chair, so obviously prepared to struggle unaided that Dan cursed under his breath.

'Let me help you, Joss. Please.'

She gave him a dark, hostile look, but in the end let him take her hands and carefully pull her upright. Her teeth sank into her bottom lip as her throbbing feet took her weight, and with a look which dared her to object Dan picked her up and carried her along the hall and out into a back entry, where a door led into a very modern little cloakroom.

'Can you manage now?' he said with constraint.

'Yes,' Joss snapped, and shut the door in his face. When she emerged Sam Armstrong was waiting outside with Dan.

'Are you all right, my dear?' he asked, winning a surprised look from his son.

'Yes, thanks,' she said philosophically. Dignity, she was learning, was a luxury abandoned with the onset of pregnancy.

Dan picked her up again, then paused in the hall. 'Where do you want to go now?' he asked.

'Put her back by the fire until our meal is ready,' said Sam with authority.

When they were alone again, Joss watched as Dan added more logs to the fire. 'I'm bidden to lunch, then.'

He shot her a wry look. 'Apparently. My father seems to take it for granted you'll stay. He doesn't entertain much. You're honoured.'

'It's very kind of him,' she said soberly.

There was an awkward silence for a moment, broken only by the clashing of pots and pans from the kitchen. At last Dan broke it to ask about her work, and Joss responded with relief, eager to abandon the topic of marriage.

'I ought to be out there, giving your father a hand,' she added impatiently at one point.

'Which you can't, so stay where you are.'

'I don't have much choice!'

Dan's mouth twisted. 'You don't have a choice in any of this,' he said bitterly. 'I remember your views on motherhood all too vividly—but an apology's just an insult.'

'And unnecessary,' she informed him.

'I disagree.' Dan stared into the fire. 'I should have been more careful. But it's too damn late to say that now.'

'Look, Dan,' Joss began, doing her best to be reasonable. 'I know that a child was never part of your plan—' She broke off, smiling as Sam Armstrong came into the room. 'I wish I could help, Mr Armstrong. Something smells delicious.'

'Just plain cooking,' he said gruffly, looking pleased. 'The same as every Sunday. You'd better lay the small table in here, Dan.'

Two hours later Joss was sitting, resigned, in Dan's car on the way back to London. 'Sorry to add to your journey,' she said eventually, as they left Dorchester.

He shot a sidelong glance at her. 'If you want to apologise it should be for letting me find out about the baby in public.'

'I didn't know you were going to be there.'

'Or you wouldn't have come within miles of Eastlegh,' he finished for her. 'As a matter of interest, when *were* you going to tell me?'

When Joss made no answer, his hands tightened, white-knuckled, on the steering wheel. 'Never?' he demanded harshly.

'What was the point? I was sure you'd refuse to believe the child was yours, especially after you found Peter Sadler in my flat that night.'

'I suppose I can understand that,' he said grudgingly, then fell silent. 'You know Joss,' he said at last, 'I'm still in the dark about certain aspects of that night. I got your message, drove like a bat out of hell to your place, and then found your door ajar. I shot up those stairs, expecting to mug a burglar at the very least.'

'I didn't send any message—but don't let's go over all that again,' she said wearily. 'It's all in the past.'

'But the child is in the future, Joss.'

'I know,' she said quietly, with a familiar tremor of apprehension at the mere thought of it.

'Have you made plans?'

She repeated her idea of hiring a nanny and returning to work as soon as possible after the birth.

'With no time at all to spare for the baby?' he demanded incredulously.

Joss made a superhuman effort to control her temper. 'As you mentioned earlier, I don't have any choice.'

'Of course you do,' he retorted grimly. 'You can stop being so damned pig-headed and marry me.'

'When you make the prospect sound so delightful,' she threw back, 'it's hard to refuse. But I do, just the same.'

'This isn't the time and place to discuss it,' said Dan coldly, as they hit heavier traffic. 'We'll talk again when we get home.'

The journey was a trial, made worse by an embarrassing request for a stop at a service station. Joss flatly refused to let Dan carry her, and after she'd hobbled back to the car with his help she sat in silence, trying to relay pleasant thoughts to the little intruder making its presence felt under her sweater. But when they were nearing London it dawned on her that Dan was taking her to his own home in Kew.

'I want to go straight to my place,' she said, very quietly.

'Not yet,' said Dan inexorably. 'We finish our talk before I drive you to Acton.'

By this time Joss was beginning to feel very weary. 'Oh, very well,' she sighed. 'But there's not really much point.'

When they arrived at the house Dan bent to lift her out of the car, but Joss held him off.

'No, please. I can walk. Well, hobble, really, but I can manage.'

Tight-lipped, he put a hand under her elbow and helped her into the house Joss had believed she'd never set foot in again. Dan released her outside the ground floor cloakroom, eyeing her warily.

'I'll make some tea. Are you hungry?'

Joss shook her head. 'I'm still full of roast lamb and your father's heavenly vegetables. But tea sounds wonderful.'

In the privacy of Dan's cloakroom Joss eyed her reflection without pleasure, tidied herself a little, then with a sigh went outside, to find Dan waiting to escort her into the comfortable, informal room which opened into the courtyard at the back of the house.

Joss sat down in a corner of Dan's vast sofa, and smiled her thanks as he pushed a couple of cushions under her feet.

'Lack of footstools here.' He handed her a beaker of tea. 'No sugar and just a splash of milk,' he said, then shot a look at her. 'Or has your taste changed lately?'

'No,' she assured him. Her taste was exactly the same, both for tea and present company. Suddenly she noticed the initial *J* in black italic on the tall white porcelain mug she held.

'I bought it when you were about to move in with me,' Dan said without inflection.

Joss bit her lip, suddenly overwhelmed by thoughts of what might have been. She sat drinking her tea, deep in reverie, then gave herself a mental shake and looked round at the comfortable, masculine room as he took a chair opposite her. 'Dan.'

'Yes?' he said swiftly.

'The night we met—'

'I haven't forgotten it,' he said dryly.

'I've just thought of something. In fact,' Joss added, 'I'm surprised I never thought of it before.'

'Go on.'

'You suggested room service at the hotel. Why were you staying there when you had this to come back to?'

To her astonishment, colour rose along his cheekbones.

'I wasn't staying there,' he said gruffly. 'But if you'd said yes I would have reserved a room while you were saying goodnight to Anna.'

Joss stared at him. 'Then you planned to get me to bed right from the first.'

'No,' he said coldly. 'You disliked the idea of a restaurant, and this place is a long way out of town. So I suggested a meal in my non-existent room. The invitation to your place came as a surprise.'

She smiled coolly. 'A convenient one, too. Look at the money I saved you.'

The dark blue eyes locked with hers. 'I would have paid anything the hotel asked, just to keep you with me a while longer.'

Joss stared back, silenced, her heart beating thickly under the sweater.

'You know I wanted you the moment I first saw you,' he went on conversationally, as though they were discussing the weather. Then his eyes lit with sudden heat. 'I still do.'

Wanting, thought Joss fiercely, wasn't enough. 'It's not much of a basis for marriage.'

'We've got a lot more going for us than that,' said Dan swiftly, sensing victory.

Joss looked at him narrowly. 'What do you mean?'

He frowned. 'The child, of course.'

Her little flame of hope flickered and died. 'Ah, yes. The child,' she repeated, as though the idea were new to her. 'Not something you ever wanted.'

'I admit I wasn't enthusiastic about the idea in theory,' he admitted. 'But now it's established fact I'm fully prepared to share the responsibility.'

'Very noble,' she snapped. 'But you don't have to marry me to do that.'

'True. But marriage is a practical option.' Dan put down his tea untouched.

Practical, she thought sadly, and smiled a little. 'You look as though you need something stronger than that.'

'Damn right I do. But I still have to drive you home.'

'There are usually taxis to be had, even in the wilds of Kew!'

He raised a sardonic eyebrow. 'And what happens if you can't make it up the stairs when you get to your place?'

Joss clenched her teeth. Crawling up her stairs on hands and knees was a lot preferable to sitting here listening to Daniel Armstrong talking about responsibility. Especially when one solitary word of love would put an end to all argument.

'I'll manage,' she said tightly.

Dan's eyes narrowed. 'Not if I keep you here until you agree to marry me.'

Her eyes flashed scornfully. 'First Regency, now the Middle Ages. You're no feudal lord, Dan, and I'm not some kidnapped heiress.'

'If you'd wanted a lord for a husband you should have aimed for Francis!'

'I don't want a husband of any kind,' lied Joss. 'I can manage on my own.'

'So I see,' said Dan with sarcasm, then took her breath away by sliding to his knees in front of her. But instead of proposing in true romantic style, as for one wild moment she'd thought he meant to, he pulled off Hugh's socks to examine her still swollen feet. 'And just how do you propose to get to work tomorrow on feet like pillows?'

'The swelling will be down tomorrow,' she croaked, choked with disappointment.

Dan slid the socks carefully back into place, then got to his feet. 'More tea?'

'No, thanks. I want to go home.' Joss put the mug down carefully on the table beside her, passionately wishing she could get to her feet unaided. Without a word Dan reached down his hands to take hers, and equally silent she took them, and allowed him to help her up.

'Stay here tonight, Joss—please,' he said urgently. 'I'll sleep in one of the spare rooms and drive you home in the morning. Once I'm sure you can walk.'

Joss gave up. She was tired, and suddenly so depressed she didn't care where she slept. 'All right,' she said listlessly. 'As long as I can go to bed right now. Will you fetch my things from the car, please?'

He scowled. 'But the whole object of your staying is to talk this through. And you should have something to eat—'

'No,' she said flatly. 'I meant it, Dan. I'm tired. I need bed—and solitude.'

His eyes hardened. 'If you object to my company that much I'll drive you back to Acton right now.'

'Which,' she said, incensed, 'is what I wanted all along.'

Joss would have given much to march out of Daniel Armstrong's house with her nose in the air, but in the end was forced to accept his arm back to the car. And once they were on their way she felt so miserable it took superhuman effort to keep from crying her eyes out. Damned hormones, she thought, sniffing, and glowered at the large hand offering a box of tissues.

'Thank you,' she said with dignity.

'Why are you crying?' asked Dan.

'I don't need a reason these days.' She sniffed loudly. 'I suppose it was a bit ambitious to travel down to Eastlegh and go to the party last night on top of a working week.'

'Why did you?'

'Because Anna felt a bit of socialising would do me good. She kept on and on about it. And Sarah was on the phone so much I wonder she had time to organise the party.'

'Francis was damned insistent where I was concerned, too.' Dan shot a glance at her. 'It was obviously a combined effort to enlighten me about the baby.'

'Probably. I made Francis swear on oath that he wouldn't tell you.'

'Which gagged him pretty effectively.'

'He thought you had a right to know.'

'Would you really have kept me in the dark, Joss? Even after the baby arrived?'

Joss shrugged, her eyes on the traffic in front of them. 'I intended to. I think I'd have kept to that. But fate— and friends—conspired against me.'

By the time they got to Acton Joss was sorry she hadn't stayed the night at Kew after all. She felt desperately tired, vaguely unwell, her feet hurt and she wished she hadn't eaten so much lunch. When Dan came to help her out of the car he took one look at her face and demanded her key.

When Joss meekly handed it over he unlocked the door and picked her up, ignoring her protests as he carried her upstairs to deposit her very carefully on her sofa. 'I'll just get your belongings, then I want no argument, Joss. You look exhausted. Before I go I want to make sure you're in bed and out of harm's way for the night.'

'Will you give me a hand to the bathroom first?' she asked, resigned.

When Dan got back with her suitcase Joss was leaning in the bathroom doorway, her face chalk-white. He leapt towards her, arms outstretched, his face suddenly as colourless as hers.

'What is it?'

'Something's wrong, Dan,' she said hoarsely.

A few hours later Joss lay propped against pillows in a hospital bed in a private room, feeling so tired it was an effort to summon a smile for Dan.

'You look terrible,' she commented, eyeing his haggard face.

'Never mind me!' He sat by the bed to take her hand. 'I had a word with the consultant, and apparently the baby's fine. But they want to keep you in for a couple of days for observation, and after that you're to stay off your feet for a while, and rest.'

'I know,' said Joss despondently. 'She told me.'

'You know what this means?' he said, his grasp tightening.

She nodded glumly. 'Time off from the job.'

'You can't go back to it at all,' he said urgently. 'If you must work, surely with your connections you can do something from home, Joss?'

'Yes. I can. But I won't earn as much money.'

'That,' he said flatly, 'is hardly a problem.'

'It is to me,' she said, eyes flashing.

'It's not a problem,' said Dan, very deliberately, 'because the solution lies in your own hands, Joss. Marry me, come and live in Kew, and work from there.'

'It sounds so cut and dried, put like that,' said Joss quietly. She looked at him intently. 'Do you really want this, Dan?'

'How many times do I have to say it? I wanted you the moment I first saw you. And I still do. But,' he added quickly, 'that needn't worry you, if you prefer a more businesslike arrangement.'

At that precise moment Joss wanted nothing more than to sink into oblivion and forget any kind of arrangement, businesslike or otherwise. She felt deeply grateful when a nurse came in to tell Dan the patient needed rest.

'I'll come to see you tomorrow,' he said, bending to kiss her cheek. 'Shall I ring Anna?'

Joss shook her head. 'No point in worrying her unnecessarily. I'll do that when I get home.' She bit her lip. 'You might ring Jack Ormond in the morning, though. Say I won't be around for a bit.'

'With the greatest pleasure,' said Dan grimly. 'Think carefully about what I said, Joss, and we'll talk about it tomorrow.'

By the time she was settled for the night Joss had made up her mind. Only a fool would turn down the chance of having the best of both worlds. If she married Dan she could still carry on with her freelancing to a certain extent, and do it in comfort, without having to worry about food and bills and all those other pressing little realities of life. Which all sounded so mercenary, she thought in distaste. Especially when she didn't really care a hang about any of it as long as she could marry Dan. And any lingering doubts disappeared next morning, when a nurse came in with a box containing a dozen yellow roses on a bed of very familiar leaves.

'Mr Armstrong rang to enquire how you are,' she said briskly. 'I'll just put these in water, then I'll have a look at you again.'

'From Dan,' said the message on the card. Joss smiled ruefully. No 'love and best wishes' from Daniel Armstrong. But the flowers were strong enough persuasion in themselves. The nurse arranged the roses against their fan of fig leaves, and when Joss was alone at last she settled back against the pillows and gazed at the perfect blooms, her hands protective on the mound moving now and then beneath the covers.

'If it's all right with you, little one,' she whispered. 'I think I'll say yes.'

CHAPTER ELEVEN

ONE brief word in the affirmative raised an instant storm of controversy about when, where, and in what style Joscelyn Georgina Hunter should be joined in marriage to Daniel Adam Francis Armstrong.

Dan, characteristically, wanted to rush her to the nearest register office the moment she said yes. Anna and her parents promptly offered Joss a reception at Glebe House, after a wedding in her father's church, while a jubilant Lord Morville urged them to both ceremony and reception at Eastlegh.

'We should have told everyone afterwards,' said Dan morosely. 'Failing that, you could at least move in with me until you decide what you do want.'

'I'm not moving to Kew until we're married,' said Joss firmly.

'Why not?'

'It fell through last time we tried it.'

'That won't happen again,' said Dan flatly.

Joss braced herself. 'Anna saw Peter Sadler the other day.'

Dan raised a hostile eyebrow. 'Did she give him the glad news?'

'Oh, yes. With great relish, she informed me.'

'Did she mention the baby?'

'Yes. That part of it didn't go down well at all.'

'No,' said Dan with grim satisfaction. 'I'm damn sure it didn't.'

They were lingering over the supper Joss had had

149

ready when Dan arrived at the flat earlier. Just like two
old marrieds, thought Joss wistfully, as they sat together
on the sofa afterwards.

'I didn't know you could cook like that,' said Dan,
stretching out his legs in comfort.

'When I'm working I don't have the time. But I first
learnt to cook with Anna's mother, when I was quite
small. She used to let us kneel up on chairs at the table
to help her.' Joss turned her head to look at him. 'Dan?'

'What's the matter?' he said instantly.

'Nothing at all.' She smiled at him. 'It's just that now
I've had time to get used to the idea I've decided how,
when and where I'd like the wedding—subject to your
approval.'

'And you want to be married in your father's church,
of course.'

'No, I don't,' she said, surprising him. 'I would miss
him too much. And though the Herricks have always
been marvellous to me I really don't feel I should put
them to the expense and bother of a reception. Not,' she
added dryly, 'that a marquee on the lawn would be necessary this time.'

Dan eyed her warily. 'Are you saying you'd prefer the
church at Eastlegh?'

'Good heavens, no! Soon enough for a wedding there
when Francis marries Sarah.' She smiled. 'Actually, I
think your idea is best. A civil ceremony first, then a
small party at your place afterwards.'

Dan looked taken aback. 'Is that what you *really*
want?'

What Joss really wanted was white silk and roses and
a choir, and a church full of people, with champagne and
witty speeches, a write-up in the *Post*'s social diary, and
a birth announcement ten months, or ten years, after-

wards. She smiled brightly and assured Dan it was exactly what she wanted.

'Then I'll get a catering firm to do the food,' he said promptly. 'How many guests were you thinking of?'

'Just the Herricks, and Anna and Hugh for me.'

'No journalists?'

'I'd rather we kept it to nearest and dearest—unless you want to invite people from your firm?'

'Not particularly.' Dan frowned, and moved closer. 'Joss, if there were no baby involved would you have preferred a bigger wedding?'

He was too quick by half. 'There wouldn't *be* a wedding without the baby,' she retorted.

'I'm hardly likely to forget!'

'I'm sorry,' she sighed. 'I didn't mean to snap.'

He gave her a dark, brooding look. 'Sometimes that tongue of yours cuts like a knife.'

So she'd actually hurt him. Joss bit her lip, her eyes filling with sudden tears, and with a stifled curse Dan closed the space between them and put his arm round her so carefully the tears turned to an unsteady chuckle.

'I won't break,' she assured him.

Dan's arm tightened a little, then his free hand reached out and touched the velvet-covered bulge for the first time. Holding her breath, Joss placed the hand over the vital spot, and Dan's entire body tensed as he stared incredulously into her eyes.

'Was that what I thought it was?'

'That's right. Miss Baby saying hello.'

'You've found out it's a girl, then?' he demanded.

'No. But it's definitely a girl. We expectant mothers know these things!' Joss looked down at the large hand, very much aware that this was the first time Dan had voluntarily touched her since they'd met up again, apart from carrying her about like a sack of potatoes.

Dan breathed in sharply as he felt kicking again, and Joss sat very still, savouring the moment of rapport. When he removed his hand at last Joss waited for him to take his arm away. But instead Dan put his hand in an inside pocket and took out a wad of tissue paper.

'This seems an appropriate time to ask if you'd like to wear this,' he said, sounding oddly unlike his normal forceful self.

'What is it?'

'Unwrap it and see.'

Joss carefully unfolded layers of tissue paper, and gazed in delight at an old-fashioned gold ring set with small diamonds interspersed with seed pearls and garnets.

Dan eyed it doubtfully. 'I could have taken you to Cartier, or whatever, but my father insisted I offer you this first.'

Joss cleared her throat. 'Was it your mother's?'

Dan nodded. 'Bought second-hand with my father's savings when they were young. If you don't care for it,' he added casually, 'we can still do the Cartier bit. No doubt Sadler gave you something more impressive.'

Joss gave him a scornful look, her heart singing as she gave him the ring. Dan must surely feel something more than just duty and responsibility to give her something so special. 'It was a small solitaire diamond—not nearly as pretty as this.' She held out her hand. 'You're supposed to put it on my finger,' she instructed, and held her breath as he slid it over her knuckle.

'I could have it made smaller,' he offered.

Joss shook her head, her eyes glued to her hand. 'No. I like it the way it is.' She looked up at him, her eyes luminous. 'It's beautiful, Dan. Is it too late to ring your father to thank him?'

'Yes,' he said firmly. 'We'll talk to him tomorrow, and tell him the plans. Maybe you can even persuade him to come up to London for the wedding.'

'But of course he must come!' said Joss, astonished.

'He doesn't like London,' Dan warned. 'He's visited me just once since I moved into the house in Kew, and even then he spent most of his time in the Gardens.'

'He'll come to the wedding,' said Joss confidently.

Now the die was cast, Joss felt better. Nothing would have made her confess it, but to refuse Dan's proposal had been the most difficult thing she'd ever done in her life. Sheer pride had forced her to say no. But from now on she could relax, prepare herself for the wedding. And if it was not the occasion of unalloyed joy it might have been in different circumstances, she was nevertheless marrying Daniel Armstrong, the father of her child. And the man she loved.

Joss obediently did her best to rest as much as possible in the time leading up to the wedding, and she was lying on her sofa with a book one morning when her doorbell rang. Her eyes lit up. Maybe Dan had called round to make sure she was following his orders. But a very different voice came over the intercom.

'Let me in, please, Joss,' said Peter Sadler urgently.

Joss stiffened. 'I will not! I'm astonished you've got the gall—'

'I've come to apologise,' he insisted. 'Talk to me just this once, Joss. *Please.*'

With reluctance Joss released the lock, and Peter ran up towards her, then stopped dead when he reached the landing, his eyes on the fall of fabric veiling her front.

'Hello, Joss,' he said, clearing his throat. His mouth twisted. 'I knew you were expecting a baby, but it's a shock just the same.'

'Hello, Peter.' She looked at him steadily for a moment, then turned and made for the sofa. 'I'm supposed to rest.'

'Anna told me you'd been in hospital,' he said, pulling out her desk chair. 'She said you'd given up your job, so I came here on the offchance of finding you in.'

'Why?' she said coldly.

'To apologise for my behaviour last time.' Colour rose in his boyish face.

'You very nearly wrecked my life,' she said without emotion.

'I was hitting out at Armstrong, not you, Joss,' he said, shamefaced.

'Just because his company turned you down!' she said incredulously.

'At the time I blamed him for everything wrong in my life. When I heard you were together it was the end. All I could think of was making him pay.'

She stared at him scornfully, then paused, frowning. 'But how on earth did you work your little scam?'

He winced. 'I'd planned it for quite a while. I conned your address from one of your pals at the *Post* beforehand. Then I came up that day, confirmed that Armstrong was in his office, and drove round here. I rang the Athena building on my carphone with the message, and waited until he was well on his way before ringing your bell. You let me in, I left your door ajar, and you know the rest.'

Joss shook her head in disbelief. 'It only worked because Dan was so frantic when he got the message he rushed straight here without ringing first.'

Peter shrugged. 'It was worth a gamble—and I won.'

She stared at him. 'So what you and I once had together meant nothing against the chance to pay Dan back for your own failure.'

His mouth twisted. 'Don't please! God, I'm sorry, Joss.' He paused. 'Besides, an apology isn't my only reason for coming.'

'Isn't it enough?' she said bitterly.

He chewed on his bottom lip, the light eyes suddenly imploring. 'Tell me the truth, Joss. Is there any chance the baby's mine?'

Joss looked at him in silence for a moment, trying to remember why she had ever thought herself in love with Peter Sadler. 'My child,' she said succinctly, 'will be born on February the fourteenth next year, give or take a day or two. You walked out in February this year. You were always a whizz with figures, Peter. Work it out.'

The following week Sam Armstrong travelled from Dorset with Francis and Sarah in the car to the house in Kew, where the three of them spent the night before the wedding with Dan.

Anna had spent a few days in Acton with Joss beforehand, looking after her like a hen with one chick, and helping in the search for a wool coat in palest creamy yellow to wear with the navy chiffon dress. Hugh and the Herricks drove up to London early on the Saturday morning to drive with them to the register office.

When Joss was in the car, holding the posy of yellow roses Dan had sent, she felt tense and apprehensive, until a sudden onset of kicking under the wickedly expensive coat reminded her that though the forthcoming ceremony was by no means compulsory, morally or any other way, she was glad Dan had insisted on a wedding. And when he came hurrying to hand her out of the car, looking magnificent in formal morning coat, her smile was so radiant he looked dazzled. Still holding Dan's hand, she reached up to kiss Sam Armstrong, who looked as magnificent as his son in formal clothes, with the addition of a fiercely stiff white collar. Then there were embraces and greetings and introductions, and half an hour later Joss was Mrs Daniel Armstrong, with marriage lines and a wide gold wedding ring to prove it. They came out to a battery of photographers from the various papers Joss worked for, and afterwards Francis and Hugh took over with their own cameras until Dan called a halt.

Dan and Joss drove back to Kew alone, leaving the rest of the party to follow behind. 'I should have hired a photographer,' he said in apology. 'Why didn't you mention it?'

'I never thought of it,' she said truthfully. 'Anyway, with Francis and Hugh snapping away, and the professional lot, we won't be short of photographs to remind us of the happy day.'

'Is it really a happy day for you?' said Dan, putting a hand on her knee.

She shot a glance at him. 'Yes. It is.'

'Then it is for me, too.' He smiled wryly. 'I wasn't sure you'd actually turn up this morning.'

Joss stared at him in astonishment. 'Were you really in any doubt?'

'Yes,' he said bluntly. 'You've been known to vanish before.'

'Not this time, Dan,' she assured him.

'You were pretty reluctant until recently. You could have changed your mind at the last minute.'

'In which case I'd have let you know, not left you waiting!'

'I kept telling myself that.' He smiled crookedly. 'But apparently brides don't hold the monopoly on wedding nerves.'

Joss laughed. '*You?* With nerves?'

'Why not? I'm human.' He glanced down at her. 'Otherwise you wouldn't be expecting my child. How is she, by the way?'

'Very lively. Must be the excitement.'

'You look very beautiful,' he said quietly, keeping his eyes on the road.

Joss gave him an oddly shy look. 'Thank you. I was so sure you'd send me yellow roses I tired Anna out in search of the coat.'

Once again his long hand, adorned now with a heavy gold ring like hers, reached out to touch Joss's knee. 'It was worth it. Motherhood seems to be adding an extra dimension to your...'

'Size?' she teased, when he paused.

'To your allure,' he said softly, in a tone which silenced her very effectively.

It was a very exuberant party which enjoyed the lunch Dan had ordered on Joss's instructions. Certain that his father would dislike picking at smart bits and pieces, Joss had ordered a conventional meal, and felt pleased when she saw Sam tucking into the salmon timbales and the roast which followed, chatting away to the Herricks as though he'd known them for years. The meal was a leisurely affair, brought to a fitting climax when a waiter brought in the wedding cake Mrs Herrick had insisted on making.

'Mother's the Annie Oakley of the icing gun,' chuckled Anna, when Sarah exclaimed on the perfection of the cake. 'She did three tiers for mine.'

'I've done two for Joss,' said Mrs Herrick, 'but I'm keeping the other one for the christening.'

There was a moment of dead silence, then Joss got up and threw her arms round Mrs Herrick and gave her a smacking kiss. 'What a lovely thought,' she said with affection, and saw Dan relax visibly before adding his own thanks.

'Come on, then, you two,' said Francis. 'Hurry up and cut the cake so I can deliver my amazingly witty speech.'

'I told him not to bother,' Dan apologised to Joss, 'but he wouldn't listen.'

'Very right and proper,' said Sam Armstrong in approval. 'It's not a wedding without speeches.'

Nor was there any lack of them. After Dan's brief speech of thanks, Francis leapt to his feet and kept everyone in gales of laughter over the combined exploits of the groom and best man in their boyhood. 'And,' he added, as the punchline, 'I insist on being godfather to the baby.'

There was a roar of applause, then Mr Herrick got up on behalf of the bride, and told Dan that though he must be congratulating himself on his lack of in-laws, he hadn't got away scot-free, since he hoped Dan would look on himself and his wife as replacements.

Then, to Dan's obvious surprise, Sam Armstrong got to his feet and raised his glass. 'It just remains for me to add my own good wishes, and ask you all to toast the happiness of my son and his lovely bride.'

At which point tears welled in the eyes of the lovely bride, and the groom efficiently whipped out a handkerchief from his pocket, having, as he informed everyone, expected this far sooner.

'It's my condition,' said Joss huskily, blowing her nose.

'A word forbidden to everyone except my wife,' warned Dan, grinning.

It was late afternoon by the time everyone bade emotional farewells, and drove off to their various destinations.

'A pity they wouldn't stay longer,' said Joss, yawning.

Dan looked down at her, lips twitching. 'You wouldn't last another ten minutes.' He held out his hands. 'Up you come.'

'Why?' she demanded.

'Time for a nap. Later on you can come down and do whatever you like for the rest of the evening, but right now you're going to rest.'

Joss knew he was right. Now everyone had gone, she felt not only tired but a little flat. 'Perhaps I will. I didn't sleep much last night.' She shrugged, smiling. 'Too excited, I suppose. And Miss Baby wasn't sleepy either, which didn't help.'

'Does she keep you awake a lot?' he asked, pulling her to her feet.

'Quite a bit.' Joss accepted Dan's hand to go upstairs. 'Where have you put my things?' she asked.

'In here.' Dan opened the door to the master bedroom. 'I'm in the room next door.'

'But I could use that,' she protested.

'You'll be more comfortable here. There's a television, and a radio, so you can stay in bed some days if you feel under the weather.'

It wasn't the first time Joss had been in Dan's rather severe bedroom. But on former occasions they'd shared the vast bed. She glanced at Dan, then away again quickly, aware that he was thinking the same thing.

'Thank you,' she said brightly.

'I've cleared out half the cupboards, but I didn't unpack your cases. I thought you'd prefer to do that your-self.' Dan showed her a buzzer on one of the bedside tables. 'This connects with my room, so if you feel ill, or you need anything, just press that.'

Secretly determined never to do any such thing, Joss wandered round the room when he was gone, picking things up and putting them down. At last she unpacked her cases and hung some of her clothes up to join the new yellow coat, put others away in drawers, then took off the beautiful chiffon dress and hung it away with the rest.

When Dan knocked on the door a couple of hours later Joss had showered, redone her face and hair and put on a comfortable brown velvet top and jersey trousers. She opened the door, smiling brightly, wondering what was required of her for their first evening as man and wife.

Dan stood leaning in the doorway, wearing a pale sweater over his favourite indigo shirt and a worn pair of navy cords.

'How do you feel?' he asked.

'Fine.'

'You look good. Are you hungry? You didn't eat much lunch.'

'I can't eat much at a time anymore. Miss Baby ob-jects.'

'In that case how about a snack? The caterers left enough food for an army. We won't have to cook for a week.'

'We?'

'You, then,' he amended. 'I'm no expert in the kitchen.'

Since he was so amazingly expert in bed, thought Joss, going ahead of him, one couldn't have everything. Though if this marriage was to be as businesslike as he suggested, it was unlikely she'd benefit from that particular expertise unless she made it plain she wanted to. Some time.

The evening was surprisingly restful. Joss put together a light meal, and afterwards they watched a film. Later Dan insisted on making tea for her before she went to bed, then switched off the television and sat down beside her while she drank it.

'Time we had a talk,' he said firmly.

Joss looked intently at the initial on her beaker. 'What shall we talk about?'

'At this point,' he began, 'most couples would be jetting off to some exotic place for a honeymoon. We can't do that, but I've taken a few days off so we can get used to living together.'

'Are you sure you won't be bored?'

'I can honestly say that one emotion I've never experienced in your company is boredom,' he said dryly.

Joss gave him a very straight look. 'But in the past, remember, we spent a lot of time making love.'

'Do you think I'm likely to forget?' He reached out to grasp the hand adorned with the rings he'd given her. 'I think we can find pleasure in each other's company, wife, just the same. For a start, first thing Monday morning I'm taking you shopping.'

Joss chuckled. 'A dangerous plan! Anything specific?'

'Clothes and bedroom furniture for Miss Baby, for starters, a new computer for her mother, plus some walking shoes. I've been reading up on the subject, and apparently short walks are beneficial. But not in four-inch heels. So, with Kew Gardens on our doorstep we'll take a daily stroll there together, weather permitting. Do they make designer hiking shoes?' he teased.

CHAPTER TWELVE

DAN was right. Boredom played no part at all in their first week of married life together. Joss felt particularly well, the weather was good, and after the purchase of the necessary shoes their walks in Kew Gardens became a daily ritual Joss enjoyed all the more because Dan so very obviously enjoyed it too. As they walked they talked without constraint, and Dan teased her about her sudden craving for sweet things, and indulged her in cakes and cappuccinos in the tea rooms, in every way as model a husband as any new bride could wish for.

Joss felt it was unreasonable to want more. But she would have traded the extravagant accessories Dan had insisted on buying for the baby, and the expensive shoes and everything else he'd bought for his wife, in exchange for one specific word of love.

Up to this point Dan's domestic arrangements had been carried out by a cleaning firm who came in once a week, but this, he told Joss, was no longer enough. Someone was now needed on a daily basis as well.

'Is that really necessary?' Joss protested.

'If not now, it will be after the baby's born. Or would you prefer a full-time nanny?'

'Absolutely not.' Joss thought about it for a while. 'If you're going to keep the cleaning firm on perhaps we could find someone to do the daily light stuff, and look after the baby for a couple of hours while I work.'

Since Dan insisted someone must be found before his

short break was over, they consulted an agency who sent them several applicants, one of whom found instant favour with both Armstrongs.

Nan Perry was in her late thirties, married with two teenage sons, lived a bus ride away in Brentford and wanted a job with shorter hours than her present hotel work.

Joss took to the brisk, attractive young woman at once, and engaged her on the spot. And after Nan's first day Dan went back to Athena, reassured that with someone on hand who was not only sensible and pleasant, but had also been through the birth process, Joss was in good hands. But Joss missed him. Without Dan's formidable presence the house seemed empty, and she was glad to have the hard-working Nan around. Except that Nan took over tasks that Joss could well have performed herself. So with time to spare for the first time in years Joss spent some of it on familiarising herself with the new computer, and decided to write regular letters to Sam Armstrong, to involve him in the approaching arrival of his grandchild. After posting the first, she dashed off a humorous article on the joys of pregnancy, which went down so well at the *Post* she was asked to contribute in the same vein regularly until the birth, then go on afterwards to report the funny side of having a new baby.

Funny side? Joss raised a wry eyebrow, wondering just how easy it would be to write hilarious little pieces if she'd been up all night with a wailing baby.

Soon afterwards the question of Christmas arose, when pressing invitations arrived from both Warwickshire and Dorset.

'What do you want to do?' asked Dan one evening over dinner.

Joss looked thoughtful.

'Frankly I don't fancy travelling that far in either direction. Couldn't we just ask your father to come here for Christmas?'

He smiled so warmly it was obvious her answer had both surprised and delighted him. 'Are you sure?'

'Yes.' Joss smiled back, suddenly so full of love for this big, sexy, sophisticated man it was almost impossible to keep from telling him. Almost, but not quite.

'You look utterly gorgeous tonight, Mrs Armstrong,' Dan said softly.

Since she'd taken a shamelessly long time over her face and hair, Joss was glad to hear it. 'That's because I'm sitting down,' she retorted, deliberately flip. 'The illusion shatters once I'm on my feet.'

'Not for me.'

'Thank you.' Joss felt her colour rise. 'Will your father come, do you think?'

'If you ask him I'm sure he will.' Dan smiled again. 'Father isn't liberal with his affections, but as far as he's concerned you can do no wrong, Joss.'

'The feeling's mutual,' she assured him.

'It was good of you to write to him.' Dan stretched out a hand to touch hers. 'Francis rang to ask about you before I left work tonight. I gather my father's softened up so much lately he's finally consented to address His Lordship by his first name.'

'Goodness!' Joss laughed. 'As soon as we can travel after—afterwards, we'll take the baby to Eastlegh and show her off.'

Dan applied himself to his dinner, unaware that his fleeting caress had deprived his wife of her appetite until he noticed her pushing food round her plate.

'What's the matter? Not hungry tonight?'

'No, not really. I shouldn't have had tea and buns with Nan this afternoon.'

'How's she shaping?'

'Very well.' Joss grinned. 'She's got a vast list of numbers taped over the kitchen telephone, ready for the first sign of Miss Baby's birthday.'

Dan nodded approvingly. 'But when that happens I'd prefer you to ring me yourself, Joss, if you can.'

'Of course I will,' she promised, then frowned as he got up to take their plates. 'I can do that.'

He shook his head. 'I'm perfectly capable of loading a dishwasher.'

Dan Armstrong was capable of anything, reflected his wife. Except the kind of love she so desperately wanted from him.

Since Joss knew, almost to the minute, when her child had been conceived, she was sure her daughter would be born on the fourteenth, St Valentine's Day, as she'd insisted all along, and she smiled to herself as she wandered next day in Kew Gardens. Dan would never agree to calling the baby Valentine. The day was bitterly cold, and Joss pulled her knitted beret low over her eyes as she turned to make for home, wishing she hadn't walked so far. Her return was slow as she avoided patches of frost the feeble winter sun had failed to melt, and by the time she reached the house Joss was shivering, and annoyed with herself for staying out so long. When she let herself in Nan came hurrying to meet her, frowning in disapproval.

'I was just coming to look for you. You've overdone it, haven't you? Let me have your coat, then you can put your feet up on the sofa and I'll bring your tea.'

'I'd rather sit with you in the kitchen,' said Joss, in need of company. But after the tea she felt no better, and in the end gave in and let Nan help her to bed. 'I feel a bit achey,' she admitted, as Nan propped pillows behind her. 'Probably coming down with something.'

'You've caught a chill, staying out in this weather.' Nan eyed her closely. 'Shall I call the doctor?'

'Heavens, no. It's probably just a cold.' Joss smiled and snuggled down into the warmth of the bed. 'I'll have a little nap.'

When Joss woke Dan was standing over her. 'Dan? You're home early!'

'Nan rang and told me you weren't well, so I called it a day and came home.' He sat on the side of the bed and put a hand on her forehead. 'You're very hot. She said you wouldn't let her call the doctor.'

'Of course not. It was cold out and I walked too far; that's all.' She smiled, touched by the anxiety in his eyes. 'Honestly, Dan, I'm all right.'

'You don't look it,' he said shortly. 'I'll have a shower and change, then I'll bring you some tea. I told Nan to go home.'

'I'll get up and put a meal on later—'

'No, you won't.' Dan wagged a finger at her. 'You stay where you are. Nan's left some kind of casserole, so we'll have supper up here together later on. No arguments,' he added, smiling.

Joss found she had no energy to make any. She felt hot and strangely light-headed, her back ached, and the thought of staying in bed was deeply attractive. When Dan had gone off to shower she forced herself to get out of bed and make for the bathroom, then came out in utter distress, sweat beading her mouth as she pressed the buzzer. Dan burst into the room, his face as white as hers when she choked out the dreaded word 'haemorrhage.'

Dan took instant charge, rang the hospital, then carried

Joss down to the car and drove as fast as the traffic allowed, talking soothingly all the way. And shortly afterwards she was on a table in a delivery room, connected to a foetal heart rate monitor, an automatic blood pressure gauge fastened on her arm and an efficient, sympathetic nurse calming her fears as her daughter made it plain that this was no false alarm, but her birthday.

Later, at some stage in the relentless process of birth, Joss was dimly aware of Dan holding her hand in a painful grip as he mopped her sweating forehead.

'She's too early,' she sobbed, tears coursing down her cheeks, and Dan, looking haggard, raised bloodshot, questioning eyes to the nurse, who assured him that a seven-month baby was no problem.

Dan was a tower of strength, up to a point, but eventually the situation was too much for his normally iron self-control. He grew so distraught he was expelled from the room and told to come back when he was called. When he was allowed in again Joss lay exhausted and ashen pale, her hand limp and cold when he took it in both of his.

'How do you feel?' he asked hoarsely.

'Tired.' She tried to smile. 'And surprised. It's not Miss Baby after all.'

Dan smoothed back her damp hair. 'No. He's a five-pound baby boy. And in remarkably good shape in the circumstances.' His face twisted. 'Better than his mother. I was sure you were going to die.'

'So I gather. I did wonder myself at one stage. Not an uncommon reaction, I'm told.' The ghost of a smile curved her dry lips. 'Feel better now?'

He nodded wryly. 'Sorry I made a fuss.'

'Did you? I was too busy to notice.' She looked away.

'They're keeping him in a special unit but we can both leave in a week or two.'

'Surely not!' Dan frowned blackly. 'We'll see about that. I'll talk to the consultant.'

Joss looked at him anxiously. 'Have you seen the baby?'

Dan nodded. 'He's frighteningly small, but with all the necessary bits and pieces, I'm told—except a name.'

'No point in calling him Valentine now,' she murmured drowsily.

Dan stared blankly, then got up as a pair of nurses came in to send him away. 'I'll see you in the morning, Joss,' he said quickly. He hesitated for a moment, then bent to kiss her pallid cheek and said goodnight.

When Dan arrived next morning, hollow-eyed, pale, and bearing yellow roses, Joss was sitting in the special care unit, the baby in a cot beside her.

'You look like a different person,' he said with relief. 'Sorry, no fig leaves available.'

'Never mind,' she said lightly. 'The roses are lovely, thank you. Someone will deal with them later.'

When Dan returned he looked at her searchingly. 'How do you feel?'

'A bit battered and bruised in places, but otherwise not too bad.' She watched, tense, as he gazed down at the sleeping baby.

'He's bigger than I expected,' said Dan. After a long, unbearable pause he shot her a penetrating blue look. '*Is* he premature, Joss?'

She met the look head-on. 'Why not rephrase the question and say what you mean?'

Dan's face twisted. 'I have a right to know if I'm his father. Not that it makes any difference.'

Her dark-ringed eyes flashed angrily. 'Of *course* it makes a difference.'

'I meant,' he said with controlled violence, 'that his mother is my wife, so I'll claim him as my son whether I'm the father or not.'

Joss clenched her hands beneath the sheets. 'How very noble,' she said, her voice shaky with scorn. 'Or is this *claim* of yours to get in before Peter Sadler can stake his?'

'Sadler's got nothing to do with it,' he flung back.

Joss looked at him, searching. 'Do you really believe that?'

'I want to—God how I want to,' he said, suddenly weary. 'So just tell me he's not the father and I'll never mention it again.'

'Do you actually think,' she said, dangerously quiet, 'I would have married you if he were?'

Dan paused an instant too long. 'No—no, or course not.'

Joss eyed him dully. 'But you're not certain.'

Dan's eyes narrowed to blazing slits of cobalt. 'The only certainty, Joss, is that you—and the child—belong to me.'

The child, thought Joss.

Dan got to his feet, looking down at her from his great height. For all the world like a god from Olympus, surveying a frail, human mortal, she thought bitterly.

'We'll talk again tonight,' he told her.

'Have you rung your father?'

'I'll do that from my office. I wanted to wait until—'

'Until what?' she asked curiously. 'Until I confirmed whether my son is yours or not?'

Dan's jaw clenched. 'No,' he said harshly. 'I was waiting until I knew for certain that you and the baby were both in good shape.'

At least 'baby' was better than 'the child.' 'Give your father my love,' said Joss. 'He'll pass the news on to Sarah and Francis, of course. But I can ring Anna myself.'

Dan nodded, and turned to go. At the door he paused, looking back. 'Have you thought of a name? Last night you were muttering something about Valentine.'

Joss shrugged. 'Delirious, probably.'

'So what shall we call him?'

'Why, Adam, of course. Adam George.' She smiled frostily. 'I was going to put in Samuel, too. But your doubts about my son's paternity rule that out.'

Dan's mouth twisted. 'Joss, listen—'

'Could you go now, please?' she interrupted with sudden force. 'I'm tired.'

The urgency drained abruptly from his face. 'Of course.' He gazed down at the baby again, then turned on his heel and strode from the room.

In the afternoon Anna and her mother came to visit, bearing books and flowers, and a parcel of exquisite knitted garments. They crooned over the baby, and sat for a while to chat, then Mrs Herrick tactfully went ahead, leaving Anna alone with Joss.

'I called into Peter's office and told him,' she said, the moment her mother was out of earshot.

'Why?' said Joss, frowning.

'I wanted to see his face when I gave him the news.' Anna pulled a face. 'But he looked so stricken I actually felt sorry for him.'

For Joss it was a poignant, but terrifying moment to hold her baby son in her arms the day they left hospital and know that from now on she was responsible for his welfare. As she cradled the warm, wool-swathed bundle she took a deep, shaky breath, and Dan, sensing her sudden apprehension, put his arm round her and kept it there as they expressed thanks to the nursing staff gathered to see them off.

Dan helped her to install the protesting baby in the small car seat, frowning as Joss coped with unfamiliar buckles and straps. 'He's a bit small for the seat yet. Will he be safe?'

'I'll sit in the back and make sure he is,' she said, and bit her lip. 'Dan, this is so scary. Being a mother, I mean. I hope I can do it.'

Dan leaned down to look at the baby, who chose that moment to look back with an unfocused stare. 'Of course you can.' He shot a look at her as she secured her safety belt. 'He's got blue eyes.'

'All babies do,' she said matter-of-factly. Peter Sadler's eyes were also blue. Ice-blue, not dark navy. But blue.

After the return to Kew Joss found her life very quickly settled into a demanding, exhausting routine of broken nights and days of endless feeding and nappy-changing, and sometimes just walking the floor in utter panic with a baby who refused to stop crying. Nan was a tower of strength. She took over the sterilising and saw to the extra laundry, assuring Joss that everything was perfectly normal, and Adam would soon settle down. And when Joss suddenly realised that Christmas was almost on them Nan insisted on taking care of Adam for an hour or two to let Joss go shopping. Once she'd been persuaded, Joss rushed round the shops, buying presents for everyone she could think of, including Nan's boys, and ordered a Christmas tree and a turkey, and got home ex-

hausted to find Dan home early for once, pacing the floor
as he waited for her.

'Where the hell have you been?' he demanded as she
came through the door, laden with parcels.

'Why? What's the matter?' she said in alarm. 'Is something wrong with Adam?'

'No. Your *son* is fine. He's with Nan. Couldn't you
have spared a thought for me for a change—realised I'd
worry?' he demanded, incensed, dumping packages on
the hall table.

'That's not fair; you're never home at this time,' she
retorted, glancing up the stairs, and with a smothered
curse Dan pulled her into their sitting room and closed
the door.

'What the hell were you doing, staying out so long?
You look shattered.'

'I've been shopping,' she flung at him. 'For the first
time since Adam arrived. I was out buying Christmas
presents—with my own money, at that.'

He seized her by the shoulders, his eyes furious. 'Do
you think I care how much money you spend? I was
worried, woman.'

Joss could cope with his anger, but his solicitude
brought tears she couldn't control, and with a sharp in-
take of breath Dan pulled her close and rubbed his cheek
against her hair.

'Don't cry, Joss. Please.' He turned her face up to his,
then took a handkerchief from his breast pocket and
mopped her face. 'Look. We can't go on like this. I'm
your husband, for better or worse, so for God's sake let's
be friends, if nothing else.'

Joss sniffed inelegantly, conscious that she'd had no
attention to spare for Dan, or anything else, since Adam's
arrival. Even their dinners together rarely went undis-

turbed by protests from the baby listener. And her broken nights were spent in the master bedroom, alone with her son.

'You're right, Dan. As usual.' She took the handkerchief from him and scrubbed at her eyes. 'Sorry to howl like Adam—' She stopped, met his eyes and began to laugh. 'And can he howl!'

Dan chuckled, his relief undisguised for once. 'Let's make a deal,' he suggested. 'If I come home early in future I'll tell you in advance.'

'Done,' said Joss, then said impulsively, 'I think you should come home early more often.'

His eyes gleamed in response. 'Then I will, Mrs Armstrong.' He bent and kissed her with such tenderness Joss had to fight to control another rush of tears. 'Come on. I'll give you a hand with Adam's bathtime.'

Joss's first Christmas as Dan's wife and Adam's mother passed in an exhausted, but oddly happy blur, and in some strange way cemented her relationship with Dan far more firmly than a less hectic kind of Christmas could have done. Sam Armstrong arrived a few days beforehand, and, far from being an extra burden, as Dan had expected, proved to be a godsend. Nan was given the week off, to spend with her family, but Joss hardly had time to miss her because Sam was always ready to hold the baby, or peel vegetables, or make cups of tea, and even, to Dan's astonishment, wheel the baby out in his pram in Kew Gardens when it was fine, so that an exhausted Joss could have a nap.

When Sam left after New Year she begged him to come back again whenever he could.

'Dan can drive you down to Eastlegh as soon as you feel up to it, my dear,' he said gruffly, and surprised his son by folding Joss, baby and all, into a loving embrace before Dan drove him to the station.

Joss waved them off with a wry little smile. Whatever doubts Dan might still harbour about Adam, Sam Armstrong had none at all.

'He looks just like you did as a baby,' he'd told Dan. 'Same eyes as me.'

Joss gradually grew less nervous about looking after Adam, but life still kept to a relentless pattern of broken nights and exhausting days. Then one night he slept the entire night through, and Joss gave a little scream of alarm next morning, and leapt out of bed to rush to the cot.

'What is it?' said Dan, as he catapulted, half-naked, into the room.

'Adam slept all night,' said Joss, and giggled, feeling utterly silly. 'Sorry to startle you.'

Dan grinned, and wagged a finger at the stirring baby. 'You scared the hell out of your mother, young man. And me. But a good night's sleep is a great idea. Try another one tonight.'

Joss hesitated. 'Are you in a hurry?'

'Why?'

'I'd love a shower before I get Adam up. Could you watch him for a few minutes?'

Dan raised an eyebrow. 'You mean you trust me with your cub, Madam Tigress?'

Joss coloured, well aware that it was an effort to trust her son to anyone. Even Dan. 'Yes, of course. I won't be long.'

When she rushed back, breathless, with her damp hair bundled up in a knot, Dan was standing at the window with the baby in his arms. He turned, grinning. 'If they ever make showering an Olympic discipline you'll win a gold medal.'

'I didn't want to hold you up,' she panted, and held out her arms.

But Dan lifted the baby high in the air, triumphant as Adam gave an unmistakable crow of approval. 'You like that? Good. We'll try it again later. But right now your mother wants you back.' He handed the baby over. 'Let Nan look after him more. She's all for it, Joss, and it won't do Adam any harm.'

Joss knew he was right. Her articles on *Life with Baby* were all written at odd moments, whenever Adam deigned to sleep. Whereas Nan, she knew, would happily wheel the baby in the park and give Joss a regular space to herself, for writing or researching, or just doing nothing. It was the reason, Joss reminded herself, why Nan had been engaged in the first place.

Adam was three months old before Joss could bring herself to let him sleep in his bedroom. She put the baby listener beside her bed, but the first night she woke every hour during the night to check on him, and just as dawn was breaking collided with Dan outside his room.

'Go back to bed,' he whispered. 'He's fine. I've just covered him up.'

Reluctantly Joss got back into the vast, lonely bed, and tried to sleep, but a few minutes later shot upright again as Dan came in.

'What's the matter?' she asked in fright, throwing back the covers.

Dan put a mug of tea on the bedside table and thrust her back again. 'Nothing's the matter. I just want you to drink that tea and sleep for a while.' He picked up the small monitor. 'I'm taking this. If Adam wakes I'll see to him until I'm ready to leave.'

Spring was showering Kew Gardens with blossom when Dan decided he could leave Athena and all its demands to his staff for a while and take a holiday.

'Time we went down to Eastlegh,' he announced.

Joss was all for it, and felt as though life was beginning to fall into place at last. Adam had sailed through his three-month check-up that morning. She had completed an article well before deadline that afternoon, while Nan had walked him in the Gardens, and even had time for a leisurely bath before they returned. Once her son was tucked up in his cot Joss had changed into a new pink sweater and black velvet jeans only one size larger than her pre-Adam days, and from the sudden leap of heat in Dan's eyes when he arrived home she knew she looked a lot more like the Eve he'd once desired so fiercely.

'I'd like that,' said Joss, pouring coffee. 'When shall we go?'

'As soon as you like.' Dan relaxed in his chair, contemplating her with approval. 'You look better these days, Joss.'

'I feel better.' She handed him his cup, smiling. 'A few hours' sleep occasionally make a world of difference.'

'I'll tell my father we'll travel down this weekend.' Dan paused. 'We could probably stay at Home Farm if you think the cottage might be a tight fit.'

'Certainly not!' said Joss indignantly. 'We stay with your father or we don't go.'

'Pax!' he said, holding up a hand. 'I was only thinking of you, Joss. As usual,' he added deliberately.

Joss flushed and looked away, and a moment later Dan got up to switch on the television for the news. She stared at the screen, wondering if her husband would ever suggest joining her in his own vast bed. If he only knew it, she longed to bridge the gap between them. It refused to heal completely because Dan, she was sure, still harboured doubts about Adam's pedigree. But if he did he never let them stand in the way between him and the baby. Adam was fast growing from the amorphous baby stage into a little person, who chuckled fatly when Dan swung him up in the air or nuzzled the moist, irresistible skin of Adam's neck. Adam responded joyfully to this large, exciting male person, who played with him far too roughly sometimes for Joss's liking. But she never said so, only too pleased to encourage any contact between the two loves of her life. And some day soon, Joss knew, she would just have to talk to Dan about the doubts and passions simmering beneath the surface of their new relationship. When they returned from Eastlegh, perhaps.

By the time they were ready to leave for Dorset the car was so crammed with necessities for Adam that Dan told Joss a second car would be necessary if she came up with another thing. 'And I demand your company on the journey,' he said firmly, 'so leave everything else behind and get in the car!'

Their welcome at Eastlegh was warm. Sam Armstrong gave Joss a swift kiss, wrung his son's hand, then reached into the back to take Adam from his car seat. For a moment the baby regarded this male person with suspicion, then his face creased into a smile, and Sam, delighted, bore him proudly into the house.

'You'd better give Home Farm a ring,' he told Dan. 'I promised I'd let them know when you arrived.'

Soon there was a noisy reunion with Francis and Sarah, with much fuss made over the baby, who lapped up the attention in a way which amused Francis enormously.

'Look at him. Cock of the walk, just like his father.

Poor lad,' he said, shaking his head. 'A beautiful mother like Joss, but he's saddled with his father's looks.'

'Francis!' cried Sarah. 'Don't be rude. You're right, though; he's the image of his daddy. Look at those eyes! But he's gorgeous just the same—aren't you, my darling? Can I hold him, Joss?'

By the time tea had been drunk and Sarah had been coaxed into relinquishing the baby it was time for Adam's bath.

'I'll see to that,' said Dan quickly, and smiled at Joss. 'I've put the gadgets in the kitchen, and the rest is up-stairs. You can sort things out while I scrub this chap.'

Francis and Sarah took reluctant leave, after extracting a promise from Joss to come over later with Dan for coffee and a drink after dinner.

'Grandpa will babysit,' said Sarah, smiling at Sam.

Joss looked doubtful. 'I don't think—'

'You go out for an hour, my girl,' said Sam firmly. 'I'll look after him. And if I can't manage I'll ring Home Farm and you can be back here in two minutes.'

'Do you good,' said Dan, and smiled wryly at the others. 'I haven't been able to persuade my wife outside the door since Adam was born.'

Joss flushed, laughing. 'I never realised motherhood was such a full-time job.'

'What you really mean,' said Dan deliberately, 'is that you're so much in love with your son you can't bear to tear yourself away from him.'

Francis put a friendly arm round Joss. 'Do come. Just for an hour. Adam's grandfather knows all about little boys, I assure you.'

Aware that Dan was eyeing them coldly, Joss detached herself, smiling. 'Right. We'll come.'

'Armed with cellphone,' said Dan dryly, and hoisted the baby higher. 'See you later.'

When Joss went upstairs she discovered what Dan had meant by a tight fit for visitors. There was one bathroom, and two bedrooms, one of which would be shared by two adults and a baby in a Moses basket.

Because his grandfather had come to watch, Adam's bathtime was not only a noisy, protracted affair, but it tired Adam out. After despatching his supper with voracious appetite the baby fell asleep in his mother's arms and settled down without a murmur in the strange bedroom.

'Wonderful!' said Dan as they began on their meal. 'It's rare that Joss and I enjoy dinner uninterrupted.'

'Well, you can tonight,' said Sam firmly, and gestured at the baby listener. 'The young rascal's snoring, so you eat up, Joscelyn, while you've got the chance.'

Adam was still fast asleep when Dan finally persuaded Joss to leave. 'He'll be fine,' he assured her as they drove over to Home Farm.

'I know.' Joss smiled guiltily. 'I never dreamed I'd be such a doting mother.'

It was very pleasant to spend an evening with Sarah and Francis, knowing that the baby was in good hands. Joss listened, relaxed, to their wedding plans, and drank an unaccustomed glass of wine, laughing as Francis began talking about the scrapes he'd used to get into with Dan. And it was Dan, in the end, who pointed out that although no call had come from their babysitter it was time to go.

'You enjoyed that,' he said, as they drove back to the cottage.

'Yes,' said Joss, yawning. 'I did. I hope Adam hasn't worn your father out.'

'It would take more than one small baby to do that,' Dan assured her, chuckling.

And he was right. When they got back Joss was astonished to find that, although Adam had woken up at ten, Sam Armstrong had coped admirably.

'I warmed up one of those bottles you left,' he said smugly. 'Then I changed him, fed him and put him back. He's fast asleep again.'

Joss exchanged a look with her highly amused husband, then gave Sam an affectionate hug. 'Thank you. You're wonderful.'

'Nonsense,' he said gruffly. 'Now you two get off to bed and get some rest while you can. And don't worry if the lad wakes in the night. I won't mind.'

Once they'd witnessed the sleeping miracle with their own eyes, Dan smiled at Joss in apology. 'I meant to give you time to yourself to get ready for bed, but old habits die hard,' he whispered. 'When my father says jump, I still jump.'

'Does he realise how unique he is in that?' queried Joss, taking off her earrings.

'Actually, he's not,' said Dan, looking down at her. 'I feel the same about you.'

She stared at him, her heart thumping. 'I seriously doubt that!'

'It's true,' he said casually, and made for the door. 'I'll use the bathroom first.'

Later, listening to snuffling baby noises from the crib beside her, Joss lay determinedly still in the darkness which was so much more intense here in the depths of the country than in London. Dan lay equally quiet beside her. And from his very stillness Joss knew that he was just as conscious of their proximity as she was. But for the entire time they spent at Eastlegh Dan scrupulously avoided any physical contact in bed, except by accident when he was asleep. Even Daniel Armstrong, thought his wife, couldn't control the odd touch when he was unconscious.

When they returned to London Dan decided to take a few more days off. 'I should spend more time with my family,' he announced, after everything was unloaded from the car. 'I'll start by giving Adam his bath while you stack his gear away. And later,' he added, as he started upstairs with the baby, 'perhaps we can achieve a peaceful meal together for once.'

Sam had sent them home laden with fresh vegetables and new-laid eggs, and after Adam was settled down for the night Joss made Spanish omelettes for supper. Dan insisted on opening a bottle of smooth red wine, but they ate in the kitchen rather than use up valuable time by laying the dining table.

'Who knows how long our son will leave us in peace?' said Dan, very deliberately.

Our son, thought Joss, and applied herself to her omelette with sudden appetite. 'Perhaps your father has sorted him out for us.'

The evening was a vivid contrast to some of those they'd tried to spend together since Adam's birth. The baby slept until ten, then woke to demand his supper, but afterwards he went down again with a promptness Joss found hard to trust.

'Will you listen for him while I have a bath?' she asked when she rejoined Dan.

He smiled at her over his paper. 'Of course. Take your time.'

Joss took him at his word. Reading in the bath was a luxury since Adam's advent, and she stretched out in hot, scented water with a sigh of pleasure, determined to con-

centrate on her novel rather than ponder over whether
Dan really believed, at last, that Adam was his son.

She succeeded so well the water got cold, and Joss
jumped out hastily, guilty at having taken so long. She
dried herself hurriedly, brushed her teeth and slapped on
some moisturiser, then pulled a thin pink lawn nightgown
over her head and hurried into the bedroom, to find her
husband sitting propped against the pillows of his vast
bed, apparently absorbed in a book.

Joss stood motionless, her heart beating like a drum as
Dan looked up.

'Before you ask, he's fast asleep,' he informed her, and
turned down the covers beside him. 'We shared a bed so
amicably at the cottage I thought we should carry on.'
His eyes met hers. 'It doesn't commit you to anything.'

Without a word, Joss crossed the room and slid into
bed beside Dan. He reached out an arm, switched off the
lamp, then lay in silence for so long that Joss was rigid
with tension by the time he turned towards her. 'This
seems the right time, at last, to ask if you'll forgive me,
Joss.'

'For what, in particular?' she whispered, breathing in
his familiar male scent.

'For doubting that Adam was my son, for a start. Not
that it would matter if he wasn't. He's mine now.'

'He always was.'

'I know.' Dan felt for her hand and held it tightly.
'Down at Eastlegh it was suddenly easy to sort out my
priorities. You, darling, are all I want. All I've ever
wanted from the moment I first saw you. But because
I'm a jealous fool I asked a stupid question that day in
the hospital and risked losing you. And losing Adam with
you.'

Joss lay very still, her entire body irradiated with heat

from his touch. 'I wouldn't have left you. I married you, Dan.'

His grasp tightened. 'If you'd wanted to go I knew damn well a few lines on a piece of paper wouldn't have kept you with me.'

'True.'

'So why did you stay?'

'Isn't it obvious?'

He pulled on her hand gently, drawing her closer. 'Are you, by any wonderful, unbelievable chance, saying you love me perhaps even a fraction as much as I love you?'

Joss fought to control her sudden trembling. This was no moment to go to pieces.

Dan waited a moment, then took her in his arms. 'If you don't love me yet I'm going to spend the rest of my life teaching you how,' he said, to her amazement, and kissed her with sudden, uncontrolled desperation. 'Do you know,' he said in her ear, his breath scorching her skin, 'how hard it was to lie with you in bed at the cottage and not touch you?'

'Yes.'

'Was it so obvious?'

'No. But I felt the same.'

Dan gave a great, relishing sigh of satisfaction, and began to kiss her in the way she had missed and longed for so desperately. His kisses were light and tender at first, but the tenderness gradually changed to a demand she answered fiercely. She shivered in delight as her body thrilled to his touch, and at last let herself gasp out her love against his lips. For a split second Dan was still, then he crushed her in a rib-cracking embrace and said a great many things which filled her with joy as he began a renewed seduction of her senses, every touch adding fuel to the fire that flamed between them at such overwhelming speed neither of them had any resistance against the bright, burning magic which consumed them in a fever of sensation so intense it was almost pain.

Long afterwards, when they had achieved something like calm, Dan raised his head slightly. 'Will you repeat that in cold blood, Mrs Armstrong?'

'My blood's not very cold yet,' she panted, 'but I'll happily repeat that I love you as often as you want. Now.'

'Why now?' he demanded.

'Now you've admitted you love *me*, of course.'

He reached out an arm and switched on the light. 'But I've told you that all along,' he said, frowning down into her flushed face.

'No,' she corrected. 'You told me you wanted me. There's a difference.'

Dan stared at her in blank astonishment. 'You mean that my choice of vocabulary was the barrier between us all this time?'

Joss shook her head. 'No. The big obstacle was your doubt about your son's pedigree.'

Dan leaned his forehead against hers. 'So if I still harboured these doubts—which I never have, in my heart of hearts—what we just shared would never have happened?'

Joss gave him a swift kiss. 'Possibly.' She leaned over to reach into her bedside drawer. 'But because you did lay claim to my baby in the end I'll give you a reward.'

'A reward?' he repeated huskily, his fingertip tracing a pattern on her bare back. 'Can I choose the reward I want?'

'I think you'll like this one,' said Joss, and handed him an envelope.

Dan's eyes narrowed incredulously as he took out a card from Peter Sadler.

'*Congratulations on the birth of your son. Arithmetic was always my strongest point,*' said the message.

Dan raised a questioning eyebrow, 'Arithmetic?'

Joss touched a hand to his face. 'If I explain will you promise not to lose your temper and storm off into the other room?'

'I'll promise the last bit,' he said, his eyes softening. 'From now on we sleep together, my darling.'

'Good.' Joss smiled at him luminously, then told him about Peter Sadler's second visit before the wedding, how he'd planned the scene Dan had walked in on purely as a means to get back at the man behind Athena.

'He did that out of petty revenge?' said Dan in outrage. 'If I'd been there I'd have rearranged his pretty little face.'

'He didn't really come to apologise. That was an excuse. He wanted to know if he was the father of my baby,' said Joss baldly.

Dan looked at her for a moment, then drew her back into his arms and smoothed her head against his shoulder. 'And you kicked him out?'

'I did better than that. I told him the baby was due on February the fourteenth.'

Dan was suddenly still. 'When did Sadler walk out on you?'

'February last year. Which is why he put the bit about arithmetic on the card.'

'So,' said Dan slowly, 'even if Adam were a full-term baby there was never any question about who was his father.'

'No.' Joss raised her head to look up into Dan's eyes, and found him looking down at her with a strange, wry expression. 'What is it?'

'Why didn't you tell me this before?'

'I objected to the idea of producing evidence that Adam was your son. This is marriage, Daniel Armstrong, not a court of law.' Joss looked at him steadily. 'I wanted you to take him—and me—on trust.'

'As I should have done,' he said heavily. 'Not that there was ever any question about the taking and keeping. But I own to one fleeting, human second of doubt. Can you forgive me for that, my darling?' he asked, in a tone which brought her face up to his for a kiss of passionate absolution. Dan caught her close and kissed her back, then they both shook with laughter as an imperious cry came through the speaker by the bed. Dan threw back the covers and pulled on a dressing gown.

'Stay where you are. I'll see to him.'

Joss looked at him uncertainly. 'Are you sure?'

'Of course I am. It's time Adam started sleeping through anyway. I'll mention it to him when I put him down.' Dan turned in the doorway, smiling. 'But don't go away. I'm coming back.'

Joss stretched luxuriously. 'When you do, perhaps we can talk about rewards again.'

'We will. And this time I'll have what *I* want,' said Dan firmly, his eyes gleaming. 'Want to guess what it is?'

'Do *I* get a reward if I'm right?'

'Anything you want, my darling.'

'I want exactly the same as you,' she said demurely, then fended him off, laughing, as he dived across the room to kiss her. 'Hurry up, your son's getting furious in there.'

'My son will just have to wait a minute while I kiss his mother,' said Dan against her lips. 'It took me far too long to get *my* priorities right. Adam can start learning about his right now.'

Modern Romance™
...seduction and
passion guaranteed

Tender Romance™
...love affairs that
last a lifetime

Sensual Romance™
...sassy, sexy and
seductive

Blaze Romance™
...the temperature's
rising

Medical Romance™
...medical drama on
the pulse

Historical Romance™
...rich, vivid and
passionate

27 new titles every month.

*With all kinds of Romance for
every kind of mood...*

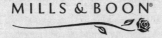

**Don't miss *Book Six* of this
BRAND-NEW 12 book
collection 'Bachelor Auction'.**

Who says
money
can't buy
love?

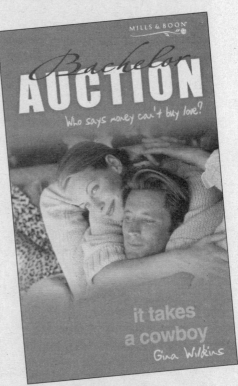

On sale 7th February

*Available at most branches of WH Smith,
Tesco, Martins, Borders, Eason, Sainsbury's,
and all good paperback bookshops.*

BA/RTL/6

Blaze Romance™

Two brand new titles each month

The temperature's rising...

GEN/14/RTL6